P9-CKY-169

# The Portable Sherwood Anderson

*The Viking Portable Library*

Each Portable Library volume is made up of representative works of a favorite modern or classic author, or is a comprehensive anthology on a special subject. The format is designed for compactness and for pleasurable reading. The books average about 700 pages in length. Each is intended to fill a need not hitherto met by any single book. Each is edited by an authority distinguished in his field, who adds a thoroughgoing introductory essay and other helpful material. Most "Portables" are available both in durable cloth and in stiff paper covers.

The Portable

# Sherwood Anderson

Edited, and with an introduction, by

Horace Gregory

The Viking Press

New York

PUBLISHED IN FEBRUARY 1949

PUBLISHED ON THE SAME DAY IN THE DOMINION OF CANADA
BY THE MACMILLAN COMPANY OF CANADA LIMITED

EIGHTH PRINTING SEPTEMBER 1966



Acknowledgment is made to Liveright Publishing Corporation for permission to include "Death in the Woods" and "A Meeting South" from *Death in the Woods,* "In Washington" from *Hello Towns,* and four sketches from *Sherwood Anderson's Notebook.*

PRINTED IN U.S.A. BY THE COLONIAL PRESS INC.

# Table of Contents

# Editor's Introduction

WHEN Sherwood Anderson died in 1941 the moment was not unlike that at the death of D. H. Lawrence eleven years earlier: a pause was felt, even though neither writer was then at the widest span of his reputation. Today Sherwood Anderson's reputation is more secure than it was in 1941, and his short novels, tales and stories, like the writings of D. H. Lawrence, have lived well beyond their day of being in or out of fashion. Like the legend of his life which he created in his autobiographies and memoirs, his tales and stories have independent life of their own, an existence no longer sustained and modified by a widely known and vivid personality. The decade following a writer's death provides, often enough, the severest test of his true vitality. Even in his lifetime, his popularity, his "fame" may suffer (as Anderson's did) polar extremes of critical approval and indifference, but the years following his death are a test of his survival in the world that he has left behind him. Of American writers of the 1920's who were also "poets" (in the same sense that some European writers of prose are given that distinction), Sherwood Anderson has achieved his promise of "immortality," and it is not surprising that his place in the literature of the twentieth century is close to that of two writers for whom he felt particular kinship, Gertrude Stein and D. H. Lawrence.

The reservation of a place in the company of Gertrude Stein and D. H. Lawrence scarcely defines the singular impression that Sherwood Anderson makes upon the imagination of the reader, yet for all the particular qualities that have set him apart from other writers of the day, it is not inappropriate to think of *Winesburg, Ohio* and *Horses and Men* as placed in the same climate in which *Sons and Lovers* and *The Prussian Officer* and Gertrude Stein's *Three Lives* exist. In each one finds something of the same temperature, the same charm, the same authentic presence of a personality.

All three writers joined in the large, and for them victorious, cause of liberating prose from a multitude of literary clichés, and thereby saving their own works from the dust that falls so thickly upon library shelves. Each gives the reader (and beyond this their kinship ends) a vision usually reserved for readers of poetry alone, a view of life, familiar to be sure in "realistic" detail, but far more "alive" than the resources of prose and of fiction commonly permit.

European readers who come to Anderson's *Winesburg, Ohio* for the first time feel the proximity of a new speech, a "new country," a fresh view of the Main Street that Sinclair Lewis had opened for them. The interrelated stories of *Winesburg, Ohio* offer something that is less foreign to them than the restless, half-satirical observant eye that guides the reader so faithfully through the pages of Lewis's realistic novel. What is felt in *Winesburg, Ohio,* felt rather than read, overheard rather than stressed, is a memory of youth, of early "joys and sorrows," and this is conveyed with the simplicity of a folk tale, a style known in all languages. To the American reader another level of almost subterranean feeling is contained in Sherwood Anderson's novels and stories. The streets and landscapes here depicted are close to the roots of an American heritage which takes its definition from the writings of Emerson, Whitman, Thoreau, Melville, and Mark Twain. Critics with as diverse opinions of Anderson as those expressed by Lionel Trilling on one hand and Van Wyck Brooks on the other have agreed in recognizing these particular features of Anderson's "Americanism," his almost instinctive and acknowledged debt to writers who represent the Emersonian aspect of the Great Tradition in American literature. It is clear enough that Anderson's writings are of that heritage and not in the Great Tradition of Hawthorne and Henry James. But why were they "instinctively" so, why were they ranged so conclusively on the side of Thoreau and Whitman? As one reads Anderson's autobiographies and memoirs, it is absurd to think of him reading Thoreau, Emerson, and Whitman in the spirit of one determined to follow a "party line" in choosing the sources of his inspiration; it is absurd to think of him surrounded by books in order to draw "ideas" and intellectual convictions from them. His sources were the air he breathed, childhood memories of talk, of the few books loaned to him by schoolmasters, by older men in small Middle Western towns who took a fancy to the brilliant, sensitive, imaginative son of a Southern drifter and tall-tale-teller. These were the essentials of Sherwood Anderson's early impressions; they are the actual sources of whatever Anderson thought and saw and felt, and all other experiences, whether of reading or of sensitively overhearing conversation which flowed around him, were superimposed upon them.

The impact on Anderson's imagination of Thoreau and Whitman came in later life, but the important impressions of his boyhood were the associations of what is now called a "democratic" heritage: the diluted forms of oratory at Fourth of July celebrations, the speeches made at county fairs, the talk overheard at race tracks, and through the swinging doors of the nineteenth-century, Middle Western, small-town saloon. In these surroundings, legends of Abraham Lincoln flourished, floating upward into Ohio from Illinois and Kentucky—stories pertinent to Anderson's own half-Southern, log-cabin origins. He, too, came from a "shiftless, drifting" family, and so he was particularly sympathetic to the picture of Lincoln reading books by the flickering, red glare thrown from a log-cabin hearth, to the figure of "the man of sorrows" and unrequited love, the shrewd country lawyer who told tall stories in the back rooms of general stores, the gaunt, distracted figure, clad in a nightshirt, pacing the floor of his bedroom in the White House, reading jokes aloud from an open book or periodical, and finally, the martyred President, who loved the North and South alike, the author of the Gettysburg Address—these pictures hung as icons in the mind of the impressionable boy.

Beneath the seeming contradictions of Anderson's discussions in his memoirs, novels, and topical essays of socialism, democracy, and the twentieth century "machine age," there lies a singular loyalty to the heritage of a Middle Western boyhood. It is in this connection that the year of his birth, 1876, and the place where he was born, Camden, Ohio, are of relevant meaning. Anderson grew up in a place that was permeated by that "religion of humanity" of which Emerson was the transcendental fountainhead, showering forth his concepts of the "oversoul" like rain from the clouds; across the prairies of the Middle West his name and Thoreau's represented New England "culture," and when their writings were read at all, which was only in small circles, they were tolerated with more respect than understanding. Those who lived through the post-bellum years of the Civil War in the Middle West demanded both more and less of their own priests of "humanity" than they did of the memory of Emerson.

The new priests of the "religion of humanity" were champions of reason and of Herbert Spencer's *First Principles,* of Henry George's *Progress and Poverty* and Edward Bellamy's *Looking Backward,* of Robert Ingersoll's lectures on The Gods ("An Honest God Is the Noblest Work of Man") and on Individuality ("Every human being should take a road of his own. . . . Every mind . . . should think, investigate and conclude for itself"). These new priests spoke in the names of "democracy," "science," "progress," and "liberty"; most of them were in revolt against the older Protestant sects and denominations of New England, against Puritan restraints and moralities, and yet the shadows of older taboos were among their obsessions. Sherwood Anderson's generation in Ohio and Illinois felt in boyhood the presence of Ingersoll's "individuality" and his faith in "science" with greater intimacy, and perhaps, greater clarity, than Thoreau's "Civil Disobedience."

Compared with Ingersoll's rhetoric, a flamboyant language of evangelical threats and promises ("Science took a tear from the cheek of unpaid labor, converted into steam, created a giant that turns with tireless arm, the countless wheels of toil."), Thoreau's writings seem austere, and his serene appreciation of solitude at Walden almost classic in feeling and Puritanical. But to Anderson's generation the voice of Ingersoll was the voice of "progress"; it promised the arrival of a "new day" for those who had been attracted to The Noble Order of the Knights of Labor, and yet it shouted down with equal vehemence the totalitarian Utopia of Bellamy's *Looking Backward.* "We are believers in individual independence," said Ingersoll. "We invent . . . we enslave the winds and waves." It was through the invention of machines, and the tools to control, improve, and mend them, that the "religion of humanity" offered its rewards on earth to members of its congregation; and to Sherwood Anderson the delight of invention for its own sake never lost its spell. To invent became part of his pleasure in telling a story, and the very inventions of the machine age, an age whose virtues he came to distrust and to criticize, never lost their fascination.

It is clear that Ingersoll, whose attacks upon Christianity defeated his political ambitions (and left him, scarcely content, with the office of Attorney-General for the State of Illinois) had assumed heroic proportions in the Middle West during the early 1890's. Even so, it may still seem strange to link Anderson's name so closely with his. Anderson had little concern for merely rational arguments in favor of science, and no respect whatever for inflated rhetoric, yet the sentiments of Ingersoll, overheard or half-heard from the lips of talkers in small-town newspaper offices and saloons, are of the same character as those that filled the young and speculative mind of George Willard in *Winesburg, Ohio*. The sentiments of Ingersoll prepared Willard for the story of the Reverend Curtis Hartman in "The Strength of God," and the same source of inspiration provides a logic of its own for the arrival of Hugh McVey, the inventor, the central figure, if not the "hero," of Anderson's *Poor White*.

As we speak of Anderson's heritage and his place in American letters, it is never appropriate to name too loudly other writers who directly influenced his writings; like D. H. Lawrence, Anderson is a singularly unbookish figure, an "original," a "maker" in his own right. He is also the self-educated writer, whose brief stay at college (The college was Wittenberg at Springfield, Ohio. "Later they called me back. They gave me a degree," he wrote in his *Memoirs.*) was the least memorable of his experiences. Yet like many self-taught writers, what he read for pleasure held a place more deeply rooted in his imagination than the place held by required reading in the minds of those who are "educated" by the thousands in colleges and universities. As one reads Anderson's stories and autobiographies, three older writers come to mind: one is Herman Melville, another Mark Twain, and the third George Borrow. In writing tributes to older writers for whom he felt a particular affinity, Anderson always remembered George Borrow, and in doing so, he showed a more profound depth of self-knowledge than many of his critics have attributed to him. Superficially, his choice of Borrow seems very far from the area of his distinctly American heritage. Even in the broad stream of nineteenth century British prose, Borrow, the author of *The Bible in Spain, Lavengro,* and *The Romany Rye,* was a distant figure to his contemporaries. But that distance, and the failure of critics to classify Borrow's books as fiction or autobiography, as stories or novels, have their relevance to the attraction that Anderson felt to Borrow. The people about whom Borrow wrote, companions of the road and alehouse, pugilists, "bruisers," tinkers, "the Flaming Tinman," boys who loved horses and ponies, gypsies, fortune-tellers, the poverty-stricken Welsh and Irish nomadic figures, are not unlike the people that Anderson knew in the American Middle West. All of Borrow's people are tellers of stories and whether Borrow retold these stories with respect for literal truth is of less importance than is the record he created of the essential life within and around them. His writings have the same peripatetic atmosphere that is sometimes felt in Anderson's *Horses and Men* or *A Story-Teller's Story:* his was an art of speech that wanders slightly, that seems to walk, that philosophizes gently in an almost absent-minded fashion. It is important also that Borrow, the accomplished linguist, called himself "the Word-Master," for Anderson, with far greater aesthetic discrimination than Borrow, knew himself to be a "Word-Master" of another, an American kind.

Anderson's liking for Borrow has an instinctive rightness beyond anything he could have learned through a conventional education. Borrow showed what a writer could do while ignoring the conventional rules for writing autobiographies and novels. This was a valuable lesson that Anderson never forgot; he became, as Thomas Seccombe wrote of Borrow, not a "matter-of-fact," but a "matter-of-fiction" man. He did not allow Borrow to influence him directly, and in matters of style, in which Borrow was notoriously uneven, Anderson greatly improved upon him. The choice of Borrow as one of his models placed Anderson on the side of those who see and feel things from the ground up, from the pavement of a city street, from the grasses of a field, from the threshold of a house. This view is always an independent view that refuses to become housebroken.

Anderson's debt to Mark Twain is less veiled than that to Borrow, for Mark Twain's *Huckleberry Finn* is literally close to an American time and place that Anderson knew. In his letters to Van Wyck Brooks, Anderson speaks authoritatively on the subject of Mark Twain, whom he sees as a distinctly American phenomenon, a figure who stands in the company of and between the figures of Lincoln and Whitman: "Twain's way lies somewhere between the roads taken by the other two men"; and in respect to Twain and Borrow, Anderson wrote, "In my own mind I have always coupled Mark Twain with George Borrow. I get the same quality of honesty in them, the same wholesome disregard of literary precedent.* Of the "real" Twain, Anderson wrote to Brooks, "Should not one go to Huck Finn for the real man, working out of a real people?" The people of Anderson's boyhood in the Middle West were but a single generation beyond Tom Sawyer and Huckleberry Finn, and there was an unbroken continuity between the two generations. Huckleberry Finn's skepticism concerning the virtues of church-going was of a piece with the world that Anderson knew, a world whose enjoyment was of the earth. Anderson's affinity to Mark Twain was as "natural," as unstudied as Anderson's memories of growing up and coming of age. Equally natural was the example of perspective taken from Borrow, choosing the life of the out-of-doors as the true center of worldly experience.

With Melville, Anderson's affinities are of a far less conscious order; they belong to the inward-looking, darkened "nocturnal" aspects of Anderson's heritage. The affinities to Twain and Borrow are of daylight character; they are clear and specific, and are sharply outlined within the lively scenes that Anderson created, but his kinship with Melville belongs to that diffused and shadowy area of his imagination which Paul Rosenfeld named as mysticism. As they spoke of his mysticism, even Anderson's best friends became confused because Anderson, like Borrow before him, distrusted philosophic generalities; for himself, he would have little or none of them; he would plead ignorance of large thoughts and pretensions, though he would gladly speak of how he came to write a story, and in *A Story-Teller's Story,* tell something very like another story to illustrate his point. He thought in symbols, in metaphors, in images, in turns of phrasing, in terms of a situation, or a scene of action—and in this language whatever is meant by his "mysticism" is half-revealed. The friendship of Ishmael, in *Moby Dick,* with the dark-skinned savage Queequeg has a quality akin to the quality of the boy's contact with Negroes in "The Man Who Became a Woman" or the sound of Negro laughter in Anderson's *Dark Laughter.* It was once fashionable to call such "mysticism" Freudian, because it touched upon the emotions of adolescent sexual experience. In Anderson those emotions are transcended in "Death in the Woods," and whatever "mysticism" may be found within them, including the expression of mystery and awe, is of an older heritage than are the teachings of Freud in America. Ishmael's decision to share a bed with Queequeg—"Better sleep with a sober cannibal than a drunken Christian"—and the horror of Queequeg's first impression upon him is closely, if broadly, allied to the mysteries, the transcendental qualities, of sexual experience in Anderson's stories, and to find that kinship one need go no further than the story "Hands" in *Winesburg, Ohio.* The diffused affinity that Anderson has with Melville is not a facile one, for Anderson made it one of his few rules to stand aside from "literary precedent," to re-create scenes of action in terms of his own experience rather than to lean upon experiences gained from reading the works of others. The kinship of Anderson's writings with *Moby Dick* embraces that side of Anderson's imagination which is "non-realistic," and which converts what is outwardly the simple telling of a story into a series of symbolic actions. The fluttering, "talking" quality of Wing Biddlebaum's "slender expressive fingers, forever active," in "Hands," is endowed with the mystery that Anderson makes his readers feel. And when the Reverend Curtis Hartman in "The Strength of God" breaks a church window with his fist, the action carries with it undertones of symbolic, almost transcendental, meaning; the impulse which drove Curtis Hartman to his action was a force greater than his will, and with appropriate irony he assigned that impulse to "the strength of God."

Throughout many of Anderson's stories and in his autobiography, *Tar: A Midwest Childhood,* the figure of the boy who is created to tell the tale bears a strong family resemblance to Melville's Ishmael, and behind this figure there is the other Ishmael, son of the bondwoman Hagar in Genesis. The figure is one who will inherit no fortune, is of nomadic character; a figure whose association with the Biblical story, half-concealed behind his obvious relationship to Huckleberry Finn, gives him a faint aura of transcendental kinship with the Old Testament. Literally, of course, the boy's mother, as she appears in *Tar,* is no Hagar, but the roving character of the family milieu is close enough to Hagar's wanderings in the desert to make explicit Waldo Frank's observations on *Winesburg, Ohio,* that Tar, growing older, is George Willard, and that "a Testamental accent and vision modulate every page of Sherwood Anderson's great story." So they do. Despite the "naturalism," despite the skepticism concerning the conventional moralities of the orthodox church-goers and the Reverend Curtis Hartmans, an atmosphere of Biblical vision and of semi-divine "animal faith" attends these movements and awakenings in the physical world of Middle Western America.

It may seem strange that Anderson, the maker of legends and stories, is not among the best of those who write autobiographies as their major work of art. Anderson's gifts as "a matter-of-fiction man," like those of George Borrow, usurped his hold upon literal facts. In the writing of *Tar* he had half-promised himself to write *the* autobiographical story, but in his foreword he explains his lack of interest in literal truth:

> It was only after I had created Tar Moorehead, had brought him to life in my own fancy, that I could sit down before my sheets and feel at ease. It was only then I faced myself, accepted myself. "If you are a born liar, a man of the fancy, why not be what you are," I said to myself, and having said it I at once began writing with a new feeling of comfort.

It was only when Anderson saw himself as a character that his re-creation of essential truths began to take on the air of remarkable candor; in his posthumously published *Memoirs* he is frankly bored with the chronological progress of events, and is deliberately careless in the naming of dates, as though everything he had to say about himself belonged to a single moment in the past that is called "once upon a time." In all his autobiographical books and sketches, it is the legend of his life that charmed him and charms his readers; his love of wandering, of men and women, of horses, of Midwestern landscapes, of county fairs, of small-town streets and houses, take on the colors of a reality that is far more convincing than the figure of their author. The real Anderson is in his stories, in George Willard of Winesburg, in "The Man Who Became a Woman," in "I'm a Fool," in Tar Moorehead, and is notably less visible whenever he assumes the personal pronoun "I" in *A Story-Teller's Story* and in his *Memoirs.*

To understand the importance of his legend a few facts (over which Anderson glided in his *Memoirs*) are pertinent: Anderson was one of seven children in a family that migrated from town to town in rural Ohio; his mother was of Italian or German origin, and his father, a man of declining fortunes, came to Ohio from the Southern United States, and was consecutively a harness dealer and a house painter. As a small boy, Anderson was known as "Jobby" Anderson, the boy who did odd jobs of great variety which later formed the general background of the experiences that came to life in his stories. From this he drifted into jobs in factories, into and out of Chicago, and then enlisted as a private in the Spanish-American War, which carried him through Southern training camps and south to Cuba. Then came his short winter at a Middle Western college, and from there he went to Chicago and wrote copy in an advertising office; and shortly after this experience he went into business and ran a small paint factory in Elyria, Ohio, only to return to Chicago and an advertising office, and at last to begin in earnest a career of writing stories. These experiences were central to a culture and an environment that he shared in part with other writers of his generation, with Theodore Dreiser, who was born in Indiana, with Edgar Lee Masters, born in Garnett, Kansas, with Vachel Lindsay, of Springfield, Illinois, with Carl Sandburg of Galesburg, Illinois—and these were writers who, like Anderson, came into wide public recognition in middle age. Anderson, in his autobiographies, had much the same story to tell as his contemporaries; all had the same unorthodox schooling, the same memories of Ingersoll, Herbert Spencer, Henry George, Edward Bellamy, William Jennings Bryan, the same vivid images of Abraham Lincoln. Anderson's autobiographies cross and recross the territory also discovered in the autobiographical writings of Dreiser, Masters, and Lindsay, or the monumental biographies of Lincoln written by Carl Sandburg. These are all of one cloth, and only the particulars of Anderson's own legend weave a distinctive pattern through the fabric. Not a few of the literal facts of his life—the classless poverty of the Middle West, in which a new job, a new life, lay at the next turning of the road or the next railway station; the experiences of a short, successful Spanish-American War, which for so many young men was almost a patriotic holiday—were of the cloth, and not of the pattern. The more valuable part of what he had to say was contained in the legend of how he made up his mind not to be a business man, how he stepped out of his paint factory in Elyria, Ohio. As he began to look about him in the small town and become absorbed in the lives of the townspeople, as he began to sit at his office desk only to "lose myself in the writing of others . . . it was all disastrous to my business," the time had arrived to pack up and go:

> I resorted to slickness, to craftiness. Already I had got a reputation for a kind of queerness among my acquaintances. Men had seen me walking somewhere in the outskirts of the town and suddenly beginning to run. . . . The impression got abroad. I perhaps encouraged it—that I was overworking, was on the point of a nervous breakdown. . . . The thought occurred to me that if men thought me a little insane they would forgive me if I lit out, left the business in which they invested their money on their hands. I did it one day —walked into my office and called the stenographer— It was a bright warm day in summer. I closed the door in my office and spoke to her. A startled look came into her eyes. "My feet are cold and wet," I said. "I have been walking too long on the bed of a river." Saying these words I walked out of the door leaving her staring after me with frightened eyes. I walked eastward along a railroad track, toward the city of Cleveland. There were five or six dollars in my pocket.

The episode has a classic ring, and it is Anderson's contribution to the legend of how poets and novelists in the Middle West found themselves: Masters, the Chicago lawyer, giving up his practice when the notoriety of *The Spoon River Anthology* awakened distrust among his clients; Sandburg creating the impression, according to his biographer, Karl Detzer, of a "wandering minstrel with a frayed shirt-collar and an old guitar"; and Lindsay trading rhymes for bread and lodging across the United States from New York to San Francisco.

Anderson's personal decision was of more than superficial likeness to the decisions made by those writers who had created the Middle Western school, "a robin's egg renaissance," as Anderson called it, in Chicago. It was consistent also with what he had to say in the novels and stories that brought him fame, and with the tradition of Ishmael, the man who walks alone, and it was finally consistent that he should be converted to socialism but then tear up the essay to which he had given the title, "Why I Am a Socialist."

II

If the "real Anderson" is seen more clearly in legendary episodes of the autobiographies than when he employs too consciously the pronoun "I," how vividly, how memorably he moves before the reader in his major novel, *Poor White.* It may seem pretentious to call so modest a book a major novel: its bulk is scarcely greater than *Winesburg, Ohio* and no greater than Anderson's *Many Marriages, Windy McPherson's Son, Marching Men, Dark Laughter,* and *Kit Brandon.* But one never measures Anderson's writings by their physical size, for he is essentially the creator of short forms in fiction, in which the short novel is included; despite his easy, deceptively rambling manner, his true concerns were for scenes and people that could be revealed in a single gesture, a single episode. When he wrote an introduction to the Modern Library edition of *Poor White,* he told his readers that the actual hero of the book was a small

Ohio town, Bidwell, Ohio, and that the people of the town, even the central figure, Hugh McVey, the "poor white" Lincolnesque inventor, were supernumeraries—they were, it is true, the life of the town, but what happened to the town was what he wished remembered. Today one reads *Poor White* almost as though it were a particular kind of historical novel; time has refreshed it and thrown into perspective the ideas, the events, the atmosphere of a late-nineteenth-century American small town that had thrust forward the fortunes of a Hugh McVey.

What values *Poor White* has gained in the years between its publication in 1920 and today are similar to those we place upon Frank Norris's *The Pit* and Dreiser's *The Titan.* The elder novels take Chicago as their center, and the scenes of the Middle Western city, with its "pioneer" competition and rapid acquisition of wealth, have now assumed, with greater force than any costume novel attempting to revive the period could have done, the character of all historical as well as "social" novels. The town of Bidwell, Ohio, and the book *Poor White* itself are parallel creations of the same period on a smaller scale. *Poor White* belongs among the few books that have restored with memorable vitality the life of an era, its hopes and desires, its conflicts between material prosperity and ethics, and its disillusionments, in a manner that stimulates the historical imagination. The book belongs to the period, those years between the middle 1870's and the first ten years of the present century, that gave Thorstein Veblen's *The Theory of the Leisure Class* (the book was first published in 1899 and it is relevant to say that its author was born in Wisconsin and taught for a number of years at the University of Chicago) its air of immediate reference. It was in *Poor White* that the ideas, the talk overheard in Anderson's boyhood, bore fruit. In the second chapter of *Poor White* we come upon the following observation:

> In even the smallest of the towns [the towns of the Middle West] inhabited only by farm laborers, a quaint interesting civilization was being developed. Men worked hard but were much in the open air and had time to think. Their minds reached out toward the solution of the mystery of existence. The schoolmaster and the country lawyer read Tom Paine's *Age of Reason* and Bellamy's *Looking Backward*. They discussed these books with their fellows. There was a feeling, ill-expressed, that America had something real and spiritual to offer to the rest of the world. . . . Long-drawn-out discussions of religious beliefs and the political destiny of America were carried on.

Anderson names some of the sources from which novelists like Dreiser and philosophic economists like Veblen drew, as he did, inspiration as if from the air, and he names the premise on which a number of their critical attitudes were founded. Anderson also described the evangelical promise of that "new force" in American life of which Ingersoll was so ardent a champion:

> A new force that was being born into American life and into life everywhere all over the world was feeding on the old dying individualistic life. The new force stirred and aroused the people. It met a need that was universal. It was meant to seal men together, to wipe out national lines, to walk under seas and fly through the air, to change the entire face of the world in which men lived. Already the giant that was to be king in the place of old kings was calling his servants and his armies to serve him. He used the methods of old kings and promised his followers booty and gain . . . The Morgans, Fricks, Goulds, Carnegies, Vanderbilts, servants of the new king, princes of the new faith, merchants all, a new kind of rulers of men, defied the world-old law of class that puts the merchant below the craftsman, and added to the confusion of men by taking on the air of creators . . .
>
> And all over the country, in the towns, the farm houses, and the growing cities of the new country, people stirred and

awakened. Thought and poetry died or passed as a heritage to feeble fawning men who also became servants of the new order. Serious young men in Bidwell and in other American towns, whose fathers had walked together on moonlight nights along Turner's Pike to talk of God, went away to technical schools. . . . The impulse had reached back to their father's fathers on moonlit roads of England, Germany, Ireland, France, and Italy, and back of these to the moonlit hills of Judea where shepherds talked and serious young men, John and Matthew and Jesus, caught the drift of the talk and made poetry of it; but the serious-minded sons of these men in the new land were swept away from thinking and dreaming. From all sides the voice of the new age that was to do definite things shouted at them. Eagerly they took up the cry and ran with it.

In these lines Anderson conveys the emotional and speculative temper of the day and region which *Poor White* re-creates concretely in the imagination of the reader; but he also gives the scenes of his novel an historical perspective, by establishing their contemporaneous disillusionments. His position is obviously neither that held by the theorist, the reformer, the economist, nor the politician, but rather the one held by the novelist, the American, non-Marxian historian, the individual who shared the hopes of those who had preached the religion of humanity.

Anderson did not reach the accomplishment of *Poor White* without preparation; in writing *Winesburg, Ohio* he had begun to discover his style, and in the last chapters of the book he had really found it. He records the importance of that discovery in his *Memoirs,* how the book came to life in a series of stories while he was living in a Chicago rooming house. But *Poor White* also has behind it *Windy McPherson's Son* and more particularly, *Marching Men,* which, Anderson afterwards wrote, should have been a poem. The book was not a poem, but a novel that failed to accomplish its intentions, and yet foreshadowed the kind of novel *Poor White* became. In theory *Marching Men* is a good idea for a book; it embraces the problem of labor leadership in America and the spectacle of American workingmen marching together to redress industrial wrong. But the good idea in the novel remained too theoretical to take on the semblance of life; its hero "Beaut" McGregor, the tall, awkward, red-haired miner's son who becomes a lawyer, and afterwards a leader of workingmen, is too thinly drawn; he is an unindividualized type, whose eventual failure as a leader of men is not felt by the reader. And the entire book is punctuated by fictional clichés. Behind the obvious failure of the book, however, Anderson gives meaning even to his all-too-typical hero, for McGregor recalls the figure of General Coxey, who in the Populist movement, during the administration of Grover Cleveland, led an army of unemployed men to Washington, D.C. McGregor also resembles another Populist hero, John Peter Altgeld, Governor of Illinois, who pardoned the Haymarket anarchists and attacked Cleveland's action in sending federal troops into Illinois to break the American Railway Union. It is important that both Coxey and Altgeld were natives of Anderson's Ohio, and though the McGregor of Anderson's book was a Pennsylvania miner's son, his temperament fits the characters of the native Populist heroes of Anderson's early manhood. It is important also to remember that the living models from which the fictional McGregor was drawn received public ridicule and abuse, and that their groups of marching men, like McGregor's, met with the extremes of spectacular notoriety and failure. The only scene in *Marching Men* that comes to life is irrelevant to the historical and social themes of the book—and that is the passionate recital of the woman problem by a minor character, a barber. In the barber's speech on his unhappy marriage and his relationship to women the accents of the future Anderson are heard; the barber's theme is expanded in *Many Marriages,* and is heard with greater clarity in *Dark Laughter.* It is sounded fitfully in Anderson's first novel, *Windy McPherson's Son.*

A too broad, too loose fictional method of writing cultural (and industrial) history begins in *Windy McPherson's Son,* grows into a more clearly discerned view of Anderson's world in *Marching Men,* and then achieves a justly proportioned design in *Poor White.* In this novel Hugh McVey, the self-educated, "poor white" inventor of farm machinery, who turns the little town of Bidwell, Ohio, into a center of industrial "progress," with war between craftsmen and machine-workers, between workers and employers, remains unaware until the closing pages of the book, of the evil and loss of spiritual heritage that his well-intentioned machines have brought to the people of the town. In leaving the Chicago of *Windy McPherson's Son* and of *Marching Men* for a scene not unlike that of *Winesburg, Ohio,* Anderson found the means of giving the people of his novels flesh and blood—and through their actions, their speculative thinking, their hopes, their sense of having made mistakes, we find the real Anderson.

His Hugh McVey, as he confessed in a letter to Van Wyck Brooks, was conceived in the physical image of Lincoln, and was "a Lincolnian type from Missouri." And because of this conception, the figure carries an aura of myth-making around it and is slightly larger than life-size. Hugh McVey, as one reads of him, becomes more than one man, and one associates him with other inventors of devices and machines, with Thomas Alva Edison and with Henry Ford. His belated emotional maturity, his devotion to mechanical crafts and skills, his near-blindness to issues that lie outside the province of making machines are characteristic of the scientific-inventor type, and lead McVey to the disillusionments he suffers in the face of industrial troubles, of strikes and lockouts, to the scene in which he looks at a group of colored stones held loosely in his hand:

> The same light that had played over the stones in his hand began to play over his mind, and for a moment he became not an inventor but a poet. The revolution within had really begun. A new declaration of independence wrote itself within him. "The gods have thrown the towns like stones over the flat country, but the stones have no color. They do not burn and change in the light," he thought.

The scene also brings Hugh McVey close to the character of his author, the real Anderson, the man of insight, who had become weary of advancing the causes of business and salesmanship in Chicago advertising offices, had felt the emptiness behind the slogans of American prosperity and progress, and had contributed to the most extreme, most experimental of non-commercial little magazines, Margaret Anderson's *The Little Review,* then edited and published in Chicago. Like D. H. Lawrence, Anderson is frequently most successful in his fiction when one of his characters reveals some aspect of his own insight and emotion.

At Hugh McVey's side, how typical of her time and place, is Clara Butterworth! Clara, the daughter of a well-to-do farmer, had gone to college and then come back home to marry. She is one of the most convincing of Anderson's portraits of women, and she is treated by him with the chivalry which, despite his candor in talking about sexual relationships, always enters into his descriptions of girls and women. The exterior manner of Anderson's portraits of women, whether he views them working at looms in a factory or as ex-hostesses of brothels (see the portrait of Aunt Sally in "A Meeting South") is that of the shrewd American provincial—but under the surface of this half-worldly, half-boyish admiration, a deeply chivalrous attitude toward woman emerges. To tough-minded, self-consciously realistic readers, Anderson's undertones of chivalry are almost shocking. But this chivalry combined with sexual candor create a paradox very close to that employed by writers of Latin origin, the French, the Italian, and it gave Anderson in his day the title of the "Ohio Pagan."

*Poor White,* a tribute to a cultural past, does not, of course, resemble the costume historical novel in any of its features: it is as plotless as though Anderson had wisely taken to heart Mark Twain's warning to the readers of *Huckleberry Finn*—"persons attempting to find a plot in it will be shot." And he drew as much from the example of Mark Twain's kind of plotlessness (which never, however, permitted a story to lack action and incident) as from the examples provided by the stories in Gertrude Stein's *Three Lives.*

No novel of the American small town in the Middle West evokes in the minds of its readers so much of the cultural heritage of its milieu as does *Poor White;* nor does Anderson in his later novels ever recapture the same richness of association, the ability to make memorable each scene in the transition from an agrarian way of living to a twentieth-century spectacle of industrial conflict with its outward display of physical comfort and wealth.

## III

One of Anderson's critics has remarked on his ability to write at his best only when the impulse to write urgently moved him, and that statement has an enlightening truth within it for anyone examining his short stories. In these he held to his position of being one whose concern for prose was like a poet's concern for verse: he was a story-teller who desired only to gratify his need to talk and to charm his listeners, with no thought of pecuniary reward. But if his standards seem often those of one who perpetuates the folk tale in its simplicity, he is also the artist, who with a limited number of brush strokes leaves his style, the impress of his personality, along with the image of an undraped figure, or a landscape, upon his canvas. And if one finds the impact of any style of plastic art in Anderson's stories, it is the style of Renoir and Pissaro, of late Impressionism. For often there seems to be light and air between his sentences, as in "The American County Fair," for example, and the same loose Impressionistic strokes introduce the reader to scenes in "The Egg" and "The Man Who Became a Woman." It is in seeming at times to wander away from his story that Anderson so often relaxes and lures his readers, and within the details of an Impressionistic haze of light and color that he often creates an "artlessness" that conceals his art.

In Anderson's stories, from the early pieces which became parts of a series in *Winesburg, Ohio,* to his masterpiece "Death in the Woods," one sees the particulars of people, rather than the types that one finds in his novels. The first edition of *The Triumph of the Egg: A Book of Impressions from American Life in Tale's and Poems* (its subtitle is not to be ignored) is illustrated by photographs of grotesques in clay by Tennessee Mitchell. The grotesques, nearly burlesque portrait heads of the people in the book, are in spirit with the stories told about these people, for their individuality is carried upward, slightly off the earth, into a higher register of fancy. Since Anderson's view is always from the earth upward, in the story of "The Egg" the flight of fancy takes off from a child's-eye-view level, and we are warned early in the story that a grotesque humor will be released: we are told, "Grotesques are born out of eggs as out of people." The scene of the story is again Bidwell, Ohio, the very setting in which the events of *Poor White* took place. The story is of chicken-farming and its failure, seen through the eyes of a child whose father was an unhappy chicken-farmer, and the grotesques which come out of the eggs, the misfits, the deformed wonders of the world—the side-show of two-headed roosters and five-legged hens—are the centers of symbolic meaning in the story. The bare story as such is painful, awkward, ridiculous, naïve, and terrifying—the story of the ex-chicken-farmer who becomes a restaurant owner and a grotesque himself—but it is a story that only Anderson could tell. And the side lights of the story illuminate a burlesque of American salesmanship, for the ex-chicken-farmer and his wife, as Anderson writes, "became ambitious. The American passion for getting up in the world took possession of them." From the child's-eye-view through which Anderson presents it, the story has the authenticity of a fable, an air of candor which saves it from falling into bad taste, and the high spirit in which it is told rescues it from a mawkish concern over the spectacle of repeated failure, for the grotesque man is no more successful as a restaurant-keeper and panic-stricken salesman than he was as a chicken-farmer. It is the kind of story that having been told once cannot be told again; it is the story that makes the entire book, *The Triumph of the Egg*, memorable, and all the other stories and verses in the volume grow pale beside it; these others seem to have been written with less urgency of impulse, and though no less lyrical in tone, are thin and diffused. The book is in fact The Triumph of the Egg.

Anderson's ventures into the higher registers of fancy

(which make it strange to think of him as a realist, as he was once classified) did not end with *The Triumph of the Egg*—the ventures had actually begun in "Hands," the first of the *Winesburg* stories, and indeed the prelude to *Winesburg* was called "The Book of the Grotesque." As the image, the theme, and the fear of being grotesque matured in Anderson's imagination, some of the most clearly inspired of his stories were possessed by it. The fears of being strange and, similarly, the painful, half-comic experiences of "growing up," pervade the stories and sketches of *Horses and Men.* The book is literally of horses and men, and no American writer of Anderson's generation or any other has caught the colors, the lights and shadows, the spirit of the race track as well as he; the race track is Anderson's milieu quite as the American county fair is, and among those who write of sports, he is in the company of Ring Lardner and Ernest Hemingway. But here also his view of the scene is a characteristic upward glance, the view of country boys in "I'm a Fool" and "The Man Who Became a Woman." The boys are grooms' helpers, "swipes," and they follow the circuit of race-track activities with the same delight with which their younger brothers would try to enter the world of the traveling wild west show or circus. The influence of George Borrow's attraction to gypsy life is active here, but Anderson translates it wholly into American sights and scenes.

Yet all this is finally only the happy choice of a decor for what he really has to say, and in "The Man Who Became a Woman" what is said touches upon the fears, the mysteries of adolescence—the fear of the boy (now grown to a man) on discovering that he is "strange," is not wholly masculine, and underlying this, the fear of sterility and death. With a touch as sure as that of D. H. Lawrence, and with none of the mechanical features of overt psychological fiction, Anderson uses, with deceptive simplicity, the scenes in the bar-room and the hay-loft, and the incident of the boy's fall, naked, into the shell of bones which was once the carcass of a horse, as the means to tell his story. None of Anderson's stories, with the exception of "Death in the Woods," is a better example of his skill in giving the so-called common experiences of familiar, everyday life, an aura of internal meaning. In this story there is also the fear of Negro laughter, a fear which enters at extended length into two of his later novels, *Dark Laughter* and *Beyond Desire.* In "The Man Who Became a Woman," that particular fear is made more convincing, more appropriate than in the novels; the boy's innocence, his lack of experience, do much to justify his fear, and the fear properly belongs to the immature, the unpoised, the ignorant.

"I'm a Fool" is done with the same turning of light upon common experience—the telling of an awkward, grotesque, foolish lie. Again it is part of the painful experience of growing up, a boyish shrewdness that failed of its desires; it is the image of the concealed, the fatal mistake made by the glib, the young, the unworldly, who parade their candor and innocence wherever they walk and breathe.

"Death in the Woods," Anderson's masterpiece among his shorter stories, is of a different temper and key than the colorful, high-spirited narratives of *Horses and Men.* It is a story which, as Anderson realized, demanded perfection of its kind: he rewrote it several times; it had originally been an episode in *Tar,* and had continued to haunt Anderson's imagination. The strong, initial impulse to write it was not enough, for the story, beyond any other story that Anderson wrote, was the summing up of a lifetime's experience, and in its final version it became Anderson's last look backward into the Middle

West of his childhood. It was the last of his *Mid-American Chants,* the book of verses in prose, the last of the prose poems in *A New Testament,* and though its external form is plainly that of a story, its internal structure is that of poetry; it has the power of saying more than prose is required to say, and saying it in the fewest words. But of more importance than the phonetic art of the story is the interplay of those prose rhythms of which Anderson had become a master, and the control of its central theme. To the editors of *The Oxford Anthology of American Literature* Anderson wrote in 1937:

> It seems to me that the theme of the story is the persistent animal hunger of man. There are these women who spend their whole lives, rather dumbly, feeding this hunger. For years I wanted to write this story.
>
> As for the technique, it was quite definitely thought out. Over a period of several years I made several attempts that had to be thrown aside. For example I thought it necessary to . . . lift the animal hunger, I wanted to get at, out of the realm of sex. Therefore my tired-out, sexless old woman, the dogs feeding from the food attached to her body after her own death.
>
> The story has its particular form . . . the young man and the German fighting over the girl in the road, the son bringing his mistress to his mother's house, the butcher, half-grudgingly and yet out of pity, giving her the meat bones, the dogs circling in the mysterious moonlit night in the forest, the men and boys of the town hurrying out of town to find the body. . . . What is wanted is something beyond the horizon, to retain the sense of mystery in life while showing at the same time, at what cost our ordinary animal hungers are sometimes fed.

Anderson's explanation is like that of a poet presenting the argument of a poem; and the story contains the kind of poetry that we associated with Wordsworth—the recollection of youthful experience, the figures of common speech, the instinctive dignity and life of the poor, the moonlit rural scene—done with the simplicity that

Wordsworth sought and attained. It is for this reason (among others) that the story transcends its regional atmosphere, and becomes the universal story that it is. One can think of it, and not inappropriately, as a story that applies to the years of cold and famine in postwar twentieth-century Europe; it has that kind of universality, one that makes possible analogies in life as well as literature. In writing it Anderson's transcendental note was clearly sounded. The note transcends, in more than one meaning of the verb, the writers from whom Anderson drew inspiration—his own contemporaries, Gertrude Stein, Dreiser, D. H. Lawrence, as well as the writers who came before him in revolt against the Puritan New England tradition—and places him not too far from the figures of Thoreau and Emerson.

To enter that dangerous ground which lies between prose and poetry, and to emerge at last, as Anderson does in "Death in the Woods," unscarred by its pitfalls, is a considerable accomplishment, one that has been achieved by few writers in America, and of this small number most are writers whose books provide larger scenes of action than are witnessed in any of Anderson's short stories or novels. It was his contribution and perhaps his destiny, to limit the size of his canvas, to give those who read him a view whose depth, like that of a picture, is greater than the span of the frame around it, and that is one of the reasons why Anderson's best stories have the penetrating quality of Ishmael's gaze in the opening chapters of *Moby Dick*.

## IV

In the years between his writing of *Windy McPherson's Son* in 1916 and his death in 1941, Anderson wrote twenty-five books, including seven novels, a half-dozen

volumes of essays, and two plays, dramatizations of scenes from *Winesburg, Ohio* and *The Triumph of the Egg.* The essays were, properly speaking, editorials on the themes that entered his novels and short stories. They supplemented his lecture tours and the editing of two small-town newspapers which occupied his time during the latter years of his life, and they were concerned with the problems of a self-consciously transitional machine age in America. Many of the subjects with which Anderson dealt, his speculations on sex, and what was spoken of as "the war of the sexes" have, at least in the terms he employed, passed out of fashion, with little likelihood of revival. Nor do such novels as *Beyond Desire, Many Marriages,* and *Dark Laughter,* bold and candid as they were at the time they were written, have much possibility of attracting the eye and ear of a later generation: they advanced themes implicit in some of the stories published in this volume, but in the novels the editorial and theoretical aspects of the "machine age" (which editorial writers now call an "atomic age") are disfigurements. And the richness, the sense of the mystery of life, which Anderson gave voice to in his stories thins to an echo of itself in the later novels.

The real Anderson of the stories, sketches, and novels collected in this volume was one who greatly enjoyed life as he found it, but his discovery of it was no easy accomplishment, and the difficulty of this discovery involves his particular genius as a writer. With the writing of the stories in *Winesburg, Ohio,* that discovery had begun, and when the book was published he was a man of forty-three, an age at which too many American writers have left their best years behind them. In Anderson a richness of personality flowered late and held within it an appreciation of the physical joy of being which in his stories is conveyed through things seen and heard, images of the race track, the sight of moonlight in winter, the stones held in the hand of Hugh McVey, or, in the last pages of *Winesburg, Ohio,* George Willard at the station platform at seven forty-five in the morning stepping on the train. In these scenes the joy of being is almost kinetic, a joy of bodily movement, of seeing things and human beings in transit, freshly and directly, and then moving on. As the unnamed spectator in his own books, Anderson often becomes the charmed and delighted visitor on earth, and the reader shares with him the sense of discovering, under drab exteriors, the strangeness and the physical beauty in what are usually passed by as ordinary things and people.

These qualities, which are felt throughout his writings, brought him the friendship of two courageous and discerning publishers, B. W. Huebsch and Horace Liveright; and to these among many were added the friendships of Dreiser, Van Wyck Brooks, Paul Rosenfeld (whose last days in 1946 were spent editing an omnibus edition of Anderson's shorter pieces), Waldo Frank, Carl Sandburg, and Gertrude Stein. But more extraordinary than these older friendships was the admiration and affection he received from younger writers. In America literary generations are so short and their figures are so quickly discarded, that to find an older man who holds the affection of the young is to discover a rarity. In this respect Anderson's qualities did not go unrewarded, bringing him the regard of many young writers, including Hart Crane, William Faulkner, Thomas Wolfe—each of whom saw in Anderson a reflection of his own concern for the arts of prose and poetry. They and many others owe a debt to the imaginative insight Anderson possessed and to the intimate, speaking voices of his prose. He was their Ishmael, their contemporary, and their master.

At a time, today, when most of the writers of Anderson's generation are highly respected and less read, Anderson's stories hold a place that is undisputed, and each new reader, welcoming his modesty, feels no constraint in reading Anderson for pleasure. This volume is edited with Anderson's new readers kept in mind, and it contains those selections from his writings which even now seem to assure him of a life beyond the horizon, beyond the moment of his own enriched experience and ours.

HORACE GREGORY

## THE CHRONOLOGY OF SHERWOOD ANDERSON'S LIFE AND BOOKS

1876. September 13, Sherwood Anderson born in Camden, Ohio.

1879-1897. The events of these years (without dates attached to them) are described in *Tar, A Story-Teller's Story,* and *Sherwood Anderson's Memoirs.* The picture is one of a family drifting from one small Ohio town to another: the father, a "story-teller" from the South who had served in the Union Army and who declined from the saddlery-and-harness business into odd jobs of house- and sign-painting, the mother, a woman of Italian or of German descent, who gave birth to seven children, of whom Sherwood Anderson was the third. Karl Anderson, the painter, was Sherwood Anderson's elder brother. The genius for story-telling, the eye for color, came to Sherwood Anderson within the circle of his family; his schooling was irregular, and was both accelerated and modified by his need to take many odd jobs; he sold newspapers, worked in cabbage fields and on racecourses, was a stable-boy and a factory hand.

1898-1912. Anderson volunteered for service in the U. S. Army during the Spanish-American War and on his return from Cuba spent a short time at Wittenberg College in Ohio. Even before the war, he had begun to write, and among the jobs he had held during a stay in Chicago was one as a copy-writer in an advertising office. He resumed this position upon leaving Wittenberg. He married and returned to Ohio, this time to Elyria, where he ran a paint factory. From running a business he turned again to an advertising office in Chicago, and began to meet young writers in Chicago.

1912-1915. Anderson began to contribute essays and stories to Margaret Anderson's and Jane Heap's *The Little Review,* and in his *Memoirs* he tells of meeting Carl Sandburg, Ben Hecht, Floyd Dell, Eunice Tietjens.

1916. The chronology of Anderson's books begins with his first novel, *Windy McPherson's Son.*

1917. *Marching Men,* a novel.

1918. *Mid-American Chants,* unrhymed poems.

1919. *Winesburg, Ohio,* a group of tales of Ohio small-town life.

1920. *Poor White,* a novel.

1921. *The Triumph of the Egg,* a book of impressions of American life in tales and poems. In this year Anderson received *The Dial* award of two thousand dollars, which, with the recognition he had received as the author of *Winesburg, Ohio* and *Poor White,* gave him a sense of well-being that permitted a holiday in Europe. He had already enlarged the orbit of his travels from areas of which Chicago was the center to New York.

1922-1923. *Many Marriages,* a novel, and *Horses and Men,* tales long and short from American life, were published. Anderson spent the greater part of the year in New Orleans, where he shared an apartment with William Faulkner.

1924. *A Story-Teller's Story,* the tale of an American writer's journey through his own imaginative world and through the world of facts. From this book one learns why Anderson disregarded dates in his autobiographies; in it he wrote: "I think it was Joseph Conrad who said that a writer only began to live after he began to write. It pleased me to think I was after all but ten years old. Plenty of time ahead for such a one. Time to look about, plenty of time to look about."

1925. "The Modern Writer," an essay; *Dark Laughter,* a novel, the only novel Anderson wrote that became commercially successful. With the money earned from this book he bought a farm near Marion, Virginia, and he also purchased and edited two newspapers in Marion. *Hands and Other Stories,* selected from *Winesburg, Ohio.*

1926. *Sherwood Anderson's Notebook; Tar: A Midwest Childhood.*

1927. *A New Testament,* poems in prose. Through this period, he continued his series of lectures throughout the country, which had become one of his ways of earning a livelihood.

1929. *Hello Towns!*, selected pieces from his newspapers; "Nearer the Grass Roots," an essay; *Alice and the Lost Novel,* stories.

1930. *The American County Fair.*

1931. *Perhaps Women,* an essay on women which continued the discussions of sex that had appeared in his novels from *Marching Men* to *Dark Laughter.*

1932. *Beyond Desire,* a novel.

1933. *Death in the Woods and Other Stories.*

1934. "No Swank," an essay. In this year he dramatized *Winesburg, Ohio,* which was put on the stage by the Hedgerow Theatre Group.

1935. *Puzzled America,* an essay.

1936. *Kit Brandon,* a novel.

1937. Four plays were published: *Winesburg, Ohio, The Triumph of the Egg, Mother,* and *They Married Later.* The last three are one-act plays.

1939. *Home Town,* a book of prose sketches.

1941. Death from peritonitis on a trip to South America; he died at Cristobal, Canal Zone.

1942. *Sherwood Anderson's Memoirs.*

1947. *The Sherwood Anderson Reader,* edited by Paul Rosenfeld.

## A SELECTED BIBLIOGRAPHY ON SHERWOOD ANDERSON

Few writers of his generation have attracted more diversified critical attention than Sherwood Anderson. The literature on Anderson is large and often contradictory. The following short list of titles presents views and opinions of him that are likely to endure through time and changes of fashion.

The best book-length study of Anderson is Cleveland B. Chase's *Sherwood Anderson* (New York: Robert M. McBride & Co., 1927). The book devotes most of its attention to *Winesburg, Ohio* and attempts to place Anderson as an important figure in the American scene of his day. In its approach to Anderson's writings the book reflects a middle-of-the-road, academic attitude which is neither profound nor stimulating; yet it represents with fair accuracy "objective" opinion during Sherwood Anderson's lifetime concerning his accomplishments as a short-story writer. The book has its value for those who wish to make a study of critical opinions on Anderson's writings without reference to Anderson's personal legend.

Harlan Hatcher's *Creating the Modern American Novel* (New York: Farrar & Rinehart, 1935) supplements Chase's book in placing Anderson among his contemporaries. Hatcher's chapter on Anderson is the first in a section which carries the spectacular title of "Freudian Psychology and the Sex Age," but the chapter itself contains many sound observations on the nature of Anderson's position in American literature. Hatcher was among the first of Anderson's critics to insist that his gifts were not those of a realist, and that he was one of "the few first-rate symbolists in America." The chapter is also valuable for its appreciation of Anderson's "instincts." Of them Hatcher wrote: "He [Anderson] has always been willing to trust these instincts and let them bring into his novels the unaccountable tumult of the soul which defies all reason." Hatcher's chapter remains the best of all academic (and sympathetic) commentaries on Anderson's place in American fiction of the nineteen-twenties.

Waldo Frank's essay on *Winesburg, Ohio* (*Story*, September–October 1941) is the most penetrating of all critical observations on the book in which Anderson "found himself." Frank observed Anderson's instinctive emotional debt to the heritage of the Old Testament, and with great persuasion and imaginative insight he convinces even the most skeptical of what he believes to be the sources of Anderson's so-called mysticism. Frank is one of the few among Anderson's friends who were able to detach the value of Anderson's writings from the charms of Anderson's personality; the piece is also one of the best of Waldo Frank's critical writings.

Of short critical commentaries on Anderson, Lionel Trilling's "Sherwood Anderson" (*Kenyon Review*, Summer 1941) is the most stimulating because it opens several views toward a final evaluation of Anderson's writings. Although it is too brief to be conclusive in itself (and Trilling seems to be of two minds regarding Anderson's contribution to American literature), the essay provides the means of discussing pros and cons of Anderson's reputation in the eyes of contemporary critics. Trilling clearly states Anderson's preoccupation with the details of adolescent emotion, and raises doubts as to its moral value. In general, and not so clearly, he relates the body of Anderson's writings to the "Whitman tradition" in American letters. He repeats a brilliant but essentially unsound and ill-informed attack on Anderson made by Wyndham Lewis in *Paleface,* and speculates upon the validity of Anderson's "truth": "Anderson's truth may have become a falsehood in his hands through limitations in himself, but one has only to take it out of his hands to see again that it is still a truth. . . ." The value of Trilling's remarks lies in the effort to discuss Anderson with appropriate seriousness; but they also show Anderson's ability (which was not unlike D. H. Lawrence's) to concern and bedevil his serious critics.

The most revealing and engaging of the personal memoirs of Anderson is in Margaret Anderson's *My Thirty Years' War* (New York: Covici, Friede, Inc., 1930). Her portrait of Anderson recalls him giving her advice on the fortunes of her magazine, *The Little Review.* Another early Chicago portrait may be found in Robert Morss Lovett's tribute to Anderson in *The Virginia Quarterly Review* (Summer 1941).

For readers who wish to study Anderson's writing at greater length, *The Sherwood Anderson Reader,* edited by Paul Rosenfeld (Boston: Houghton, Mifflin, 1947), and *The Letters of Sherwood Anderson,* edited by Howard Mumford Jones and Walter B. Rideout (Boston: Little, Brown, 1953), are recommended.

# From
# WINESBURG, OHIO

## EDITOR'S NOTE

*Winesburg, Ohio* is Sherwood Anderson's fourth book and his first collection of tales, and was published in 1919. Some of the stories had already appeared in *The Little Review*, then published in Chicago, which was the most high-spirited of the "little magazines" in the years 1914-1928. Within its pages, James Joyce's *Ulysses* as well as stories by Sherwood Anderson and poems by Hart Crane made an early appearance. Of its editor, Margaret Anderson—she was not related to the writer—Sherwood Anderson wrote in *A Story-Teller's Story:* "Miss Anderson and myself had in common a fondness for rather striking clothes and for strutting a bit upon the stage of life that drew us closely together but being at bottom fellow Chicagoans we were bound not to take each other too seriously—at least not under the rose." And of him, Miss Anderson wrote in *My Thirty Years' War:* "Floyd Dell and I talked of Pater and of living with the hard gem-like flame. Sherwood Anderson used to listen to us in a certain amazement (resembling fear) and indicating clearly that nothing would induce him into such fancy realms. But I liked Sherwood—because he, too, was a talker and of a highly special type. He didn't talk ideas—he told stories. (It sounds bad but the stories were good. So was the telling.) He said to everyone: You don't mind if I use that story you've just told, do you? No one minded. Sherwood's story never bore any relation to the original. He read us the manuscript of *Windy McPherson's Son.* Floyd was passionate about it —I, a little less so. It was a new prose but I knew by Sherwood's look that he would do something even better."

In a lecture called "A Writer's Conception of Realism," published in 1939, Anderson said of *Winesburg, Ohio:* "The book was written in a crowded tenement district of Chicago. The hint for almost every character was taken from my fellow lodgers in a large rooming house, many of whom had never lived in a village. . . . Most people are afraid to trust their imagination and the artist is not. . . . Realism, in so far as the word means reality to life, is always bad art." These statements explain what Miss Anderson meant when she said "Sherwood's story never bore any relation to the original." They also explain why the stories of *Winesburg, Ohio,* although they are set in the remembered atmosphere of a small town in America, have a "universal" quality.

If one remembers the moment when *Winesburg, Ohio* first appeared as a book, it is little wonder that the book became a landmark in American fiction. At that moment it held the same relationship to prose as Edgar Lee Masters' *The Spoon River Anthology* held to verse. It was admired for its candor and for its realism, and for its success in shocking the sensibilities of insensible people. Because of its success, it accomplished a revolution in the American short story, but, as the moment of the book's arrival falls into the past, certain stories in *Winesburg, Ohio* hold the reader's attention better than others, and one also becomes aware that some of Anderson's later stories repeat with greater art and deeper insight a few of the episodes, scenes, and themes which first appeared in *Winesburg,*

*Ohio.* For this reason the present editor has omitted one death scene in *Winesburg, Ohio* so that its theme and emotion may be given their complete and mature expression in "Death in the Woods," and Sherwood Anderson's remarks on the grotesque which introduce the reader to *Winesburg, Ohio* are omitted in favor of the best of his grotesque stories—the story of "The Egg." The loose construction of *Winesburg, Ohio* makes it possible to present the best of its stories without loss to the reader, and it should be remembered that the tales of *Winesburg, Ohio* were conceived and written as short stories before they appeared under the title of a book.

# Hands

(CONCERNING WING BIDDLEBAUM)

UPON the half-decayed veranda of a small frame house that stood near the edge of a ravine near the town of Winesburg, Ohio, a fat little old man walked nervously up and down. Across a long field that had been seeded for clover but that had produced only a dense crop of yellow mustard weeds, he could see the public highway along which went a wagon filled with berry pickers returning from the fields. The berry pickers, youths and maidens, laughed and shouted boisterously. A boy clad in a blue shirt leaped from the wagon and attempted to drag after him one of the maidens who screamed and protested shrilly. The feet of the boy in the road kicked up a cloud of dust that floated across the face of the departing sun. Over the long field came a thin girlish voice. "Oh, you Wing Biddlebaum, comb your hair, it's falling into your eyes," commanded the voice to the man, who was bald and whose nervous little hands fiddled about the bare white forehead as though arranging a mass of tangled locks.

Wing Biddlebaum, forever frightened and beset by a ghostly band of doubts, did not think of himself as in any way a part of the life of the town where he had lived for twenty years. Among all the people of Winesburg but one had come close to him. With George Willard, son of Tom Willard, the proprietor of the new Willard House, he had formed something like a friendship. George Willard was the reporter on the *Winesburg Eagle* and sometimes in the evenings he walked out along the highway to Wing Biddlebaum's house. Now as the old man walked up and down on the veranda, his hands moving nervously about, he was hoping that George Willard would come and spend the evening with him. After the wagon containing the berry pickers had passed, he went across the field through the tall mustard weeds and climbing a rail fence peered anxiously along the road to the town. For a moment he stood thus, rubbing his hands together and looking up and down the road, and then, fear overcoming him, ran back to walk again upon the porch on his own house.

In the presence of George Willard, Wing Biddlebaum, who for twenty years had been the town mystery, lost something of his timidity, and his shadowy personality, submerged in a sea of doubts, came forth to look at the world. With the young reporter at his side, he ventured in the light of day into Main Street or strode up and down on the rickety front porch of his own house, talking excitedly. The voice that had been low and trembling became shrill and loud. The bent figure straightened. With a kind of wriggle, like a fish returned to the brook by the fisherman, Biddlebaum the silent began to talk, striving to put into words the ideas that had been accumulated by his mind during long years of silence.

Wing Biddlebaum talked much with his hands. The slender expressive fingers, forever active, forever striving to conceal themselves in his pockets or behind his back, came forth and became the piston rods of his machinery of expression.

The story of Wing Biddlebaum is a story of hands. Their restless activity, like unto the beating of the wings of an imprisoned bird, had given him his name. Some obscure poet of the town had thought of it. The hands alarmed their owner. He wanted to keep them hidden away and looked with amazement at the quiet inexpressive hands of other men who worked beside him in the fields, or passed, driving sleepy teams on country roads.

When he talked to George Willard, Wing Biddlebaum closed his fists and beat with them upon a table or on the walls of his house. The action made him more comfortable. If the desire to talk came to him when the two were walking in the fields, he sought out a stump or the top board of a fence and with his hands pounding busily talked with renewed ease.

The story of Wing Biddlebaum's hands is worth a book in itself. Sympathetically set forth it would tap many strange, beautiful qualities in obscure men. It is a job for a poet. In Winesburg the hands had attracted attention merely because of their activity. With them Wing Biddlebaum had picked as high as a hundred and forty quarts of strawberries in a day. They became his distinguishing feature, the source of his fame. Also they made more grotesque an already grotesque and elusive individuality. Winesburg was proud of the hands of Wing Biddlebaum in the same spirit in which it was proud of Banker White's new stone house and Wesley Moyer's bay stallion, Tony Tip, that had won the two-fifteen trot at the fall races in Cleveland.

As for George Willard, he had many times wanted to ask about the hands. At times an almost overwhelming curiosity had taken hold of him. He felt that there must be a reason for their strange activity and their inclination to keep hidden away and only a growing respect for Wing Biddlebaum kept him from blurting out the questions that were often in his mind.

Once he had been on the point of asking. The two were walking in the fields on a summer afternoon and had stopped to sit upon a grassy bank. All afternoon Wing Biddlebaum had talked as one inspired. By a fence he had stopped and beating like a giant woodpecker upon the top board had shouted at George Willard, condemning his tendency to be too much influenced by the people about him. "You are destroying yourself," he cried. "You have the inclination to be alone and to dream and you are afraid of dreams. You want to be like others in town here. You hear them talk and you try to imitate them."

On the grassy bank Wing Biddlebaum had tried again to drive his point home. His voice became soft and reminiscent, and with a sigh of contentment he launched into a long rambling talk, speaking as one lost in a dream.

Out of the dream Wing Biddlebaum made a picture for George Willard. In the picture men lived again in a kind of pastoral golden age. Across a green open country came clean-limbed young men, some afoot, some mounted upon horses. In crowds the young men came to gather about the feet of an old man who sat beneath a tree in a tiny garden and who talked to them.

Wing Biddlebaum became wholly inspired. For once he forgot the hands. Slowly they stole forth and lay upon George Willard's shoulders. Something new and bold came into the voice that talked. "You must try to forget all you have learned," said the old man. "You must begin to dream. From this time on you must shut your ears to the roaring of the voices."

Pausing in his speech, Wing Biddlebaum looked long and earnestly at George Willard. His eyes glowed. Again he raised the hands to caress the boy and then a look of horror swept over his face.

With a convulsive movement of his body, Wing Biddlebaum sprang to his feet and thrust his hands deep into his trousers pockets. Tears came to his eyes. "I must be getting along home. I can talk no more with you," he said nervously.

Without looking back, the old man had hurried down the hillside and across a meadow, leaving George Willard perplexed and frightened upon the grassy slope. With a shiver of dread the boy arose and went along the road toward town. "I'll not ask him about his hands," he thought, touched by the memory of the terror he had seen in the man's eyes. "There's something wrong, but I don't want to know what it is. His hands have something to do with his fear of me and of everyone."

And George Willard was right. Let us look briefly into the story of the hands. Perhaps our talking of them will arouse the poet who will tell the hidden wonder story of the influence for which the hands were but fluttering pennants of promise.

In his youth Wing Biddlebaum had been a school teacher in a town in Pennsylvania. He was not then known as Wing Biddlebaum, but went by the less euphonic name of Adolph Myers. As Adolph Myers he was much loved by the boys of his school.

Adolph Myers was meant by nature to be a teacher of youth. He was one of those rare, little-understood men who rule by a power so gentle that it passes as a lovable weakness. In their feeling for the boys under their charge such men are not unlike the finer sort of women in their love of men.

And yet that is but crudely stated. It needs the poet there. With the boys of his school, Adolph Myers had walked in the evening or had sat talking until dusk upon the schoolhouse steps lost in a kind of dream. Here and there went his hands, caressing the shoulders of the boys, playing about the tousled heads. As he talked his voice became soft and musical. There was a caress in that also. In a way the voice and the hands, the stroking of the shoulders and the touching of the hair was a part of the schoolmaster's effort to carry a dream into the young minds. By the caress that was in his fingers he expressed himself. He was one of those men in whom the force that creates life is diffused, not centralized. Under the caress of his hands doubt and disbelief went out of the minds of the boys and they began also to dream.

And then the tragedy. A half-witted boy of the school became enamored of the young master. In his bed at night he imagined unspeakable things and in the morning went forth to tell his dreams as facts. Strange hideous accusations fell from his loose-hung lips. Through the Pennsylvania town went a shiver. Hidden, shadowy doubts that had been in men's minds concerning Adolph Myers were galvanized into beliefs.

The tragedy did not linger. Trembling lads were jerked out of bed and questioned. "He put his arms about me," said one. "His fingers were always playing in my hair," said another.

One afternoon a man of the town, Henry Bradford, who kept a saloon, came to the schoolhouse door. Calling Adolph Myers into the school yard he began to beat him with his fists. As his hard knuckles beat down into the frightened face of the schoolmaster, his wrath became more and more terrible. Screaming with dismay, the children ran here and there like disturbed insects. "I'll teach you to put your hands on my boy, you beast," roared the saloon keeper, who, tired of beating the master, had begun to kick him about the yard.

Adolph Myers was driven from the Pennsylvania town in the night. With lanterns in their hands a dozen men came to the door of the house where he lived alone and commanded that he dress and come forth. It was raining and one of the men had a rope in his hands. They had intended to hang the schoolmaster, but something in his figure, so small, white, and pitiful, touched their hearts and they let him escape. As he ran away into the darkness they repented of their weakness and ran after him, swearing and throwing sticks and great balls of soft mud at the figure that screamed and ran faster and faster into the darkness.

For twenty years Adolph Myers had lived alone in Winesburg. He was but forty but looked sixty-five. The name of Biddlebaum he got from a box of goods seen at a freight station as he hurried through an eastern Ohio town. He had an aunt in Winesburg, a black-toothed old woman who raised chickens, and with her he lived until she died. He had been ill for a year after the experience in Pennsylvania, and after his recovery worked as a day laborer in the fields, going timidly about and striving to conceal his hands. Although he did not understand what had happened he felt that the hands must be to blame. Again and again the fathers of the boys had talked of the hands. "Keep your hands to yourself," the saloon keeper had roared, dancing with fury in the schoolhouse yard.

Upon the veranda of his house by the ravine, Wing Biddlebaum continued to walk up and down until the sun had disappeared and the road beyond the field was lost in the gray shadows. Going into his house he cut slices of bread and spread honey upon them. When the rumble of the evening train that took away the express cars loaded with the day's harvest of berries had passed and restored the silence of the summer night, he went again to walk upon the veranda. In the darkness he could not see the hands and they became quiet.

Although he still hungered for the presence of the boy, who was the medium through which he expressed his love of man, the hunger became again a part of his loneliness and his waiting. Lighting a lamp, Wing Biddlebaum washed the few dishes soiled by his simple meal and, setting up a folding cot by the screen door that led to the porch, prepared to undress for the night. A few stray white bread crumbs lay on the cleanly washed floor by the table; putting the lamp on a low stool he began to pick up the crumbs, carrying them to his mouth one by one with unbelievable rapidity. In the dense blotch of light beneath the table, the kneeling figure looked like a priest engaged in some service of his church. The nervous expressive fingers, flashing in and out of the light, might well have been mistaken for the fingers of the devotee going swiftly through decade after decade of his rosary.

# The Philosopher

(CONCERNING DOCTOR PARCIVAL)

DOCTOR PARCIVAL was a large man with a drooping mouth covered by a yellow mustache. He always wore a dirty white waistcoat out of the pockets of which protruded a number of the kind of black cigars known as stogies. His teeth were black and irregular and there was something strange about his eyes. The lid of the left eye twitched; it fell down and snapped up; it was exactly as though the lid of the eye were a window shade and someone stood inside the doctor's head playing with the cord.

Doctor Parcival had a liking for the boy, George Willard. It began when George had been working for a year on the *Winesburg Eagle* and the acquaintanceship was entirely a matter of the doctor's own making.

In the late afternoon Will Henderson, owner and editor of the *Eagle*, went over to Tom Willy's saloon. Along an alleyway he went and slipping in at the back door of the saloon began drinking a drink made of a combination of sloe gin and soda water. Will Henderson was a sensualist and had reached the age of forty-five. He imagined the gin renewed the youth in him. Like most sensualists he enjoyed talking of women, and for an hour he lingered about gossiping with Tom Willy. The saloon keeper was a short, broad-shouldered man with peculiarly marked hands. That flaming kind of birthmark that sometimes paints with red the faces of men and women had touched with red Tom Willy's fingers and the backs of his hands. As he stood by the bar talking to Will Henderson he rubbed the hands together. As he grew more and more excited the red of his fingers deepened. It was as though the hands had been dipped in blood that had dried and faded.

As Will Henderson stood at the bar looking at the red hands and talking of women, his assistant, George Willard, sat in the office of the *Winesburg Eagle* and listened to the talk of Doctor Parcival.

Doctor Parcival appeared immediately after Will Henderson had disappeared. One might have supposed that the doctor had been watching from his office window and had seen the editor going along the alleyway. Coming in at the front door and finding himself a chair, he lighted one of the stogies and crossing his legs began to talk. He seemed intent upon convincing the boy of the advisability of adopting a line of conduct that he was himself unable to define.

"If you have your eyes open you will see that although I call myself a doctor I have mighty few patients," he began. "There is a reason for that. It is not an accident and it is not because I do not know as much of medicine as anyone here. I do not want patients. The reason, you see, does not appear on the surface. It lies in fact in my character, which has, if you think about it, many strange turns. Why I want to talk to you of the matter I don't know. I might keep still and get more credit in your eyes. I have a desire to make you admire me, that's a fact. I don't know why. That's why I talk. It's very amusing, eh?"

Sometimes the doctor launched into long tales concerning himself. To the boy the tales were very real and full of meaning. He began to admire the fat unclean-looking man and, in the afternoon when Will Henderson had gone, looked forward with keen interest to the doctor's coming.

Doctor Parcival had been in Winesburg about five years. He came from Chicago and when he arrived was drunk and got into a fight with Albert Longworth, the baggageman. The fight concerned a trunk and ended by the doctor's being escorted to the village lockup. When he was released he rented a room above a shoe-repairing shop at the lower end of Main Street and put out the sign that announced himself as a doctor. Although he had but few patients and these of the poorer sort who were unable to pay, he seemed to have plenty of money for his needs. He slept in the office that was unspeakably dirty and dined at Biff Carter's lunchroom in a small frame building opposite the railroad station. In the summer the lunchroom was filled with flies and Biff Carter's white apron was more dirty than his floor. Doctor Parcival did not mind. Into the lunchroom he stalked and deposited twenty cents upon the counter. "Feed me what you wish for that," he said laughing. "Use up food that you wouldn't otherwise sell. It makes no difference to me. I am a man of distinction, you see. Why should I concern myself with what I eat."

The tales that Doctor Parcival told George Willard began nowhere and ended nowhere. Sometimes the boy thought they must all be inventions, a pack of lies. And then again he was convinced that they contained the very essence of truth.

"I was a reporter like you here," Doctor Parcival began. "It was in a town in Iowa—or was it in Illinois? I don't remember and anyway it makes no difference. Perhaps I am trying to conceal my identity and don't want to be very definite. Have you ever thought it strange that I have money for my needs although I do nothing? I may have stolen a great sum of money or been involved in a murder before I came here. There is food for thought in that, eh? If you were a really smart newspaper reporter you would look me up. In Chicago there was a Doctor Cronin who was murdered. Have you heard of that? Some men murdered him and put him in a trunk. In the early morning they hauled the trunk across the city. It sat on the back of an express wagon and they were on the seat as unconcerned as anything. Along they went through quiet streets where everyone was asleep. The sun was just coming up over the lake. Funny, eh—just to think of them smoking pipes and chattering as they drove along as unconcerned as I am now. Perhaps I was one of those men. That would be a strange turn of things, now wouldn't it, eh?" Again Doctor Parcival began his tale: "Well, anyway there I was, a reporter on a paper just as you are here, running about and getting little items to print. My mother was poor. She took in washing. Her dream was to make me a Presbyterian minister and I was studying with that end in view.

"My father had been insane for a number of years. He was in an asylum over at Dayton, Ohio. There you see I have let it slip out! All of this took place in Ohio, right here in Ohio. There is a clew if you ever get the notion of looking me up.

"I was going to tell you of my brother. That's the object of all this. That's what I'm getting at. My brother was a railroad painter and had a job on the Big Four. You know that road runs through Ohio here. With other men he lived in a box car and away they went from town to town painting the railroad property—switches, crossing gates, bridges, and stations.

"The Big Four paints its stations a nasty orange color. How I hated that color! My brother was always covered with it. On pay days he used to get drunk and come home wearing his paint-covered clothes and bringing his money with him. He did not give it to mother but laid it in a pile on our kitchen table.

"About the house he went in the clothes covered with the nasty orange-colored paint. I can see the picture. My mother, who was small and had red, sad-looking eyes, would come into the house from a little shed at the back. That's where she spent her time over the washtub scrubbing people's dirty clothes. In she would come and stand by the table, rubbing her eyes with her apron that was covered with soap-suds.

" 'Don't touch it! Don't you dare touch that money,' my brother roared, and then he himself took five or ten dollars and went tramping off to the saloons. When he had spent what he had taken he came back for more. He never gave my mother any money at all but stayed about until he had spent it all, a little at a time. Then he went back to his job with the painting crew on the railroad. After he had gone things began to arrive at our house, groceries and such things. Sometimes there would be a dress for mother or a pair of shoes for me.

"Strange, eh? My mother loved my brother much more than she did me, although he never said a kind word to either of us and always raved up and down threatening us if we dared so much as touch the money that sometimes lay on the table three days.

"We got along pretty well. I studied to be a minister and prayed. I was a regular ass about saying prayers. You should have heard me. When my father died I prayed all night, just as I did sometimes when my brother was in town drinking and going about buying the things for us. In the evening after supper I knelt by the table where the money lay and prayed for hours. When no one was looking I stole a dollar or two and put it in my pocket. That makes me laugh now but then it was terrible. It was on my mind all the time. I got six dollars a week from my job on the paper and always took it straight home to mother. The few dollars I stole from my brother's pile I spent on myself, you know, for trifles, candy and cigarettes and such things.

"When my father died at the asylum over at Dayton, I went over there. I borrowed some money from the man for whom I worked and went on the train at night. It was raining. In the asylum they treated me as though I were a king.

"The men who had jobs in the asylum had found out I was a newspaper reporter. That made them afraid. There had been some negligence, some carelessness, you see, when father was ill. They thought perhaps I would write it up in the paper and make a fuss. I never intended to do anything of the kind.

"Anyway, in I went to the room where my father lay dead and blessed the dead body. I wonder what put that notion into my head. Wouldn't my brother, the painter, have laughed, though. There I stood over the dead body and spread out my hands. The superintendent of the asylum and some of his helpers came in and stood about looking sheepish. It was very amusing. I spread out my hands and said, 'Let peace brood over this carcass.' That's what I said."

Jumping to his feet and breaking off the tale, Doctor Parcival began to walk up and down in the office of the *Winesburg Eagle* where George Willard sat listening. He was awkward and, as the office was small, continually knocked against things. "What a fool I am to be talking," he said. "That is not my object in coming here and forcing my acquaintanceship upon you. I have something else in mind. You are a reporter just as I was once and you have attracted my attention. You may end by becoming just such another fool. I want to warn you and keep on warning you. That's why I seek you out."

Doctor Parcival began talking of George Willard's attitude toward men. It seemed to the boy that the man had but one object in view, to make everyone seem despicable. "I want to fill you with hatred and contempt so that you will be a superior being," he declared. "Look at my brother. There was a fellow, eh? He despised everyone, you see. You have no idea with what contempt he looked upon mother and me. And was he not our superior? You know he was. You have not seen him and yet I have made you feel that. I have given you a sense of it. He is dead. Once when he was drunk he lay down on the tracks and the car in which he lived with the other painters ran over him."

One day in August Doctor Parcival had an adventure in Winesburg. For a month George Willard had been going each morning to spend an hour in the doctor's office. The visits came about through a desire on the part of the doctor to read to the boy from the pages of a book he was in the process of writing. To write the book Doctor Parcival declared was the object of his coming to Winesburg to live.

On the morning in August before the coming of the boy, an incident had happened in the doctor's office. There had been an accident on Main Street. A team of horses had been frightened by a train and had run away. A little girl, the daughter of a farmer, had been thrown from a buggy and killed.

On Main Street everyone had become excited and a cry for doctors had gone up. All three of the active practitioners of the town had come quickly but had found the child dead. From the crowd someone had run to the office of Doctor Parcival who had bluntly refused to go down out of his office to the dead child. The useless cruelty of his refusal had passed unnoticed. Indeed, the man who had come up the stairway to summon him had hurried away without hearing the refusal.

All of this Doctor Parcival did not know and when George Willard came to his office he found the man shaking with terror. "What I have done will arouse the people of this town," he declared excitedly. "Do I not know human nature? Do I not know what will happen? Word of my refusal will be whispered about. Presently men will get together in groups and talk of it. They will come here. We will quarrel and there will be talk of hanging. Then they will come again bearing a rope in their hands."

Doctor Parcival shook with fright. "I have a presentiment," he declared emphatically. "It may be that what I am talking about will not occur this morning. It may be put off until tonight but I will be hanged. Everyone will get excited. I will be hanged to a lamppost on Main Street."

Going to the door of his dirty little office, Doctor Parcival looked timidly down the stairway leading to the street. When he returned the fright that had been in his eyes was beginning to be replaced by doubt. Coming on tip-toe across the room he tapped George Willard on the shoulder. "If not now, sometime," he whispered, shaking his head. "In the end I will be crucified, uselessly crucified."

Doctor Parcival began to plead with George Willard. "You must pay attention to me," he urged. "If something happens perhaps you will be able to write the book that I may never get written. The idea is very simple, so simple that if you are not careful you will forget it. It is this—that everyone in the world is Christ and they are all crucified. That's what I want to say. Don't you forget that. Whatever happens, don't you dare let yourself forget."

# Godliness

(CONCERNING JESSE BENTLEY)

## PART ONE

THERE were always three or four old people sitting on the front porch of the house or puttering about the garden of the Bentley farm. Three of the old people were women and sisters to Jesse. They were a colorless, soft-voiced lot. Then there was a silent old man with thin white hair who was Jesse's uncle.

The farmhouse was built of wood, a board outer-covering over a framework of logs. It was in reality not one house but a cluster of houses joined together in a rather haphazard manner. Inside, the place was full of surprises. One went up steps from the living room into the dining room and there were always steps to be ascended or descended in passing from one room to another. At meal times the place was like a beehive. At one moment all was quiet, then doors began to open, feet clattered on stairs, a murmur of soft voices arose and people appeared from a dozen obscure corners.

Beside the old people, already mentioned, many others lived in the Bentley house. There were four hired men, a woman named Aunt Callie Beebe, who was in charge of the housekeeping, a dull-witted girl named Eliza Stoughton, who made beds and helped with the milking, a boy who worked in the stables, and Jesse Bentley himself, the owner and overlord of it all.

By the time the American Civil War had been over for twenty years, that part of Northern Ohio where the Bentley farms lay had begun to emerge from pioneer life. Jesse then owned machinery for harvesting grain. He had built modern barns and most of his land was drained with carefully laid tile drain, but in order to understand the man we will have to go back to an earlier day.

The Bentley family had been in Northern Ohio for several generations before Jesse's time. They came from New York State and took up land when the country was new and land could be had at a low price. For a long time they, in common with all the other Middle Western people, were very poor. The land they had settled upon was heavily wooded and covered with fallen logs and underbrush. After the long hard labor of clearing these away and cutting the timber, there were still the stumps to be reckoned with. Plows run through the fields caught on hidden roots, stones lay all about, on the low places water gathered, and the young corn turned yellow, sickened and died.

When Jesse Bentley's father and brothers had come into their ownership of the place, much of the harder part of the work of clearing had been done, but they clung to old traditions and worked like driven animals. They lived as practically all of the farming people of the time lived. In the spring and through most of the winter the highways leading into the town of Winesburg were a sea of mud. The four young men of the family worked hard all day in the fields, they ate heavily of coarse, greasy food, and at night slept like tired beasts on beds of straw. Into their lives came little that was not coarse and brutal and outwardly they were themselves coarse and brutal. On Saturday afternoons they hitched a team of horses to a three-seated wagon and went off to town. In town they stood about the stoves in the stores talking to other farmers or to the store keepers. They were dressed in overalls and in the winter wore heavy coats that were flecked with mud. Their hands as they stretched them out to the heat of the stoves were cracked and red. It was difficult for them to talk and so they for the most part kept silent. When they had bought meat, flour, sugar, and salt, they went into one of the Winesburg saloons and drank beer. Under the influence of drink the naturally strong lusts of their natures, kept suppressed by the heroic labor of breaking up new ground, were released. A kind of crude and animal-like poetic fervor took possession of them. On the road home they stood up on the wagon seats and shouted at the stars. Sometimes they fought long and bitterly and at other times they broke forth into songs. Once Enoch Bentley, the older one of the boys, struck his father, old Tom Bentley, with the butt of a teamster's whip, and the old man seemed likely to die. For days Enoch lay hid in the straw in the loft of the stable ready to flee if the result of his momentary passion turned out to be murder. He was kept alive with food brought by his mother who also kept him informed of the injured man's condition. When all turned out well he emerged from his hiding place and went back to the work of clearing land as though nothing had happened.

The Civil War brought a sharp turn to the fortunes of the Bentleys and was responsible for the rise of the youngest son, Jesse. Enoch, Edward, Harry, and Will Bentley all enlisted and before the long war ended they were all killed. For a time after they went away to the South, old Tom tried to run the place, but he was not successful. When the last of the four had been killed he sent word to Jesse that he would have to come home.

Then the mother, who had not been well for a year, died suddenly, and the father became altogether discouraged. He talked of selling the farm and moving into town. All day he went about shaking his head and muttering. The work in the fields was neglected and weeds grew high in the corn. Old Tom hired men but he did not use them intelligently. When they had gone away to the fields in the morning he wandered into the woods and sat down on a log. Sometimes he forgot to come home at night and one of the daughters had to go in search of him.

When Jesse Bentley came home to the farm and began to take charge of things he was a slight, sensitive-looking man of twenty-two. At eighteen he had left home to go to school to become a scholar and eventually to become a minister of the Presbyterian Church. All through his boyhood he had been what in our country was called an "odd sheep" and had not got on with his brothers. Of all the family only his mother had understood him and she was now dead. When he came home to take charge of the farm, that had at that time grown to more than six hundred acres, everyone on the farms about and in the nearby town of Winesburg smiled at the idea of his trying to handle the work that had been done by his four strong brothers.

There was indeed good cause to smile. By the standards of his day Jesse did not look like a man at all. He was small and very slender and womanish of body and, true to the traditions of young ministers, wore a long black coat and a narrow black string tie. The neighbors were amused when they saw him, after the years away, and they were even more amused when they saw the woman he had married in the city.

As a matter of fact, Jesse's wife did soon go under. That was perhaps Jesse's fault. A farm in Northern Ohio in the hard years after the Civil War was no place for a delicate woman, and Katherine Bentley was delicate. Jesse was hard with her as he was with everybody about him in those days. She tried to do such work as all the neighbor women about her did and he let her go on without interference. She helped to do the milking and did part of the housework; she made the beds for the men and prepared their food. For a year she worked every day from sunrise until late at night and then after giving birth to a child she died.

As for Jesse Bentley—although he was a delicately built man there was something within him that could not easily be killed. He had brown curly hair and gray eyes that were at times hard and direct, at times wavering and uncertain. Not only was he slender but he was also short of stature. His mouth was like the mouth of a sensitive and very determined child. Jesse Bentley was a fanatic. He was a man born out of his time and place and for this he suffered and made others suffer. Never did he succeed in getting what he wanted out of life and he did not know what he wanted. Within a very short time after he came home to the Bentley farm he made everyone there a little afraid of him, and his wife, who should have been close to him as his mother had been, was afraid also. At the end of two weeks after his coming, old Tom Bentley made over to him the entire ownership of the place and retired into the background. Everyone retired into the background. In spite of his youth and inexperience, Jesse had the trick of mastering the souls of his people. He was so in earnest in everything he did and said that no one understood him. He made everyone on the farm work as they had never worked before and yet there was no joy in the work. If things went well they went well for Jesse and never for the people who were his dependents. Like a thousand other strong men who have come into the world here in America in these later times, Jesse was but half strong. He could master others but he could not master himself. The running of the farm as it had never been run before was easy for him. When he came home from Cleveland where he had been in school, he shut himself off from all of his people and began to make plans. He thought about the farm night and day and that made him successful. Other men on the farms about him worked too hard and were too tired to think, but to think of the farm and to be everlastingly making plans for its success was a relief to Jesse. It partially satisfied something in his passionate nature. Immediately after he came home he had a wing built onto the old house and in a large room facing the west he had windows that looked into the barnyard and other windows that looked off across the fields. By the window he sat down to think. Hour after hour and day after day he sat and looked over the land and thought out his new place in life. The passionate burning thing in his nature flamed up and his eyes became hard. He wanted to make the farm produce as no farm in his state had ever produced before and then he wanted something else. It was the indefinable hunger within that made his eyes waver and that kept him always more and more silent before people. He would have given much to achieve peace and in him was a fear that peace was the thing he could not achieve.

All over his body Jesse Bentley was alive. In his small frame was gathered the force of a long line of strong men. He had always been extraordinarily alive when he was a small boy on the farm and later when he was a young man in school. In the school he had studied and thought of God and the Bible with his whole mind and heart. As time passed and he grew to know people better, he began to think of himself as an extraordinary man, one set apart from his fellows. He wanted terribly to make his life a thing of great importance, and as he looked about at his fellow men and saw how like clods they lived it seemed to him that he could not bear to become also such a clod. Although in his absorption in himself and in his own destiny he was blind to the fact that his young wife was doing a strong woman's work even after she had become large with child and that she was killing herself in his service, he did not intend to be unkind to her. When his father, who was old and twisted with toil, made over to him the ownership of the farm and seemed content to creep away to a corner and wait for death, he shrugged his shoulders and dismissed the old man from his mind.

In the room by the window overlooking the land that

had come down to him sat Jesse thinking of his own affairs. In the stables he could hear the tramping of his horses and the restless movement of his cattle. Away in the fields he could see other cattle wandering over green hills. The voices of men, his men who worked for him, came in to him through the window. From the milkhouse there was the steady thump, thump of a churn being manipulated by the half-witted girl, Eliza Stoughton. Jesse's mind went back to the men of Old Testament days who had also owned lands and herds. He remembered how God had come down out of the skies and talked to these men and he wanted God to notice and to talk to him also. A kind of feverish boyish eagerness to in some way achieve in his own life the flavor of significance that had hung over these men took possession of him. Being a prayerful man he spoke of the matter aloud to God and the sound of his own words strengthened and fed his eagerness.

"I am a new kind of man come into possession of these fields," he declared. "Look upon me, O God, and look Thou also upon my neighbors and all the men who have gone before me here! O God, create in me another Jesse, like that one of old, to rule over men and to be the father of sons who shall be rulers!" Jesse grew excited as he talked aloud and jumping to his feet walked up and down in the room. In fancy he saw himself living in old times and among old peoples. The land that lay stretched out before him became of vast significance, a place peopled by his fancy with a new race of men sprung from himself. It seemed to him that in his day as in those other and older days, kingdoms might be created and new impulses given to the lives of men by the power of God speaking through a chosen servant. He longed to be such a servant. "It is God's work I have come to the land to do," he declared in a loud voice and his short figure straightened and he thought that something like a halo of Godly approval hung over him.

It will perhaps be somewhat difficult for the men and women of a later day to understand Jesse Bentley. In the last fifty years a vast change has taken place in the lives of our people. A revolution has in fact taken place. The coming of industrialism, attended by all the roar and rattle of affairs, the shrill cries of millions of new voices that have come among us from over seas, the going and coming of trains, the growth of cities, the building of the interurban car lines that weave in and out of towns and past farmhouses, and now in these later days the coming of the automobiles has worked a tremendous change in the lives and in the habits of thought of our people of Mid-America. Books, badly imagined and written though they may be in the hurry of our times, are in every household, magazines circulate by the millions of copies, newspapers are everywhere. In our day a farmer standing by the stove in the store in his village has his mind filled to overflowing with the words of other men. The newspapers and the magazines have pumped him full. Much of the old brutal ignorance that had in it also a kind of beautiful childlike innocence is gone forever. The farmer by the stove is brother to the men of the cities, and if you listen you will find him talking as glibly and as senselessly as the best city man of us all.

In Jesse Bentley's time and in the country districts of the whole Middle West in the years after the Civil War it was not so. Men labored too hard and were too tired to read. In them was no desire for words printed upon paper. As they worked in the fields, vague, half-formed thoughts took possession of them. They believed in God and in God's power to control their lives. In the little Protestant churches they gathered on Sunday to hear of God and his works. The churches were the center of the social and intellectual life of the times. The figure of God was big in the hearts of men.

And so, having been born an imaginative child and having within him a great intellectual eagerness, Jesse Bentley had turned wholeheartedly toward God. When the war took his brothers away, he saw the hand of God in that. When his father became ill and could no longer attend to the running of the farm, he took that also as a sign from God. In the city, when the word came to him, he walked about at night through the streets thinking of the matter and when he had come home and had got the work on the farm well under way, he went again at night to walk through the forests and over the low hills and to think of God.

As he walked the importance of his own figure in some divine plan grew in his mind. He grew avaricious and was impatient that the farm contained only six hundred acres. Kneeling in a fence corner at the edge of some meadow, he sent his voice abroad into the silence and looking up he saw the stars shining down at him.

One evening, some months after his father's death, and when his wife Katherine was expecting at any moment to be laid abed of childbirth, Jesse left his house and went for a long walk. The Bentley farm was situated in a tiny valley watered by Wine Creek, and Jesse walked along the banks of the stream to the end of his own land and on through the fields of his neighbors. As he walked the valley broadened and then narrowed again. Great open stretches of field and wood lay before him. The moon came out from behind clouds, and, climbing a low hill, he sat down to think.

Jesse thought that as the true servant of God the

entire stretch of country through which he had walked should have come into his possession. He thought of his dead brothers and blamed them that they had not worked harder and achieved more. Before him in the moonlight the tiny stream ran down over stones, and he began to think of the men of old times who like himself had owned flocks and lands.

A fantastic impulse, half fear, half greediness, took possession of Jesse Bentley. He remembered how in the old Bible story the Lord had appeared to that other Jesse and told him to send his son David to where Saul and the men of Israel were fighting the Philistines in the Valley of Elah. Into Jesse's mind came the conviction that all of the Ohio farmers who owned land in the valley of Wine Creek were Philistines and enemies of God. "Suppose," he whispered to himself, "there should come from among them one who, like Goliath the Philistine of Gath, could defeat me and take from me my possessions." In fancy he felt the sickening dread that he thought must have lain heavy on the heart of Saul before the coming of David. Jumping to his feet, he began to run through the night. As he ran he called to God. His voice carried far over the low hills. "Jehovah of Hosts," he cried, "send to me this night out of the womb of Katherine, a son. Let Thy grace alight upon me. Send me a son to be called David who shall help me to pluck at last all of these lands out of the hands of the Philistines and turn them to Thy service and to the building of Thy kingdom on earth."

## PART TWO

David Hardy of Winesburg, Ohio was the grandson of Jesse Bentley, the owner of Bentley farms. When he was twelve years old he went to the old Bentley place to live. His mother, Louise Bentley, the girl who came into the world on that night when Jesse ran through the fields crying to God that he be given a son, had grown to womanhood on the farm and had married young John Hardy of Winesburg who became a banker. Louise and her husband did not live happily together and everyone agreed that she was to blame. She was a small woman with sharp gray eyes and black hair. From childhood she had been inclined to fits of temper and when not angry she was often morose and silent. In Winesburg it was said that she drank. Her husband, the banker, who was a careful, shrewd man, tried hard to make her happy. When he began to make money he bought for her a large brick house on Elm Street in Winesburg and he was the first man in that town to keep a manservant to drive his wife's carriage.

But Louise could not be made happy. She flew into half-insane fits of temper during which she was sometimes silent, sometimes noisy and quarrelsome. She swore and cried out in her anger. She got a knife from the kitchen and threatened her husband's life. Once she deliberately set fire to the house, and often she hid herself away for days in her own room and would see no one. Her life, lived as a half recluse, gave rise to all sorts of stories concerning her. It was said that she took drugs and that she hid herself away from people because she was often so under the influence of drink that her condition could not be concealed. Sometimes on summer afternoons she came out of the house and got into her carriage. Dismissing the driver she took the reins in her own hands and drove off at top speed through the streets. If a pedestrian got in her way she drove straight ahead and the frightened citizen had to escape as best he could. To the people of the town it seemed as though she wanted to run them down. When she had driven through several streets, tearing around corners and beating the horses with the whip, she drove off into the country. On the country roads after she had gotten out of sight of the houses she let the horses slow down to a walk and her wild, reckless mood passed. She became thoughtful and muttered words. Sometimes tears came into her eyes. And then when she came back into town she again drove furiously through the quiet streets. But for the influence of her husband and the respect he inspired in people's minds she would have been arrested more than once by the town marshal.

Young David Hardy grew up in the house with this woman and as can well be imagined there was not much joy in his childhood. He was too young then to have opinions of his own about people, but at times it was difficult for him not to have very definite opinions about the woman who was his mother. David was always a quiet orderly boy and for a long time was thought by the people of Winesburg to be something of a dullard. His eyes were brown and as a child he had a habit of looking at things and people a long time without appearing to see what he was looking at. When he heard his mother spoken of harshly or when he overheard her berating his father, he was frightened and ran away to hide. Sometimes he could not find a hiding place and that confused him. Turning his face toward a tree or if he were indoors toward the wall, he closed his eyes and tried not to think of anything. He had a habit of talking aloud to himself, and early in life a spirit of quiet sadness often took possession of him.

On the occasions when David went to visit his grandfather on the Bentley farm, he was altogether contented and happy. Often he wished that he would never have to go back to town and once when he had come home from the farm after a long visit, something happened that had a lasting effect on his mind.

David had come back into town with one of the hired men. The man was in a hurry to go about his own affairs and left the boy at the head of the street in which the Hardy house stood. It was early dusk of a fall evening and the sky was overcast with clouds. Something happened to David. He could not bear to go into the house where his mother and father lived, and on an impulse he decided to run away from home. He intended to go back to the farm and to his grandfather, but lost his way and for hours he wandered weeping and frightened on country roads. It started to rain and lightning flashed in the sky. The boy's imagination was excited and he fancied that he could see and hear strange things in the darkness. Into his mind came the conviction that he was walking and running in some terrible void where no one had ever been before. The darkness about him seemed limitless. The sound of the wind blowing in trees was terrifying. When a team of horses approached along the road in which he walked he was frightened and climbed a fence. Through a field he ran until he came into another road and getting upon his knees felt of the soft ground with his fingers. But for the figure of his grandfather, whom he was afraid he would never find in the darkness, he thought the world must be altogether empty. When his cries were heard by a farmer who was walking home from town and he was brought back to his father's house, he was so tired and excited that he did not know what was happening to him.

By chance David's father knew that he had disappeared. On the street he had met the farm hand from the Bentley place and knew of his son's return to town. When the boy did not come home an alarm was set up and John Hardy with several men of the town went to search the country. The report that David had been kidnapped ran about through the streets of Winesburg. When he came home there were no lights in the house, but his mother appeared and clutched him eagerly in her arms. David thought she had suddenly become another woman. He could not believe that so delightful a thing had happened. With her own hands Louise Hardy bathed his tired young body and cooked him food. She would not let him go to bed but, when he had put on his nightgown, blew out the lights and sat down in a chair to hold him in her arms. For an hour the woman sat in the darkness and held her boy. All the time she kept talking in a low voice. David could not understand what had so changed her. Her habitually dissatisfied face had become, he thought, the most peaceful and lovely thing he had ever seen. When he began to weep she held him more and more tightly. On and on went her voice. It was not harsh or shrill as when she talked to her husband, but was like rain falling on trees. Presently men began coming to the door to report that he had not been found, but she made him hide and be silent until she had sent them away. He thought it must be a game his mother and the men of the town were playing with him and laughed joyously. Into his mind came the thought that his having been lost and frightened in the darkness was an altogether unimportant matter. He thought that he would have been willing to go through the frightful experience a thousand times to be sure of finding at the end of the long black road a thing so lovely as his mother had suddenly become.

During the last years of young David's boyhood he saw his mother but seldom and she became for him just a woman with whom he had once lived. Still he could not get her figure out of his mind and as he grew older it became more definite. When he was twelve years old he went to the Bentley farm to live. Old Jesse came into town and fairly demanded that he be given charge of the boy. The old man was excited and determined on having his own way. He talked to John Hardy in the office of the Winesburg Savings Bank and then the two men went to the house on Elm Street to talk with Louise. They both expected her to make trouble but were mistaken. She was very quiet and when Jesse had explained his mission and had gone on at some length about the advantages to come through having the boy out of doors and in the quiet atmosphere of the old farmhouse, she nodded her head in approval. "It is an atmosphere not corrupted by my presence," she said sharply. Her shoulders shook and she seemed about to fly into a fit of temper. "It is a place for a man child, although it was never a place for me," she went on. "You never wanted me there and of course the air of your house did me no good. It was like poison in my blood but it will be different with him."

Louise turned and went out of the room, leaving the two men to sit in embarrassed silence. As very often happened she later stayed in her room for days. Even when the boy's clothes were packed and he was taken away she did not appear. The loss of her son made a sharp break in her life and she seemed less inclined to quarrel with her husband. John Hardy thought it had all turned out very well indeed.

And so young David went to live in the Bentley farmhouse with Jesse. Two of the old farmer's sisters were alive and still lived in the house. They were afraid of Jesse and rarely spoke when he was about. One of the women who had been noted for her flaming red hair when she was younger was a born mother and became the boy's caretaker. Every night when he had gone to bed she went into his room and sat on the floor until he fell asleep. When he became drowsy she became bold and whispered things that he later thought he must have dreamed.

Her soft low voice called him endearing names and he dreamed that his mother had come to him and that she had changed so that she was always as she had been that time after he ran away. He also grew bold and reaching out his hand stroked the face of the woman on the floor so that she was ecstatically happy. Everyone in the old house became happy after the boy went there. The hard insistent thing in Jesse Bentley that had kept the people in the house silent and timid and that had never been dispelled by the presence of the girl Louise was apparently swept away by the coming of the boy. It was as though God had relented and sent a son to the man.

The man who had proclaimed himself the only true servant of God in all the valley of Wine Creek, and who had wanted God to send him a sign of approval by way of a son out of the womb of Katherine, began to think that at last his prayers had been answered. Although he was at that time only fifty-five years old he looked seventy and was worn out with much thinking and scheming. The effort he had made to extend his land holdings had been successful and there were few farms in the valley that did not belong to him, but until David came he was a bitterly disappointed man.

There were two influences at work in Jesse Bentley and all his life his mind had been a battleground for these influences. First there was the old thing in him. He wanted to be a man of God and a leader among men of God. His walking in the fields and through the forests at night had brought him close to nature and there were forces in the passionately religious man that ran out to the forces in nature. The disappointment that had come to him when a daughter and not a son had been born to Katherine had fallen upon him like a blow struck by some unseen hand and the blow had somewhat softened his egotism. He still believed that God might at any moment make himself manifest out of the winds or the clouds, but he no longer demanded such recognition. Instead he prayed for it. Sometimes he was altogether doubtful and thought God had deserted the world. He regretted the fate that had not let him live in a simpler and sweeter time when at the beckoning of some strange cloud in the sky men left their lands and houses and went forth into the wilderness to create new races. While he worked night and day to make his farms more productive and to extend his holdings of land, he regretted that he could not use his own restless energy in the building of temples, the slaying of unbelievers and in general in the work of glorifying God's name on earth.

That is what Jesse hungered for and then also he hungered for something else. He had grown into maturity in America in the years after the Civil War and he, like all men of his time, had been touched by the deep influences that were at work in the country during those years when modern industrialism was being born. He began to buy machines that would permit him to do the work of the farms while employing fewer men and he sometimes thought that if he were a younger man he would give up farming altogether and start a factory in Winesburg for the making of machinery. Jesse formed the habit of reading newspapers and magazines. He invented a machine for the making of fence out of wire. Faintly he realized that the atmosphere of old times and places that he had always cultivated in his own mind was strange and foreign to the thing that was growing up in the minds of others. The beginning of the most materialistic age in the history of the world, when wars would be fought without patriotism, when men would forget God and only pay attention to moral standards, when the will to power would replace the will to serve and beauty would be well-nigh forgotten in the terrible headlong rush of mankind toward the acquiring of possessions, was telling its story to Jesse the man of God as it was to the men about him. The greedy thing in him wanted to make money faster than it could be made by tilling the land. More than once he went into Winesburg to talk with his son-in-law John Hardy about it. "You are a banker and you will have chances I never had," he said and his eyes shone. "I am thinking about it all the time. Big things are going to be done in the country and there will be more money to be made than I ever dreamed of. You get into it. I wish I were younger and had your chance." Jesse Bentley walked up and down in the bank office and grew more and more excited as he talked. At one time in his life he had been threatened with paralysis and his left side remained somewhat weakened. As he talked his left eyelid twitched. Later when he drove back home and when night came on and the stars came out it was harder to get back the old feeling of a close and personal God who lived in the sky overhead and who might at any moment reach out his hand, touch him on the shoulder, and appoint for him some heroic task to be done. Jesse's mind was fixed upon the things read in newspapers and magazines, on fortunes to be made almost without effort by shrewd men who bought and sold. For him the coming of the boy David did much to bring back with renewed force the old faith and it seemed to him that God had at last looked with favor upon him.

As for the boy on the farm, life began to reveal itself to him in a thousand new and delightful ways. The kindly attitude of all about him expanded his quiet nature and he lost the half-timid, hesitating manner he had always had with his people. At night when he went to bed after a long day of adventures in the stables, in the fields, or driving about from farm to farm with his grandfather he wanted to embrace everyone in the house. If Sherley Bentley, the woman who came each night to sit on the floor by his bedside, did not appear at once, he went to the head of the stairs and shouted, his young voice ringing through the narrow halls where for so long there had been a tradition of silence. In the morning when he awoke and lay still in bed, the sounds that came in to him through the windows filled him with delight. He thought with a shudder of the life in the house in Winesburg and of his mother's angry voice that had always made him tremble. There in the country all sounds were pleasant sounds. When he awoke at dawn the barnyard back of the house also awoke. In the house people stirred about. Eliza Stoughton the half-witted girl was poked in the ribs by a farm hand and giggled noisily, in some distant field a cow bawled and was answered by the cattle in the stables, and one of the farm hands spoke sharply to the horse he was grooming by the stable door. David leaped out of bed and ran to a window. All of the people stirring about excited his mind, and he wondered what his mother was doing in the house in town.

From the windows of his own room he could not see directly into the barnyard where the farm hands had now all assembled to do the morning chores, but he could hear the voices of the men and the neighing of the horses. When one of the men laughed, he laughed also. Leaning out at the open window, he looked into an orchard where a fat sow wandered about with a litter of tiny pigs at her heels. Every morning he counted the pigs. "Four, five, six, seven," he said slowly, wetting his finger and making straight up and down marks on the window ledge. David ran to put on his trousers and shirt. A feverish desire to get out of doors took possession of him. Every morning he made such a noise coming downstairs that Aunt Callie, the housekeeper, declared he was trying to tear the house down. When he had run through the long old house, shutting doors behind him with a bang, he came into the barnyard and looked about with an amazed air of expectancy. It seemed to him that in such a place tremendous things might have happened during the night. The farm hands looked at him and laughed. Henry Strader, an old man who had been on the farm since Jesse came into possession and who before David's time had never been known to make a joke, made the same joke every morning. It amused David so that he laughed and clapped his hands. "See, come here and look," cried the old man, "Grandfather Jesse's white mare has torn the black stocking she wears on her foot."

Day after day through the long summer, Jesse Bentley drove from farm to farm up and down the valley of Wine Creek, and his grandson went with him. They rode in a comfortable old phaeton drawn by the white horse. The old man scratched his thin white beard and talked to himself of his plans for increasing the productiveness of the fields they visited and of God's part in the plans all men made. Sometimes he looked at David and smiled happily and then for a long time he appeared to forget the boy's existence. More and more every day now his mind turned back again to the dreams that had filled his mind when he had first come out of the city to live on the land. One afternoon he startled David by letting his dreams take entire possession of him. With the boy as a witness, he went through a ceremony and brought about an accident that nearly destroyed the companionship that was growing up between them.

Jesse and his grandson were driving in a distant part of the valley some miles from home. A forest came down to the road and through the forest Wine Creek wriggled its way over stones toward a distant river. All the afternoon Jesse had been in a meditative mood and now he began to talk. His mind went back to the night when he had been frightened by thoughts of a giant that might come to rob and plunder him of his possessions, and again as on that night when he had run through the fields crying for a son, he became excited to the edge of insanity. Stopping the horse he got out of the buggy and asked David to get out also. The two climbed over a fence and walked along the bank of the stream. The boy paid no attention to the muttering of his grandfather, but ran along beside him and wondered what was going to happen. When a rabbit jumped up and ran away through the woods, he clapped his hands and danced with delight. He looked at the tall trees and was sorry that he was not a little animal to climb high in the air without being frightened. Stooping, he picked up a small stone and threw it over the head of his grandfather into a clump of bushes. "Wake up, little animal. Go and climb to the top of the trees," he shouted in a shrill voice.

Jesse Bentley went along under the trees with his head bowed and with his mind in a ferment. His earnestness affected the boy who presently became silent and a little alarmed. Into the old man's mind had come the notion that now he could bring from God a word or a sign out of the sky, that the presence of the boy and man on their knees in some lonely spot in the forest would make the miracle he had been waiting for almost inevitable. "It was in just such a place as this that other David tended the sheep when his father came and told him to go down unto Saul," he muttered.

Taking the boy rather roughly by the shoulder, he climbed over a fallen log and when he had come to an open place among the trees, he dropped upon his knees and began to pray in a loud voice.

A kind of terror he had never known before took possession of David. Crouching beneath a tree he watched the man on the ground before him and his own knees began to tremble. It seemed to him that he was in the presence, not only of his grandfather but of someone else, someone who might hurt him, someone who was not kindly but dangerous and brutal. He began to cry and reaching down picked up a small stick which he held tightly gripped in his fingers. When Jesse Bentley, absorbed in his own idea, suddenly arose and advanced toward him, his terror grew until his whole body shook. In the woods an intense silence seemed to lie over everything and suddenly out of the silence came the old man's harsh and insistent voice. Gripping the boy's shoulders, Jesse turned his face to the sky and shouted. The whole left side of his face twitched and his hand on the boy's shoulder twitched also. "Make a sign to me, God," he cried, "here I stand with the boy David. Come down to me out of the sky and make Thy presence known to me."

With a cry of fear, David turned and shaking himself loose from the hands that held him, ran away through the forest. He did not believe that the man who turned up his face and in a harsh voice shouted at the sky, was his grandfather at all. The man did not look like his grandfather. The conviction that something strange and terrible had happened, that by some miracle a new and dangerous person had come into the body of the kindly old man took possession of him. On and on he ran down the hillside sobbing as he ran. When he fell over the roots of a tree and in falling struck his head, he arose and tried to run on again. His head hurt so that presently he fell down and lay still, but it was only after Jesse had carried him to the buggy and he awoke to find the old man's hand stroking his head tenderly, that the terror left him. "Take me away. There is a terrible man back there in the woods," he declared firmly, while Jesse looked away over the tops of the trees and again his lips cried out to God. "What have I done that Thou doest not approve of me," he whispered softly, saying the words over and over as he drove rapidly along the road with the boy's cut and bleeding head held tenderly against his shoulder.

# The Strength of God

(CONCERNING THE REVEREND CURTIS HARTMAN)

THE Reverend Curtis Hartman was pastor of the Presbyterian Church of Winesburg, and had been in that position ten years. He was forty years old, and by his nature very silent and reticent. To preach, standing in the pulpit before the people, was always a hardship for him and from Wednesday morning until Saturday evening he thought of nothing but the two sermons that must be preached on Sunday. Early on Sunday morning he went into a little room called a study in the bell tower of the church and prayed. In his prayers there was one note that always predominated. "Give me strength and courage for Thy work, O Lord!" he plead, kneeling on the bare floor and bowing his head in the presence of the task that lay before him.

The Reverend Hartman was a tall man with a brown beard. His wife, a stout, nervous woman, was the daughter of a manufacturer of underwear at Cleveland, Ohio. The minister himself was rather a favorite in the town. The elders of the church liked him because he was quiet and unpretentious and Mrs. White, the banker's wife, thought him scholarly and refined.

The Presbyterian Church held itself somewhat aloof from the other churches of Winesburg. It was larger and more imposing and its minister was better paid. He even had a carriage of his own and on summer evenings sometimes drove about town with his wife. Through Main Street and up and down Buckeye Street he went, bowing gravely to the people, while his wife, afire with secret pride, looked at him out of the corners of her eyes and worried lest the horse become frightened and run away.

For a good many years after he came to Winesburg things went well with Curtis Hartman. He was not one to arouse keen enthusiasm among the worshippers in his church but on the other hand he made no enemies. In reality he was much in earnest and sometimes suffered prolonged periods of remorse because he could not go crying the word of God in the highways and byways of the town. He wondered if the flame of the spirit really burned in him and dreamed of a day when a strong sweet new current of power would come like a great wind into his voice and his soul and the people would tremble before the spirit of God made manifest in him. "I am a poor stick and that will never really happen to me," he mused dejectedly and then a patient smile lit up his features. "Oh well, I suppose I'm doing well enough," he added philosophically.

The room in the bell tower of the church, where on Sunday mornings the minister prayed for an increase in him of the power of God, had but one window. It was long and narrow and swung outward on a hinge like a door. On the window, made of little leaded panes, was a design showing the Christ laying his hand upon the head of a child. One Sunday morning in the summer as he sat by his desk in the room with a large Bible opened before him, and the sheets of his sermon scattered about, the minister was shocked to see, in the upper room of the house next door, a woman lying in her bed and smoking a cigarette while she read a book. Curtis Hartman went on tiptoe to the window and closed it softly. He was horror stricken at the thought of a woman smoking and trembled also to think that his eyes, just raised from the pages of the book of God, had looked upon the bare shoulders and white throat of a woman. With his brain in a whirl he went down into the pulpit and preached a long sermon without once thinking of his gestures or his voice. The sermon attracted unusual attention because of its power and clearness. "I wonder if she is listening, if my voice is carrying a message into her soul," he thought and began to hope that on future Sunday mornings he might be able to say words that would touch and awaken the woman apparently far gone in secret sin.

The house next door to the Presbyterian Church, through the windows of which the minister had seen the sight that had so upset him, was occupied by two women. Aunt Elizabeth Swift, a gray competent-looking widow with money in the Winesburg National Bank, lived there with her daughter Kate Swift, a school teacher. The school teacher was thirty years old and had a neat trim-looking figure. She had few friends and bore a reputation of having a sharp tongue. When he began to think about her, Curtis Hartman remembered that she had been to Europe and had lived for two years in New York City. "Perhaps after all her smoking means nothing," he thought. He began to remember that when he was a student in college and occasionally read novels, good, although somewhat worldly women, had smoked through the pages of a book that had once fallen into his hands. With a rush of new determination he worked on his sermons all through the week and forgot, in his zeal to reach the ears and the soul of this new listener, both his embarrassment in the pulpit and the necessity of prayer in the study on Sunday mornings.

Reverend Hartman's experience with women had been somewhat limited. He was the son of a wagon maker from Muncie, Indiana, and had worked his way through college. The daughter of the underwear manufacturer had boarded in a house where he lived during his school days and he had married her after a formal and prolonged courtship, carried on for the most part by the girl herself. On his marriage day the underwear manufacturer had given his daughter five thousand dollars and he promised to leave her at least twice that amount in his will. The minister had thought himself fortunate in marriage and had never permitted himself to think of other women. He did not want to think of other women. What he wanted was to do the work of God quietly and earnestly.

In the soul of the minister a struggle awoke. From wanting to reach the ears of Kate Swift, and through his sermons to delve into her soul, he began to want also to look again at the figure lying white and quiet in the bed. On a Sunday morning when he could not sleep because of his thoughts he arose and went to walk in the streets. When he had gone along Main Street almost to the old Richmond place he stopped and picking up a stone rushed off to the room in the bell tower. With the stone he broke out a corner of the window and then locked the door and sat down at the desk before the open Bible to wait. When the shade of the window to Kate Swift's room was raised he could see, through the hole, directly into her bed, but she was not there. She also had arisen and had gone for a walk and the hand that raised the shade was the hand of Aunt Elizabeth Swift.

The minister almost wept with joy at this deliverance from the carnal desire to "peep" and went back to his own house praising God. In an ill moment he forgot, however, to stop the hole in the window. The piece of glass broken out at the corner of the window just nipped off the bare heel of the boy standing motionless and looking with rapt eyes into the face of the Christ.

Curtis Hartman forgot his sermon on that Sunday morning. He talked to his congregation and in his talk said that it was a mistake for people to think of their minister as a man set aside and intended by nature to lead a blameless life. "Out of my own experience I know that we, who are the ministers of God's word, are beset by the same temptations that assail you," he declared. "I have been tempted and have surrendered to temptation. It is only the hand of God, placed beneath my head, that has raised me up. As he has raised me so also will he raise you. Do not despair. In your hour of sin raise your eyes to the skies and you will be again and again saved."

Resolutely the minister put the thoughts of the woman in the bed out of his mind and began to be something like a lover in the presence of his wife. One evening when they drove out together he turned the horse out of Buckeye Street and in the darkness on Gospel Hill, above Waterworks Pond, put his arm about Sarah Hartman's waist. When he had eaten breakfast in the morning and was ready to retire to his study at the back of his house he went around the table and kissed his wife on the cheek. When thoughts of Kate Swift came into his head, he smiled and raised his eyes to the skies. "Intercede for me, Master," he muttered, "keep me in the narrow path intent on Thy work."

And now began the real struggle in the soul of the brown-bearded minister. By chance he discovered that Kate Swift was in the habit of lying in her bed in the evenings and reading a book. A lamp stood on a table by the side of the bed and the light streamed down upon her white shoulders and bare throat. On the evening when he made the discovery the minister sat at the desk in the study from nine until after eleven and when her light was put out stumbled out of the church to spend two more hours walking and praying in the streets. He did not want to kiss the shoulders and the throat of Kate Swift and had not allowed his mind to dwell on such thoughts. He did not know what he wanted. "I am God's child and he must save me from myself," he cried, in the darkness under the trees as he wandered in the streets. By a tree he stood and looked at the sky that was covered with hurrying clouds. He began to talk to God intimately and closely. "Please, Father, do not forget me. Give me power to go tomorrow and repair the hole in the window. Lift my eyes again to the skies. Stay with me, Thy servant, in his hour of need."

Up and down through the silent streets walked the minister and for days and weeks his soul was troubled. He could not understand the temptation that had come to him nor could he fathom the reason for its coming. In a way he began to blame God, saying to himself that he had tried to keep his feet in the true path and had not run about seeking sin. "Through my days as a young man and all through my life here I have gone quietly about my work," he declared. "Why now should I be tempted? What have I done that this burden should be laid on me?"

Three times during the early fall and winter of that year Curtis Hartman crept out of his house to the room in the bell tower to sit in the darkness looking at the figure of Kate Swift lying in her bed and later went to walk and pray in the streets. He could not understand himself. For weeks he would go along scarcely thinking of the school teacher and telling himself that he had conquered the carnal desire to look at her body. And then something would happen. As he sat in the study of his own house, hard at work on a sermon, he would become nervous and begin to walk up and down the room. "I will go out into the streets," he told himself and even as he let himself in at the church door he persistently denied to himself the cause of his being there. "I will not repair the hole in the window and I will train myself to come here at night and sit in the presence of this woman without raising my eyes. I will not be defeated in this thing. The Lord has devised this temptation as a test of my soul and I will grope my way out of darkness into the light of righteousness."

One night in January when it was bitter cold and snow lay deep on the streets of Winesburg Curtis Hartman paid his last visit to the room in the bell tower of the church. It was past nine o'clock when he left his own house and he set out so hurriedly that he forgot to put on his overshoes. In Main Street no one was abroad but Hop Higgins the night watchman and in the whole town no one was awake but the watchman and young George Willard, who sat in the office of the *Winesburg Eagle* trying to write a story. Along the street to the church went the minister, plowing through the drifts and thinking that this time he would utterly give way to sin. "I want to look at the woman and to think of kissing her shoulders and I am going to let myself think what I choose," he declared bitterly and tears came into his eyes. He began to think that he would get out of the ministry and try some other way of life. "I shall go to some city and get into business," he declared. "If my nature is such that I cannot resist sin, I shall give myself over to sin. At least I shall not be a hypocrite, preaching the word of God with my mind thinking of the shoulders and neck of a woman who does not belong to me."

It was cold in the room of the bell tower of the church on that January night and almost as soon as he came into the room Curtis Hartman knew that if he stayed he would be ill. His feet were wet from tramping in the snow and there was no fire. In the room in the house next door Kate Swift had not yet appeared. With grim determination the man sat down to wait. Sitting in the chair and gripping the edge of the desk on which lay the Bible he stared into the darkness thinking the blackest thoughts of his life. He thought of his wife and for the moment almost hated her. "She has always been ashamed of passion and has cheated me," he thought. "Man has a right to expect living passion and beauty in a woman. He has no right to forget that he is an animal and in me there is something that is Greek. I will throw off the woman of my bosom and seek other women. I will besiege this school teacher. I will fly in the face of all men and if I am a creature of carnal lusts I will live then for my lusts."

The distracted man trembled from head to foot, partly from cold, partly from the struggle in which he was engaged. Hours passed and a fever assailed his body. His throat began to hurt and his teeth chattered. His feet on the study floor felt like two cakes of ice. Still he would not give up. "I will see this woman and will think the thoughts I have never dared to think," he told himself, gripping the edge of the desk and waiting.

Curtis Hartman came near dying from the effects of that night of waiting in the church, and also he found in the thing that happened what he took to be the way of life for him. On other evenings when he had waited he had not been able to see, through the little hole in the glass, any part of the school teacher's room except that occupied by her bed. In the darkness he had waited until the woman suddenly appeared sitting in the bed in her white night-robe. When the light was turned up she propped herself up among the pillows and read a book. Sometimes she smoked one of the cigarettes. Only her bare shoulders and throat were visible.

On the January night, after he had come near dying with cold and after his mind had two or three times actually slipped away into an odd land of fantasy so that he had by an exercise of will power to force himself back into consciousness, Kate Swift appeared. In the room next door a lamp was lighted and the waiting man stared into an empty bed. Then upon the bed before his eyes a naked woman threw herself. Lying face downward she wept and beat with her fists upon the pillow. With a final outburst of weeping she half arose, and in the presence of the man who had waited to look and to think thoughts the woman of sin began to pray. In the lamplight her figure, slim and strong, looked like the figure of the boy in the presence of the Christ on the leaded window.

Curtis Hartman never remembered how he got out of the church. With a cry he arose, dragging the heavy desk along the floor. The Bible fell, making a great clatter in the silence. When the light in the house next door went out he stumbled down the stairway and into the street. Along the street he went and ran in at the door of the *Winesburg Eagle.* To George Willard, who was tramping up and down in the office undergoing a struggle of his own, he began to talk half-incoherently. "The ways of God are beyond human understanding," he cried, running in quickly and closing the door. He began to advance upon the young man, his eyes glowing and his voice ringing with fervor. "I have found the light," he cried. "After ten years in this town, God has manifested himself to me in the body of a woman." His voice dropped and he began to whisper. "I did not understand," he said. "What I took to be a trial of my soul was only a preparation for a new and more beautiful fervor of the spirit. God has appeared to me in the person of Kate Swift, the school teacher, kneeling naked on a bed. Do you know Kate Swift? Although she may not be aware of it, she is an instrument of God, bearing the message of truth."

Reverend Curtis Hartman turned and ran out of the office. At the door he stopped, and after looking up and down the deserted street, turned again to George Willard. "I am delivered. Have no fear." He held up a bleeding fist for the young man to see. "I smashed the glass of the window," he cried. "Now it will have to be wholly replaced. The strength of God was in me and I broke it with my fist."

# The Teacher

(CONCERNING KATE SWIFT)

SNOW lay deep in the streets of Winesburg. It had begun to snow about ten o'clock in the morning and a wind sprang up and blew the snow in clouds along Main Street. The frozen mud roads that led into town were fairly smooth and in places ice covered the mud. "There will be good sleighing," said Will Henderson, standing by the bar in Ed Griffith's saloon. Out of the saloon he went and met Sylvester West the druggist stumbling along in the kind of heavy overshoes called arctics. "Snow will bring the people into town on Saturday," said the druggist. The two men stopped and discussed their affairs. Will Henderson, who had on a light overcoat and no overshoes, kicked the heel of his left foot with the toe of the right. "Snow will be good for the wheat," observed the druggist sagely.

Young George Willard, who had nothing to do, was glad because he did not feel like working that day. The weekly paper had been printed and taken to the post office on Wednesday evening and the snow began to fall on Thursday. At eight o'clock, after the morning train had passed, he put a pair of skates in his pocket and went up to Waterworks Pond but did not go skating. Past the pond and along a path that followed Wine Creek he went until he came to a grove of beech trees. There he built a fire against the side of a log and sat down at the end of the log to think. When the snow began to fall and the wind to blow he hurried about getting fuel for the fire.

The young reporter was thinking of Kate Swift who had once been his school teacher. On the evening before he had gone to her house to get a book she wanted him to read and had been alone with her for an hour. For the fourth or fifth time the woman had talked to him with great earnestness and he could not make out what she meant by her talk. He began to believe she might be in love with him and the thought was both pleasing and annoying.

Up from the log he sprang and began to pile sticks on the fire. Looking about to be sure he was alone he talked aloud pretending he was in the presence of the woman. "Oh, you're just letting on, you know you are," he declared. "I am going to find out about you. You wait and see."

The young man got up and went back along the path toward town leaving the fire blazing in the wood. As he went through the streets the skates clanked in his pocket. In his own room in the New Willard House he built a fire in the stove and lay down on top of the bed. He began to have lustful thoughts and pulling down the shade of the window closed his eyes and turned his face to the wall. He took a pillow into his arms and embraced it thinking first of the school teacher, who by her words had stirred something within him and later of Helen White, the slim daughter of the town banker, with whom he had been for a long time half in love.

By nine o'clock of that evening snow lay deep in the streets and the weather had become bitter cold. It was difficult to walk about. The stores were dark and the people had crawled away to their houses. The evening train from Cleveland was very late but nobody was interested in its arrival. By ten o'clock all but four of the eighteen hundred citizens of the town were in bed.

Hop Higgins, the night watchman, was partially awake. He was lame and carried a heavy stick. On dark nights he carried a lantern. Between nine and ten o'clock he went his rounds. Up and down Main Street he stumbled through the drifts trying the doors of the stores. Then he went into alleyways and tried the back doors. Finding all tight he hurried around the corner to the New Willard House and beat on the door. Through the rest of the night he intended to stay by the stove. "You go to bed. I'll keep the stove going," he said to the boy who slept on a cot in the hotel office.

Hop Higgins sat down by the stove and took off his shoes. When the boy had gone to sleep he began to think of his own affairs. He intended to paint his house in the spring and sat by the stove calculating the cost of paint and labor. That led him into other calculations. The night watchman was sixty years old and wanted to retire. He had been a soldier in the Civil War and drew a small pension. He hoped to find some new method of making a living and aspired to become a professional breeder of ferrets. Already he had four of the strangely shaped savage little creatures, that are used by sportsmen in the pursuit of rabbits, in the cellar of his house. "Now I have one male and three females," he mused. "If I am lucky by spring I shall have twelve or fifteen. In another year I shall be able to begin advertising ferrets for sale in the sporting papers."

The night watchman settled into his chair and his mind became a blank. He did not sleep. By years of practice he had trained himself to sit for hours through the long nights neither asleep nor awake. In the morning he was almost as refreshed as though he had slept.

With Hop Higgins safely stowed away in the chair behind the stove only three people were awake in

Winesburg. George Willard was in the office of the *Eagle* pretending to be at work on the writing of a story but in reality continuing the mood of the morning by the fire in the wood. In the bell tower of the Presbyterian Church the Reverend Curtis Hartman was sitting in the darkness preparing himself for a revelation from God, and Kate Swift, the school teacher, was leaving her house for a walk in the storm.

It was past ten o'clock when Kate Swift set out and the walk was unpremeditated. It was as though the man and the boy, by thinking of her, had driven her forth into the wintry streets. Aunt Elizabeth Swift had gone to the county seat concerning some business in connection with mortgages in which she had money invested and would not be back until the next day. By a huge stove, called a base burner, in the living room of the house sat the daughter reading a book. Suddenly she sprang to her feet and, snatching a cloak from a rack by the front door, ran out of the house.

At the age of thirty Kate Swift was not known in Winesburg as a pretty woman. Her complexion was not good and her face was covered with blotches that indicated ill health. Alone in the night in the winter streets she was lovely. Her back was straight, her shoulders square and her features were as the features of a tiny goddess on a pedestal in a garden in the dim light of a summer evening.

During the afternoon the school teacher had been to see Dr. Welling concerning her health. The doctor had scolded her and had declared she was in danger of losing her hearing. It was foolish for Kate Swift to be abroad in the storm, foolish and perhaps dangerous.

The woman in the streets did not remember the words of the doctor and would not have turned back had she remembered. She was very cold but after walking for five minutes no longer minded the cold. First she went to the end of her own street and then across a pair of hay scales set in the ground before a feed barn and into Trunion Pike. Along Trunion Pike she went to Ned Winter's barn and turning east followed a street of low frame houses that led over Gospel Hill and into Sucker Road that ran down a shallow valley past Ike Smead's chicken farm to Waterworks Pond. As she went along, the bold, excited mood that had driven her out of doors passed and then returned again.

There was something biting and forbidding in the character of Kate Swift. Everyone felt it. In the schoolroom she was silent, cold, and stern, and yet in an odd way very close to her pupils. Once in a long while something seemed to have come over her and she was happy. All of the children in the schoolroom felt the effect of her happiness. For a time they did not work but sat back in their chairs and looked at her.

With hands clasped behind her back the school teacher walked up and down in the schoolroom and talked very rapidly. It did not seem to matter what subject came into her mind. Once she talked to the children of Charles Lamb and made up strange intimate little stories concerning the life of the dead writer. The stories were told with the air of one who had lived in a house with Charles Lamb and knew all the secrets of his private life. The children were somewhat confused, thinking Charles Lamb must be someone who had once lived in Winesburg.

On another occasion the teacher talked to the children of Benvenuto Cellini. That time they laughed. What a bragging, blustering, brave, lovable fellow she made of the old artist! Concerning him also she invented anecdotes. There was one of a German music teacher who had a room above Cellini's lodgings in the city of Milan that made the boys guffaw. Sugars McNutts, a fat boy with red cheeks, laughed so hard that he became dizzy and fell off his seat and Kate Swift laughed with him. Then suddenly she became again cold and stern.

On the winter night when she walked through the deserted snow-covered streets, a crisis had come into the life of the school teacher. Although no one in Winesburg would have suspected it, her life had been very adventurous. It was still adventurous. Day by day as she worked in the schoolroom or walked in the streets, grief, hope, and desire fought within her. Behind a cold exterior the most extraordinary events transpired in her mind. The people of the town thought of her as a confirmed old maid and because she spoke sharply and went her own way thought her lacking in all the human feeling that did so much to make and mar their own lives. In reality she was the most eagerly passionate soul among them, and more than once, in the five years since she had come back from her travels to settle in Winesburg and become a school teacher, had been compelled to go out of the house and walk half through the night fighting out some battle raging within. Once on a night when it rained she had stayed out six hours and when she came home had a quarrel with Aunt Elizabeth Swift. "I am glad you're not a man," said the mother sharply. "More than once I've waited for your father to come home, not knowing what new mess he had got into. I've had my share of uncertainty and you cannot blame me if I do not want to see the worst side of him reproduced in you."

Kate Swift's mind was ablaze with thoughts of George Willard. In something he had written as a school boy she thought she had recognized the spark of genius and wanted to blow on the spark. One day in the summer she had gone to the *Eagle* office and finding the boy unoccupied had taken him out Main Street to the fair ground, where the two sat on a grassy bank and talked. The school teacher tried to bring home to the mind of the boy some conception of the difficulties he would have to face as a writer. "You will have to know life," she declared, and her voice trembled with earnestness. She took hold of George Willard's shoulders and turned him about so that she could look into his eyes. A passer-by might have thought them about to embrace. "If you are to become a writer you'll have to stop fooling with words," she explained. "It would be better to give up the notion of writing until you are better prepared. Now it's time to be living. I don't want to frighten you, but I would like to make you understand the import of what you think of attempting. You must not become a mere peddler of words. The thing to learn is to know what people are thinking about, not what they say."

On the evening before that stormy Thursday night, when the Reverend Curtis Hartman sat in the bell tower of the church waiting to look at her body, young Willard had gone to visit the teacher and to borrow a book. It was then the thing happened that confused and puzzled the boy. He had the book under his arm and was preparing to depart. Again Kate Swift talked with great earnestness. Night was coming on and the light in the room grew dim. As he turned to go she spoke his name softly and with an impulsive movement took hold of his hand. Because the reporter was rapidly becoming a man something of his man's appeal, combined with the winsomeness of the boy, stirred the heart of the lonely woman. A passionate desire to have him understand the import of life, to learn to interpret it truly and honestly, swept over her. Leaning forward, her lips brushed his cheek. At the same moment he for the first time became aware of the marked beauty of her features. They were both embarrassed, and to relieve her feeling she became harsh and domineering. "What's the use? It will be ten years before you begin to understand what I mean when I talk to you," she cried passionately.

On the night of the storm and while the minister sat in the church waiting for her, Kate Swift went to the office of the *Winesburg Eagle,* intending to have another talk with the boy. After the long walk in the snow she was cold, lonely, and tired. As she came through Main Street she saw the light from the print shop window shining on the snow and on an impulse opened the door and went in. For an hour she sat by the stove in the office talking of life. She talked with passionate earnestness. The impulse that had driven her out into the snow poured itself out into talk. She became inspired as she sometimes did in the presence of the children in school. A great eagerness to open the door of life to the boy, who had been her pupil and whom she thought might possess a talent for the understanding of life, had possession of her. So strong was her passion that it became something physical. Again her hands took hold of his shoulders and she turned him about. In the dim light her eyes blazed. She arose and laughed, not sharply as was customary with her, but in a queer, hesitating way. "I must be going," she said. "In a moment, if I stay, I'll be wanting to kiss you."

In the newspaper office a confusion arose. Kate Swift turned and walked to the door. She was a teacher but she was also a woman. As she looked at George Willard, the passionate desire to be loved by a man, that had a thousand times before swept like a storm over her body, took possession of her. In the lamplight George Willard looked no longer a boy, but a man ready to play the part of a man.

The school teacher let George Willard take her into his arms. In the warm little office the air became suddenly heavy and the strength went out of her body. Leaning against a low counter by the door she waited. When he came and put a hand on her shoulder she turned and let her body fall heavily against him. For George Willard the confusion was immediately increased. For a moment he held the body of the woman tightly against his body and then it stiffened. Two sharp little fists began to beat on his face. When the school teacher had run away and left him alone, he walked up and down in the office swearing furiously.

It was into this confusion that the Reverend Curtis Hartman protruded himself. When he came in George Willard thought the town had gone mad. Shaking a bleeding fist in the air, the minister proclaimed the woman George had only a moment before held in his arms an instrument of God bearing a message of truth.

George blew out the lamp by the window and locking the door of the print shop went home. Through the hotel office, past Hop Higgins lost in his dream of the raising of ferrets, he went and up into his own room. The fire in the stove had gone out and he undressed in the cold. When he got into bed the sheets were like blankets of dry snow.

George Willard rolled about in the bed on which he had lain in the afternoon hugging the pillow and thinking thoughts of Kate Swift. The words of the minister, who he thought had gone suddenly insane, rang in his ears. His eyes stared about the room. The resentment, natural to the baffled male, passed and he tried to understand what had happened. He could not make it out. Over and over he turned the matter in his mind. Hours passed and he began to think it must be time for another day to come. At four o'clock he pulled the covers up about his neck and tried to sleep. When he became drowsy and closed his eyes, he raised a hand and with it groped about in the darkness. "I have missed something. I have missed something Kate Swift was trying to tell me," he muttered sleepily. Then he slept and in all Winesburg he was the last soul on that winter night to go to sleep.

# Loneliness

(CONCERNING ENOCH ROBINSON)

HE WAS the son of Mrs. Al Robinson who once owned a farm on a side road leading off Trunion Pike, east of Winesburg and two miles beyond the town limits. The farmhouse was painted brown and the blinds to all of the windows facing the road were kept closed. In the road before the house a flock of chickens, accompanied by two guinea hens, lay in the deep dust. Enoch lived in the house with his mother in those days and when he was a young boy went to school at the Winesburg High School. Old citizens remembered him as a quiet, smiling youth inclined to silence. He walked in the middle of the road when he came into town and sometimes read a book. Drivers of teams had to shout and swear to make him realize where he was so that he would turn out of the beaten track and let them pass.

When he was twenty-one years old Enoch went to New York City and was a city man for fifteen years. He studied French and went to an art school, hoping to develop a faculty he had for drawing. In his own mind he planned to go to Paris and to finish his art education among the masters there, but that never turned out.

Nothing ever turned out for Enoch Robinson. He could draw well enough and he had many odd delicate thoughts hidden away in his brain that might have expressed themselves through the brush of a painter, but he was always a child and that was a handicap to his worldly development. He never grew up and of course he couldn't understand people and he couldn't make people understand him. The child in him kept bumping against things, against actualities like money and sex and opinions. Once he was hit by a streetcar and thrown against an iron post. That made him lame. It was one of the many things that kept things from turning out for Enoch Robinson.

In New York City, when he first went there to live and before he became confused and disconcerted by the facts of life, Enoch went about a good deal with young men. He got into a group of other young artists, both men and women, and in the evenings they sometimes came to visit him in his room. Once he got drunk and was taken to a police station where a police magistrate frightened him horribly, and once he tried to have an affair with a woman of the town met on the sidewalk before his lodging house. The woman and Enoch walked together three blocks and then the young man grew afraid and ran away. The woman had been drinking and the incident amused her. She leaned against the wall of a building and laughed so heartily that another man stopped and laughed with her. The two went away together, still laughing, and Enoch crept off to his room trembling and vexed.

The room in which young Robinson lived in New York faced Washington Square and was long and narrow like a hallway. It is important to get that fixed in your mind. The story of Enoch is in fact the story of a room almost more than it is the story of a man.

And so into the room in the evening came young Enoch's friends. There was nothing particularly striking about them except that they were artists of the kind that talk. Everyone knows of the talking artists. Throughout all of the known history of the world they have gathered in rooms and talked. They talk of art and are passionately, almost feverishly, in earnest about it. They think it matters much more than it does.

And so these people gathered and smoked cigarettes and talked and Enoch Robinson, the boy from the farm near Winesburg, was there. He stayed in a corner and for the most part said nothing. How his big blue child-like eyes stared about! On the walls were pictures he had made, crude things, half-finished. His friends talked of these. Leaning back in their chairs, they talked and talked with their heads rocking from side to side. Words were said about line and values and composition, lots of words, such as are always being said.

Enoch wanted to talk too but he didn't know how. He was too excited to talk coherently. When he tried he sputtered and stammered and his voice sounded strange and squeaky to him. That made him stop talking. He knew what he wanted to say, but he knew also that he could never by any possibility say it. When a picture he had painted was under discussion, he wanted to burst out with something like this: "You don't get the point," he wanted to explain, "the picture you see doesn't consist of the things you see and say words about. There is something else, something you don't see at all, something you aren't intended to see. Look at this one over here, by the door here, where the light from the window falls on it. The dark spot by the road that you might not notice at all is, you see, the beginning of everything. There is a clump of elders there such as used to grow beside the road before our house back in Winesburg, Ohio, and in among the elders there is something hidden. It is a woman, that's what it is. She has been thrown from a horse and the horse has run away out of sight. Do you not see how the old man who drives a cart looks anxiously about? That is Thad Grayback who has a farm up the road. He is taking corn to Winesburg to be ground into meal at Comstock's mill. He knows there is something in the elders, something hidden away, and yet he doesn't quite know.

"It's a woman you see, that's what it is! It's a woman and, oh, she is lovely! She is hurt and is suffering but she makes no sound. Don't you see how it is? She lies quite still, white and still, and the beauty comes out from her and spreads over everything. It is in the sky back there and all around everywhere. I didn't try to paint the woman, of course. She is too beautiful to be painted. How dull to talk of composition and such things! Why do you not look at the sky and then run away as I used to do when I was a boy back there in Winesburg, Ohio?"

That is the kind of thing young Enoch Robinson trembled to say to the guests who came into his room when he was a young fellow in New York City, but he always ended by saying nothing. Then he began to doubt his own mind. He was afraid the things he felt were not getting expressed in the pictures he painted. In a half-indignant mood he stopped inviting people into his room and presently got into the habit of locking the door. He began to think that enough people had visited him, that he did not need people any more. With quick imagination he began to invent his own people to whom he could really talk and to whom he explained the things he had been unable to explain to living people. His room began to be inhabited by the spirits of men and women among whom he went, in his turn saying words. It was as though everyone Enoch Robinson had ever seen had left with him some essence of himself, something he could mold and change to suit his own fancy, something that understood all about such things as the wounded woman behind the elders in the pictures.

The mild, blue-eyed young Ohio boy was a complete egotist, as all children are egotists. He did not want friends for the quite simple reason that no child wants friends. He wanted most of all the people of his own mind, people with whom he could really talk, people he could harangue and scold by the hour, servants, you see, to his fancy. Among these people he was always self-confident and bold. They might talk, to be sure, and even have opinions of their own, but always he talked last and best. He was like a writer busy among the figures of his brain, a kind of tiny blue-eyed king he was, in a six-dollar room facing Washington Square in the city of New York.

Then Enoch Robinson got married. He began to get lonely and to want to touch actual flesh and bone people with his hands. Days passed when his room seemed empty. Lust visited his body and desire grew in his mind. At night strange fevers, burning within, kept him awake. He married a girl who sat in a chair next to his own in the art school and went to live in an apartment house in Brooklyn. Two children were born to the woman he married, and Enoch got a job in a place where illustrations are made for advertisements.

That began another phase of Enoch's life. He began to play at a new game. For a while he was very proud of himself in the role of producing citizen of the world. He dismissed the essence of things and played with realities. In the fall he voted at an election and he had a newspaper thrown on his porch each morning. When in the evening he came home from work he got off a streetcar and walked sedately along behind some business man, striving to look very substantial and important. As a payer of taxes he thought he should post himself on how things are run. "I'm getting to be of some moment, a real part of things, of the state and the city and all that," he told himself with an amusing miniature air of dignity. Once coming home from Philadelphia, he had a discussion with a man met on a train. Enoch talked about the advisability of the government's owning and operating the railroads and the man gave him a cigar. It was Enoch's notion that such a move on the part of the government would be a good thing, and he grew quite excited as he talked. Later he remembered his own words with pleasure. "I gave him something to think about, that fellow," he muttered to himself as he climbed the stairs to his Brooklyn apartment.

To be sure, Enoch's marriage did not turn out. He himself brought it to an end. He began to feel choked and walled in by the life in the apartment, and to feel toward his wife and even toward his children as he had felt concerning the friends who once came to visit him. He began to tell little lies about business engagements that would give him freedom to walk alone in the street at night and, the chance offering, he secretly re-rented the room facing Washington Square. Then Mrs. Al Robinson died on the farm near Winesburg, and he got eight thousand dollars from the bank that acted as trustee of her estate. That took Enoch out of the world of men altogether. He gave the money to his wife and told her he could not live in the apartment any more. She cried and was angry and threatened, but he only stared at her and went his own way. In reality the wife did not care much. She thought Enoch slightly insane and was a little afraid of him. When it was quite sure that he would never come back, she took the two children and went to a village in Connecticut where she had lived as a girl. In the end she married a man who bought and sold real estate and was contented enough.

And so Enoch Robinson stayed in the New York room among the people of his fancy, playing with them, talking to them, happy as a child is happy. They were an odd lot, Enoch's people. They were made, I suppose, out of real people he had seen and who had for some obscure reason made an appeal to him. There was a woman with a sword in her hand, an old man with a long white beard who went about followed by a dog, a young girl whose stockings were always coming down and hanging over her shoe tops. There must have been two dozen of the shadow people, invented by the child-mind of Enoch Robinson, who lived in the room with him.

And Enoch was happy. Into the room he went and locked the door. With an absurd air of importance he talked aloud, giving instructions, making comments on life. He was happy and satisfied to go on making his living in the advertising place until something happened. Of course something did happen. That is why he went back to live in Winesburg and why we know about him. The thing that happened was a woman. It would be that way. He was too happy. Something had to come into his world. Something had to drive him out of the New York room to live out his life, an obscure, jerky little figure, bobbing up and down on the streets of an Ohio town at evening when the sun was going down behind the roof of Wesley Moyer's livery barn.

About the thing that happened. Enoch told George Willard about it one night. He wanted to talk to someone, and he chose the young newspaper reporter because the two happened to be thrown together at a time when the younger man was in a mood to understand.

Youthful sadness, young man's sadness, the sadness of a growing boy in a village at the year's end opened the lips of the old man. The sadness was in the heart of George Willard and was without meaning, but it appealed to Enoch Robinson.

It rained on the evening when the two met and talked, a drizzly wet October rain. The fruition of the year had come and the night should have been fine with a moon in the sky and the crisp sharp promise of frost in the air, but it wasn't that way. It rained and little puddles of water shone under the street lamps on Main Street. In the woods in the darkness beyond the Fair Ground water dripped from the black trees. Beneath the trees wet leaves were pasted against tree roots that protruded from the ground. In gardens back of houses in Winesburg dry shriveled potato vines lay sprawling on the ground. Men who had finished the evening meal and who had planned to go uptown to talk the evening away with other men at the back of some store changed their minds. George Willard tramped about in the rain and was glad that it rained. He felt that way. He was like Enoch Robinson on the evenings when the old man came down out of his room and wandered alone in the streets. He was like that only that George Willard had become a tall young man and did not think it manly to weep and carry on. For a month his mother had been very ill and that had something to do with his sadness, but not much. He thought about himself and to the young that always brings sadness.

Enoch Robinson and George Willard met beneath a wooden awning that extended out over the sidewalk before Voight's wagon shop on Maumee Street just off the main street of Winesburg. They went together from there through the rain-washed streets to the older man's room on the third floor of the Heffner Block. The young reporter went willingly enough. Enoch Robinson asked him to go after the two had talked for ten minutes. The boy was a little afraid but had never been more curious in his life. A hundred times he had heard the old man spoken of as a little off his head and he thought himself rather brave and manly to go at all. From the very beginning, in the street in the rain, the old man talked in a queer way, trying to tell the story of the room in Washington Square and of his life in the room. "You'll understand if you try hard enough," he said conclusively. "I have looked at you when you went past me on the street and I think you can understand. It isn't hard. All you have to do is to believe what I say, just listen and believe, that's all there is to it."

It was past eleven o'clock that evening when Old Enoch, talking to George Willard in the room in the Heffner Block, came to the vital thing, the story of the woman and of what drove him out of the city to live out his life alone and defeated in Winesburg. He sat on a cot by the window with his head in his hand and George Willard was in a chair by a table. A kerosene lamp sat on the table and the room, although almost bare of furniture, was scrupulously clean. As the man talked George Willard began to feel that he would like to get out of the chair and sit on the cot also. He wanted to put his arms about the little old man. In the half darkness the man talked and the boy listened, filled with sadness.

"She got to coming in there after there hadn't been anyone in the room for years," said Enoch Robinson. "She saw me in the hallway of the house and we got acquainted. I don't know just what she did in her own room. I never went there. I think she was a musician and played a violin. Every now and then she came and knocked at the door and I opened it. In she came and sat down beside me, just sat and looked about and said nothing. Anyway, she said nothing that mattered."

The old man arose from the cot and moved about the room. The overcoat he wore was wet from the rain and drops of water kept falling with a soft little thump on the floor. When he again sat upon the cot George Willard got out of the chair and sat beside him.

"I had a feeling about her. She sat there in the room with me and she was too big for the room. I felt that she was driving everything else away. We just talked of little things, but I couldn't sit still. I wanted to touch her with my fingers and to kiss her. Her hands were so strong and her face was so good and she looked at me all the time."

The trembling voice of the old man became silent and his body shook as from a chill. "I was afraid," he whispered. "I was terribly afraid. I didn't want to let her come in when she knocked at the door but I couldn't sit still. 'No, no,' I said to myself, but I got up and opened the door just the same. She was so grown up, you see. She was a woman. I thought she would be bigger than I was there in that room."

Enoch Robinson stared at George Willard, his childlike blue eyes shining in the lamplight. Again he shivered. "I wanted her and all the time I didn't want her," he explained. "Then I began to tell her about my people, about everything that meant anything to me. I tried to keep quiet, to keep myself to myself, but I couldn't. I felt just as I did about opening the door. Sometimes I ached to have her go away and never come back any more."

The old man sprang to his feet and his voice shook with excitement. "One night something happened. I became mad to make her understand me and to know what a big thing I was in that room. I wanted her to see how important I was. I told her over and over. When she tried to go away, I ran and locked the door. I followed her about. I talked and talked and then all of a sudden things went to smash. A look came into her eyes and I knew she did understand. Maybe she had understood all the time. I was furious. I couldn't stand it. I wanted her to understand but, don't you see, I couldn't let her understand. I felt that then she would know everything, that I would be submerged, drowned out, you see. That's how it is. I don't know why."

The old man dropped into a chair by the lamp and the boy listened, filled with awe. "Go away, boy," said the man. "Don't stay here with me any more. I thought it might be a good thing to tell you but it isn't. I don't want to talk any more. Go away."

George Willard shook his head and a note of command came into his voice. "Don't stop now. Tell me the rest of it," he commanded sharply. "What happened? Tell me the rest of the story."

Enoch Robinson sprang to his feet and ran to the window that looked down into the deserted main street of Winesburg. George Willard followed. By the window the two stood, the tall awkward boy-man and the little wrinkled man-boy. The childish, eager voice carried forward the tale. "I swore at her," he explained. "I said vile words. I ordered her to go away and not to come back. Oh, I said terrible things. At first she pretended not to understand but I kept at it. I screamed and stamped on the floor. I made the house ring with my curses. I didn't want ever to see her again and I knew, after some of the things I said, that I never would see her again."

The old man's voice broke and he shook his head. "Things went to smash," he said quietly and sadly. "Out she went through the door and all the life there had been in the room followed her out. She took all of my people away. They all went out through the door after her. That's the way it was."

George Willard turned and went out of Enoch Robinson's room. In the darkness by the window, as he went through the door, he could hear the thin old voice whimpering and complaining. "I'm alone, all alone here," said the voice. "It was warm and friendly in my room but now I'm all alone."

# Departure

(CONCERNING GEORGE WILLARD)

YOUNG George Willard got out of bed at four in the morning. It was April and the young tree leaves were just coming out of their buds. The trees along the residence streets in Winesburg are maple and the seeds are winged. When the wind blows they whirl crazily about, filling the air and making a carpet underfoot.

George came downstairs into the hotel office carrying a brown leather bag. His trunk was packed for departure. Since two o'clock he had been awake thinking of the journey he was about to take and wondering what he would find at the end of his journey. The boy who slept in the hotel office lay on a cot by the door. His mouth was open and he snored lustily. George crept past the cot and went out into the silent deserted main street. The east was pink with the dawn and long streaks of light climbed into the sky where a few stars still shone.

Beyond the last house on Trunion Pike in Winesburg there is a great stretch of open fields. The fields are owned by farmers who live in town and drive homeward at evening along Trunion Pike in light creaking wagons. In the fields are planted berries and small fruits. In the late afternoon in the hot summers when the road and the fields are covered with dust, a smoky haze lies over the great flat basin of land. To look across it is like looking out across the sea. In the spring when the land is green the effect is somewhat different. The land becomes a wide green billiard table on which tiny human insects toil up and down.

All through his boyhood and young manhood George Willard had been in the habit of walking on Trunion Pike. He had been in the midst of the great open place on winter nights when it was covered with snow and only the moon looked down at him; he had been there in the fall when bleak winds blew and on summer evenings when the air vibrated with the song of insects. On the April morning he wanted to go there again, to walk again in the silence. He did walk to where the road dipped down by a little stream two miles from town and then turned and walked silently back again. When he got to Main Street clerks were sweeping the sidewalks before the stores. "Hey you George. How does it feel to be going away?" they asked.

The westbound train leaves Winesburg at seven forty-five in the morning. Tom Little is conductor. His train runs from Cleveland to where it connects with a great trunk line railroad with terminals in Chicago and New York. Tom has what in railroad circles is called an "easy run." Every evening he returned to his family. In the fall and spring he spends his Sundays fishing in Lake Erie. He has a round red face and small blue eyes. He knows the people in the towns along his railroad better than a city man knows the people who live in his apartment building.

George came down the little incline from the New Willard House at seven o'clock. Tom Willard carried his bag. The son had become taller than the father.

On the station platform everyone shook the young man's hand. More than a dozen people waited about. Then they talked of their own affairs. Even Will Henderson, who was lazy and often slept until nine, had got out of bed. George was embarrassed. Gertrude Wilmot, a tall thin woman of fifty who worked in the Winesburg post office, came along the station platform. She had never before paid any attention to George. Now she stopped and put out her hand. In two words she voiced what everyone felt. "Good luck," she said sharply and then turning went on her way.

When the train came into the station George felt relieved. He scampered hurriedly aboard. Helen White came running along Main Street hoping to have a parting word with him, but he had found a seat and did not see her. When the train started Tom Little punched his ticket, grinned and, although he knew George well and knew on what adventure he was just setting out, made no comment. Tom had seen a thousand George

Willards go out of their towns to the city. It was a commonplace enough incident with him. In the smoking car there was a man who had just invited Tom to go on a fishing trip to Sandusky Bay. He wanted to accept the invitation and talk over details.

George glanced up and down the car to be sure no one was looking then took out his pocketbook and counted his money. His mind was occupied with a desire not to appear green. Almost the last words his father had said to him concerned the matter of his behavior when he got to the city. "Be a sharp one," Tom Willard had said. "Keep your eyes on your money. Be awake. That's the ticket. Don't let anyone think you're a greenhorn."

After George counted his money he looked out of the window and was surprised to see that the train was still in Winesburg.

The young man, going out of his town to meet the adventure of life, began to think but he did not think of anything very big or dramatic. Things like his mother's death, his departure from Winesburg, the uncertainty of his future life in the city, the serious and larger aspects of his life did not come into his mind.

He thought of little things—Turk Smallet wheeling boards through the main street of his town in the morning, a tall woman, beautifully gowned, who had once stayed overnight at his father's hotel, Butch Wheeler the lamplighter of Winesburg hurrying through the streets on a summer evening and holding a torch in his hand, Helen White standing by a window in the Winesburg post office and putting a stamp on an envelope.

The young man's mind was carried away by his growing passion for dreams. One looking at him would not have thought him particularly sharp. With the recollection of little things occupying his mind he closed his eyes and leaned back in the car seat. He stayed that way for a long time and when he aroused himself and again looked out of the car window the town of Winesburg had disappeared and his life there had become but a background on which to paint the dreams of his manhood.

# POOR WHITE

## A Novel

## EDITOR'S NOTE

*Poor White* was first published in 1920. In his introduction to The Modern Library edition of the book (1925) Anderson wrote of how he conceived its characters while he was on the deck of a ship in the Gulf of Mexico; as he describes their arrival in his imagination, one is reminded of Edgar Lee Masters' description of how the people in his *Spoon River Anthology* came to life, interrupting the conduct of his affairs in his law office in Chicago. Both Masters and Anderson possessed strong historical imaginations, and each re-created in his own fashion the cultural life of the Middle West as it existed between the decade following the Civil War and 1900.

Of Anderson's seven novels, *Poor White* and *Dark Laughter* represent him writing at the height of his narrative style, but *Poor White* is richer in texture than *Dark Laughter*, and with its evocation of an American past already into the twentieth century has more to say to a present generation of readers. In that sense *Poor White* reintroduces the readers of the present mid-century to relatives of their ancestors, and readers will rediscover them, not as they are seen in faded photographs and formal portraits, but as active men and women whose emotions and ideas were shaped by the transition from agrarian to industrial civilization.

# Book One

## CHAPTER I

HUGH McVEY was born in a little hole of a town stuck on a mud bank on the western shore of the Mississippi River in the State of Missouri. It was a miserable place in which to be born. With the exception of a narrow strip of black mud along the river, the land for ten miles back from the town—called in derision by river men "Mudcat Landing"—was almost entirely worthless and unproductive. The soil, yellow, shallow and stony, was tilled, in Hugh's time, by a race of long gaunt men who seemed as exhausted and no-account as the land on which they lived. They were chronically discouraged, and the merchants and artisans of the town were in the same state. The merchants, who ran their stores—poor tumble-down ramshackle affairs—on the credit system, could not get pay for the goods they handed out over their counters and the artisans, the shoemakers, carpenters and harnessmakers, could not get pay for the work they did. Only the town's two saloons prospered. The saloon keepers sold their wares for cash and, as the men of the town and the farmers who drove into town felt that without drink life was unbearable, cash always could be found for the purpose of getting drunk.

Hugh McVey's father, John McVey, had been a farm hand in his youth but before Hugh was born had moved into town to find employment in a tannery. The tannery ran for a year or two and then failed, but John McVey stayed in town. He also became a drunkard. It was the easy obvious thing for him to do. During the time of his employment in the tannery he had been married and his son had been born. Then his wife died and the idle workman took his child and went to live in a tiny fishing shack by the river. How the boy lived through the next few years no one ever knew. John McVey loitered in the streets and on the river bank and only awakened out of his habitual stupor when, driven by hunger or the craving for drink, he went for a day's work in some farmer's field at harvest time or joined a number of other idlers for an adventurous trip down river on a lumber raft. The baby was left shut up in the shack by the river or carried about wrapped in a soiled blanket. Soon after he was old enough to walk he was compelled to find work in order that he might eat. The boy of ten went listlessly about town at the heels of his father. The two found work, which the boy did while the man lay sleeping in the sun. They cleaned cisterns, swept out stores and saloons and at night went with a wheelbarrow and a box to remove and dump in the river the contents of outhouses. At fourteen Hugh was as tall as his father and almost without education. He could read a little and could write his own name, had picked up these accomplishments from other boys who came to fish with him in the river, but he had never been to school. For days sometimes he did nothing but lie half asleep in the shade of a bush on the river bank. The fish he caught on his more industrious days he sold for a few cents to some housewife, and thus got money to buy food for his big growing indolent body. Like an animal that has come to its maturity he turned away from his father, not because of resentment for his hard youth, but because he thought it time to begin to go his own way.

In his fourteenth year and when the boy was on the

point of sinking into the sort of animal-like stupor in which his father had lived, something happened to him. A railroad pushed its way down along the river to his town and he got a job as man of all work for the station master. He swept out the station, put trunks on trains, mowed the grass in the station yard and helped in a hundred odd ways the man who held the combined jobs of ticket seller, baggage master and telegraph operator at the little out-of-the-way place.

Hugh began a little to awaken. He lived with his employer, Henry Shepard, and his wife, Sarah Shepard, and for the first time in his life sat down regularly at table. His life, lying on the river bank through long summer afternoons or sitting perfectly still for endless hours in a boat, had bred in him a dreamy detached outlook on life. He found it hard to be definite and to do definite things, but for all his stupidity the boy had a great store of patience, a heritage perhaps from his mother. In his new place the station master's wife, Sarah Shepard, a sharp-tongued, good-natured woman, who hated the town and the people among whom fate had thrown her, scolded at him all day long. She treated him like a child of six, told him how to sit at table, how to hold his fork when he ate, how to address people who came to the house or to the station. The mother in her was aroused by Hugh's helplessness and, having no children of her own, she began to take the tall awkward boy to her heart. She was a small woman and when she stood in the house scolding the great stupid boy who stared down at her with his small perplexed eyes, the two made a picture that afforded endless amusement to her husband, a short fat bald-headed man who went about clad in blue overalls and a blue cotton shirt. Coming to the back door of his house, that was within a stone's throw of the station, Henry Shepard stood with his hand on the doorjamb and watched the woman and the boy. Above the scolding voice of the woman his own voice arose. "Look out, Hugh," he called. "Be on the jump, lad! Perk yourself up. She'll be biting you if you don't go mighty careful in there."

Hugh got little money for his work at the railroad station but for the first time in his life he began to fare well. Henry Shepard bought the boy clothes, and his wife, Sarah, who was a master of the art of cooking, loaded the table with good things to eat. Hugh ate until both the man and woman declared he would burst if he did not stop. Then when they were not looking he went into the station yard and crawling under a bush went to sleep. The station master came to look for him. He cut a switch from the bush and began to beat the boy's bare feet. Hugh awoke and was overcome with confusion. He got to his feet and stood trembling, half afraid he was to be driven away from his new home. The man and the confused blushing boy confronted each other for a moment and then the man adopted the method of his wife and began to scold. He was annoyed at what he thought the boy's indolence and found a hundred little tasks for him to do. He devoted himself to finding tasks for Hugh, and when he could think of no new ones, invented them. "We will have to keep the big lazy fellow on the jump. That's the secret of things," he said to his wife.

The boy learned to keep his naturally indolent body moving and his clouded sleepy mind fixed on definite things. For hours he plodded straight ahead, doing over and over some appointed task. He forgot the purpose of the job he had been given to do and did it because it was a job and would keep him awake. One morning he was told to sweep the station platform and as his employer had gone away without giving him additional tasks and as he was afraid that if he sat down he would fall into the odd detached kind of stupor in which he had spent so large a part of his life, he continued to sweep for two or three hours. The station platform was built of rough boards and Hugh's arms were very powerful. The broom he was using began to go to pieces. Bits of it flew about and after an hour's work the platform looked more uncleanly than when he began. Sarah Shepard came to the door of her house and stood watching. She was about to call to him and to scold him again for his stupidity when a new impulse came to her. She saw the serious determined look on the boy's long gaunt face and a flash of understanding came to her. Tears came into her eyes and her arms ached to take the great boy and hold him tightly against her breast. With all her mother's soul she wanted to protect Hugh from a world she was sure would treat him always as a beast of burden and would take no account of what she thought of as the handicap of his birth. Her morning's work was done and without saying anything to Hugh, who continued to go up and down the platform laboriously sweeping, she went out at the front door of the house and to one of the town stores. There she bought a half dozen books, a geography, an arithmetic, a speller and two or three readers. She had made up her mind to become Hugh McVey's school teacher and with characteristic energy did not put the matter off, but went about it at once. When she got back to her house and saw the boy still going doggedly up and down the platform, she did not scold but spoke to him with a new gentleness in her manner. "Well, my boy, you may put the broom away now and come to the house," she suggested. "I've made up my mind to take you for my own boy and I don't want to be ashamed of you. If you're going to live with me I can't have you growing up to be a lazy good-for-nothing like your father and the other men in this hole of a place.

You'll have to learn things and I suppose I'll have to be your teacher.

"Come on over to the house at once," she added sharply, making a quick motion with her hand to the boy who with the broom in his hands stood stupidly staring. "When a job is to be done there's no use putting it off. It's going to be hard work to make an educated man of you, but it has to be done. We might as well begin on your lessons at once."

Hugh McVey lived with Henry Shepard and his wife until he became a grown man. After Sarah Shepard became his school teacher things began to go better for him. The scolding of the New England woman, that had but accentuated his awkwardness and stupidity, came to an end and life in his adopted home became so quiet and peaceful that the boy thought of himself as one who had come into a kind of paradise. For a time the two older people talked of sending him to the town school, but the woman objected. She had begun to feel so close to Hugh that he seemed a part of her own flesh and blood and the thought of him, so huge and ungainly, sitting in a schoolroom with the children of the town, annoyed and irritated her. In imagination she saw him being laughed at by other boys and could not bear the thought. She did not like the people of the town and did not want Hugh to associate with them.

Sarah Shepard had come from a people and a country quite different in its aspect from that in which she now lived. Her own people, frugal New Englanders, had come west in the year after the Civil War to take up cut-over timber land in the southern end of the State of Michigan. The daughter was a grown girl when her father and mother took up the westward journey, and after they arrived at the new home, had worked with her father in the fields. The land was covered with huge stumps and was difficult to farm but the New Englanders were accustomed to difficulties and were not discouraged. The land was deep and rich and the people who had settled upon it were poor but hopeful. They felt that every day of hard work done in clearing the land was like laying up treasure against the future. In New England they had fought against a hard climate and had managed to find a living on stony unproductive soil. The milder climate and the rich deep soil of Michigan was, they felt, full of promise. Sarah's father like most of his neighbors had gone into debt for his land and for tools with which to clear and work it and every year spent most of his earnings in paying interest on a mortgage held by a banker in a nearby town, but that did not discourage him. He whistled as he went about his work and spoke often of a future of ease and plenty. "In a few years and when the land is cleared we'll make money hand over fist," he declared.

When Sarah grew into young womanhood and went about among the young people in the new country, she heard much talk of mortgages and of the difficulty of making ends meet, but everyone spoke of the hard conditions as temporary. In every mind the future was bright with promise. Throughout the whole Mid-American country, in Ohio, Northern Indiana and Illinois, Wisconsin and Iowa a hopeful spirit prevailed. In every breast hope fought a successful war with poverty and discouragement. Optimism got into the blood of the children and later led to the same kind of hopeful courageous development of the whole western country. The sons and daughters of these hardy people no doubt had their minds too steadily fixed on the problem of the paying off of mortgages and getting on in the world, but there was courage in them. If they, with the frugal and sometimes niggardly New Englanders from whom they were sprung, have given modern American life a too material flavor, they have at least created a land in which a less determinedly materialistic people may in their turn live in comfort.

In the midst of the little hopeless community of beaten men and yellow defeated women on the bank of the Mississippi River, the woman who had become Hugh McVey's second mother and in whose veins flowed the blood of the pioneers, felt herself undefeated and unbeatable. She and her husband would, she felt, stay in the Missouri town for a while and then move on to a larger town and a better position in life. They would move on and up until the little fat man was a railroad president or a millionaire. It was the way things were done. She had no doubt of the future. "Do everything well," she said to her husband, who was perfectly satisfied with his position in life and had no exalted notions as to his future. "Remember to make your reports out neatly and clearly. Show them you can do perfectly the task given you to do, and you will be given a chance at a larger task. Some day when you least expect it something will happen. You will be called up into a position of power. We won't be compelled to stay in this hole of a place very long."

The ambitious energetic little woman, who had taken the son of the indolent farm hand to her heart, constantly talked to him of her own people. Every afternoon when her housework was done she took the boy into the front room of the house and spent hours laboring with him over his lessons. She worked upon the problem of rooting the stupidity and dullness out of his mind as her father had worked at the problem of rooting the stumps out of the Michigan land. After the lesson for the day had been gone over and over until Hugh was in a stupor of mental weariness, she put the books aside and talked to him. With glowing fervor she made for him a picture of her own youth and the people and places where she had lived. In the picture she represented the New Englanders of the Michigan farming community as a strong godlike race, always honest, always frugal, and always pushing ahead. His own people she utterly condemned. She pitied him for the blood in his veins. The boy had then and all his life certain physical difficulties she could never understand. The blood did not flow freely through his long body. His feet and hands were always cold and there was for him an almost sensual satisfaction to be had from just lying perfectly still in the station yard and letting the hot sun beat down on him.

Sarah Shepard looked upon what she called Hugh's laziness as a thing of the spirit. "You have got to get over it," she declared. "Look at your own people—poor white trash—how lazy and shiftless they are. You can't be like them. It's a sin to be so dreamy and worthless."

Swept along by the energetic spirit of the woman, Hugh fought to overcome his inclination to give himself up to vaporous dreams. He became convinced that his own people were really of inferior stock, that they were to be kept away from and not to be taken into account. During the first year after he came to live with the Shepards, he sometimes gave way to a desire to return to his old lazy life with his father in the shack by the river. People got off steamboats at the town and took the train to other towns lying back from the river. He earned a little money by carrying trunks filled with clothes or traveling men's samples up an incline from the steamboat landing to the railroad station. Even at fourteen the strength in his long gaunt body was so great that he could outlift any man in town, and he put one of the trunks on his shoulder and walked slowly and stolidly away with it as a farm horse might have walked along a country road with a boy of six perched on his back.

The money earned in this way Hugh for a time gave to his father, and when the man had become stupid with drink he grew quarrelsome and demanded that the boy return to live with him. Hugh had not the spirit to refuse and sometimes did not want to refuse. When neither the station master nor his wife was about he slipped away and went with his father to sit for a half day with his back against the wall of the fishing shack, his soul at peace. In the sunlight he sat and stretched forth his long legs. His small sleepy eyes stared out over the river. A delicious feeling crept over him and for the moment he thought of himself as completely happy and made up his mind that he did not want to return again to the railroad station and to the woman who was so determined to arouse him and make of him a man of her own people.

Hugh looked at his father asleep and snoring in the long grass on the river bank. An odd feeling of disloyalty crept over him and he became uncomfortable. The man's mouth was open and he snored lustily. From his greasy and threadbare clothing arose the smell of fish. Flies gathered in swarms and alighted on his face. Disgust took possession of Hugh. A flickering but ever recurring light came into his eyes. With all the strength of his awakening soul he struggled against the desire to give way to the inclination to stretch himself out beside the man and sleep. The words of the New England woman, who was, he knew, striving to lift him out of slothfulness and ugliness into some brighter and better way of life, echoed dimly in his mind. When he arose and went back along the street to the station master's house and when the woman there looked at him reproachfully and muttered words about the poor white trash of the town, he was ashamed and looked at the floor.

Hugh began to hate his own father and his own people. He connected the man who had bred him with the dreaded inclination toward sloth in himself. When the farm hand came to the station and demanded the money he had earned by carrying trunks, he turned away and went across a dusty road to the Shepards' house. After a year or two he paid no more attention to the dissolute farm hand who came occasionally to the station to mutter and swear at him; and, when he had earned a little money, gave it to the woman to keep for him. "Well," he said, speaking slowly and with the hesitating drawl characteristic of his people, "if you give me time I'll learn. I want to be what you want me to be. If you stick to me I'll try to make a man of myself."

Hugh McVey lived in the Missouri town under the tutelage of Sarah Shepard until he was nineteen years old. Then the station master gave up railroading and went back to Michigan. Sarah Shepard's father had died after having cleared one hundred and twenty acres of the cut-over timber land and it had been left to her. The dream that had for years lurked in the back of the little woman's mind and in which she saw bald-headed, good-natured Henry Shepard become a power in the railroad world had begun to fade. In newspapers and magazines she read constantly of other men who, starting from a humble position in the railroad service, soon became rich and powerful, but nothing of the kind seemed likely to happen to her husband. Under her watchful eye he did his work well and carefully but nothing came of it. Officials of the railroad sometimes passed through the town riding in private cars hitched to the end of one of the through trains, but the trains did not stop and the officials did not alight and, calling Henry out of the station, reward his faithfulness by piling new responsibilities upon him, as railroad officials did in such cases in the stories she read. When her father died and she saw a chance to again turn her face eastward and to live again among her own people, she told her husband to resign his position with the air of one accepting an undeserved defeat. The station master managed to get Hugh appointed in his place, and the two people went away one gray morning in October, leaving the tall ungainly young man in charge of affairs. He had books to keep, freight waybills to make out, messages to receive, dozens of definite things to do. Early in the morning before the train that was to take her away came to the station, Sarah Shepard called the young man to her and repeated the instructions she had so often given her husband. "Do everything neatly and carefully," she said. "Show yourself worthy of the trust that has been given you."

The New England woman wanted to assure the boy, as she had so often assured her husband, that if he would but work hard and faithfully promotion would inevitably come; but in the face of the fact that Henry Shepard had for years done without criticism the work Hugh was to do and had received neither praise nor blame from those above him, she found it impossible to say the words that arose to her lips. The woman and the son of the people among whom she had lived for five years and had so often condemned, stood beside each other in embarrassed silence. Stripped of her assurance as to the purpose of life and unable to repeat her accustomed formula, Sarah Shepard had nothing to say. Hugh's tall figure, leaning against the post that supported the roof of the front porch of the little house where she had taught him his lessons day after day, seemed to her suddenly old and she thought his long solemn face suggested a wisdom older and more mature than her own. An odd revulsion of feeling swept over her. For the moment she began to doubt the advisability of trying to be smart and to get on in life. If Hugh had been somewhat smaller of frame so that her mind could have taken hold of the fact of his youth and immaturity, she would no doubt have taken him into her arms and said words regarding her doubts. Instead she also became silent and the minutes slipped away as the two people stood before each other and stared at the floor of the porch. When the train on which she was to leave blew a warning whistle, and Henry Shepard called to her from the station platform, she put a hand on the lapel of Hugh's coat and drawing his face down, for the first time kissed him on the cheek. Tears came into her eyes and into the eyes of the young man. When he stepped across the porch to get her bag Hugh stumbled awkwardly against a chair. "Well, you do the best you can here," Sarah Shepard said quickly and then out of long habit and half unconsciously did repeat her formula. "Do little things well and big opportunities are bound to come," she declared as she walked briskly along beside Hugh across the narrow road and to the station and the train that was to bear her away.

After the departure of Sarah and Henry Shepard Hugh continued to struggle with his inclination to give way to dreams. It seemed to him a struggle it was necessary to win in order that he might show his respect and appreciation of the woman who had spent so many long hours laboring with him. Although, under her tutelage, he had received a better education than any other young man of the river town, he had lost none of his physical desire to sit in the sun and do nothing. When he worked, every task had to be consciously carried on from minute to minute. After the woman left, there were days when he sat in the chair in the telegraph office and fought a desperate battle with himself. A queer determined light shone in his small gray eyes. He arose from the chair and walked up and down the station platform. Each time as he lifted one of his long feet and set it slowly down a special little effort had to be made. To move about at all was a painful performance, something he did not want to do. All physical acts were to him dull but necessary parts of his training for a vague and glorious future that was to come to him some day in a brighter and more beautiful land that lay in the direction thought of rather indefinitely as the East. "If I do not move and keep moving I'll become like father, like all of the people about here," Hugh said to himself. He thought of the man who had bred him and whom he occasionally saw drifting aimlessly along Main Street or sleeping away a drunken stupor on the river bank. He was disgusted with him and had come to share the opinion the station master's wife had always held concerning the people of the Missouri village. "They're a lot of miserable lazy louts," she had declared a thousand times, and Hugh agreed with her, but sometimes wondered if in the end he might not also become a lazy lout. That possibility he knew was in him and for the sake of the woman as well as for his own sake he was determined it should not be so.

The truth is that the people of Mudcat Landing were totally unlike any of the people Sarah Shepard had ever known and unlike the people Hugh was to know during his mature life. He who had come from a people not smart was to live among smart energetic men and women and be called a big man by them without in the least understanding what they were talking about.

Practically all of the people of Hugh's home town were of Southern origin. Living originally in a land where all physical labor was performed by slaves, they had come to have a deep aversion to physical labor. In the South their fathers, having no money to buy slaves of their own and being unwilling to compete with slave labor, had tried to live without labor. For the most part they lived in the mountains and the hill country of Kentucky and Tennessee, on land too poor and unproductive to be thought worth cultivating by their rich slave-owning neighbors of the valleys and plains. Their food was meager and of an enervating sameness and their bodies degenerate. Children grew up long and gaunt and yellow like badly nourished plants. Vague indefinite hungers took hold of them and they gave themselves over to dreams. The more energetic among them, sensing dimly the unfairness of their position in life, became vicious and dangerous. Feuds started among them and they killed each other to express their hatred of life. When, in the years preceding the Civil War, a few of them pushed north along the rivers and settled in Southern Indiana and Illinois and in Eastern Missouri and Arkansas, they seemed to have exhausted their energy in making the voyage and slipped quickly back into their old slothful way of life. Their impulse to emigrate did not carry them far and but a few of them ever reached the rich corn lands of central Indiana, Illinois or Iowa or the equally rich land back from the river in Missouri or Arkansas. In Southern Indiana and Illinois they were merged into the life about them and with the infusion of new blood they a little awoke. They have tempered the quality of the peoples of those regions, made them perhaps less harshly energetic than their forefathers, the pioneers. In many of the Missouri and Arkansas river towns they have changed but little. A visitor to these parts may see them there today, long, gaunt, and lazy, sleeping their lives away and awakening out of their stupor only at long intervals and at the call of hunger.

As for Hugh McVey, he stayed in his home town and among his own people for a year after the departure of the man and woman who had been father and mother to him, and then he also departed. All through the year he worked constantly to cure himself of the curse of indolence. When he awoke in the morning he did not dare lie in bed for a moment for fear indolence would overcome him and he would not be able to arise at all. Getting out of bed at once he dressed and went to the station. During the day there was not much work to be done and he walked for hours up and down the station platform. When he sat down he at once took up a book and put his mind to work. When the pages of the book became indistinct before his eyes and he felt within him the inclination to drift off into dreams, he again arose and walked up and down the platform. Having accepted the New England woman's opinion of his own people and not wanting to associate with them, his life became utterly lonely and his loneliness also drove him to labor.

Something happened to him. Although his body would not and never did become active, his mind began suddenly to work with feverish eagerness. The vague thoughts and feelings that had always been a part of him but that had been indefinite, ill-defined things, like clouds floating far away in a hazy sky, began to grow definite. In the evening after his work was done and he had locked the station for the night, he did not go to the town hotel where he had taken a room and where he ate his meals, but wandered about town and along the road that ran south beside the great mysterious river. A hundred new and definite desires and hungers awoke in him. He began to want to talk with people, to know men and most of all to know women, but the disgust for his fellows in the town, engendered in him by Sarah Shepard's words and most of all by the things in his nature that were like their natures, made him draw back. When in the fall at the end of the year after the Shepards had left and he began living alone, his father was killed in a senseless quarrel with a drunken river man over the ownership of a dog, a sudden, and what seemed to him at the moment heroic, resolution came to him. He went early one morning to one of the town's two saloon keepers, a man who had been his father's nearest approach to a friend and companion, and gave him money to bury the dead man. Then he wired to the headquarters of the railroad company telling them to send a man to Mudcat Landing to take his place. On the afternoon of the day on which his father was buried, he bought himself a handbag and packed his few belongings. Then he sat down alone on the steps of the railroad station to wait for the evening train that would bring the man who was to replace him and that would at the same time take him away. He did not know where he intended to go, but knew that he wanted to push out into a new land and get among new people. He thought he would go east and north. He remembered the long summer evenings in the river town when the station master slept and his wife talked. The boy who listened had wanted to sleep also, but with the eyes of Sarah Shepard fixed on him, had not dared to do so. The woman had talked of a land dotted with towns where the houses were all painted in bright colors, where young girls dressed in white dresses went about in the evening, walking under trees beside streets paved with bricks, where there was no dust or mud, where stores were gay bright places filled with beautiful wares that the people had money to buy in abundance and where everyone was alive and doing things worth while and none was slothful and lazy. The boy who had now become a man wanted to go to such a place. His work in the railroad station had given him some idea of the geography of the country and, although he could not have told whether the woman who had talked so enticingly had in mind her childhood in New England or her girlhood in Michigan, he knew in a general way that to reach the land and the people who were to show him by their lives the better way to form his own life, he must go east. He decided that the further east he went the more beautiful life would become, and that he had better not try going too far in the beginning. "I'll go into the northern part of Indiana or Ohio," he told himself. "There must be beautiful towns in those places."

Hugh was boyishly eager to get on his way and to become at once a part of the life in a new place. The gradual awakening of his mind had given him courage, and he thought of himself as armed and ready for association with men. He wanted to become acquainted with and be the friend of people whose lives were beautifully lived and who were themselves beautiful and full of significance. As he sat on the steps of the railroad station in the poor little Missouri town with his bag beside him, and thought of all the things he wanted to do in life, his mind became so eager and restless that some of its restlessness was transmitted to his body. For perhaps the first time in his life he arose without conscious effort and walked up and down the station platform out of an excess of energy. He thought he could not bear to wait until the train came and brought the man who was to take his place. "Well, I'm going away, I'm going away to be a man among men," he said to himself over and over. The saying became a kind of refrain and he said it unconsciously. As he repeated the words his heart beat high in anticipation of the future he thought lay before him.

## CHAPTER II

Hugh McVey left the town of Mudcat Landing in early September of the year eighteen eighty-six. He was then twenty years old and was six feet and four inches tall. The whole upper part of his body was immensely strong but his long legs were ungainly and lifeless. He secured a pass from the railroad company that had employed him, and rode north along the river in the night train until he came to a large town named Burlington in the State of Iowa. There a bridge went over the river, and the railroad tracks joined those of a trunk line and ran eastward toward Chicago; but Hugh did not continue his journey on that night. Getting off the train he went to a nearby hotel and took a room for the night.

It was a cool clear evening and Hugh was restless. The town of Burlington, a prosperous place in the midst of a rich farming country, overwhelmed him with its stir and bustle. For the first time he saw brick-paved streets and streets lighted with lamps. Although it was nearly ten o'clock at night when he arrived, people still walked about in the streets and many stores were open.

The hotel where he had taken a room faced the railroad tracks and stood at the corner of a brightly lighted street. When he had been shown to his room Hugh sat for a half hour by an open window, and then as he could not sleep, decided to go for a walk. For a time he walked in the streets where the people stood about before the doors of the stores but, as his tall figure attracted attention and he felt people staring at him, he went presently into a side street.

In a few minutes he became utterly lost. He went through what seemed to him miles of streets lined with frame and brick houses, and occasionally passed people, but was too timid and embarrassed to ask his way. The street climbed upward and after a time he got into open country and followed a road that ran along a cliff overlooking the Mississippi River. The night was clear and the sky brilliant with stars. In the open, away from the multitude of houses, he no longer felt awkward and afraid, and went cheerfully along. After a time he stopped and stood facing the river. Standing on a high cliff and with a grove of trees at his back, the stars seemed to have all gathered in the eastern sky. Below him the water of the river reflected the stars. They seemed to be making a pathway for him into the East.

The tall Missouri countryman sat down on a log near the edge of the cliff and tried to see the water in the river below. Nothing was visible but a bed of stars that danced and twinkled in the darkness. He had made his way to a place far above the railroad bridge, but presently a through passenger train from the West passed over it and the lights of the train looked also like stars, stars that moved and beckoned and that seemed to fly like flocks of birds out of the West into the East.

For several hours Hugh sat on the log in the darkness. He decided that it was hopeless for him to find his way back to the hotel, and was glad of the excuse for staying abroad. His body for the first time in his life felt light and strong and his mind was feverishly awake. A buggy in which sat a young man and woman went along the road at his back, and after the voices had died away silence came, broken only at long intervals during the hours when he sat thinking of his future by the barking of a dog in some distant house or the churning of the paddle wheels of a passing river boat.

All of the early formative years of Hugh McVey's life had been spent within sound of the lapping of the waters of the Mississippi River. He had seen it in the hot summer when the water receded and the mud lay baked and cracked along the edge of the water; in the spring when the floods raged and the water went whirling past, bearing tree logs and even parts of houses; in the winter when the water looked deathly cold and ice floated past; and in the fall when it was quiet and still and lovely, and seemed to have sucked an almost human quality of warmth out of the red trees that lined its shores. Hugh had spent hours and days sitting or lying in the grass beside the river. The fishing shack in which he had lived with his father until he was fourteen years old was within a half dozen long strides of the river's edge, and the boy had often been left there alone for a week at a time. When his father had gone for a trip on a lumber raft or to work for a few days on some farm in the country back from the river, the boy, left often without money and with but a few loaves of bread, went fishing when he was hungry and when he was not did nothing but idle the days away in the grass on the river bank. Boys from the town came sometimes to spend an hour with him, but in their presence he was embarrassed and a little annoyed. He wanted to be left alone with his dreams. One of the boys, a sickly, pale, undeveloped lad of ten, often stayed with him through an entire summer afternoon. He was the son of a merchant in the town and grew quickly tired when he tried to follow other boys about. On the river bank he lay beside Hugh in silence. The two got into Hugh's boat and went fishing and the merchant's son grew animated and talked. He taught Hugh to write his own name and to read a few words. The shyness that kept them apart had begun to break down, when the merchant's son caught some childhood disease and died.

In the darkness above the cliff that night in Burlington Hugh remembered things concerning his boyhood that had not come back to his mind in years. The very thoughts that had passed through his mind during those long days of idling on the river bank came streaming back.

After his fourteenth year when he went to work at the railroad station Hugh had stayed away from the river. With his work at the station, and in the garden back of Sarah Shepard's house, and the lessons in the afternoons, he had little idle time. On Sundays however things were different. Sarah Shepard did not go to church after she came to Mudcat Landing, but she would have no work done on Sundays. On Sunday afternoons in the summer she and her husband sat in chairs beneath a tree beside the house and went to sleep. Hugh got into the habit of going off by himself. He wanted to sleep also, but did not dare. He went along the river bank by the road that ran south from the town, and when he had followed it two or three miles, turned into a grove of trees and lay down in the shade.

The long summer Sunday afternoons had been delightful times for Hugh, so delightful that he finally gave them up, fearing they might lead him to take up again his old sleepy way of life. Now as he sat in the darkness above the same river he had gazed on through the long Sunday afternoons, a spasm of something like loneliness swept over him. For the first time he thought about leaving the river country and going into a new land with a keen feeling of regret.

On the Sunday afternoons in the woods south of Mudcat Landing Hugh had lain perfectly still in the grass for hours. The smell of dead fish that had always been present about the shack where he spent his boyhood, was gone and there were no swarms of flies. Above his head a breeze played through the branches of the trees, and insects sang in the grass. Everything about him was clean. A lovely stillness pervaded the river and the woods. He lay on his belly and gazed down over the river out of sleep-heavy eyes into hazy distances. Half-formed thoughts passed like visions through his mind. He dreamed, but his dreams were unformed and vaporous. For hours the half-dead, half-alive state into which he had got, persisted. He did not sleep but lay in a land between sleeping and waking. Pictures formed in his mind. The clouds that floated in the sky above the river took on strange, grotesque shapes. They began to move. One of the clouds separated itself from the others. It moved swiftly away into the dim distance and then returned. It became a half-human thing and seemed to be marshaling the other clouds. Under its influence they became agitated and moved restlessly about. Out of the body of the most active of the clouds long vaporous arms were extended. They pulled and hauled at the other clouds making them also restless and agitated.

Hugh's mind, as he sat in the darkness on the cliff above the river that night in Burlington, was deeply stirred. Again he was a boy lying in the woods above his river, and the visions that had come to him there returned with startling clearness. He got off the log and lying in the wet grass, closed his eyes. His body became warm.

Hugh thought his mind had gone out of his body and up into the sky to join the clouds and the stars, to play with them. From the sky he thought he looked down on the earth and saw rolling fields, hills and forests. He had no part in the lives of the men and women of the earth, but was torn away from them, left to stand by himself. From his place in the sky above the earth he saw the great river going majestically along. For a time it was quiet and contemplative as the sky had been when he was a boy down below lying on his belly in the wood. He saw men pass in boats and could hear their voices dimly. A great quiet prevailed and he looked abroad beyond the wide expanse of the river and saw fields and towns. They were all hushed and still. An air of waiting hung over them. And then the river was whipped into action by some strange unknown force, something that had come out of a distant place, out of the place to which the cloud had gone and from which it had returned to stir and agitate the other clouds.

The river now went tearing along. It overflowed its banks and swept over the land, uprooting trees and forests and towns. The white faces of drowned men and children, borne along by the flood, looked up into the mind's eye of the man Hugh, who, in the moment of his setting out into the definite world of struggle and defeat, had let himself slip back into the vaporous dreams of his boyhood.

As he lay in the wet grass in the darkness on the cliff Hugh tried to force his way back to consciousness, but for a long time was unsuccessful. He rolled and writhed about and his lips muttered words. It was useless. His mind also was swept away. The clouds of which he felt himself a part flew across the face of the sky. They blotted out the sun from the earth, and darkness descended on the land, on the troubled towns, on the hills that were torn open, on the forests that were destroyed, on the peace and quiet of all places. In the country stretching away from the river where all had been peace and quiet, all was now agitation and unrest. Houses were destroyed and instantly rebuilt. People gathered in whirling crowds.

The dreaming man felt himself a part of something significant and terrible that was happening to the earth and to the peoples of the earth. Again he struggled to awake, to force himself back out of the dream world into consciousness. When he did awake, day was breaking and he sat on the very edge of the cliff that looked down upon the Mississippi River, gray now in the dim morning light.

The towns in which Hugh lived during the first three years after he began his eastward journey were all small places containing a few hundred people, and were scattered through Illinois, Indiana and Western Ohio. All of the people among whom he worked and lived during that time were farmers and laborers. In the spring of the first year of his wandering he passed through the city of Chicago and spent two hours there, going in and out at the same railroad station.

He was not tempted to become a city man. The huge commercial city at the foot of Lake Michigan, because of its commanding position in the very center of a vast farming empire, had already become gigantic. He never forgot the two hours he spent standing in the station in the heart of the city and walking in the street adjoining the station. It was evening when he came into the roaring, clanging place. On the long wide plains west of the city he saw farmers at work with their spring plowing as the train went flying along. Presently the farms grew small and the whole prairie dotted with towns. In these the train did not stop but ran into a crowded network of streets filled with multitudes of people. When he got into the big dark station Hugh saw thousands of people rushing about like disturbed insects. Unnumbered thousands of people were going out of the city at the end of their day of work and trains waited to take them to towns on the prairies. They came in droves, hurrying along like distraught cattle, over a bridge and into the station. The inbound crowds that had alighted from through trains coming from cities of the East and West climbed up a stairway to the street, and those that were outbound tried to descend by the same stairway and at the same time. The result was a whirling churning mass of humanity. Everyone pushed and crowded his way along. Men swore, women grew angry, and children cried. Near the doorway that opened into the street a long line of cab drivers shouted and roared.

Hugh looked at the people who were whirled along past him, and shivered with the nameless fear of multitudes, common to country boys in the city. When the rush of people had a little subsided he went out of the station and, walking across a narrow street, stood by a brick store building. Presently the rush of people began again, and again men, women, and boys came hurrying across the bridge and ran wildly in at the doorway leading into the station. They came in waves as water washes along a beach during a storm. Hugh had a feeling that if he were by some chance to get caught in the crowd he would be swept away into some unknown and terrible place. Waiting until the rush had a little subsided, he went across the street and on to the bridge to look at the river that flowed past the station. It was narrow and filled with ships, and the water looked gray and dirty. A pall of black smoke covered the sky. From all sides of him and even in the air above his head a great clatter and roar of bells and whistles went on.

With the air of a child venturing into a dark forest Hugh went a little way into one of the streets that led westward from the station. Again he stopped and stood by a building. Near at hand a group of young city roughs stood smoking and talking before a saloon. Out of a nearby building came a young girl who approached and spoke to one of them. The man began to swear furiously. "You tell her I'll come in there in a minute and smash her face," he said, and, paying no more attention to the girl, turned to stare at Hugh. All of the young men lounging before the saloon turned to stare at the tall country man. They began to laugh and one of them walked quickly toward him.

Hugh ran along the street and into the station followed by the shouts of the young roughs. He did not venture out again, and when his train was ready, got aboard and went gladly out of the great complex dwelling-place of modern Americans.

Hugh went from town to town always working his way eastward, always seeking the place where happiness was to come to him and where he was to achieve companionship with men and women. He cut fence posts in a forest on a large farm in Indiana, worked in the fields, and in one place was a section hand on the railroad.

On a farm in Indiana, some forty miles east of Indianapolis, he was for the first time powerfully touched by the presence of a woman. She was the daughter of the farmer who was Hugh's employer, and was an alert, handsome woman of twenty-four who had been a school teacher but had given up the work because she was about to be married. Hugh thought the man who was to marry her the most fortunate being in the world. He lived in Indianapolis and came by train to spend the week ends at the farm. The woman prepared for his coming by putting on a white dress and fastening a rose in her hair. The two people walked about in an orchard beside the house or went for a ride along the country roads. The young man, who, Hugh had been told, worked in a bank, wore stiff white collars, a black suit and a black derby hat.

On the farm Hugh worked in the field with the farmer and ate at table with his family, but did not get acquainted with them. On Sunday when the young man came he took the day off and went into a nearby town. The courtship became a matter very close to him and he lived through the excitement of the weekly visits as though he had been one of the principals. The daughter of the house, sensing the fact that the silent farm hand was stirred by her presence, became interested in him. Sometimes in the evening as he sat on a little porch before the house, she came to join him, and sat looking at him with a peculiarly detached and interested air. She tried to make talk, but Hugh answered all her advances so briefly and with such a half-frightened manner that she gave up the attempt. One Saturday evening when her sweetheart had come she took him for a ride in the family carriage, and Hugh concealed himself in the hayloft of the barn to wait for their return.

Hugh had never seen or heard a man express in any way his affection for a woman. It seemed to him a terrifically heroic thing to do and he hoped by concealing himself in the barn to see it done. It was a bright moonlight night and he waited until nearly eleven o'clock before the lovers returned. In the hayloft there was an opening high up under the roof. Because of his great height he could reach and pull himself up, and when he had done so, found a footing on one of the beams that formed the framework of the barn. The lovers stood unhitching the horse in the barnyard below. When the city man had led the horse into the stable he hurried quickly out again and went with the farmer's daughter along a path toward the house. The two people laughed and pulled at each other like children. They grew silent and when they had come near the house, stopped by a tree to embrace.

Hugh saw the man take the woman into his arms and hold her tightly against his body. He was so excited that he nearly fell off the beam. His imagination was inflamed and he tried to picture himself in the position of the young city man. His fingers gripped the boards to which he clung and his body trembled. The two figures standing in the dim light by the tree became one. For a long time they clung tightly to each other and then drew apart. They went into the house and Hugh climbed down from his place on the beam and lay in the hay. His body shook as with a chill and he was half ill of jealousy, anger, and an overpowering sense of defeat. It did not seem to him at the moment that it was worth while for him to go further east or to try to find a place where he would be able to mingle freely with men and women, or where such a wonderful thing as had happened to the man in the barnyard below might happen to him.

Hugh spent the night in the hayloft and at daylight crept out and went into a nearby town. He returned to the farmhouse late on Monday when he was sure the city man had gone away. In spite of the protest of the farmer he packed his clothes at once and declared his intention of leaving. He did not wait for the evening meal but hurried out of the house. When he got into the road and had started to walk away, he looked back and saw the daughter of the house standing at an open door and looking at him. Shame for what he had done on the night before swept over him. For a moment he stared at the woman who, with an intense, interested air stared back at him, and then putting down his head he hurried away. The woman watched him out of sight and later, when her father stormed about the house, blaming Hugh for leaving so suddenly and declaring the tall Missourian was no doubt a drunkard who wanted to go off on a drunk, she had nothing to say. In her own heart she knew what was the matter with her father's farm hand and was sorry he had gone before she had more completely exercised her power over him.

None of the towns Hugh visited during his three years of wandering approached realization of the sort of life Sarah Shepard had talked to him about. They were all very much alike. There was a main street with a dozen stores on each side, a blacksmith shop, and perhaps an elevator for the storage of grain. All day the town was deserted, but in the evening the citizens gathered on Main Street. On the sidewalks before the stores young farm hands and clerks sat on store boxes or on the curbing. They did not pay any attention to Hugh who, when he went to stand near them, remained silent and kept himself in the background. The farm hands talked of their work and boasted of the number of bushels of corn they could pick in a day, or of their skill in plowing. The clerks were intent upon playing practical jokes which pleased the farm hands immensely. While one of them talked loudly of his skill in his work a clerk crept out of the door of one of the stores and approached him. He held a pin in his hand and with it jabbed the talker in the back. The crowd yelled and shouted with delight. If the victim became angry a quarrel started, but this did not often happen. Other men came to join the party and the joke was told to them. "Well, you should have seen the look on his face. I thought I would die," one of the bystanders declared.

Hugh got a job with a carpenter who specialized in

the building of barns and stayed with him all through one fall. Later he went to work as a section hand on a railroad. Nothing happened to him. He was like one compelled to walk through life with a bandage over his eyes. On all sides of him, in the towns and on the farms, an undercurrent of life went on that did not touch him. In even the smallest of the towns, inhabited only by farm laborers, a quaint interesting civilization was being developed. Men worked hard but were much in the open air and had time to think. Their minds reached out toward the solution of the mystery of existence. The schoolmaster and the country lawyer read Tom Paine's *Age of Reason* and Bellamy's *Looking Backward.* They discussed these books with their fellows. There was a feeling, ill-expressed, that America had something real and spiritual to offer to the rest of the world. Workmen talked to each other of the new tricks of their trades, and after hours of discussion of some new way to cultivate corn, shape a horseshoe or build a barn, spoke of God and his intent concerning man. Long-drawn-out discussions of religious beliefs and the political destiny of America were carried on.

And across the background of these discussions ran tales of action in a sphere outside the little world in which the inhabitants of the towns lived. Men who had been in the Civil War and who had climbed fighting over hills and in the terror of defeat had swum wide rivers, told the tale of their adventures.

In the evening, after his day of work in the field or on the railroad with the section hands, Hugh did not know what to do with himself. That he did not go to bed immediately after the evening meal was due to the fact that he looked upon his tendency to sleep and to dream as an enemy to his development; and a peculiarly persistent determination to make something alive and worth while out of himself—the result of the five years of constant talking on the subject by the New England woman—had taken possession of him. "I'll find the right place and the right people and then I'll begin," he continually said to himself.

And then, worn out with weariness and loneliness, he went to bed in one of the little hotels or boarding houses where he lived during those years, and his dreams returned. The dream that had come that night as he lay on the cliff above the Mississippi River near the town of Burlington, came back time after time. He sat upright in bed in the darkness of his room and after he had driven the cloudy, vague sensation out of his brain, was afraid to go to sleep again. He did not want to disturb the people of the house and so got up and dressed and without putting on his shoes walked up and down in the room. Sometimes the room he occupied had a low ceiling and he was compelled to stoop. He crept out of the house carrying his shoes in his hand and sat down on the sidewalk to put them on. In all the towns he visited, people saw him walking alone through the streets late at night or in the early hours of the morning. Whispers concerning the matter ran about. The story of what was spoken of as his queerness came to the men with whom he worked, and they found themselves unable to talk freely and naturally in his presence. At the noon hour when the men ate the lunch they had carried to work, when the boss was gone and it was customary among the workers to talk of their own affairs, they went off by themselves. Hugh followed them about. They went to sit under a tree, and when Hugh came to stand nearby, they became silent or the more vulgar and shallow among them began to show off. While he worked with a half dozen other men as a section hand on the railroad, two men did all the talking. Whenever the boss went away an old man who had a reputation as a wit told stories concerning his relations with women. A young man with red hair took the cue from him. The two men talked loudly and kept looking at Hugh. The younger of the two wits turned to another workman who had a weak, timid face. "Well, you," he cried, "what about your old woman? What about her? Who is the father of your son? Do you dare tell?"

In the towns Hugh walked about in the evening and tried always to keep his mind fixed on definite things. He felt that humanity was for some unknown reason drawing itself away from him, and his mind turned back to the figure of Sarah Shepard. He remembered that she had never been without things to do. She scrubbed her kitchen floor and prepared food for cooking; she washed, ironed, kneaded dough for bread, and mended clothes. In the evening, when she made the boy read to her out of one of the school books or do sums on a slate, she kept her hands busy knitting socks for him or for her husband. Except when something had crossed her so that she scolded and her face grew red, she was always cheerful. When the boy had nothing to do at the station and had been sent by the station master to work about the house, to draw water from the cistern for a family washing, or pull weeds in the garden, he heard the woman singing as she went about the doing of her innumerable petty tasks. Hugh decided that he also must do small tasks, fix his mind upon definite things. In the town where he was employed as a section hand, the cloud dream in which the world became a whirling, agitated center of disaster came to him almost every night. Winter came on and he walked through the streets at night in the darkness and through the deep snow. He was almost frozen; but as the whole lower part of his body was habitually cold he did not much mind the added discomfort, and so great was the reserve of strength in his big frame that the loss of sleep did not affect his ability to labor all day without effort.

Hugh went into one of the residence streets of the town and counted the pickets in the fences before the houses. He returned to the hotel and made a calculation as to the number of pickets in all the fences in town. Then he got a rule at the hardware store and carefully measured the pickets. He tried to estimate the number of pickets that could be cut out of certain sized trees and that gave his mind another opening. He counted the number of trees in every street in town. He learned to tell at a glance and with relative accuracy how much lumber could be cut out of a tree. He built imaginary houses with lumber cut from the trees that lined the streets. He even tried to figure out a way to utilize the small limbs cut from the tops of the trees, and one Sunday went into the wood back of the town and cut a great armful of twigs, which he carried to his room and later with great patience wove into the form of a basket.

# Book Two

## CHAPTER III

Bidwell, Ohio, was an old town as the ages of towns go in the Central West, long before Hugh McVey, in his search for a place where he could penetrate the wall that shut him off from humanity, went there to live and to try to work out his problem. It is a busy manufacturing town now and has a population of nearly a hundred thousand people; but the time for the telling of the story of its sudden and surprising growth has not yet come.

From the beginning Bidwell has been a prosperous place. The town lies in the valley of a deep, rapid-flowing river that spreads out just above the town, becomes for the time wide and shallow, and goes singing swiftly along over stones. South of the town the river not only spreads out, but the hills recede. A wide flat valley stretches away to the north. In the days before the factories came the land immediately about town was cut up into small farms devoted to fruit and berry raising, and beyond the area of small farms lay larger tracts that were immensely productive and that raised huge crops of wheat, corn, and cabbage.

When Hugh was a boy sleeping away his days in the grass beside his father's fishing shack by the Mississippi River, Bidwell had already emerged out of the hardships of pioneer days. On the farms that lay in the wide valley to the north the timber had been cut away and the stumps had all been rooted out of the ground by a generation of men that had passed. The soil was easy to cultivate and had lost little of its virgin fertility. Two railroads, the Lake Shore and Michigan Central—later a part of the great New York Central System—and a less important coal-carrying road, called the Wheeling and Lake Erie, ran through the town. Twenty-five hundred people lived then in Bidwell. They were for the most part descendants of the pioneers who had come into the country by boat through the Great Lakes or by wagon roads over the mountains from the States of New York and Pennsylvania.

The town stood on a sloping incline running up from the river, and the Lake Shore and Michigan Central

Railroad had its station on the river bank at the foot of Main Street. The Wheeling Station was a mile away to the north. It was to be reached by going over a bridge and along a piked road that even then had begun to take on the semblance of a street. A dozen houses had been built facing Turner's Pike and between these were berry fields and an occasional orchard planted to cherry, peach or apple trees. A hard path went down to the distant station beside the road, and in the evening this path, wandering along under the branches of the fruit trees that extended out over the farm fences, was a favorite walking place for lovers.

The small farms lying close about the town of Bidwell raised berries that brought top prices in the two cities, Cleveland and Pittsburgh, reached by its two railroads, and all of the people of the town who were not engaged in one of the trades—in shoemaking, carpentry, horseshoeing, house-painting or the like—or who did not belong to the small merchant and professional classes, worked in summer on the land. On summer mornings, men, women and children went into the fields. In the early spring when planting went on and all through late May, June and early July when berries and fruit began to ripen, everyone was rushed with work and the streets of the town were deserted. Everyone went to the fields. Great hay wagons loaded with children, laughing girls, and sedate women set out from Main Street at dawn. Beside them walked tall boys, who pelted the girls with green apples and cherries from the trees along the road, and men who went along behind smoking their morning pipes and talking of the prevailing prices of the products of their fields. In the town after they had gone a Sabbath quiet prevailed. The merchants and clerks loitered in the shade of the awnings before the doors of the stores, and only their wives and the wives of the two or three rich men in town came to buy and to disturb their discussions of horse racing, politics and religion.

In the evening when the wagons came home, Bidwell awoke. The tired berry pickers walked home from the fields in the dust of the roads swinging their dinner pails. The wagons creaked at their heels, piled high with boxes of berries ready for shipment. In the stores after the evening meal crowds gathered. Old men lit their pipes and sat gossiping along the curbing at the edge of the sidewalks on Main Street; women with baskets on their arms did the marketing for the next day's living; the young men put on stiff white collars and their Sunday clothes, and girls, who all day had been crawling over the fields between the rows of berries or pushing their way among the tangled masses of raspberry bushes, put on white dresses and walked up and down before the men. Friendships begun between boys and girls in the fields ripened into love. Couples walked along residence streets under the trees and talked with subdued voices. They became silent and embarrassed. The bolder ones kissed. The end of the berry picking season brought each year a new outbreak of marriages to the town of Bidwell.

In all the towns of Midwestern America it was a time of waiting. The country having been cleared and the Indians driven away into a vast distant place spoken of vaguely as the West, the Civil War having been fought and won, and there being no great national problems that touched closely their lives, the minds of men were turned in upon themselves. The soul and its destiny was spoken of openly on the streets. Robert Ingersoll came to Bidwell to speak in Terry's Hall, and after he had gone the question of the divinity of Christ for months occupied the minds of the citizens. The ministers preached sermons on the subject and in the evening it was talked about in the stores. Everyone had something to say. Even Charley Mook, who dug ditches, who stuttered so that not a half dozen people in town could understand him, expressed his opinion.

In all the great Mississippi Valley each town came to have a character of its own, and the people who lived in the towns were to each other like members of a great family. The individual idiosyncrasies of each member of the great family stood forth. A kind of invisible roof beneath which everyone lived spread itself over each town. Beneath the roof boys and girls were born, grew up, quarreled, fought, and formed friendships with their fellows, were introduced into the mysteries of love, married, and became the fathers and mothers of children, grew old, sickened, and died.

Within the invisible circle and under the great roof everyone knew his neighbor and was known to him. Strangers did not come and go swiftly and mysteriously and there was no constant and confusing roar of machinery and of new projects afoot. For the moment mankind seemed about to take time to try to understand itself.

In Bidwell there was a man named Peter White who was a tailor and worked hard at his trade, but who once or twice a year got drunk and beat his wife. He was arrested each time and had to pay a fine, but there was a general understanding of the impulse that led to the beating. Most of the women knowing the wife sympathized with Peter. "She is a noisy thing and her jaw is never still," the wife of Henry Teeters, the grocer, said to her husband. "If he gets drunk it's only to forget he's married to her. Then he goes home to sleep it off and she begins jawing at him. He stands it as long as he can. It takes a fist to shut up that woman. If he strikes her it's the only thing he can do."

Allie Mulberry the half-wit was one of the highlights of life in the town. He lived with his mother in a tumbledown house at the edge of town on Medina Road. Besides being a half-wit he had something the matter with his legs. They were trembling and weak and he could only move them with great difficulty. On summer afternoons when the streets were deserted, he hobbled along Main Street with his lower jaw hanging down. Allie carried a large club, partly for the support of his weak legs and partly to scare off dogs and mischievous boys. He liked to sit in the shade with his back against a building and whittle, and he liked to be near people and have his talent as a whittler appreciated. He made fans out of pieces of pine, long chains of wooden beads, and he once achieved a singular mechanical triumph that won him wide renown. He made a ship that would float in a beer bottle half-filled with water and laid on its side. The ship had sails and three tiny wooden sailors who stood at attention with their hands to their caps in salute. After it was constructed and put into the bottle it was too large to be taken out through the neck. How Allie got it in no one ever knew. The clerks and merchants who crowded about to watch him at work discussed the matter for days. It became a never-ending wonder among them. In the evening they spoke of the matter to the berry pickers who came into the stores, and in the eyes of the people of Bidwell Allie Mulberry became a hero. The bottle, half-filled with water and securely corked, was laid on a cushion in the window of Hunter's Jewelry Store. As it floated about on its own little ocean crowds gathered to look at it. Over the bottle was a sign with the words—"Carved by

Allie Mulberry of Bidwell"—prominently displayed. Below these words a query had been printed. "How Did He Get It Into The Bottle?" was the question asked. The bottle stayed in the window for months and merchants took the traveling men who visited them, to see it. Then they escorted their guests to where Allie, with his back against the wall of a building and his club beside him, was at work on some new creation of the whittler's art. The travelers were impressed and told the tale abroad. Allie's fame spread to other towns. "He has a good brain," the citizen of Bidwell said, shaking his head. "He don't appear to know very much, but look what he does! He must be carrying all sorts of notions around inside of his head."

Jane Orange, widow of a lawyer, and with the single exception of Thomas Butterworth, a farmer who owned over a thousand acres of land and lived with his daughter on a farm a mile south of town, the richest person in town, was known to everyone in Bidwell, but was not liked. She was called stingy and it was said that she and her husband had cheated everyone with whom they had dealings in order to get their start in life. The town ached for the privilege of doing what they called "bringing them down a peg." Jane's husband had once been the Bidwell town attorney and later had charge of the settlement of an estate belonging to Ed Lucas, a farmer who died leaving two hundred acres of land and two daughters. The farmer's daughters, everyone said, "came out at the small end of the horn," and John Orange began to grow rich. It was said he was worth fifty thousand dollars. All during the latter part of his life the lawyer went to the city of Cleveland on business every week, and when he was at home and even in the hottest weather he went about dressed in a long black coat. When she went to the stores to buy supplies for her house, Jane Orange was watched closely by the merchants. She was suspected of carrying away small articles that could be slipped into the pockets of her dress. One afternoon in Toddmore's grocery, when she thought no one was looking, she took a half dozen eggs out of a basket and looking quickly around to be sure she was unobserved, put them into her dress pocket. Harry Toddmore, the grocer's son who had seen the theft, said nothing, but went unobserved out at the back door. He got three or four clerks from other stores and they waited for Jane Orange at a corner. When she came along they hurried out and Harry Toddmore fell against her. Throwing out his hand he struck the pocket containing the eggs a quick, sharp blow. Jane Orange turned and hurried away toward home, but as she half ran through Main Street clerks and merchants came out of the stores, and from the assembled crowd a voice called attention to the fact that the contents of the stolen eggs having run down the inside of her dress and over her stockings began to make a stream on the sidewalk. A pack of town dogs excited by the shouts of the crowd ran at her heels, barking and sniffing at the yellow stream that dripped from her shoes.

An old man with a long white beard came to Bidwell to live. He had been a carpetbag Governor of a Southern state in the reconstruction days after the Civil War and had made money. He bought a house on Turner's Pike close beside the river and spent his days puttering about in a small garden. In the evening he came across the bridge into Main Street and went to loaf in Birdie Spinks' drugstore. He talked with great frankness and candor of his life in the South during the terrible time when the country was trying to emerge from the black gloom of defeat, and brought to the Bidwell men a new point of view on their old enemies, the "Rebs."

The old man—the name by which he had introduced himself in Bidwell was that of Judge Horace Hanby—believed in the manliness and honesty of purpose of the men he had for a time governed and who had fought a long grim war with the North, with the New Englanders and sons of New Englanders from the West and Northwest. "They're all right," he said with a grin. "I cheated them and made some money, but I liked them. Once a crowd of them came to my house and threatened to kill me and I told them that I did not blame them very much, so they let me alone." The judge, an ex-politician from the city of New York who had been involved in some affair that made it uncomfortable for him to return to live in that city, grew prophetic and philosophic after he came to live in Bidwell. In spite of the doubt everyone felt concerning his past, he was something of a scholar and a reader of books, and won respect by his apparent wisdom. "Well, there's going to be a new war here," he said. "It won't be like the Civil War, just shooting off guns and killing peoples' bodies. At first it's going to be a war between individuals to see to what class a man must belong; then it is going to be a long, silent war between classes, between those who have and those who can't get. It'll be the worst war of all."

The talk of Judge Hanby, carried along and elaborated almost every evening before a silent, attentive group in the drugstore, began to have an influence on the minds of Bidwell young men. At his suggestion several of the town boys, Cliff Bacon, Albert Small, Ed Prawl, and two or three others, began to save money for the purpose of going east to college. Also at his suggestion Tom Butterworth the rich farmer sent his daughter away to school. The old man made many prophecies concerning what would happen in America.

"I tell you, the country isn't going to stay as it is," he said earnestly. "In eastern towns the change has already come. Factories are being built and everyone is going to work in the factories. It takes an old man like me to see how that changes their lives. Some of the men stand at one bench and do one thing not only for hours but for days and years. There are signs hung up saying they mustn't talk. Some of them make more money than they did before the factories came, but I tell you it's like being in prison. What would you say if I told you all America, all you fellows who talk so big about freedom, are going to be put in a prison, eh?

"And there's something else. In New York there are already a dozen men who are worth a million dollars. Yes, sir, I tell you it's true, a million dollars. What do you think of that, eh?"

Judge Hanby grew excited and, inspired by the absorbed attention of his audience, talked of the sweep of events. In England, he explained, the cities were constantly growing larger, and already almost everyone either worked in a factory or owned stock in a factory. "In New England it is getting the same way fast," he explained. "The same thing'll happen here. Farming'll be done with tools. Almost everything now done by hand'll be done by machinery. Some'll grow rich and some poor. The thing is to get educated, yes, sir, that's the thing, to get ready for what's coming. It's the only way. The younger generation has got to be sharper and shrewder."

The words of the old man, who had been in many places and had seen men and cities, were repeated in the streets of Bidwell. The blacksmith and the wheelwright repeated his words when they stopped to exchange news of their affairs before the post office. Ben Peeler, the carpenter, who had been saving money to buy a house and a small farm to which he could retire when he became too old to climb about on the framework of buildings, used the money instead to send his son to Cleveland to a new technical school. Steve Hunter, the son of Abraham Hunter the Bidwell jeweler, declared that he was going to get up with the times, and when he went into a factory, would go into the office, not into the shop. He went to Buffalo, New York, to attend a business college.

The air of Bidwell began to stir with talk of new times. The evil things said of the new life coming were soon forgotten. The youth and optimistic spirit of the country led it to take hold of the hand of the giant, industrialism, and lead him laughing into the land. The cry, "get on in the world," that ran all over America at that period and that still echoes in the pages of American newspapers and magazines, rang in the streets of Bidwell.

In the harness shop belonging to Joseph Wainsworth it one day struck a new note. The harness maker was a tradesman of the old school and was vastly independent. He had learned his trade after five years' service as apprentice, and had spent an additional five years in going from place to place as a journeyman workman, and felt that he knew his business. Also he owned his shop and his home and had twelve hundred dollars in the bank. At noon one day when he was alone in the shop, Tom Butterworth came in and told him he had ordered four sets of farm work harness from a factory in Philadelphia. "I came in to ask if you'll repair them if they get out of order," he said.

Joe Wainsworth began to fumble with the tools on his bench. Then he turned to look the farmer in the eye and to do what he later spoke of to his cronies as "laying down the law." "When the cheap things begin to go to pieces take them somewhere else to have them repaired," he said sharply. He grew furiously angry. "Take the damn things to Philadelphia where you got 'em," he shouted at the back of the farmer who had turned to go out of the shop.

Joe Wainsworth was upset and thought about the incident all the afternoon. When farmer-customers came in and stood about to talk of their affairs he had nothing to say. He was a talkative man and his apprentice, Will Sellinger, son of the Bidwell house painter, was puzzled by his silence.

When the boy and the man were alone in the shop, it was Joe Wainsworth's custom to talk of his days as a journeyman workman when he had gone from place to place working at his trade. If a trace were being stitched or a bridle fashioned, he told how the thing was done at a shop where he had worked in the city of Boston and in another shop at Providence, Rhode Island. Getting a piece of paper he made drawings illustrating the cuts of leather that were made in the other places and the methods of stitching. He claimed to have worked out his own method for doing things, and that his method was better than anything he had seen in all his travels. To the men who came into the shop to loaf during winter afternoons he presented a smiling front and talked of their affairs, of the price of cabbage in Cleveland or the effect of a cold snap on the winter wheat, but alone with the boy, he talked only of harness making. "I don't say anything about it. What's the good bragging? Just the same, I could learn something to all the harness makers I've ever seen, and I've seen the best of them," he declared emphatically.

During the afternoon, after he had heard of the four factory-made work harnesses brought into what he had always thought of as a trade that belonged to him by the rights of a first-class workman, Joe remained silent for two or three hours. He thought of the words of old Judge Hanby and the constant talk of the new times now coming. Turning suddenly to his apprentice, who was puzzled by his long silence and who knew nothing of the incident that had disturbed his employer, he broke forth into words. He was defiant and expressed his defiance. "Well, then, let 'em go to Philadelphia, let 'em go any damn place they please," he growled, and then, as though his own words had re-established his self-respect, he straightened his shoulders and glared at the puzzled and alarmed boy. "I know my trade and do not have to bow down to any man," he declared. He expressed the old tradesman's faith in his craft and the rights it gave the craftsman. "Learn your trade. Don't listen to talk," he said earnestly. "The man who knows his trade is a man. He can tell everyone to go to the devil."

## CHAPTER IV

Hugh McVey was twenty-three years old when he went to live in Bidwell. The position of telegraph operator at the Wheeling station a mile north of town became vacant and, through an accidental encounter with a former resident of a neighboring town, he got the place.

The Missourian had been at work during the winter in a sawmill in the country near a Northern Indiana town. During the evenings he wandered on country roads and in the town streets, but he did not talk to anyone. As had happened to him in other places, he had the reputation of being queer. His clothes were worn threadbare and, although he had money in his pockets, he did not buy new ones. In the evening when he went through the town streets and saw the smartly dressed clerks standing before the stores, he looked at his own shabby person and was ashamed to enter. In his boyhood Sarah Shepard had always attended to the buying of his clothes, and he made up his mind that he would go to the place in Michigan to which she and her husband had retired, and pay her a visit. He wanted Sarah Shepard to buy him a new outfit of clothes, but wanted also to talk with her.

Out of the three years of going from place to place and working with other men as a laborer, Hugh had got no big impulse that he felt would mark the road his life should take; but the study of mathematical problems, taken up to relieve his loneliness and to cure his inclination to dreams, was beginning to have an effect on his character. He thought that if he saw Sarah Shepard again he could talk to her and through her get into the way of talking to others. In the sawmill where he worked he answered the occasional remarks made to him by his fellow workers in a slow, hesitating drawl, and his body was still awkward and his gait shambling, but he did his work more quickly and accurately. In the presence of his foster-mother and garbed in new clothes, he believed he could now talk to her in a way that had been impossible during his youth. She would see the change in his character and would be encouraged about him. They would get on to a new basis and he would feel respect for himself in another.

Hugh went to the railroad station to make inquiry regarding the fare to the Michigan town and there had the adventure that upset his plans. As he stood at the window of the ticket office, the ticket seller, who was also the telegraph operator, tried to engage him in conversation. When he had given the information asked, he followed Hugh out of the building and into the darkness of a country railroad station at night, and the two men stopped and stood together beside an empty baggage truck. The ticket agent spoke of the loneliness of life in the town and said he wished he could go back to his own place and be again with his own people. "It may not be any better in my own town, but I know everybody there," he said. He was curious concerning Hugh as were all the people of the Indiana town, and hoped to get him into talk in order that he might find out why he walked alone at night, why he sometimes worked all evening over books and figures in his room at the country hotel, and why he had so little to say to his fellows. Hoping to fathom Hugh's silence he abused the town in which they both lived. "Well," he began, "I guess I understand how you feel. You want to get out of this place." He explained his own predicament in life. "I got married," he said. "Already I have three children. Out here a man can make more money railroading than he can in my state, and living is pretty cheap. Just today I had an offer of a job in a good town near my own place in Ohio, but I can't take it. The job only pays forty a month. The town's all right, one of the best in the northern part of the State, but you see the job's no good. Lord, I wish I could go. I'd like to live again among people such as live in that part of the country."

The railroad man and Hugh walked along the street that ran from the station up into the main street of the town. Wanting to meet the advances that had been made by his companion and not knowing how to go about it, Hugh adopted the method he had heard his fellow laborers use with one another. "Well," he said slowly, "come have a drink."

The two men went into a saloon and stood by the bar. Hugh made a tremendous effort to overcome his embarrassment. As he and the railroad man drank foaming glasses of beer he explained that he also had once been a railroad man and knew telegraphy, but that for several years he had been doing other work. His companion looked at his shabby clothes and nodded his head. He made a motion with his head to indicate that he wanted Hugh to come with him outside into the darkness. "Well, well," he exclaimed, when they had again got outside and had started along the street toward the station. "I understand now. They've all been wondering about you and I've heard lots of talk. I won't say anything, but I'm going to do something for you."

Hugh went to the station with his new-found friend and sat down in the lighted office. The railroad man got out a sheet of paper and began to write a letter. "I'm going to get you that job," he said. "I'm writing the letter now and I'll get it off on the midnight train. You've got to get on your feet. I was a boozer myself, but I cut it all out. A glass of beer now and then, that's my limit."

He began to talk of the town in Ohio where he proposed to get Hugh the job that would set him up in the world and save him from the habit of drinking, and described it as an earthly paradise in which lived bright, clear-thinking men and beautiful women. Hugh was reminded sharply of the talk he had heard from the lips of Sarah Shepard, when in his youth she spent long evenings telling him of the wonder of her own Michigan and New England towns and people, and contrasted the life lived there with that lived by the people of his own place.

Hugh decided not to try to explain away the mistake made by his new acquaintance, and to accept the offer of assistance in getting the appointment as telegraph operator.

The two men walked out of the station and stood again in the darkness. The railroad man felt like one who has been given the privilege of plucking a human soul out of the darkness of despair. He was full of words that poured from his lips and he assumed a knowledge of Hugh and his character entirely unwarranted by the circumstances. "Well," he exclaimed heartily, "you see I've given you a send-off. I have told them you're a good man and a good operator, but that you will take the place with its small salary because you've been sick and just now can't work very hard." The excited man followed Hugh along the street. It was late and the store lights had been put out. From one of the town's two saloons that lay in their way arose a clatter of voices. The old boyhood dream of finding a place and a people among whom he could, by sitting still and inhaling the air breathed by others, come into a warm closeness with life, came back to Hugh. He stopped before the saloon to listen to the voices within, but the railroad man plucked at his coat sleeve and protested. "Now, now, you're going to cut it out, eh?" he asked anxiously and then hurriedly explained his anxiety. "Of course I know what's the matter with you. Didn't I tell you I've been there myself? You've been working around. I know why that is. You don't have to tell me. If there wasn't something the matter with him, no man who knows telegraphy would work in a sawmill.

"Well, there's no good talking about it," he added thoughtfully. "I've given you a send-off. You're going to cut it out, eh?"

Hugh tried to protest and to explain that he was not addicted to the habit of drinking, but the Ohio man would not listen. "It's all right," he said again, and then they came to the hotel where Hugh lived and he turned to go back to the station and wait for the midnight train that would carry the letter away and that would, he felt, carry also his demand that a fellow-human, who had slipped from the modern path of work and progress should be given a new chance. He felt magnanimous and wonderfully gracious. "It's all right, my boy," he said heartily. "No use talking to me. Tonight when you came to the station to ask the fare to that hole of a place in Michigan I saw you were embarrassed. 'What's the matter with that fellow?' I said to myself. I got to thinking. Then I came uptown with you and right away you bought me a drink. I wouldn't have thought anything about that if I hadn't been there myself. You'll get on your feet. Bidwell, Ohio, is full of good men. You get in with them and they'll help you and stick by you. You'll like those people. They've got get-up to them. The place you'll work at there is far out of town. It's away out about a mile at a little kind of outside-like place called Pickleville. There used to be a saloon there and a factory for putting up cucumber pickles, but they've both gone now. You won't be tempted to slip in that place. You'll have a chance to get on your feet. I'm glad I thought of sending you there."

The Wheeling and Lake Erie ran along a little wooded depression that cut across the wide expanse of open farm lands north of the town of Bidwell. It brought coal from the hill country of West Virginia and Southeastern Ohio to ports on Lake Erie, and did not pay much attention to the carrying of passengers. In the morning a train consisting of a combined express and baggage car and two passenger coaches went north and west toward the lake, and in the evening the same train returned, bound southeast into the hills. The Bidwell station of the road was, in an odd way, detached from the town's life. The invisible roof under which the life of the town and the surrounding country was lived did not cover it. As the Indiana railroad man had told Hugh, the station itself stood on a spot known locally as Pickleville. Back of the station there was a small building for the storage of freight and near at hand four or five houses facing Turner's Pike. The pickle factory, now deserted and with its windows gone, stood across the tracks from the station and beside a small stream that ran under a bridge and across country through a grove of trees to the river. On hot summer days a sour, pungent smell arose from the old factory, and at night its presence lent a ghostly flavor to the tiny corner of the world in which lived perhaps a dozen people.

All day and at night an intense persistent silence lay over Pickleville, while in Bidwell a mile away the stir of new life began. In the evenings and on rainy afternoons when men could not work in the fields, old Judge Hanby went along Turner's Pike and across the wagon bridge into Bidwell and sat in a chair at the back of Birdie Spinks' drugstore. He talked. Men came in to listen to him and went out. New talk ran through the town. A new force that was being born into American life and into life everywhere all over the world was feeding on the old dying individualistic life. The new force stirred and aroused the people. It met a need that was universal. It was meant to seal men together, to wipe out national lines, to walk under seas and fly through the air, to change the entire face of the world in which men lived. Already the giant that was to be king in the place of old kings was calling his servants and his armies to serve him. He used the methods of old kings and promised his followers booty and gain. Everywhere he went unchallenged, surveying the land, raising a new class of men to positions of power. Railroads had already been pushed out across the plains; great coal fields from which was to be taken food to warm the blood in the body of the giant were being opened up; iron fields were being discovered; the roar and clatter of the breathing of the terrible new thing, half-hideous, half-beautiful in its possibilities, that was for so long to drown the voices and confuse the thinking of men, was heard not only in the towns but even in lonely farm houses, where its willing servants, the newspapers and magazines, had begun to circulate in ever increasing numbers. At the town of Gibsonville, near Bidwell, Ohio, and at Lima and Finley, Ohio, oil and gas fields were discovered. At Cleveland, Ohio, a precise, definite-minded man named Rockefeller bought and sold oil. From the first he served the new thing well and he soon found others to serve with him. The Morgans, Fricks, Goulds, Carnegies, Vanderbilts, servants of the new king, princes of the new faith, merchants all, a new kind of rulers of men, defied the world-old law of class that puts the merchant below the craftsman, and added to the confusion of men by taking on the air of creators. They were merchants glorified and dealt in giant things, in the lives of men and in mines, forests, oil and gas fields, factories, and railroads.

And all over the country, in the towns, the farm houses, and the growing cities of the new country, people stirred and awakened. Thought and poetry died or passed as a heritage to feeble fawning men who also became servants of the new order. Serious young men in Bidwell and in other American towns, whose fathers had walked together on moonlight nights along Turner's Pike to talk of God, went away to technical schools. Their fathers had walked and talked and thoughts had grown up in them. The impulse had reached back to their father's fathers on moonlit roads of England, Germany, Ireland, France, and Italy, and back of these to the moonlit hills of Judea where shepherds talked and serious young men, John and Matthew and Jesus, caught the drift of the talk and made poetry of it; but the serious-minded sons of these men in the new land were swept away from thinking and dreaming. From all sides the voice of the new age that was to do definite things shouted at them. Eagerly they took up the cry and ran with it. Millions of voices arose. The clamor became terrible, and confused the minds of all men. In making way for the newer, broader brotherhood into which men are some day to emerge, in extending the invisible roofs of the towns and cities to cover the world, men cut and crushed their way through the bodies of men.

And while the voices became louder and more excited and the new giant walked about making a preliminary survey of the land, Hugh spent his days at the quiet, sleepy railroad station at Pickleville and tried to adjust his mind to the realization of the fact that he was not to be accepted as fellow by the citizens of the new place to which he had come. During the day he sat in the tiny telegraph office or, pulling an express truck to the open window near his telegraph instrument, lay on his back with a sheet of paper propped on his bony knees and did sums. Farmers driving past on Turner's Pike saw him there and talked of him in the stores in town. "He's a queer silent fellow," they said. "What do you suppose he's up to?"

Hugh walked in the streets of Bidwell at night as he had walked in the streets of towns in Indiana and Illinois. He approached groups of men loafing on a street corner and then went hurriedly past them. On quiet streets as he went along under the trees, he saw women sitting in the lamplight in the houses and hungered to have a house and a woman of his own. One afternoon a woman school teacher came to the station to make inquiry regarding the fare to a town in West Virginia. As the station agent was not about Hugh gave her the information she sought and she lingered for a few moments to talk with him. He answered the questions she asked with monosyllables and she soon went away, but he was delighted and looked upon the incident as an adventure. At night he dreamed of the school teacher and when he awoke, pretended she was with him in his bedroom. He put out his hand and touched the pillow. It was soft and smooth as he imagined the cheek of a woman would be. He did not know the school teacher's name but invented one for her. "Be quiet, Elizabeth. Do not let me disturb your sleep," he murmured into the darkness. One evening he went to the house where the school teacher boarded and stood in the shadow of a tree until he saw her come out and go toward Main Street. Then he went by a roundabout way and walked past her on the sidewalk before the lighted stores. He did not look at her, but in passing her dress touched his arm and he was so excited later that he could not sleep and spent half the night walking about and thinking of the wonderful thing that had happened to him.

The ticket, express, and freight agent for the Wheeling and Lake Erie at Bidwell, a man named George Pike, lived in one of the houses near the station, and besides attending to his duties for the railroad company, owned and worked a small farm. He was a slender, alert, silent man with a long drooping mustache. Both he and his wife worked as Hugh had never seen a man and woman work before. Their arrangement of the division of labor was not based on sex but on convenience. Sometimes Mrs. Pike came to the station to sell tickets, load express boxes and trunks on the passenger trains and deliver heavy boxes of freight to draymen and farmers, while her husband worked in the fields back of his house or prepared the evening meal, and sometimes the matter was reversed and Hugh did not see Mrs. Pike for several days at a time.

During the day there was little for the station agent or his wife to do at the station and they disappeared.

George Pike had made an arrangement of wires and pulleys connecting the station with a large bell hung on top of his house, and when someone came to the station to receive or deliver freight Hugh pulled at the wire and the bell began to ring. In a few minutes either George Pike or his wife came running from the house or fields, dispatched the business and went quickly away again.

Day after day Hugh sat in a chair by a desk in the station or went outside and walked up and down the station platform. Engines pulling long caravans of coal cars ground past. The brakemen waved their hands to him and then the train disappeared into the grove of trees that grew beside the creek along which the tracks of the road were laid. In Turner's Pike a creaking farm wagon appeared and then disappeared along the tree-lined road that led to Bidwell. The farmer turned on his wagon seat to stare at Hugh but unlike the railroad men did not wave his hand. Adventurous boys came out along the road from town and climbed, shouting and laughing, over the rafters in the deserted pickle factory across the tracks or went to fish in the creek in the shade of the factory walls. Their shrill voices added to the loneliness of the spot. It became almost unbearable to Hugh. In desperation he turned from the rather meaningless doing of sums and working out of problems regarding the number of fence pickets that could be cut from a tree or the number of steel rails or railroad ties consumed in building a mile of railroad, the innumerable petty problems with which he had been keeping his mind busy, and returned to more definite and practical problems. He remembered an autumn he had put in cutting corn on a farm in Illinois and, going into the station, waved his long arms about, imitating the movements of a man in the act of cutting corn. He wondered if a machine might not be made that would do the work, and tried to make drawings of the parts of such a machine. Feeling his inability to handle so difficult a problem he sent away for books and began the study of mechanics. He joined a correspondence school started by a man in Pennsylvania, and worked for days on the problems the man sent him to do. He asked questions and began a little to understand the mystery of the application of power. Like the other young men of Bidwell he began to put himself into touch with the spirit of the age, but unlike them he did not dream of suddenly acquired wealth. While they embraced new and futile dreams he worked to destroy the tendency to dreams in himself.

Hugh came to Bidwell in the early spring and during May, June and July the quiet station at Pickleville awoke for an hour or two each evening. A certain percentage of the sudden and almost overwhelming increase in express business that came with the ripening of the fruit and berry crop came to the Wheeling, and every evening a dozen express trucks, piled high with berry boxes, waited for the southbound train.

When the train came into the station a small crowd had assembled. George Pike and his stout wife worked madly, throwing the boxes in at the door of the express car. Idlers standing about became interested and lent a hand. The engineer climbed out of his locomotive, stretched his legs and crossing a narrow road got a drink from the pump in George Pike's yard.

Hugh walked to the door of his telegraph office and standing in the shadows watched the busy scene. He wanted to take part in it, to laugh and talk with the men standing about, to go to the engineer and ask questions regarding the locomotive and its construction, to help George Pike and his wife, and perhaps cut through their silence and his own enough to become acquainted with them. He thought of all these things but stayed in the shadow of the door that led to the telegraph office until, at a signal given by the train conductor, the engineer climbed into his engine and the train began to move away into the evening darkness. When Hugh came out of his office the station platform was deserted again. In the grass across the tracks and beside the ghostly looking old factory, crickets sang. Tom Wilder, the Bidwell hack driver, had got a traveling man off the train and the dust left by the heels of his team still hung in the air over Turner's Pike. From the darkness that brooded over the trees that grew along the creek beyond the factory came the hoarse croak of frogs. On Turner's Pike a half-dozen Bidwell young men accompanied by as many town girls walked along the path beside the road under the trees. They had come to the station to have somewhere to go, had made up a party to come, but now the half-unconscious purpose of their coming was apparent. The party split itself up into couples and each strove to get as far away as possible from the others. One of the couples came back along the path toward the station and went to the pump in George Pike's yard. They stood by the pump, laughing and pretending to drink out of a tin cup, and when they got again into the road the others had disappeared. They became silent. Hugh went to the end of the platform and watched as they walked slowly along. He became furiously jealous of the young man who put his arm about the waist of his companion and then, when he turned and saw Hugh staring at him, took it away again.

The telegraph operator went quickly along the platform until he was out of range of the young man's eyes, and, when he thought the gathering darkness would hide him, returned and crept along the path beside the road after him. Again a hungry desire to enter into the lives of the people about him took possession of the Missourian. To be a young man dressed in a stiff white collar, wearing neatly made clothes, and in the evening to walk about with young girls seemed like getting on the road to happiness. He wanted to run shouting along the path beside the road until he had overtaken the young man and woman, to beg them to take him with them, to accept him as one of themselves, but when the momentary impulse had passed and he returned to the telegraph office and lighted a lamp, he looked at his long awkward body and could not conceive of himself as ever by any chance becoming the thing he wanted to be. Sadness swept over him and his gaunt face, already cut and marked with deep lines, became longer and more gaunt. The old boyhood notion, put into his mind by the words of his foster-mother, Sarah Shepard, that a town and a people could remake him and erase from his body the marks of what he thought of as his inferior birth, began to fade. He tried to forget the people about him and turned with renewed energy to the study of the problems in the books that now lay in a pile upon his desk. His inclination to dreams, balked by the persistent holding of his mind to definite things, began to reassert itself in a new form, and his brain played no more with pictures of clouds and men in agitated movement but took hold of steel, wood, and iron. Dumb masses of materials taken out of the earth and the forests were molded by his mind into fantastic shapes. As he sat in the telegraph office during the day or walked alone through the streets of Bidwell at night, he saw in fancy a thousand new machines, formed by his hands and brain, doing the work that had been done by the hands of men. He had come to Bidwell, not only in the hope that there he would at last find companionship, but also because his mind was really aroused and he wanted leisure to begin trying to do tangible things. When the citizens of Bidwell would not take him into their town life but left him standing to one side, as the tiny dwelling place for men called Pickleville where he lived stood aside out from under the invisible roof of the town, he decided to try to forget men and to express himself wholly in work.

## CHAPTER V

Hugh's first inventive effort stirred the town of Bidwell deeply. When word of it ran about, the men who had been listening to the talk of Judge Horace Hanby and whose minds had turned toward the arrival of the new forward-pushing impulse in American life thought they saw in Hugh the instrument of its coming to Bidwell. From the day of his coming to live among them, there had been much curiosity in the stores and houses regarding the tall, gaunt, slow-speaking stranger at Pickleville. George Pike had told Birdie Spinks the druggist how Hugh worked all day over books, and how he made drawings for parts of mysterious machines and left them on his desk in the telegraph office. Birdie Spinks told others and the tale grew. When Hugh walked alone in the streets during the evening and thought no one took account of his presence, hundreds of pairs of curious eyes followed him about.

A tradition in regard to the telegraph operator began to grow up. The tradition made Hugh a gigantic figure, one who walked always on a plane above that on which other men lived. In the imagination of his fellow citizens of the Ohio town, he went about always thinking great thoughts, solving mysterious and intricate problems that had to do with the new mechanical age Judge Hanby talked about to the eager listeners in the drugstore. An alert, talkative people saw among them one who could not talk and whose long face was habitually serious, and could not think of him as having daily to face the same kind of minor problems as themselves.

The Bidwell young man who had come down to the Wheeling station with a group of other young men, who had seen the evening train go away to the south, who had met at the station one of the town girls and had, in order to escape the others and be alone with her, taken her to the pump in George Pike's yard on the pretense of wanting a drink, walked away with her into the darkness of the summer evening with his mind fixed on Hugh. The young man's name was Ed Hall and he was apprentice to Ben Peeler, the carpenter who had sent his son to Cleveland to a technical school. He wanted to marry the girl he had met at the station and did not see how he could manage it on his salary as a carpenter's apprentice. When he looked back and saw Hugh standing on the station platform, he took the arm he had put around the girl's waist quickly away and began to talk. "I'll tell you what," he said earnestly, "if things don't pretty soon get on the stir around here I'm going to get out. I'll go over by Gibsonburg and get a job in the oil fields, that's what I'll do. I've got to have more money." He sighed heavily and looked over the girl's head into the darkness. "They say that telegraph fellow back there at the station is up to something," he ventured. "It's all the talk. Birdie Spinks says he is an inventor; says George Pike told him; says he is working all the time on new inventions to do things by machinery; that his passing off as a telegraph operator is only a bluff. Some think maybe he was sent here to see about starting a factory to make one of his inventions, sent by rich men maybe in Cleveland or some other place. Everybody says they'll bet there'll be factories here in

Bidwell before very long now. I wish I knew. I don't want to go away if I don't have to, but I got to have more money. Ben Peeler won't never give me a raise so I can get married or nothing. I wish I knew that fellow back there so I could ask him what's up. They say he's smart. I suppose he wouldn't tell me nothing. I wish I was smart enough to invent something and maybe get rich. I wish I was the kind of fellow they say he is."

Ed Hall again put his arm about the girl's waist and walked away. He forgot Hugh and thought of himself and of how he wanted to marry the girl whose young body nestled close to his own—wanted her to be utterly his. For a few hours he passed out of Hugh's growing sphere of influence on the collective thought of the town, and lost himself in the immediate deliciousness of kisses.

And as he passed out of Hugh's influence others came in. On Main Street in the evening everyone speculated on the Missourian's purpose in coming to Bidwell. The forty dollars a month paid him by the Wheeling railroad could not have tempted such a man. They were sure of that. Steve Hunter the jeweler's son had returned to town from a course in a business college at Buffalo, New York, and hearing the talk became interested. Steve had in him the making of a live man of affairs, and he decided to investigate. It was not, however, Steve's method to go at things directly, and he was impressed by the notion, then abroad in Bidwell, that Hugh had been sent to town by someone, perhaps by a group of capitalists who intended to start factories there.

Steve thought he would go easy. In Buffalo, where he had gone to the business college, he had met a girl whose father, E. P. Horn, owned a soap factory; had become acquainted with her at church and had been introduced to her father. The soap maker, an assertive positive man who manufactured a product called Horn's

Household Friend Soap, had his own notion of what a young man should be and how he should make his way in the world, and had taken pleasure in talking to Steve. He told the Bidwell jeweler's son of how he had started his own factory with but little money and had succeeded and gave Steve many practical hints on the organization of companies. He talked a great deal of a thing called "control." "When you get ready to start for yourself keep that in mind," he said. "You can sell stock and borrow money at the bank, all you can get, but don't give up control. Hang on to that. That's the way I made my success. I always kept the control."

Steve wanted to marry Ernestine Horn, but felt that he should show what he could do as a business man before he attempted to thrust himself into so wealthy and prominent a family. When he returned to his own town and heard the talk regarding Hugh McVey and his inventive genius, he remembered the soap maker's words regarding control, and repeated them to himself. One evening he walked along Turner's Pike and stood in the darkness by the old pickle factory. He saw Hugh at work under a lamp in the telegraph office and was impressed. "I'll lay low and see what he's up to," he told himself. "If he's got an invention, I'll get up a company. I'll get money in and I'll start a factory. The people here'll tumble over each other to get into a thing like that. I don't believe anyone sent him here. I'll bet he's just an inventor. That kind always are queer. I'll keep my mouth shut and watch my chance. If there is anything starts, I'll start it and I'll get into control, that's what I'll do, I'll get into control."

In the country stretching away north beyond the fringe of small berry farms lying directly about town, were other and larger farms. The land that made up these larger farms was also rich and raised big crops. Great stretches of it were planted to cabbage for which a market had been built up in Cleveland, Pittsburgh, and Cincinnati. Bidwell was often in derision called Cabbageville by the citizens of nearby towns. One of the largest of the cabbage farms belonged to a man named Ezra French, and was situated on Turner's Pike, two miles from town and a mile beyond the Wheeling station.

On spring evenings when it was dark and silent about the station and when the air was heavy with the smell of new growth and of land fresh-turned by the plow, Hugh got out of his chair in the telegraph office and walked in the soft darkness. He went along Turner's Pike to town, saw groups of men standing on the sidewalks before the stores and young girls walking arm in arm along the street, and then came back to the silent station. Into his long and habitually cold body the warmth of desire began to creep. The spring rains came and soft winds blew down from the hill country to the south. One evening when the moon shone he went around the old pickle factory to where the creek went chattering under leaning willow trees, and as he stood in the heavy shadows by the factory wall, tried to imagine himself as one who had become suddenly clean-limbed, graceful, and agile. A bush grew beside the stream near the factory and he took hold of it with his powerful hands and tore it out by the roots. For a moment the strength in his shoulders and arms gave him an intense masculine satisfaction. He thought of how powerfully he could hold the body of a woman against his body and the spark of the fires of spring that had touched him became a flame. He felt new-made and tried to leap lightly and gracefully across the stream, but stumbled and fell in the water. Later he went soberly back to the station and tried again to lose himself in the study of the problems he had found in his books.

The Ezra French farm lay beside Turner's Pike a mile north of the Wheeling station and contained two hundred acres of land of which a large part was planted to cabbages. It was a profitable crop to raise and required no more care than corn, but the planting was a terrible task. Thousands of plants that had been raised from seeds planted in a seed-bed back of the barn had to be laboriously transplanted. The plants were tender and it was necessary to handle them carefully. The planter crawled slowly and painfully along, and from the road looked like a wounded beast striving to make his way to a hole in a distant wood. He crawled forward a little and then stopped and hunched himself up into a ball-like mass. Taking the plant, dropped on the ground by one of the plant droppers, he made a hole in the soft ground with a small three-cornered hoe, and with his hands packed the earth about the plant roots. Then he crawled on again.

Ezra the cabbage farmer had come west from one of the New England states and had grown comfortably wealthy, but he would not employ extra labor for the plant setting and the work was done by his sons and daughters. He was a short, bearded man whose leg had been broken in his youth by a fall from the loft of a barn. As it had not mended properly he could do little work and limped painfully about. To the men of Bidwell he was known as something of a wit, and in the winter he went to town every afternoon to stand in the stores and tell the Rabelaisian stories for which he was famous; but when spring came he became restlessly active, and in his own house and on the farm, became a tyrant. During the time of the cabbage setting he drove his sons and daughters like slaves. When in the evening the moon came up, he made them go back to the fields immediately after supper and work until midnight. They went in sullen silence, the girls to limp slowly along dropping the plants out of baskets carried on their arms, and the boys to crawl after them and set the plants. In the half darkness the little group of humans went slowly up and down the long fields. Ezra hitched a horse to a wagon and brought the plants from the seed-bed behind the barn. He went here and there swearing and protesting against every delay in the work. When his wife, a tired little old woman, had finished the evening's work in the house, he made her come also to the fields. "Come, come," he said, sharply, "we need every pair of hands we can get." Although he had several thousand dollars in the Bidwell bank and owned mortgages on two or three neighboring farms, Ezra was afraid of poverty, and to keep his family at work pretended to be upon the point of losing all his possessions. "Now is our chance to save ourselves," he declared. "We must get in a big crop. If we do not work hard now we'll starve." When in the field his sons found themselves unable to crawl longer without resting, and stood up to stretch their tired bodies, he stood by the fence at the field's edge and swore. "Well, look at the mouths I have to feed, you lazies!" he shouted. "Keep at the work. Don't be idling around. In two weeks it'll be too late for planting and then you can rest. Now every plant we set will help to save us from ruin. Keep at the job. Don't be idling around."

In the spring of his second year in Bidwell, Hugh went often in the evening to watch the plant setters at work in the moonlight on the French farm. He did not make his presence known but hid himself in a fence corner behind bushes and watched the workers. As he saw the stooped misshapen figures crawling slowly along and heard the words of the old man driving them like cattle, his heart was deeply touched and he wanted to protest. In the dim light the slowly moving figures of women appeared, and after them came the crouched crawling men. They came down the long row toward him, wriggling into his line of sight like grotesquely misshapen animals driven by some god of the night to the performance of a terrible task. An arm went up. It came down again swiftly. The three-cornered hoe sank into the ground. The slow rhythm of the crawler was broken. He reached with his disengaged hand for the plant that lay on the ground before him and lowered it into the hole the hoe had made. With his fingers he packed the earth about the roots of the plant and then again began the slow crawl forward. There were four of the French boys and the two older ones worked in silence. The younger boys complained. The three girls and their mother, who were attending to the plant dropping, came to the end of the row and turning, went away into the darkness. "I'm going to quit this slavery," one of the younger boys said. "I'll get a job over in town. I hope it's true what they say, that factories are coming."

The four young men came to the end of the row and, as Ezra was not in sight, stood a moment by the fence near where Hugh was concealed. "I'd rather be a horse or a cow than what I am," the complaining voice went on. "What's the good being alive if you have to work like this?"

For a moment as he listened to the voices of the complaining workers, Hugh wanted to go to them and ask them to let him share in their labor. Then another thought came. The crawling figures came sharply into his line of vision. He no longer heard the voice of the youngest of the French boys that seemed to come out of the ground. The machine-like swing of the bodies of the plant setters suggested vaguely to his mind the possibility of building a machine that would do the work they were doing. His mind took eager hold of that thought and he was relieved. There had been something in the crawling figures and in the moonlight out of which the voices came that had begun to awaken in his mind the fluttering, dreamy state in which he had spent so much of his boyhood. To think of the possibility of building a plant-setting machine was safer. It fitted into what Sarah Shepard had so often told him was the safe way of life. As he went back through the darkness to the railroad station, he thought about the matter and decided that to become an inventor would be the sure way of placing his feet at last upon the path of progress he was trying to find.

Hugh became absorbed in the notion of inventing a machine that would do the work he had seen the men doing in the field. All day he thought about it. The notion once fixed in his mind gave him something tangible to work upon. In the study of mechanics, taken up in a purely amateur spirit, he had not gone far enough to feel himself capable of undertaking the actual construction of such a machine, but thought the difficulty might be overcome by patience and by experimenting with combinations of wheels, gears and levers whittled out of pieces of wood. From Hunter's Jewelry Store he got a cheap clock and spent days taking it apart and putting it together again. He dropped the doing of mathematical problems and sent away for books describing the construction of machines. Already the flood of new inventions, that was so completely to change the methods of cultivating the soil in America, had begun to spread over the country, and many new and strange kinds of agricultural implements arrived at the Bidwell freight house of the Wheeling railroad. There Hugh saw a harvesting machine for cutting grain, a mowing machine for cutting hay and a long-nosed strange-looking implement that was intended to root potatoes out of the ground very much after the method pursued by energetic pigs. He studied these carefully. For a time his mind turned away from the hunger for human contact and he was content to remain an isolated figure, absorbed in the workings of his own awakening mind.

An absurd and amusing thing happened. After the impulse to try to invent a plant-setting machine came to him, he went every evening to conceal himself in the fence corner and watch the French family at their labors. Absorbed in watching the mechanical movements of the men who crawled across the fields in the moonlight, he forgot they were human. After he had watched them crawl into sight, turn at the end of the rows, and crawl away again into the hazy light that had reminded him of the dim distances of his own Mississippi River country, he was seized with a desire to crawl after them and to try to imitate their movements. Certain intricate mechanical problems, that had already come into his mind in connection with the proposed machine, he thought could be better understood if he could get the movements necessary to plant setting into his own body. His lips began to mutter words and getting out of the fence corner where he had been concealed he began to crawl across the field behind the French boys. "The down stroke will go so," he muttered, and bringing up his arm swung it above his head. His fist descended into the soft ground. He had forgotten the rows of new set plants and crawled directly over them, crushing them into the soft ground. He stopped crawling and waved his arm about. He tried to relate his arms to the mechanical arms of the machine that was being created in his mind. Holding one arm stiffly in front of him he moved it up and down. "The stroke will be shorter than that. The machine must be built close to the ground. The wheels and the horses will travel in paths between the rows. The wheels must be broad to provide traction. I will gear from the wheels to get power for the operation of the mechanism," he said aloud.

Hugh arose and stood in the moonlight in the cabbage field, his arms still going stiffly up and down. The great length of his figure and his arms was accentuated by the wavering uncertain light. The laborers, aware of some strange presence, sprang to their feet and stood listening and looking. Hugh advanced toward them, still muttering words and waving his arms. Terror took hold of the workers. One of the woman plant droppers screamed and ran away across the field, and the others ran crying at her heels. "Don't do it. Go away," the older of the French boys shouted, and then he with his brothers also ran.

Hearing the voices Hugh stopped and stared about. The field was empty. Again he lost himself in his mechanical calculations. He went back along the road to the Wheeling station and to the telegraph office where he worked half the night on a rude drawing he was trying to make of the parts of his plant setting machine, oblivious to the fact that he had created a myth that would run through the whole countryside. The French boys and their sisters stoutly declared that a ghost had come into the cabbage fields and had threatened them with death if they did not go away and quit working at night. In a trembling voice their mother backed up their assertion. Ezra French, who had not seen the apparition and did not believe the tale, scented a revolution. He swore. He threatened the entire family with starvation. He declared that a lie had been invented to deceive and betray him.

However, the work at night in the cabbage fields on the French farm was at an end. The story was told in the town of Bidwell, and as the entire French family except Ezra swore to its truth, was generally believed. Tom Foresby, an old citizen who was a spiritualist, claimed to have heard his father say that there had been in early days an Indian burying-ground on the Turner Pike.

The cabbage field on the French farm became locally famous. Within a year two other men declared they had seen the figure of a gigantic Indian dancing and singing a funeral dirge in the moonlight. Farmer boys, who had been for an evening in town and were returning late at night to lonely farmhouses, whipped their horses into a run when they came to the farm. When it was far behind them they breathed more freely. Although he continued to swear and threaten, Ezra never again succeeded in getting his family into the fields at night. In Bidwell he declared that the story of the ghost invented by his lazy sons and daughters had ruined his chance for making a decent living out of his farm.

## CHAPTER VI

Steve Hunter decided that it was time something was done to wake up his native town. The call of the spring wind awoke something in him as in Hugh. It came up from the south bringing rain followed by warm fair days. Robins hopped about on the lawns before the houses on the residence streets of Bidwell, and the air was again sweet with the pregnant sweetness of new-plowed ground. Like Hugh, Steve walked about alone through the dark, dimly lighted residence streets during the spring evenings, but he did not try awkwardly to leap over creeks in the darkness or pull bushes out of the ground, nor did he waste his time dreaming of being physically young, clean-limbed and beautiful.

Before the coming of his great achievements in the industrial field, Steve had not been highly regarded in his home town. He had been a noisy boastful youth and had been spoiled by his father. When he was twelve years old what were called safety bicycles first came into use and for a long time he owned the only one in town. In the evening he rode it up and down Main Street, frightening the horses and arousing the envy of the town boys. He learned to ride without putting his hands on the handle-bars and the other boys began to call him Smarty Hunter and later, because he wore a stiff, white collar that folded down over his shoulders, they gave him a girl's name. "Hello, Susan," they shouted, "don't fall and muss your clothes."

In the spring that marked the beginning of his great industrial adventure, Steve was stirred by the soft spring winds into dreaming his own kind of dreams. As he walked about through the streets, avoiding the other young men and women, he remembered Ernestine, the daughter of the Buffalo soap maker, and thought a great deal about the magnificence of the big stone house in which she lived with her father. His body ached for her, but that was a matter he felt could be managed. How he could achieve a financial position that would make it possible for him to ask for her hand was a more difficult problem. Since he had come back from the business college to live in his home town, he had secretly, and at the cost of two new five dollar dresses, arranged a physical alliance with a girl named Louise Trucker whose father was a farm laborer, and that left his mind free for other things. He intended to become a manufacturer, the first one in Bidwell, to make himself a leader in the new movement that was sweeping over the country. He had thought out what he wanted to do and it only remained to find something for him to manufacture to put his plans through. First of all he had selected with great care certain men he intended to ask to go in with him. There was John Clark the banker, his own father, E. H. Hunter the town jeweler, Thomas Butterworth the rich farmer, and young Gordon Hart, who had a job as assistant cashier in the bank. For a month he had been dropping hints to these men of something mysterious and important about to happen. With the exception of his father who had infinite faith in the shrewdness and ability of his son, the men he wanted to impress were only amused. One day Thomas Butterworth went into the bank and stood talking the matter over with John Clark. "The young squirt was always a smart aleck and a blowhard," he said. "What's he up to now? What's he nudging and whispering about?"

As he walked in the main street of Bidwell, Steve began to acquire that air of superiority that later made him so respected and feared. He hurried along with a peculiarly intense absorbed look in his eyes. He saw his fellow townsmen as through a haze, and sometimes did not see them at all. As he went along he took papers from his pocket, read them hurriedly, and then quickly put them away again. When he did speak—perhaps to a man who had known him from boyhood—there was in his manner something gracious to the edge of condescension. One morning in March he met Zebe Wilson the town shoemaker on the sidewalk before the post-office. Steve stopped and smiled. "Well, good morning, Mr. Wilson," he said, "and how is the quality of leather you are getting from the tanneries now?"

Word regarding this strange salutation ran about among the merchants and artisans. "What's he up to now?" they asked each other. "Mr. Wilson, indeed! Now what's wrong between that young squirt and Zebe Wilson?"

In the afternoon, four clerks from the Main Street stores and Ed Hall the carpenter's apprentice, who had a half day off because of rain, decided to investigate. One by one they went along Hamilton Street to Zebe Wilson's shop and stepped inside to repeat Steve Hunter's salutation. "Well, good afternoon, Mr. Wilson," they said, "and how is the quality of leather you are getting from the tanneries now?" Ed Hall, the last of the five who went into the shop to repeat the formal and polite inquiry, barely escaped with his life. Zebe Wilson threw a shoemaker's hammer at him and it went through the glass in the upper part of the shop door.

Once when Tom Butterworth and John Clark the banker were talking of the new air of importance he was assuming, and half-indignantly speculated on what he meant by his whispered suggestion of something significant about to happen, Steve came along Main Street past the front door of the bank. John Clark called him in. The three men confronted each other and the jeweler's son sensed the fact that the banker and the rich farmer were amused by his pretensions. At once he proved himself to be what all Bidwell later acknowledged him to be, a man who could handle men and affairs. Having at that time nothing to support his pretensions he decided to put up a bluff. With a wave of his hand and an air of knowing just what he was about, he led the two men into the back room of the bank and shut the door leading into the large room to which the general public was admitted. "You would have thought he owned the place," John Clark afterward said with a note of admiration in his voice to young Gordon Hart when he described what took place in the back room.

Steve plunged at once into what he had to say to the

two solid moneyed citizens of his town. "Well, now, look here, you two," he began earnestly. "I'm going to tell you something, but you got to keep still." He went to the window that looked out upon an alleyway and glanced about as though fearful of being overheard, then sat down in the chair usually occupied by John Clark on the rare occasions when the directors of the Bidwell bank held a meeting. Steve looked over the heads of the two men who in spite of themselves were beginning to be impressed. "Well," he began, "there is a fellow out at Pickleville. You have maybe heard things said about him. He's telegraph operator out there. Perhaps you have heard how he is always making drawings of parts of machines. I guess everybody in town has been wondering what he's up to."

Steve looked at the two men and then got nervously out of the chair and walked about the room. "That fellow is my man. I put him there," he declared. "I didn't want to tell anyone yet."

The two men nodded and Steve became lost in the notion created in his fancy. It did not occur to him that what he had just said was untrue. He began to scold the two men. "Well, I suppose I'm on the wrong track there," he said. "My man has made an invention that will bring millions in profits to those who get into it. In Cleveland and Buffalo I'm already in touch with big bankers. There's to be a big factory built, but you see yourself how it is, here I'm at home. I was raised as a boy here."

The excited young man plunged into an exposition of the spirit of the new times. He grew bold and scolded the older men. "You know yourself that factories are springing up everywhere, in towns all over the state," he said. "Will Bidwell wake up? Will we have factories here? You know well enough we won't, and I know why. It's because a man like me who was raised here has to go to a city to get money to back his plans. If I talked to you fellows you would laugh at me. In a few years I might make you more money than you have made in your whole lives, but what's the use talking? I'm Steve Hunter; you knew me when I was a kid. You'd laugh. What's the use my trying to tell you fellows my plans?"

Steve turned as though to go out of the room, but Tom Butterworth took hold of his arm and led him back to a chair. "Now, you tell us what you're up to," he demanded. In turn he grew indignant. "If you've got something to manufacture you can get backing here as well as anyplace," he said. He became convinced that the jeweler's son was telling the truth. It did not occur to him that a Bidwell young man would dare lie to such solid men as John Clark and himself. "You let them city bankers alone," he said emphatically. "You tell us your story. What you got to tell?"

In the silent little room the three men stared at each other. Tom Butterworth and John Clark in their turn began to have dreams. They remembered the tales they had heard of vast fortunes made quickly by men who owned new and valuable inventions. The land was at that time full of such tales. They were blown about on every wind. Quickly they realized that they had made a mistake in their attitude toward Steve, and were anxious to win his regard. They had called him into the bank to bully him and to laugh at him. Now they were sorry. As for Steve, he only wanted to get away—to get by himself and think. An injured look crept over his face. "Well," he said, "I thought I'd give Bidwell a chance. There are three or four men here. I have spoken to all of you and dropped a hint of something in the wind, but I'm not ready to be very definite yet."

Seeing the new look of respect in the eyes of the two men Steve became bold. "I was going to call a meeting when I was ready," he said pompously. "You two do what I've been doing. You keep your mouths shut. Don't go near that telegraph operator and don't talk to a soul. If you mean business I'll give you a chance to make barrels of money, more'n you ever dreamed of, but don't be in a hurry." He took a bundle of letters out of his inside coat pocket, and beat with them on the edge of the table that occupied the center of the room. Another bold thought came into his mind.

"I've got letters here offering me big money to take my factory either to Cleveland or Buffalo," he declared emphatically. "It isn't money that's hard to get. I can tell you men that. What a man wants in his home town is respect. He don't want to be looked on as a fool because he tries to do something to rise in the world."

Steve walked boldly out of the bank and into Main Street. When he had got out of the presence of the two men he was frightened. "Well, I've done it. I've made a fool of myself," he muttered aloud. In the bank he had said that Hugh McVey the telegraph operator was his man, that he had brought the fellow to Bidwell. What a fool he had been. In his anxiety to impress the two older men he had told a story, the falsehood of which could be discovered in a few minutes. Why had he not kept his dignity and waited? There had been no occasion for being so definite. He had gone too far, had been carried away. To be sure he had told the two men not to go near the telegraph operator, but that would no doubt but serve to arouse their suspicions of the thinness of his story. They would talk the matter over and start an investigation of their own. Then they would find out he had lied. He imagined the two men as already engaged in a whispered conversation regarding the probability of his tale. Like most shrewd men he had an exalted notion regarding the shrewdness of others. He walked a little away from the bank and then turned to look back. A shiver ran over his body. Into his mind came the sickening fear that the telegraph operator at Pickleville was not an inventor at all. The town was full of tales, and in the bank he had taken advantage of that fact to make an impression; but what proof had he? No one had seen one of the inventions supposed to have been worked out by the mysterious stranger from Missouri. There had after all been nothing but whispered suspicions, old wives' tales, fables invented by men who had nothing to do but loaf in the drugstore and make up stories.

The thought that Hugh McVey might not be an inventor overpowered him and he put it quickly aside. He had something more immediate to think about. The story of the bluff he had just made in the bank would be found out and the whole town would rock with laughter at his expense. The young men of the town did not like him. They would roll the story over on their tongues. Ribald old fellows who had nothing else to do would take up the story with joy and would elaborate it. Fellows like the cabbage farmer Ezra French, who had a talent for saying cutting things, would exercise it. They would make up imaginary inventions, grotesque, absurd inventions. Then they would get young fellows to come to him and propose that he take them up, promote them, and make everyone rich. Men would shout jokes at him as he went along Main Street. His dignity would be gone forever. He would be made a fool of by the very school boys as he had been in his youth when he bought the bicycle and rode it about before the eyes of other boys in the evenings.

Steve hurried out of Main Street and went over the bridge that crossed the river into Turner's Pike. He did not know what he intended to do, but felt there was much at stake and that he would have to do something at once. It was a warm, cloudy day and the road that led to Pickleville was muddy. During the night before it had rained and more rain was promised. The path beside the road was slippery, and so absorbed was he that as he plunged along, his feet slipped out from under him and he sat down in a small pool of water. A farmer driving past along the road turned to laugh at him. "You go to hell," Steve shouted. "You just mind your own business and go to hell."

The distracted young man tried to walk sedately along the path. The long grass that grew beside the path wet his shoes, and his hands were wet and muddy. Farmers turned on their wagon seats to stare at him. For some obscure reason he could not himself understand, he was terribly afraid to face Hugh McVey. In the bank he had been in the presence of men who were trying to get the best of him, to make a fool of him, to have fun at his expense. He had felt that and had resented it. The knowledge had given him a certain kind of boldness; it had enabled his mind to make up the story of the inventor secretly employed at his own expense and the city bankers anxious to furnish him capital. Although he was terribly afraid of discovery, he felt a little glow of pride at the thought of the boldness with which he had taken the letters out of his pocket and had challenged the two men to call his bluff.

Steve, however, felt there was something different about the man in the telegraph office in Pickleville. He had been in town for nearly two years and no one knew anything about him. His silence might be indicative of anything. He was afraid the tall silent Missourian might decide to have nothing to do with him, and pictured himself as being brushed rudely aside, being told to mind his own business.

Steve knew instinctively how to handle business men. One simply created the notion of money to be made without effort. He had done that to the two men in the bank and it had worked. After all he had succeeded in making them respect him. He had handled the situation. He wasn't such a fool at that kind of a thing. The other thing he had to face might be very different. Perhaps after all Hugh McVey was a big inventor, a man with a powerful creative mind. It was possible he had been sent to Bidwell by a big business man of some city. Big business men did strange, mysterious things; they put wires out in all directions, controlled a thousand little avenues for the creation of wealth.

Just starting out on his own career as a man of affairs, Steve had an overpowering respect for what he thought of as the subtlety of men of affairs. With all the other American youths of his generation he had been swept off his feet by the propaganda that then went on and is still going on, and that is meant to create the illusion of greatness in connection with the ownership of money. He did not then know and, in spite of his own later success and his own later use of the machinery by which illusion is created, he never found out that in an industrial world reputations for greatness of mind are made as a Detroit manufacturer would make automobiles. He did not know that men are employed to bring up the name of a politician so that he may be called a statesman, as a new brand of breakfast food that it may be sold; that most modern great men are mere illusions sprung out of a national hunger for greatness. Some day a wise man, one who has not read too many books but who has gone about among men, will discover and set forth a very interesting thing about America. The land is vast and there is a national hunger for vastness in individuals. One wants an Illinois-sized man for Illinois, an Ohio-sized man for Ohio, and a Texas-sized man for Texas.

To be sure, Steve Hunter had no notion of all this. He never did get a notion of it. The men he had already begun to think of as great and to try to imitate were like the strange and gigantic protuberances that sometimes grow on the side of unhealthy trees, but he did not know it. He did not know that throughout the country, even in that early day, a system was being built up to create the myth of greatness. At the seat of the American government at Washington, hordes of somewhat clever and altogether unhealthy young men were already being employed for the purpose. In a sweeter age many of these young men might have become artists, but they had not been strong enough to stand against the growing strength of dollars. They had become instead newspaper correspondents and secretaries to politicians. All day and every day they used their minds and their talents as writers in the making of puffs and the creating of myths concerning the men by whom they were employed. They were like the trained sheep that are used at great slaughterhouses to lead other sheep into the killing pens. Having befouled their own minds for hire, they made their living by befouling the minds of others. Already they had found out that no great cleverness was required for the work they had to do. What was required was constant repetition. It was only necessary to say over and over that the man by whom they were employed was a great man. No proof had to be brought forward to substantiate the claims they made; no great deeds had to be done by the men who were thus made great, as brands of crackers or breakfast food are made salable. Stupid and prolonged and insistent repetition was what was necessary.

As the politicians of the industrial age have created

a myth about themselves, so also have the owners of dollars, the big bankers, the railroad manipulators, the promoters of industrial enterprise. The impulse to do so is partly sprung from shrewdness but for the most part it is due to a hunger within to be of some real moment in the world. Knowing that the talent that had made them rich is but a secondary talent, and being a little worried about the matter, they employ men to glorify it. Having employed a man for the purpose, they are themselves children enough to believe the myth they have paid money to have created. Every rich man in the country unconsciously hates his press agent.

Although he had never read a book, Steve was a constant reader of the newspapers and had been deeply impressed by the stories he had read regarding the shrewdness and ability of the American captains of industry. To him they were supermen and he would have crawled on his knees before a Gould or a Cal Price—the commanding figures among moneyed men of that day. As he went down along Turner's Pike that day when industry was born in Bidwell, he thought of these men and of lesser rich men of Cleveland and Buffalo, and was afraid that in approaching Hugh he might be coming into competition with one of these men. As he hurried along under the gray sky, he however realized that the time for action had come and that he must at once put the plans that he had formed in his mind to the test of practicability; that he must at once see Hugh McVey, find out if he really did have an invention that could be manufactured, and if he did try to secure some kind of rights of ownership over it. "If I do not act at once, either Tom Butterworth or John Clark will get in ahead of me," he thought. He knew they were both shrewd capable men. Had they not become well-to-do? Even during the talk in the bank, when they had seemed to be impressed by his words, they might well have been making plans to get the better of him. They would act, but he must act first.

Steve hadn't the courage of the lie he had told. He did not have imagination enough to understand how powerful a thing is a lie. He walked quickly along until he came to the Wheeling Station at Pickleville, and then, not having the courage to confront Hugh at once, went past the station and crept in behind the deserted pickle factory that stood across the tracks. Through a broken window at the back he climbed, and crept like a thief across the earth floor until he came to a window that looked out upon the station. A freight train rumbled slowly past and a farmer came to the station to get a load of goods that had arrived by freight. George Pike came running from his house to attend to the wants of the farmer. He went back to his house and Steve was left alone in the presence of the man on whom he felt all of his future depended. He was as excited as a village girl in the presence of a lover. Through the windows of the telegraph office he could see Hugh seated at a desk with a book before him. The presence of the book frightened him. He decided that the mysterious Missourian must be some strange sort of intellectual giant. He was sure that one who could sit quietly reading hour after hour in such a lonely isolated place could be of no ordinary clay. As he stood in the deep shadows inside the old building and stared at the man he was trying to find courage to approach, a citizen of Bidwell named Dick Spearsman came to the station and going inside, talked to the telegraph operator. Steve trembled with anxiety. The man who had come to the station was an insurance agent who also owned a small berry farm at the edge of town. He had a son who had gone west to take up land in the State of Kansas, and the father thought of visiting him. He came to the station to make inquiry regarding the railroad fare, but when Steve saw him talking to Hugh, the thought came into his mind that John Clark or Thomas Butterworth might have sent him to the station to make an investigation of the truth of the statements he had made in the bank. "It would be like them to do it that way," he muttered to himself. "They wouldn't come themselves. They would send someone they thought I wouldn't suspect. They would play safe, damn 'em."

Trembling with fear, Steve walked up and down in the empty factory. Cobwebs hanging down brushed against his face and he jumped aside as though a hand had reached out of the darkness to touch him. In the corners of the old building shadows lurked and distorted thoughts began to come into his head. He rolled and lighted a cigarette and then remembered that the flare of the match could probably be seen from the station. He cursed himself for his carelessness. Throwing the cigarette on the earth floor he ground it under his heel. When at last Dick Spearsman had disappeared up the road that led to Bidwell and he came out of the old factory and got again into Turner's Pike, he felt that he was in no shape to talk of business but nevertheless must act at once. In front of the factory he stopped in the road and tried to wipe the mud off the seat of his trousers with a handkerchief. Then he went to the creek and washed his soiled hands. With wet hands he arranged his tie and straightened the collar of his coat. He had an air of one about to ask a woman to become his wife. Striving to look as important and dignified as possible, he went along the station platform and into the telegraph office to confront Hugh and to find out at once and finally what fate the gods had in store for him.

It no doubt contributed to Steve's happiness in after life, in the days when he was growing rich, and later when he reached out for public honors, contributed to campaign funds, and even in secret dreamed of getting into the United States Senate or being Governor of his state, that he never knew how badly he overreached himself that day in his youth when he made his first business deal with Hugh at the Wheeling Station at Pickleville. Later Hugh's interest in the Steven Hunter industrial enterprises was taken care of by a man who was as shrewd as Steve himself. Tom Butterworth, who had made money and knew how to make and handle money, managed such things for the inventor, and Steve's chance was gone forever.

That is, however, a part of the story of the development of the town of Bidwell and a story that Steve never understood. When he overreached himself that day he did not know what he had done. He made a deal with Hugh and was happy to escape the predicament he thought he had got himself into when he talked too much to the two men in the bank.

Although Steve's father had always a great faith in his son's shrewdness and when he talked to other men represented him as a peculiarly capable and unappreciated man, the two did not in private get on well. In the Hunter household they quarreled and snarled at each other. Steve's mother had died when he was a small boy and his one sister, two years older than himself, kept herself always in the house and seldom appeared on the streets. She was a semi-invalid. Some obscure nervous disease had twisted her body out of shape, and her face twitched incessantly. One morning in the barn back of the Hunter house Steve, then a lad of fourteen, was oiling his bicycle when his sister appeared and stood watching him. A small wrench lay on the ground and she picked it up. Suddenly and without warning she began to beat him on the head. He was compelled to knock her down in order to tear the wrench out of her hand. After the incident she was ill in bed for a month.

Elsie Hunter was always a source of unhappiness to her brother. As he began to get up in life Steve had a growing passion for being respected by his fellows. It got to be something of an obsession with him and among other things he wanted very much to be thought of as one who had good blood in his veins. A man whom he hired searched out his ancestry, and with the exception of his immediate family it seemed very satisfactory. The sister, with her twisted body and her face that twitched so persistently, seemed to be everlastingly sneering at him. He grew half-afraid to come into her presence. After he began to grow rich he married Ernestine, the daughter of the soap maker at Buffalo, and when her father died she also had a great deal of money. His own father died and he set up a household of his own. That was in the time when big houses began to appear at the edge of the berry lands and on the hills south of Bidwell. On his father's death Steve became guardian for his sister. The jeweler had left a small estate and it was entirely in the son's hands. Elsie lived with one servant in a small house in town and was put in the position of being entirely dependent on her brother's bounty. In a sense it might be said that she lived by her hatred of him. When on rare occasions he came to her house she would not see him. A servant came to the door and reported her asleep. Almost every month she wrote a letter demanding that her share of her father's money be handed over to her, but it did no good. Steve occasionally spoke to an acquaintance of his difficulty with her. "I am more sorry for the woman than I can say," he declared. "It's the dream of my life to make the poor afflicted soul happy. You see yourself that I provide her with every comfort of life. Ours is an old family. I have it from an expert in such matters that we are descendants of one Hunter, a courtier in the court of Edward the Second of England. Our blood has perhaps become a little thin. All the vitality of the family was centered in me. My sister does not understand me and that has been the cause of much unhappiness and heart burning, but I shall always do my duty by her."

In the late afternoon of the spring day that was also the most eventful day of his life, Steve went quickly along the Wheeling Station platform to the door of the telegraph office. It was a public place, but before going in he stopped, again straightened his tie and brushed his clothes, and then knocked at the door. As there was no response he opened the door softly and looked in. Hugh was at his desk but did not look up. Steve went in and closed the door. By chance the moment of his entrance was also a big moment in the life of the man he had come to see. The mind of the young inventor, that had for so long been dreamy and uncertain, had suddenly become extraordinarily clear and free. One of the inspired moments that come to intense natures, working intensely, had come to him. The mechanical problem he was trying so hard to work out became clear. It was one of the moments that Hugh afterwards thought of as justifying his existence, and in later life he came to live for such moments. With a nod of his head to Steve he arose and hurried out to the building that was used by the Wheeling as a freight warehouse. The jeweler's son ran at his heels. On an elevated platform before the freight warehouse sat an odd-looking agricultural implement, a machine for rooting potatoes out of the ground that had been received on the day before and was now awaiting delivery to some farmer. Hugh dropped to his knees beside the machine and examined it closely. Muttered exclamations broke from his lips. For the first time in his life he was not embarrassed in the presence of another person. The two men, the one almost grotesquely tall, the other short of stature and already inclined toward corpulency, stared at each other. "What is it you're inventing? I came to see you about that," Steve said timidly.

Hugh did not answer the question directly. He stepped across the narrow platform to the freight warehouse and began to make a rude drawing on the side of the building. Then he tried to explain his plant-setting machine. He spoke of it as a thing already achieved. At the moment he thought of it in that way. "I had not thought of the use of a large wheel with the arms attached at regular intervals," he said absent-mindedly. "I will have to find money now. That'll be the next step. It will be necessary to make a working model of the machine now. I must find out what changes I'll have to make in my calculations."

The two men returned to the telegraph office and while Hugh listened Steve made his proposal. Even then he did not understand what the machine that was to be made was to do. It was enough for him that a machine was to be made and he wanted to share in its ownership at once. As the two men walked back from the freight warehouse, his mind took hold of Hugh's remark about getting money. Again he was afraid. "There's someone in the background," he thought. "Now I must make a proposal he can't refuse. I mustn't leave until I've made a deal with him."

Fairly carried away by his anxiety, Steve proposed

to provide money out of his own pocket to make the model of the machine. "We'll rent the old pickle factory across the track," he said, opening the door and pointing with a trembling finger. "I can get it cheap. I'll have windows and a floor put in. Then I'll get you a man to whittle out a model of the machine. Allie Mulberry can do it. I'll get him for you. He can whittle anything if you only show him what you want. He's half-crazy and won't get on to our secret. When the model is made, leave it to me, you just leave it to me."

Rubbing his hands together Steve walked boldly to the telegrapher's desk and picking up a sheet of paper began to write out a contract. It provided that Hugh was to get a royalty of ten per cent of the selling price on the machine he had invented and that was to be manufactured by a company to be organized by Steven Hunter. The contract also stated that a promoting company was to be organized at once and money provided for the experimental work Hugh had yet to do. The Missourian was to begin getting a salary at once. He was to risk nothing, as Steve elaborately explained. When he was ready for them mechanics were to be employed and their salaries paid. When the contract had been written and read aloud, a copy was made and Hugh, who was again embarrassed beyond words, signed his name.

With a flourish of his hand Steve laid a little pile of money on the desk. "That's for a starter," he said and turned to frown at George Pike who at that moment came to the door. The freight agent went quickly away and the two men were left alone together. Steve shook hands with his new partner. He went out and then came in again. "You understand," he said mysteriously. "The fifty dollars is your first month's salary. I was ready for you. I brought it along. You just leave everything to me, just you leave it to me." Again he went out and

Hugh was left alone. He saw the young man go across the tracks to the old factory and walk up and down before it. When a farmer came along and shouted at him, he did not reply, but stepping back into the road swept the deserted old building with his eyes as a general might have looked over a battlefield. Then he went briskly down the road toward town and the farmer turned on his wagon seat to stare after him.

Hugh McVey also stared. When Steve had gone away, he walked to the end of the station platform and looked along the road toward town. It seemed to him wonderful that he had at last held conversation with a citizen of Bidwell. A little of the import of the contract he had signed came to him, and he went into the station and got his copy of it and put it in his pocket. Then he came out again. When he read it over and realized anew that he was to be paid a living wage and have time and help to work out the problem that had now become vastly important to his happiness, it seemed to him that he had been in the presence of a kind of god. He remembered the words of Sarah Shepard concerning the bright alert citizens of eastern towns and realized that he had been in the presence of such a being, that he had in some way become connected in his new work with such a one. The realization overcame him completely. Forgetting entirely his duties as a telegrapher, he closed the office and went for a walk across the meadows and in the little patches of woodlands that still remained standing in the open plain north of Pickleville. He did not return until late at night, and when he did, had not solved the puzzle as to what had happened. All he got out of it was the fact that the machine he had been trying to make was of great and mysterious importance to the civilization into which he had come to live and of which he wanted so keenly to be a part. There seemed to him something almost sacred in that fact. A new determination to complete and perfect his plant-setting machine had taken possession of him.

The meeting to organize a promotion company that would in turn launch the first industrial enterprise in the town of Bidwell was held in the back room of the Bidwell bank one afternoon in June. The berry season had just come to an end and the streets were full of people. A circus had come to town and at one o'clock there was a parade. Before the stores horses belonging to visiting country people stood hitched in two long rows. The meeting in the bank was not held until four o'clock, when the banking business was at an end for the day. It had been a hot, stuffy afternoon and a storm threatened. For some reason the whole town had an inkling of the fact that a meeting was to be held on that day, and in spite of the excitement caused by the coming of the circus, it was in everybody's mind. From the very beginning of his upward journey in life, Steve Hunter had the faculty of throwing an air of mystery and importance about everything he did. Everyone saw the workings of the machinery by which the myth concerning himself was created, but was nevertheless impressed. Even the men of Bidwell who retained the ability to laugh at Steve could not laugh at the things he did.

For two months before the day on which the meeting was held, the town had been on edge. Everyone knew that Hugh McVey had suddenly given up his place in the telegraph office and that he was engaged in some enterprise with Steve Hunter. "Well, I see he has thrown off the mask, that fellow," said Alban Foster, superintendent of the Bidwell schools, in speaking of the matter to the Reverend Harvey Oxford, the minister of the Baptist Church.

Steve saw to it that although everyone was curious the curiosity was unsatisfied. Even his father was left in the dark. The two men had a sharp quarrel about the matter, but as Steve had three thousand dollars of his own, left him by his mother, and was well past his twenty-first year, there was nothing his father could do.

At Pickleville the windows and doors at the back of the deserted factory were bricked up, and over the windows and the door at the front, where a floor had been laid, iron bars specially made by Lew Twining the Bidwell blacksmith had been put. The bars over the door locked the place at night and gave the factory the air of a prison. Every evening before he went to bed Steve walked to Pickleville. The sinister appearance of the building at night gave him a peculiar satisfaction. "They'll find out what I'm up to when I want 'em to," he said to himself. Allie Mulberry worked at the factory during the day. Under Hugh's direction he whittled pieces of wood into various shapes, but had no idea of what he was doing. No one but the half-wit and Steve Hunter were admitted to the society of the telegraph operator. When Allie Mulberry came into the Main Street at night, everyone stopped him and a thousand questions were asked, but he only shook his head and smiled foolishly. On Sunday afternoons crowds of men and women walked down Turner's Pike to Pickleville and stood looking at the deserted building, but no one tried to enter. The bars were in place and window shades were drawn over the windows. Above the door that faced the road there was a large sign. "Keep Out. This Means You," the sign said.

The four men who met Steve in the bank knew vaguely that some sort of invention was being perfected, but did not know what it was. They spoke in an offhand way of the matter to their friends and that increased the general curiosity. Everyone tried to guess what was up. When Steve was not about, John Clark and young Gordon Hart pretended to know everything but gave the impression of men sworn to secrecy. The fact that Steve told them nothing seemed to them a kind of insult. "The young upstart, I believe yet he's a bluff," the banker declared to his friend, Tom Butterworth.

On Main Street the old and young men who stood about before the stores in the evening tried also to make light of the jeweler's son and the air of importance he constantly assumed. They also spoke of him as a young upstart and a windbag, but after the beginning of his connection with Hugh McVey, something of conviction went out of their voices. "I read in the paper that a man in Toledo made thirty thousand dollars out of an invention. He got it up in less than a day. He just thought of it. It's a new kind of way for sealing fruit cans," a man in the crowd before Birdie Spinks' drugstore absent-mindedly observed.

Inside the drugstore by the empty stove, Judge Hanby talked persistently of the time when factories would come. He seemed to those who listened a sort of John the Baptist crying out of the coming of the new day. One evening in May of that year, when a goodly crowd was assembled, Steve Hunter came in and bought a cigar. Everyone became silent. Birdie Spinks was for some mysterious reason a little upset. In the store something happened that, had there been someone there to record it, might later have been remembered as the moment that marked the coming of the new age to Bidwell. The druggist, after he had handed out the cigar, looked at the young man whose name had so suddenly come upon everyone's lips and whom he had known from babyhood, and then addressed him as no young man of his age had ever before been addressed by an older citizen of the town. "Well, good evening, Mr. Hunter," he said respectfully. "And how do you find yourself this evening?"

To the men who met him in the bank, Steve described the plant-setting machine and the work it was intended to do. "It's the most perfect thing of its kind I've ever seen," he said with the air of one who has spent his life as an expert examiner of machinery. Then, to the amazement of everyone, he produced sheets covered with figures estimating the cost of manufacturing the machine. To the men present it seemed as though the question as to the practicability of the machine had already been settled. The sheets covered with figures made the actual beginning of manufacturing seem near at hand. Without raising his voice and quite as a matter of course, Steve proposed that the men present subscribe each three thousand dollars to the stock of a promotion company, the money to be used to perfect the machine and put it actually to work in the fields, while a larger company for the building of a factory was being organized. For the three thousand dollars each of the men would receive later six thousand dollars in stock in the larger company. They would make one hundred per cent on their first investment. As for himself he owned the invention and it was very valuable. He had already received many offers from other men in other places. He wanted to stick to his own town and to the men who had known him since he was a boy. He would retain a controlling interest in the larger company and that would enable him to take care of his friends. John Clark he proposed to make treasurer of the promotion company. Everyone could see he would be the right man. Gordon Hart should be manager. Tom Butterworth could, if he could find time to give it, help him in the actual organization of the larger company. He did not propose to do anything in a small way. Much stock would have to be sold to farmers, as well as to townspeople, and he could see no reason why a certain commission for the selling of stock should not be paid.

The four men came out of the back room of the bank just as the storm that had all day been threatening broke on Main Street. They stood together by the front window and watched the people scurry along past the stores homeward-bound from the circus. Farmers jumping into their wagons started their horses away on the trot. The whole street was populous with people shouting and running. To an observing person standing at the bank window, Bidwell, Ohio, might have seemed no longer a quiet town filled with people who lived quiet lives and thought quiet thoughts, but a tiny section of some giant modern city. The sky was extraordinarily black as from the smoke of a mill. The hurrying people might have been workmen escaping from the mill at the end of the day. Clouds of dust swept through the street. Steve Hunter's imagination was aroused. For some reason the black clouds of dust and the running people gave him a tremendous sense of power. It almost seemed to him that he had filled the sky with clouds and that something latent in him had startled the people. He was anxious to get away from the men who had just agreed to join him in his first great industrial adventure. He felt that they were after all mere puppets, creatures he could use, men who were being swept along by him as the people running along the streets were being swept along by the storm. He and the storm were in a way akin to each other. He had an impulse to be alone with the storm, to walk dignified and upright in the face of it as he felt that in the future he would walk dignified and upright in the face of men.

Steve went out of the bank and into the street. The men inside shouted at him, telling him he would get wet, but he paid no attention to their warning. When he had gone and when his father had run quickly across the street to his jewelry store, the three men who were left in the bank looked at each other and laughed. Like the loiterers before Birdie Spinks' drugstore, they wanted to belittle him and had an inclination to begin calling him names; but for some reason they could not do it. Something had happened to them. They looked at each other with a question in their eyes. Each man waited for the others to speak. "Well, whatever happens we can't lose much of anything," John Clark finally observed.

And over the bridge and out into Turner's Pike walked Steve Hunter, the embryo industrial magnate. Across the great stretches of fields that lay beside the road the wind ran furiously, tearing leaves off trees, carrying great volumes of dust before it. The hurrying black clouds in the sky were, he fancied, like clouds of smoke pouring out of the chimneys of factories owned by himself. In fancy also he saw his town become a city, bathed in the smoke of his enterprises. As he looked abroad over the fields swept by the storm of wind, he realized that the road along which he walked would in time become a city street. "Pretty soon I'll get an option on this land," he said meditatively. An exalted mood took possession of him and when he got to Pickleville he did not go into the shop where Hugh and Allie Mulberry were at work, but turning, walked back toward town in the mud and the driving rain.

It was a time when Steve wanted to be by himself, to feel himself the one great man of the community. He had intended to go into the old pickle factory and escape the rain, but when he got to the railroad tracks, had turned back because he realized suddenly that in the presence of the silent, intent inventor he had never been able to feel big. He wanted to feel big on that evening and so, unmindful of the rain and of his hat, that was caught up by the wind and blown away into a field, he went along the deserted road thinking great thoughts. At a place where there were no houses he stopped for a moment and lifted his tiny hands to the skies. "I'm a man. I tell you what, I'm a man. Whatever anyone says, I tell you what, I'm a man," he shouted into the void.

## CHAPTER VII

Modern men and women who live in industrial cities are like mice that have come out of the fields to live in houses that do not belong to them. They live within the dark walls of the houses where only a dim light penetrates, and so many have come that they grow thin and haggard with the constant toil of getting food and warmth. Behind the walls the mice scamper about in droves, and there is much squealing and chattering. Now and then a bold mouse stands upon his hind legs and addresses the others. He declares he will force his way through the walls and conquer the gods who have built the house. "I will kill them," he declares. "The mice shall rule. You shall live in the light and the warmth. There shall be food for all and no one shall go hungry."

The little mice, gathered in the darkness out of sight in the great houses, squeal with delight. After a time when nothing happens they become sad and depressed. Their minds go back to the time when they lived in the fields, but they do not go out of the walls of the houses, because long living in droves has made them afraid of the silence of long nights and the emptiness of skies. In the houses giant children are being reared. When the children fight and scream in the houses and in the streets, the dark spaces between the walls rumble with strange and appalling noises.

The mice are terribly afraid. Now and then a single mouse for a moment escapes the general fear. A mood comes over such a one and a light comes into his eyes. When the noises run through the houses he makes up stories about them. "The horses of the sun are hauling wagon loads of days over the tops of trees," he says and looks quickly about to see if he has been heard. When he discovers a female mouse looking at him he runs away with a flip of his tail and the female follows. While other mice are repeating his saying and getting some little comfort from it, he and the female mouse find a warm dark corner and lie close together. It is because of them that mice continue to be born to dwell within the walls of the houses.

When the first small model of Hugh McVey's plant-setting machine had been whittled out by the half-wit Allie Mulberry, it replaced the famous ship, floating in the bottle, that for two or three years had been lying in the window of Hunter's jewelry store. Allie was inordinately proud of the new specimen of his handiwork. As he worked under Hugh's directions at a bench in a corner of the deserted pickle factory, he was like a strange dog that has at last found a master. He paid no attention to Steve Hunter who, with the air of one bearing in his breast some gigantic secret, came in and went out at the door twenty times a day, but kept his eyes on the silent Hugh who sat at a desk and made drawings on sheets of paper. Allie tried valiantly to follow the instructions given him and to understand what his master was trying to do, and Hugh, finding himself unembarrassed by the presence of the half-wit, sometimes spent hours trying to explain the workings of some intricate part of the proposed machine. Hugh made each part crudely out of great pieces of board and Allie reproduced the part in miniature. Intelligence began to come into the eyes of the man who all his life had whittled meaningless wooden chains, baskets formed out of peach stones, and ships intended to float in bottles. Love and understanding began a little to do for him what words could not have done. One day when a part Hugh had fashioned would not work the half-wit himself made the model of a part that worked perfectly. When Hugh incorporated it in the machine, he was so happy that he could not sit still, and walked up and down cooing with delight.

When the model of the machine appeared in the jeweler's window, a fever of excitement took hold of the minds of the people. Everyone declared himself either for or against it. Something like a revolution took place. Parties were formed. Men who had no interest in the success of the invention, and in the nature of things could not have, were ready to fight anyone who dared to doubt its success. Among the farmers who drove into town to see the new wonder were many who said the machine would not, could not, work. "It isn't practical," they said. Going off by themselves and forming groups, they whispered warnings. A hundred objections sprang to their lips. "See all the little wheels and cogs the thing has," they said. "You see it won't work. You take now in a field where there are stones and old tree roots, maybe, sticking in the ground. There you'll see. Fools'll buy the machine, yes. They'll spend their money. They'll put in plants. The plants'll die. The money'll be wasted. There'll be no crop." Old men, who had been cabbage farmers in the country north of Bidwell all their lives, and whose bodies were all twisted out of shape by the terrible labor of the cabbage fields, came hobbling into town to look at the model of the new machine. Their opinions were anxiously sought by the merchant, the carpenter, the artisan, the doctor—by all the townspeople. Almost without exception they shook their heads in doubt. Standing on the sidewalk before the jeweler's window, they stared at the machine and then, turning to the crowd that had gathered about, they shook their heads in doubt. "Huh," they exclaimed, "a thing of wheels and cogs, eh? Well, so young Hunter expects that thing to take the place of a man. He's a fool. I always said that boy was a fool." The merchants and townspeople, their ardor a little dampened by the adverse decision of the men who knew plant-setting, went off by themselves. They went into Birdie Spinks' drugstore, but did not listen to the talk of Judge Hanby. "If the machine works, the town'll wake up," someone declared. "It means factories, new people coming in, houses to be built, goods to be bought." Visions of suddenly acquired wealth began to float in their minds. Young Ed Hall, apprentice to Ben Peeler the carpenter, grew angry. "Hell," he exclaimed, "why listen to a lot of damned old calamity howlers? It's the town's duty to get out and plug for that machine. We got to wake up here. We got to forget what we used to think about Steve Hunter. Anyway, he saw a chance, didn't he? and he took it. I wish I was him. I only wish I was him. And what about that fellow we thought was maybe just a telegraph operator? He fooled us all slick, now didn't he? I tell you we ought to be proud to have such men as him and Steve Hunter living in Bidwell. That's what I say. I tell you it's the town's duty to get out and plug for them and for that machine. If we don't, I know what'll happen. Steve Hunter's a live one. I been thinking maybe he was. He'll take that invention and that inventor of his to some other town or to a city. That's what he'll do. Damn it, I tell you we got to get out and back them fellows up. That's what I say."

On the whole the town of Bidwell agreed with young Hall. The excitement did not die, but grew every day more intense. Steve Hunter had a carpenter come to his father's store and build in the show window facing Main Street, a long shallow box formed in the shape of a field. This he filled with pulverized earth and then by an arrangement of strings and pulleys connected with a clockwork device the machine was pulled across the field. In a receptacle at the top of the machine had been placed some dozens of tiny plants no larger than pins. When the clockwork was started and the strings pulled to imitate applied horse power, the machine crept slowly forward, an arm came down and made a hole in the ground, the plant dropped into the hole and spoon-like hands appeared and packed the earth about the plant roots. At the top of the machine there was a tank filled with water, and when the plant was set, a portion of water, nicely calculated as to quantity, ran down a pipe and was deposited at the plant roots.

Evening after evening the machine crawled forward across the tiny field, setting the plants in perfect order. Steve Hunter busied himself with it; he did nothing else; and rumors of a great company to be formed in Bidwell to manufacture the device were whispered about. Every evening a new tale was told. Steve went to Cleveland for a day and it was said that Bidwell was to lose its chance, that big moneyed men had induced Steve to take his factory project to the city. Hearing Ed Hall berate a farmer who doubted the practicability of the machine, Steve took him aside and talked to him. "We're going to need live young men who know how to handle other men for jobs as superintendent and things like that," he said. "I make no promises. I only want to tell you that I like live young fellows who can see the hole in a bushel basket. I like that kind. I like to see them get up in the world."

Steve heard the farmers continually expressing their skepticism about making the plants that had been set by the machine grow into maturity, and had the carpenter build another tiny field in a side window of the store. He had the machine moved and plants set in the new field. He let these grow. When some of the plants showed signs of dying he came secretly at night and replaced them with sturdier shoots so that the miniature field showed always a brave, vigorous front to the world.

Bidwell became convinced that the most rigorous of all forms of human labor practiced by its people was at an end. Steve made and had hung in the store window a large sheet showing the relative cost of planting an acre of cabbage with the machine, and by what was already called "the old way," by hand. Then he formally announced that a stock company would be formed in Bidwell and that everyone would have a chance to get into it. He printed an article in the weekly paper in which he said that many offers had come to him to take his project to the city or to other and larger towns. "Mr. McVey, the celebrated inventor, and I both want to stick to our own people," he said, regardless of the fact that Hugh knew nothing of the article and had never been taken into the lives of the people addressed. A day was set for the beginning of the taking of stock subscriptions, and in private conversations Steve whispered of huge profits to be made. The matter was talked over in every household and plans were made for raising money to buy stock. John Clark agreed to lend a certain percentage on the value of the town property and Steve secured a long-time option on all the land facing Turner's Pike clear down to Pickleville. When the town heard of this it was filled with wonder. "Gee," the loiterers before the store exclaimed, "old Bidwell is going to grow up. Now look at that, will you? There are going to be houses clear down to Pickleville." Hugh went to Cleveland to see about having one of his new machines made in steel and wood and in a size that would permit its actual use in the field. He returned, a hero in the town's eyes. His silence made it possible for the people, who could not entirely forget their former lack of faith in Steve, to let their minds take hold of something they thought was truly heroic.

In the evening, after going again to see the machine in the window of the jewelry store, crowds of young and old men wandered down along Turner's Pike to the Wheeling Station where a new man had come to replace Hugh. They hardly saw the evening train when it came in. Like devotees before a shrine they gazed with something like worship in their eyes at the old pickle factory, and when by chance Hugh came among them, unconscious of the sensation he was creating, they became embarrassed as he was always embarrassed by their presence. Everyone dreamed of becoming suddenly rich by the power of the man's mind. They thought of him as thinking always great thoughts. To be sure, Steve Hunter might be more than half bluff and blow and pretense, but there was no bluff and blow about Hugh. He didn't waste his time in words. He thought, and out of his thought sprang almost unbelievable wonders.

In every part of the town of Bidwell, the new impulse toward progress was felt. Old men, who had become settled in their ways and who had begun to pass their days in a sort of sleepy submission to the idea of the gradual passing away of their lives, awoke and went into Main Street in the evening to argue with skeptical farmers. Beside Ed Hall, who had become a Demosthenes on the subject of progress and the duty of the town to awake and stick to Steve Hunter and the machine, a dozen other men held forth on the street corners. Oratorical ability awoke in the most unexpected places. Rumors flew from lip to lip. It was said that within a year Bidwell was to have a brick factory covering acres of ground, that there would be paved streets and electric lights.

Oddly enough the most persistent decrier of the new spirit in Bidwell was the man who, if the machine turned out to be a success, would profit most from its use. Ezra French, the profane, refused to be convinced. When pressed by Ed Hall, Dr. Robinson, and other enthusiasts, he fell back upon the word of that God whose name had been so much upon his lips. The decrier of God became the defender of God. "The thing, you see, can't be done. It ain't all right. Something awful'll happen. The rains won't come and the plants'll dry up and die. It'll be like it was in Egypt in the Bible times," he declared. The old farmer with the twisted leg stood before the crowd in the drugstore and proclaimed the truth of God's word. "Don't it say in the Bible men shall work and labor by the sweat of their brows?" he asked sharply. "Can a machine like that sweat? You know it can't. And it can't do the work either. No, siree. Men've got to do it. That's the way things have been since Cain killed Abel in the Garden of Eden. God intended it so and there can't be no telegraph operator or no smart young squirt like Steve Hunter—fellows in a town like this—set themselves up before me to change the workings of God's laws. It can't be done, and if it could be done it would be wicked and ungodly to try. I'll have nothing to do with it. It ain't right. That's what I say and all your smart talk ain't a-going to change me."

It was in the year 1892 that Steve Hunter organized the first industrial enterprise that came to Bidwell. It was called the Bidwell Plant-Setting Machine Company, and in the end it turned out to be a failure. A large factory was built on the river bank facing the New York Central tracks. It is now occupied by an enterprise called the Hunter Bicycle Company and is what in industrial parlance is called a live, going concern.

For two years Hugh worked faithfully trying to perfect the first of his inventions. After the working models of the plant-setter were brought from Cleveland, two trained mechanics were employed to come to Bidwell and work with him. In the old pickle factory an engine was installed and lathes and other tool-making machines were set up. For a long time Steve, John Clark, Tom Butterworth, and the other enthusiastic promoters of the enterprise had no doubt as to the final outcome. Hugh wanted to perfect the machine, had his heart set on doing the job he had set out to do, but he had then and, for that matter, he continued during his whole life to have but little conception of the import in the lives of the people about him of the things he did. Day after day, with two city mechanics and Allie Mulberry to drive the team of horses Steve had provided, he went into a rented field north of the factory. Weak places developed in the complicated mechanism, and new and stronger parts were made. For a time the machine worked perfectly. Then other defects appeared and other parts had to be strengthened and changed. The machine became too heavy to be handled by one team.

It would not work when the soil was either too wet or too dry. It worked perfectly in both wet and dry sand but would do nothing in clay. During the second year and when the factory was nearing completion and much machinery had been installed, Hugh went to Steve and told him of what he thought were the limitations of the machine. He was depressed by his failure, but in working with the machine, he felt he had succeeded in educating himself as he never could have done by studying books. Steve decided that the factory should be started and some of the machines made and sold. "You keep the two men you have and don't talk," he said. "The machine may yet turn out to be better than you think. One can never tell. I have made it worth their while to keep still." On the afternoon of the day on which he had his talk with Hugh, Steve called the four men who were associated with him in the promotion of the enterprise into the back room of the bank and told them of the situation. "We're up against something here," he said. "If we let word of the failure of this machine get out, where'll we be? It is a case of the survival of the fittest."

Steve explained his plan to the men in the room. After all, he said, there was no occasion for any of them to get excited. He had taken them into the thing and he proposed to get them out. "I'm that kind of a man," he said pompously. In a way, he declared, he was glad things had turned out as they had. The four men had little actual money invested. They had all tried honestly to do something for the town and he would see to it that everything came out all right. "We'll be honest with everyone," he said. "The stock in the company has all been sold. We'll make some of the machines and sell them. If they're failures, as this inventor thinks, it will not be our fault. The plant, you see, will have to be sold cheap. When that time comes we five will have to save ourselves and the future of the town. The machinery we have bought, is, you see, iron and woodworking machinery, the very latest kind. It can be used to make some other thing. If the plant-setting machine is a failure we'll simply buy up the plant at a low price and make something else. Perhaps it'll be better for the town to have the entire stock control in our hands. You see we few men have got to run things here. It's going to be on our shoulders to see that labor is employed. A lot of small stockholders are a nuisance. As man to man I'm going to ask each of you not to sell his stock, but if anyone comes to you and asks about its value, I expect you to be loyal to our enterprise. I'll begin looking about for something to replace the plant-setting machine, and when the shop closes we'll start right up again. It isn't every day men get a chance to sell themselves a fine plant full of new machinery as we can do in a year or so now."

Steve went out of the bank and left the four men staring at each other. Then his father got up and went out. The other men, all connected with the bank, arose and wandered out. "Well," said John Clark, somewhat heavily, "he's a smart man. I suppose after all it is up to us to stick with him and with the town. As he says, labor has got to be employed. I can't see that it does a carpenter or a farmer any good to own a little stock in a factory. It only takes their minds off their work. They have foolish dreams of getting rich and don't attend to their own affairs. It would be an actual benefit to the town if a few men owned the factory. The banker lighted a cigar and going to a window stared out into the main street of Bidwell. Already the town had changed. Three new brick buildings were being erected on Main Street within sight of the bank window. Workmen employed in the building of the factory had come to town to live, and many new houses were being built. Everywhere things were astir. The stock of the company had been oversubscribed, and almost every day men came into the bank and spoke of wanting to buy more. Only the day before a farmer had come in with two thousand dollars. The banker's mind began to secrete the poison of his age. "After all, it's men like Steve Hunter, Tom Butterworth, Gordon Hart, and myself that have to take care of things, and to be in shape to do it we have to look out for ourselves," he soliloquized. Again he stared into Main Street. Tom Butterworth went out at the front door. He wanted to be by himself and think his own thoughts. Gordon Hart returned to the empty back room and standing by a window looked out into an alleyway. His thoughts ran in the same channel as those that played through the mind of the bank president. He also thought of men who wanted to buy stock in the company that was doomed to failure. He began to doubt the judgment of Hugh McVey in the matter of failure. "Such fellows are always pessimists," he told himself. From the window at the back of the bank, he could see over the roofs of a row of small sheds and down a residence street to where two new workingmen's houses were being built. His thoughts only differed from the thoughts of John Clark because he was a younger man. "A few men of the younger generation, like Steve and myself will have to take hold of things," he muttered aloud. "We'll have to have money to work with. We'll have to take the responsibility of the ownership of money."

At the front of the bank John Clark puffed at his cigar. He felt like a soldier weighing the chances of battle. Vaguely he thought of himself as a general, a kind of U. S. Grant of industry. The lives and happiness of many people, he told himself, depended on the clear working of his brain. "Well," he thought, "when factories start coming to a town and it begins to grow as this town is growing no man can stop it. The fellow who thinks of individual men, little fellows with their savings invested, who may be hurt by an industrial failure, is just a weakling. Men have to face the duties life brings. The few men who see clearly have to think first of themselves. They have to save themselves in order that they may save others."

Things kept on the stir in Bidwell and the gods of chance played into the hands of Steve Hunter. Hugh invented an apparatus for lifting a loaded coal-car off the railroad tracks, carrying it high up into the air and dumping its contents into a chute. By its use an entire car of coal could be emptied with a roaring rush into the hold of a ship or the engine room of a factory. A model of the new invention was made and a patent secured. Then Steve Hunter carried it off to New York. He received two hundred thousand dollars in cash for it, half of which went to Hugh. Steve's faith in the inventive genius of the Missourian was renewed and strengthened. He looked forward with a feeling almost approaching pleasure to the time when the town would be forced to face the fact that the plant-setting machine was a failure, and the factory with its new machinery would have to be thrown on the market. He knew that his associates in the promotion of the enterprise were secretly selling their stock. One day he went to Cleveland and had a long talk with a banker there. Hugh was at work on a corn-cutting machine and already he had secured an option on it. "Perhaps when the time comes to sell the factory there'll be more than one bidder," he told Ernestine, the soap maker's daughter, who had married him within a month after the sale of the car-unloading device. He grew indignant when he told her of the disloyalty of the two men in the bank, and the rich farmer, Tom Butterworth. "They're selling their shares and letting the small stockholders lose their money," he declared. "I told 'em not to do it. Now if anything happens to spoil their plans they'll not have me to blame."

Nearly a year had been spent in stirring up the people of Bidwell to the point of becoming investors. Then things began to stir. The ground was broken for the erection of the factory. No one knew of the difficulties that had been encountered in attempting to perfect the machine and word was passed about that in actual tests in the fields it had proven itself entirely practical. The skeptical farmers who came into town on Saturdays were laughed at by the town enthusiasts. A field, that had been planted during one of the brief periods when the machine finding ideal soil conditions had worked perfectly, was left to grow. As when he operated the tiny model in the store window, Steve took no chances. He engaged Ed Hall to go at night and replace the plants that did not live. "It's fair enough," he explained to Ed. "A hundred things can cause the plants to die, but if they die it'll be blamed on the machine. What will become of the town if we don't believe in the thing we're going to manufacture here?"

The crowds of people, who in the evenings walked out along Turner's Pike to look at the field with its long rows of sturdy young cabbages, moved restlessly about and talked of the new days. From the field they went along the railroad tracks to the site of the factory. The brick walls began to mount up into the sky. Machinery began to arrive and was housed under temporary sheds against the time when it could be installed.

An advance horde of workmen came to town and new faces appeared on Main Street in the evening. The thing that was happening in Bidwell happened in towns all over the Middle West. Out through the coal and iron regions of Pennsylvania, into Ohio and Indiana, and on westward into the states bordering on the Mississippi River, industry crept. Gas and oil were discovered in Ohio and Indiana. Overnight, towns grew into cities. A madness took hold of the minds of the people. Villages like Lima and Findlay, Ohio, and like Muncie and Anderson in Indiana, became small cities within a few weeks. To some of these places, so anxious were the people to get to them and to invest their money, excursion trains were run. Town lots that a few weeks before the discovery of oil or gas could have been bought for a few dollars sold for thousands. Wealth seemed to be spurting out of the very earth. On farms in Indiana and Ohio giant gas wells blew the drilling machinery out of the ground, and the fuel so essential to modern industrial development rushed into the open. A wit, standing in the presence of one of the roaring gas wells exclaimed, "Papa, Earth has indigestion; he has gas on his stomach. His face will be covered with pimples."

Having, before the factories came, no market for the gas, the wells were lighted and at night great torches of flame lit the skies. Pipes were laid on the surface of the ground and by a day's work a laborer earned enough to heat his house at tropical heat through an entire winter. Farmers owning oil-producing land went to bed in the evening poor and owing money at the bank, and awoke in the morning rich. They moved into the towns and invested their money in the factories that sprang up everywhere. In one county in southern Michigan, over five hundred patents for woven wire farm fencing were taken out in one year, and almost every patent was a magnet about which a company for the manufacture of fence formed itself. A vast energy seemed to come out of the breast of earth and infect the people. Thousands of the most energetic men of the Middle States wore themselves out in forming companies, and when the companies failed, immediately formed others. In the fast-growing towns, men who were engaged in organizing companies representing a capital of millions lived in houses thrown hurriedly together by carpenters who, before the time of the great awakening, were engaged in building barns. It was a time of hideous architecture, a time when thought and learning paused. Without music, without poetry, without beauty in their lives or impulses, a whole people, full of the native energy and strength of lives lived in a new land, rushed pell-mell into a new age. A man in Ohio, who had been a dealer in horses, made a million dollars out of a patent churn he had bought for the price of a farm horse, took his wife to visit Europe and in Paris bought a painting for fifty thousand dollars. In another state of the Middle West, a man who sold patent medicine from door to door through the country began dealing in oil leases, became fabulously rich, bought himself three daily newspapers, and before he had reached the age of thirty-five succeeded in having himself elected Governor of his state. In the glorification of his energy his unfitness as a statesman was forgotten.

In the days before the coming of industry, before the time of the mad awakening, the towns of the Middle West were sleepy places devoted to the practice of the old trades, to agriculture and to merchandising. In the morning the men of the towns went forth to work in the fields or to the practice of the trade of carpentry, horseshoeing, wagon making, harness repairing, and the making of shoes and clothing. They read books and believed in a God born in the brains of men who came out of a civilization much like their own. On the farms and in the houses in the towns the men and women worked toward the same ends in life. They lived in small frame houses set on the plains like boxes, but very substantially built. The carpenter who built a farmer's house differentiated it from the barn by putting what he called scroll work up under the eaves and by building at the front a porch with carved posts. After one of the poor little houses had been lived in for a long time, after children had been born and men had died, after men and women had suffered and had moments of joy together in the tiny rooms under the low roofs, a subtle change took place. The houses became almost beautiful in their old humanness. Each of the houses began vaguely to shadow forth the personality of the people who lived within its walls.

In the farmhouses and in the houses on the side streets in the villages, life awoke at dawn. Back of each of the houses there was a barn for the horses and cows, and sheds for pigs and chickens. At daylight a chorus of neighs, squeals, and cries broke the silence. Boys and men came out of the houses. They stood in the open spaces before the barns and stretched their bodies like sleepy animals. The arms extended upward seemed to be supplicating the gods for fair days, and the fair days came. The men and boys went to a pump beside the house and washed their faces and hands in the cold water. In the kitchens there was the smell and sound of the cooking of food. The women also were astir. The men went into the barns to feed the animals and then hurried to the houses to be themselves fed. A continual grunting sound came from the sheds where pigs were eating corn, and over the houses a contented silence brooded.

After the morning meal men and animals went together to the fields and to the doing of their tasks, and in the houses the women mended clothes, put fruit in cans against the coming of winter and talked of woman's affairs. On the streets of the towns on fair days lawyers, doctors, the officials of the county courts, and the merchants walked about in their shirt sleeves. The house painter went along with his ladder on his shoulder. In the stillness there could be heard the hammers of the carpenters building a new house for the son of a merchant who had married the daughter of a blacksmith. A sense of quiet growth awoke in sleeping minds. It was the time for art and beauty to awake in the land.

Instead, the giant, Industry, awoke. Boys, who in the schools had read of Lincoln, walking for miles through the forest to borrow his first book, and of Garfield, the towpath lad who became president, began to read in the newspapers and magazines of men who by developing their faculty for getting and keeping money had become suddenly and overwhelmingly rich. Hired writers called these men great, and there was no maturity of mind in the people with which to combat the force of the statement, often repeated. Like children the people believed what they were told.

While the new factory was being built with the carefully saved dollars of the people, young men from Bidwell went out to work in other places. After oil and gas were discovered in neighboring states, they went to the fast-growing towns and came home telling wonder tales. In the boom towns men earned four, five and even six dollars a day. In secret and when none of the older people were about, they told of adventures on which they had gone in the new places; of how, attracted by the flood of money, women came from the cities; and the times they had been with these women. Young Harley Parsons, whose father was a shoemaker and who had learned the blacksmith trade, went to work in one of the new oil fields. He came home wearing a fancy silk vest and astonished his fellows by buying and smoking ten-cent cigars. His pockets were bulging with money. "I'm not going to stay long in this town, you can bet on that," he declared one evening as he stood, surrounded by a group of admirers before Fanny Twist's Millinery Shop on lower Main Street. "I have been with a Chinese woman, and an Italian, and with one from South America." He took a puff of his cigar and spat on the sidewalk. "I'm out to get what I can out of life," he declared. "I'm going back and I'm going to make a record. Before I get through I'm going to be with a woman of every nationality on earth, that's what I'm going to do."

Joseph Wainsworth the harness maker, who had been the first man in Bidwell to feel the touch of the heavy finger of industrialism, could not get over the effect of the conversation had with Butterworth, the farmer who had asked him to repair harnesses made by machines in a factory. He became a silent disgruntled man and muttered as he went about his work in the shop. When Will Sellinger his apprentice threw up his place and went to Cleveland he did not get another boy but for a time worked alone in the shop. He got the name of being disagreeable, and on winter afternoons the farmers no longer came into his place to loaf. Being a sensitive man, Joe felt like a pigmy, a tiny thing walking always in the presence of a giant that might at any moment and by a whim destroy him. All his life he had been somewhat off-hand with his customers. "If they don't like my work, let 'em go to the devil," he said to his apprentices. "I know my trade and I don't have to bow down to anyone here."

When Steve Hunter organized the Bidwell Plant-Setting Machine Company, the harness maker put his savings, twelve hundred dollars, into the stock of the company. One day, during the time when the factory was building, he heard that Steve had paid twelve hundred dollars for a new lathe that had just arrived by freight and had been set on the floor of the uncompleted building. The promoter had told a farmer that the lathe would do the work of a hundred men, and the farmer had come into Joe's shop and repeated the statement. It stuck in Joe's mind and he came to believe that the twelve hundred dollars he had invested in stock had been used for the purchase of the lathe. It was money he had earned in a long lifetime of effort and it had now bought a machine that would do the work of a hundred men. Already his money had increased by a hundredfold and he wondered why he could not be happy about the matter. On some days he was happy, and then his happiness was followed by an odd fit of depression. Suppose, after all, the plant-setting machine wouldn't work? What then could be done with the lathe, with the machine bought with his money?

One evening after dark and without saying anything to his wife, he went down along Turner's Pike to the old factory at Pickleville where Hugh with the half-wit Allie Mulberry, and the two mechanics from the city, were striving to correct the faults in the plant-setting machine. Joe wanted to look at the tall gaunt man from the West, and had some notion of trying to get into conversation with him and of asking his opinion of the possibilities of the success of the new machine. The man of the age of flesh and blood wanted to walk in the presence of the man who belonged to the new age of iron and steel. When he got to the factory it was dark and on an express truck in front of the Wheeling Station the two city workmen sat smoking their evening pipes. Joe walked past them to the station door and then returned along the platform and got again into Turner's Pike. He stumbled along the path beside the road and presently saw Hugh McVey coming toward him. It was one of the evenings when Hugh, overcome with loneliness, and puzzled that his new position in the town's life did not bring him any closer to people, had gone to town to walk through Main Street, half-hoping someone would break through his embarrassment and enter into conversation with him.

When the harness maker saw Hugh walking in the path, he crept into a fence corner, and crouching down, watched the man as Hugh had watched the French boys at work in the cabbage fields. Strange thoughts came into his head. He thought the extraordinarily tall figure before him in some way terrible. He became childishly angry and for a moment thought that if he had a stone in his hand he would throw it at the man, the workings of whose brain had so upset his own life. Then as the figure of Hugh went away along the path another mood came. "I have worked all my life for twelve hundred dollars, for money that will buy one machine that this man thinks nothing about," he muttered aloud. "Perhaps I'll get more money than I invested: Steve Hunter says maybe I will. If machines kill the harness-making trade what's the difference? I'll be all right. The thing to do is to get in with the new times, to wake up, that's the ticket. With me it's like with everyone else: nothing venture nothing gain."

Joe crawled out of the fence corner and went stealthily along the road behind Hugh. A fervor seized him and he thought he would like to creep close and touch with his finger the hem of Hugh's coat. Afraid to try anything so bold his mind took a new turn. He ran in the darkness along the road toward town and, when he had crossed the bridge and come to the New York Central tracks, turned west and went along the tracks until he came to the new factory. In the darkness the half-completed walls stuck up into the sky, and all about were piles of building materials. The night had been dark and cloudy, but now the moon began to push its way through the clouds. Joe crawled over a pile of bricks and through a window into the building. He felt his way along the walls until he came to a mass of iron covered by a rubber blanket. He was sure it must be the lathe his money had bought, the machine that was to do the work of a hundred men and that was to make him comfortably rich in his old age. No one had spoken of any other machine having been brought in on the factory floor. Joe knelt on the floor and put his hands about the heavy iron legs of the machine. "What a strong thing it is! It will not break easily," he thought. He had an impulse to do something he knew would be foolish, to kiss the iron legs of the machine or to say a prayer as he knelt before it. Instead he got to his feet and crawling out again through the window, went home. He felt renewed and full of new courage because of the experiences of the night, but when he got to his own house and stood at the door outside, he heard his neighbor, David Chapman, a wheelwright who worked in Charlie Collins' wagon shop, praying in his bedroom before an open window. Joe listened for a moment and, for some reason he couldn't understand, his new-found faith was destroyed by what he heard. David Chapman, a devout Methodist, was praying for Hugh McVey and for the success of his invention. Joe knew his neighbor had also invested his savings in the stock of the new company. He had thought that he alone was doubtful of success, but it was apparent that doubt had come also into the mind of the wheelwright. The pleading voice of the praying man, as it broke the stillness of the night, cut across and for the moment utterly destroyed his confidence. "O God, help the man Hugh McVey to remove every obstacle that stands in his way," David Chapman prayed. "Make the plant-setting machine a success. Bring light into the dark places. O Lord, help Hugh McVey, thy servant, to build successfully the plant-setting machine."

# Book Three

## CHAPTER VIII

When Clara Butterworth, the daughter of Tom Butterworth, was eighteen years old she graduated from the town high school. Until the summer of her seventeenth year, she was a tall, strong, hard-muscled girl, shy in the presence of strangers and bold with people she knew well. Her eyes were extraordinarily gentle.

The Butterworth house on Medina Road stood back of an apple orchard and there was a second orchard beside the house. The Medina Road ran south from Bidwell and climbed gradually upward toward a country of low hills, and from the side porch of the Butterworth house the view was magnificent. The house itself was a large brick affair with a cupola on top and was considered at that time the most pretentious place in the county.

Behind the house were several great barns for the horses and cattle. Most of Tom Butterworth's farm land lay north of Bidwell, and some of his fields were five miles from his home; but as he did not himself work the land it did not matter. The farms were rented to men who worked them on shares. Beside the business of farming Tom carried on other affairs. He owned two hundred acres of hillside land near his house and, with the exception of a few fields and a strip of forest land, it was devoted to the grazing of sheep and cattle. Milk and cream were delivered each morning to the householders of Bidwell by two wagons driven by his employees. A half-mile to the west of his residence there was a slaughterhouse on a side road and at the edge of a field where cattle were killed for the Bidwell market. Tom owned it and employed the men who did the killing. A creek that came down out of the hills through one of the fields past his house had been dammed, and south of the pond there was an icehouse. He also supplied the town with ice. In his orchards beneath the trees stood more than a hundred beehives and every year he shipped honey to Cleveland. The farmer himself was a man who appeared to do nothing, but his shrewd mind was always at work. In the summer throughout the long sleepy afternoons, he drove about over the county buying sheep and cattle, stopping to trade horses with some farmer, dickering for new pieces of land, everlastingly busy. He had one passion. He loved fast trotting horses, but would not humor himself by owning one. "It's a game that only gets you into trouble and debt," he said to his friend John Clark, the banker. "Let other men own the horses and go broke racing them. I'll go to the races. Every fall I can go to Cleveland to the grand circuit. If I go crazy about a horse I can bet ten dollars he'll win. If he doesn't I'm out ten dollars. If I owned him I would maybe be out hundreds for the expense of training and all that." The farmer was a tall man with a white beard, broad shoulders, and rather small slender white hands. He chewed tobacco, but in spite of the habit kept both himself and his white beard scrupulously clean. His wife had died while he was yet in the full vigor of life, but he had no eye for women. His mind, he once told one of his friends, was too much occupied with his own affairs and with thoughts of the fine horses he had seen to concern itself with any such nonsense.

For many years the farmer did not appear to pay much attention to his daughter Clara, who was his only child. Throughout her childhood she was under the care of one of his five sisters, all of whom except the one who lived with him and managed his household being comfortably married. His own wife had been a somewhat frail woman, but his daughter had inherited his own physical strength.

When Clara was seventeen, she and her father had a quarrel that eventually destroyed their relationship. The quarrel began late in July. It was a busy summer on the farms and more than a dozen men were employed about the barns, in the delivery of ice and milk to the town, and at the slaughtering pens a half-mile away. During that summer something happened to the girl. For hours she sat in her own room in the house reading books, or lay in a hammock in the orchard and looked up through the fluttering leaves of the apple trees at the summer sky. A light, strangely soft and enticing, sometimes came into her eyes. Her figure that had been boyish and strong began to change. As she went about the house she sometimes smiled at nothing. Her aunt hardly noticed what was happening to her, but her father, who all her life had seemed hardly to take account of her existence, was interested. In her presence he began to feel like a young man. As in the days of his courtship of her mother and before the possessive passion in him destroyed his ability to love, he began to feel vaguely that life about him was full of significance. Sometimes in the afternoon when he went for one of his long drives through the country he asked his daughter to accompany him, and although he had little to say a kind of gallantry crept into his attitude toward the awakening girl. While she was in the buggy with him, he did not chew tobacco, and after one or two attempts to indulge in the habit without having the smoke blow in her face, he gave up smoking his pipe during the drives.

Always before that summer Clara had spent the months when there was no school in the company of the farm hands. She rode on wagons, visited the barns, and when she grew weary of the company of older people, went into town to spend an afternoon with one of her friends among the town girls.

In the summer of her seventeenth year she did none of these things. At the table she ate in silence. The Butterworth household was at that time run on the old-fashioned American plan, and the farm hands, the men who drove the ice and milk wagons and even the men who killed and dressed cattle and sheep, ate at the same table with Tom Butterworth, his sister, who was the housekeeper, and his daughter. Three hired girls were employed in the house and after all had been served they also came and took their places at table. The older men among the farmer's employees, many of whom had known her from childhood, had got into the habit of teasing the daughter of the house. They made comments concerning town boys, young fellows who clerked in stores or who were apprenticed to some tradesman and one of whom had perhaps brought the girl home at night from a school party or from one of the affairs called "socials" that were held at the town churches. After they had eaten in the peculiar silent intent way common to hungry laborers, the farm hands leaned back in their chairs and winked at each other. Two of them began an elaborate conversation touching on some incident in the girl's life. One of the older men, who had been on the farm for many years and who had a reputation among the others of being something of a wit, chuckled softly. He began to talk, addressing no one in particular. The man's name was Jim Priest, and although the Civil War had come upon the country when he was past forty, he had been a soldier. In Bidwell he was looked upon as something of a rascal, but his employer was very fond of him. The two men often talked together for hours concerning the merits of well-known trotting horses. In the war Jim had been what was called a bounty man, and it was whispered about town that he had also been a deserter and a bounty jumper. He did not go to town with the other men on Saturday afternoons, and had never attempted to get into the Bidwell chapter of the G. A. R. On Saturdays when the other farm hands washed, shaved and dressed themselves in their Sunday clothes preparatory to the weekly flight to town, he called one of them into the barn, slipped a quarter into his hand, and said, "Bring me a half pint and don't you forget it." On Sunday afternoons he crawled into the hayloft of one of the barns, drank his weekly portion of whiskey, got drunk, and sometimes did not appear again until time to go to work on Monday morning. In the fall Jim took his savings and went to spend a week at the grand circuit trotting meeting at Cleveland, where he bought a costly present for his employer's daughter and then bet the rest of his money on the races. When he was lucky he stayed on in Cleveland, drinking and carousing until his winnings were gone.

It was Jim Priest who always led the attacks of teasing at the table, and in the summer of her seventeenth year, when she was no longer in the mood for such horse-play, it was Jim who brought the practice to an end. At the table Jim leaned back in his chair, stroked his red bristly beard, now rapidly graying, looked out of a window over Clara's head, and told a tale concerning an attempt at suicide on the part of a young man in love with Clara. He said the young man, a clerk in a Bidwell store, had taken a pair of trousers from a shelf, tied one leg about his neck and the other to a bracket in the wall. Then he jumped off a counter and had only been saved from death because a town girl, passing the store, had seen him and had rushed in and cut him down. "Now what do you think of that?" he cried. "He was in love with our Clara, I tell you."

After the telling of the tale, Clara got up from the table and ran out of the room. The farm hands joined by her father laughed heartily. Her aunt shook her finger at Jim Priest, the hero of the occasion. "Why don't you let her alone?" she asked. "She'll never get married if she stays here where you make fun of every young man who pays her any attention." At the door Clara stopped and, turning, put out her tongue at Jim Priest. Another roar of laughter arose. Chairs were scraped along the floor and the men filed out of the house to go back to the work in the barns and about the farm.

In the summer when the change came over her Clara sat at the table and did not hear the tales told by Jim Priest. She thought the farm hands who ate so greedily were vulgar, a notion she had never had before, and wished she did not have to eat with them. One afternoon as she lay in the hammock in the orchard, she heard several of the men in a nearby barn discussing the change that had come over her. Jim Priest was explaining what had happened. "Our fun's over with Clara," he said. "Now we'll have to treat her in a new way. She's no longer a kid. We'll have to let her alone or pretty soon she won't speak to any of us. It's a thing that happens when a girl begins to think about being a woman. The sap has begun to run up the tree."

The puzzled girl lay in the hammock and looked up at the sky. She thought about Jim Priest's words and tried to understand what he meant. Sadness crept over her and tears came into her eyes. Although she did not know what the old man meant by the words about the sap and the tree, she did, in a detached subconscious way, understand something of the import of the words, and she was grateful for the thoughtfulness that had led to his telling the others to stop trying to tease her at the table. The half worn-out old farm hand, with the bristly beard and the strong old body, became a figure full of significance to her mind. She remembered with gratitude that, in spite of all of his teasing, Jim Priest had never said anything that had in any way hurt her. In the new mood that had come upon her that meant much. A greater hunger for understanding, love, and friendliness took possession of her. She did not think of turning to her father or to her aunt, with whom she had never talked of anything intimate or close to herself, but turned instead to the crude old man. A hundred minor points in the character of Jim Priest she had never thought of before came sharply into her mind. In the barns he had never mistreated the animals as the other farm hands sometimes did. When on Sunday afternoons he was drunk and went staggering through the barns, he did not strike the horses or swear at them.

She wondered if it would be possible for her to talk to Jim Priest, to ask him questions about life and people and what he meant by his words regarding the sap and the tree. The farm hand was old and unmarried. She wondered if in his youth he had ever loved a woman. She decided he had. His words about the sap were, she was sure, in some way connected with the idea of love. How strong his hands were. They were gnarled and rough, but there was something beautifully powerful about them. She half-wished the old man had been her father. In his youth, in the darkness at night or when he was alone with a girl, perhaps in a quiet wood in the late afternoon when the sun was going down, he had put his hands on her shoulders. He had drawn the girl to him. He had kissed her.

Clara jumped quickly out of the hammock and walked about under the trees in the orchard. Her thoughts of Jim Priest's youth startled her. It was as though she had walked suddenly into a room where a man and woman were making love. Her cheeks burned and her hands trembled. As she walked slowly through the clumps of grass and weeds that grew between the trees where the sunlight struggled through, bees coming home to the hives heavily laden with honey flew in droves about her head. There was something heady and purposeful about the song of labor that arose out of the beehives. It got into her blood and her step quickened. The words of Jim Priest that kept running through her mind seemed a part of the same song the bees were singing. "The sap has begun to run up the tree," she repeated aloud. How significant and strange the words seemed! They were the kind of words a lover might use in speaking to his beloved. She had read many novels, but they contained no such words. It was better so. It was better to hear them from human lips. Again she thought of Jim Priest's youth and boldly wished he were still young. She told herself that she would like to see him young and married to a beautiful young woman. She stopped by a fence that looked out upon a hillside meadow. The sun seemed extraordinarily bright, the grass in the meadow greener than she had ever seen it before. Two birds in a tree nearby made love to each other. The female flew madly about and was pursued by the male bird. In his eagerness he was so intent that he flew directly before the girl's face, his wing nearly touching her cheek. She went back through the orchard to the barns and through one of them to the open door of a long shed that was used for housing wagons and buggies, her mind occupied with the idea of finding Jim Priest, of standing perhaps near him. He was not about, but in the open space before the shed, John May, a young man of twenty-two who had just come to work on the farm, was oiling the wheels of a wagon. His back was turned and as he handled the heavy wagon wheels the muscles could be seen playing beneath his thin cotton shirt. "It is so Jim Priest must have looked in his youth," the girl thought.

The farm girl wanted to approach the young man, to speak to him, to ask him questions concerning many strange things in life she did not understand. She knew that under no circumstances would she be able to do such a thing, that it was but a meaningless dream that had come into her head, but the dream was sweet. She did not, however, want to talk to John May. At the moment she was in a girlish period of being disgusted at what she thought of as the vulgarity of the men who worked on the place. At the table they ate noisily and greedily like hungry animals. She wanted youth that was like her own youth, crude and uncertain perhaps, but reaching eagerly out into the unknown. She wanted to draw very near to something young, strong, gentle, insistent, beautiful. When the farm hand looked up and saw her standing and looking intently at him, she was embarrassed. For a moment the two young animals, so unlike each other, stood staring at each other and then, to relieve her embarrassment, Clara began to play a game. Among the men employed on the farm she had always passed for something of a tomboy. In the hay-fields and in the barns she had wrestled and fought playfully with both the old and the young men. To them she had always been a privileged person. They liked her and she was the boss's daughter. One did not get rough with her or say or do rough things. A basket of corn stood just within the door of the shed, and running to it Clara took an ear of the yellow corn and threw it at the farm hand. It struck a post of the barn just above his head. Laughing shrilly Clara ran into the shed among the wagons, and the farm hand pursued her.

John May was a very determined man. He was the son of a laborer in Bidwell and for two or three years had been employed about the stable of a doctor. Something had happened between him and the doctor's wife and he had left the place because he had a notion that the doctor was becoming suspicious. The experience had taught him the value of boldness in dealing with women. Ever since he had come to work on the Butterworth farm, he had been having thoughts regarding the girl who had now, he imagined, given him a direct challenge. He was a little amazed by her boldness but did not stop to ask himself questions. She had openly invited him to pursue her. That was enough. His accustomed awkwardness and clumsiness went away and he leaped lightly over the extended tongues of wagons and buggies. He caught Clara in a dark corner of the shed.

Without a word he took her tightly into his arms and kissed her, first upon the neck and then on the mouth. She lay trembling and weak in his arms and he took hold of the collar of her dress and tore it open. Her brown neck and one of her hard, round breasts were exposed. Clara's eyes grew big with fright. Strength came back into her body. With her sharp hard little fist she struck John May in the face; and when he stepped back she ran quickly out of the shed. John May did not understand. He thought she had sought him out once and would return. "She's a little green. I was too fast. I scared her. Next time I'll go a little easy," he thought.

Clara ran through the barn and then walked slowly to the house and went upstairs to her own room. A farm dog followed her up the stairs and stood at her door wagging his tail. She shut the door in his face. For the moment everything that lived and breathed seemed to her gross and ugly. Her cheeks were pale and she pulled shut the blinds to the window and sat down on the bed, overcome with the strange new fear of life. She did not want even the sunlight to come into her presence. John May had followed her through the barn and now stood in the barnyard staring at the house. She could see him through the cracks of the blinds and wished it were possible to kill him with a gesture of her hand.

The farm hand, full of male confidence, waited for her to come to the window and look down at him. He wondered if there were anyone else in the house. Perhaps she would beckon to him. Something of the kind had happened between him and the doctor's wife and it had turned out that way. When after five or ten minutes he did not see her, he went back to the work of oiling the wagon wheels. "It's going to be a slower thing. She's shy, a green girl,'" he told himself.

One evening a week later Clara sat on the side porch

of the house with her father when John May came into the barnyard. It was a Wednesday evening and the farm hands were not in the habit of going into town until Saturday, but he was dressed in his Sunday clothes and had shaved and oiled his hair. On the occasion of a wedding or a funeral the laborers put oil in their hair. It was indicative of something very important about to happen. Clara looked at him, and in spite of the feeling of repugnance that swept over her, her eyes glistened. Ever since the affair in the barn she had managed to avoid meeting him but she was not afraid. He had in fact taught her something. There was a power within her with which she could conquer men. The touch of her father's shrewdness, that was a part of her nature, had come to her rescue. She wanted to laugh at the silly pretensions of the man, to make a fool of him. Her cheeks flushed with pride in her mastery of the situation.

John May walked almost to the house and then turned along the path that led to the road. He made a gesture with his hand and by chance Tom Butterworth, who had been looking off across the open country toward Bidwell, turned and saw both the movement and the leering confident smile on the farm hand's face. He arose and followed John May into the road, astonishment and anger fighting for possession of him. The two men stood talking for three minutes in the road before the house and then returned. The farm hand went to the barn and then came back along the path to the road carrying under his arm a grain bag containing his work clothes. He did not look up as he went past. The farmer returned to the porch.

The misunderstanding that was to wreck the tender relationship that had begun to grow up between father and daughter began on that evening. Tom Butterworth was furious. He muttered and clinched his fists. Clara's heart beat heavily. For some reason she felt guilty, as though she had been caught in an intrigue with the man. For a long time her father remained silent and then he, like the farm hand, made a furious and brutal attack on her. "Where have you been with that fellow? What you been up to?" he asked harshly.

For a time Clara did not answer her father's question. She wanted to scream, to strike him in the face with her fist as she had struck the man in the shed. Then her mind struggled to take hold of the new situation. The fact that her father had accused her of seeking the thing that had happened made her hate John May less heartily. She had someone else to hate.

Clara did not think the matter out clearly on that first evening but, after denying that she had ever been anywhere with John May, burst into tears and ran into the house. In the darkness of her own room she began to think of her father's words. For some reason she could not understand, the attack made on her spirit seemed more terrible and unforgivable than the attack upon her body made by the farm hand in the shed. She began to understand vaguely that the young man had been confused by her presence on that warm sunshiny afternoon as she had been confused by the words uttered by Jim Priest, by the song of the bees in the orchard, by the love-making of the birds, and by her own uncertain thoughts. He had been confused and he was stupid and young. There had been an excuse for his confusion. It was understandable and could be dealt with. She had now no doubt of her own ability to deal with John May. As for her father—it was all right for him to be suspicious regarding the farm hand, but why had he been suspicious of her?

The perplexed girl sat down in the darkness on the

edge of the bed, and a hard look came into her eyes. After a time her father came up the stairs and knocked at her door. He did not come in but stood in the hall-way outside and talked. She remained calm while the conversation lasted, and that confused the man who had expected to find her in tears. That she was not seemed to him an evidence of guilt.

Tom Butterworth, in many ways a shrewd, observ-ing man, never understood the quality of his own daughter. He was an intensely possessive man and once, when he was newly married, there had been a suspicion in his mind that there was something between his wife and a young man who had worked on the farm where he then lived. The suspicion was unfounded, but he discharged the man and one evening, when his wife had gone into town to do some shopping and did not return at the accustomed time, he followed, and when he saw her on the street stepped into a store to avoid a meeting. She was in trouble. Her horse had become suddenly lame and she had to walk home. Without letting her see him the husband followed along the road. It was dark and she heard the footsteps in the road behind her and becoming frightened ran the last half-mile to her own house. He waited until she had entered and then fol-lowed her in, pretending he had just come from the barns. When he heard her story of the accident to the horse and of her fright in the road he was ashamed; but as the horse, that had been left in a livery stable, seemed all right when he went for it the next day he became suspicious again.

As he stood outside the door of his daughter's room, the farmer felt as he had felt that evening long before when he followed his wife along the road. When on the porch downstairs he had looked up suddenly and had seen the gesture made by the farm hand, he had also looked quickly at his daughter. She looked confused and, he thought, guilty. "Well, it is the same thing over again," he thought bitterly, "like mother, like daughter —they are both of the same stripe." Getting quickly out of his chair he had followed the young man into the road and had discharged him. "Go, tonight. I don't want to see you on the place again," he said. In the darkness before the girl's room he thought of many bitter things he wanted to say. He forgot she was a girl and talked to her as he might have talked to a mature, sophisticated, and guilty woman. "Come," he said, "I want to know the truth. If you have been with that farm hand you are starting young. Has anything happened between you?"

Clara walked to the door and confronted her father. The hatred of him, born in that hour and that never left her, gave her strength. She did not know what he was talking about, but had a keen sense of the fact that he, like the stupid, young man in the shed, was trying to violate something very precious in her nature. "I don't know what you are talking about," she said calmly, "but I know this. I am no longer a child. Within the last week I've become a woman. If you don't want me in your house, if you don't like me any more, say so and I'll go away."

The two people stood in the darkness and tried to look at each other. Clara was amazed by her own strength and by the words that had come to her. The words had clarified something. She felt that if her father would but take her into his arms or say some kindly understanding word, all could be forgotten. Life could be started over again. In the future she would understand much that she had not understood. She and her father could draw close to each other. Tears came into her eyes and a sob trembled in her throat. As her father, however, did not answer her words and turned to go silently away, she shut the door with a loud bang and afterward lay awake all night, white and furious with anger and disappointment.

Clara left home to become a college student that fall, but before she left had another passage at arms with her father. In August a young man who was to teach in the town schools came to Bidwell, and she met him at a supper given in the basement of the church. He walked home with her and came on the following Sunday afternoon to call. She introduced the young man, a slender fellow with black hair, brown eyes, and a serious face, to her father who answered by nodding his head and walking away. She and the young man walked along a country road and went into a wood. He was five years older than herself and had been to college, but she felt much the older and wiser. The thing that happens to so many women had happened to her. She felt older and wiser than all the men she had ever seen. She had decided, as most women finally decide, that there are two kinds of men in the world, those who are kindly, gentle, well-intentioned children, and those who, while they remain children, are obsessed with stupid, male vanity and imagine themselves born to be masters of life. Clara's thoughts on the matter were not very clear. She was young and her thoughts were indefinite. She had, however, been shocked into an acceptance of life and she was made of the kind of stuff that survives the blows life gives.

In the wood with the young school teacher, Clara began an experiment. Evening came on and it grew dark. She knew her father would be furious that she did not come home but she did not care. She led the school teacher to talk of love and the relationships of men and women. She pretended an innocence that was not hers.

School girls know many things that they do not apply to themselves until something happens to them such as had happened to Clara. The farmer's daughter became conscious. She knew a thousand things she had not known a month before and began to take her revenge upon men for their betrayal of her. In the darkness as they walked home together, she tempted the young man into kissing her, and later lay in his arms for two hours, entirely sure of herself, striving to find out, without risk to herself, the things she wanted to know about life.

That night she again quarreled with her father. He tried to scold her for remaining out late with a man, and she shut the door in his face. On another evening she walked boldly out of the house with the school teacher. The two walked along a road to where a bridge went over a small stream. John May, who was still determined that the farmer's daughter was in love with him, had on that evening followed the school teacher to the Butterworth house and had been waiting outside intending to frighten his rival with his fists. On the bridge something happened that drove the school teacher away. John May came up to the two people and began to make threats. The bridge had just been repaired and a pile of small, sharp-edged stones lay close at hand. Clara picked one of them up and handed it to the school teacher. "Hit him," she said. "Don't be afraid. He's only a coward. Hit him on the head with the stone."

The three people stood in silence waiting for something to happen. John May was disconcerted by Clara's words. He had thought she wanted him to pursue her. He stepped toward the school teacher, who dropped the stone that had been put into his hand and ran away. Clara went back along the road toward her own house followed by the muttering farm hand who, after her speech at the bridge, did not dare approach. "Maybe she was making a bluff. Maybe she didn't want that young fellow to get on to what is between us," he muttered, as he stumbled along in the darkness.

In the house Clara sat for a half-hour at a table in the lighted living room beside her father, pretending to read a book. She half-hoped he would say something that would permit her to attack him. When nothing happened she went upstairs and to bed, only again to spend the night awake and white with anger at the thought of the cruel and unexplainable things life seemed trying to do to her.

In September Clara left the farm to attend the State University at Columbus. She was sent there because Tom Butterworth had a sister who was married to a manufacturer of plows and lived at the State Capital. After the incident with the farm hand and the misunderstanding that had sprung up between himself and his daughter, he was uncomfortable with her in the house and was glad to have her away. He did not want to frighten his sister by telling of what had happened, and when he wrote, tried to be diplomatic. "Clara has been too much among the rough men who work on my farms and had become a little rough," he wrote. "Take her in hand. I want her to become more of a lady. Get her acquainted with the right kind of people." In secret he hoped she would meet and marry some young man while she was away. Two of his sisters had gone away to school and it had turned out that way.

During the month before his daughter left home the farmer tried to be somewhat more human and gentle in his attitude toward her, but did not succeed in dispelling the dislike of himself that had taken deep root in her nature. At table he made jokes at which the farm hands laughed boisterously. Then he looked at his daughter who did not appear to have been listening. Clara ate quickly and hurried out of the room. She did not go to visit her girl friends in town and the young school teacher came no more to see her. During the long summer afternoons she walked in the orchard among the beehives or climbed over fences and went into a wood, where she sat for hours on a fallen log staring at the trees and the sky. Tom Butterworth also hurried out of his house. He pretended to be busy and every day drove far and wide over the country. Sometimes he thought he had been brutal and crude in his treatment of his daughter, and decided he would speak to her regarding the matter and ask her to forgive him. Then his suspicion returned. He struck the horse with the whip and drove furiously along the lonely roads. "Well, there's something wrong," he muttered aloud. "Men don't just look at women and approach them boldly, as that young fellow did with Clara. He did it before my very eyes. He's been given some encouragement." An old suspicion awoke in him. "There was something wrong with her mother, and there's something wrong with her. I'll be glad when the time comes for her to marry and settle down, so I can get her off my hands," he thought bitterly.

On the evening when Clara left the farm to go to the train that was to take her away, her father said he had a headache, a thing he had never been known to complain of before, and told Jim Priest to drive her to the station. Jim took the girl to the station, saw to the checking of her baggage, and waited about until her train came in. Then he boldly kissed her on the cheek. "Good-by, little girl," he said gruffly. Clara was so grateful she could not reply. On the train she spent an hour weeping softly. The rough gentleness of the old farm hand had done much to take the growing bitterness out of her heart. She felt that she was ready to begin life anew, and wished she had not left the farm without coming to a better understanding with her father.

## CHAPTER IX

The Woodburns of Columbus were wealthy by the standards of their day. They lived in a large house and kept two carriages and four servants, but had no children. Henderson Woodburn was small of stature, wore a gray beard, and was neat and precise about his person. He was treasurer of the plow manufacturing company and was also treasurer of the church he and his wife attended. In his youth he had been called "Hen" Woodburn and had been bullied by larger boys, and when he grew to be a man and after his persistent shrewdness and patience had carried him into a position of some power in the business life of his native city he in turn became something of a bully to the men beneath him. He thought his wife Priscilla had come from a better family than his own and was a little afraid of her. When they did not agree on any subject, she expressed her opinion gently but firmly, while he blustered for a time and then gave in. After a misunderstanding his wife put her arms about his neck and kissed the bald spot on the top of his head. Then the subject was forgotten.

Life in the Woodburn house was lived without words. After the stir and bustle of the farm, the silence of the house for a long time frightened Clara. Even when she was alone in her own room she walked about on tiptoe. Henderson Woodburn was absorbed in his work, and when he came home in the evening, ate his dinner in silence and then worked again. He brought home account books and papers from the office and spread them out on a table in the living room. His wife Priscilla sat in a large chair under a lamp and knitted children's stockings. They were, she told Clara, for the children of the poor. As a matter of fact the stockings never left her house. In a large trunk in her room upstairs lay hundreds of pairs knitted during the twenty-five years of her family life.

Clara was not very happy in the Woodburn household, but on the other hand, was not very unhappy. She attended to her studies at the University passably well and in the late afternoons took a walk with a girl classmate, attended a matinée at the theater, or read a book. In the evening she sat with her aunt and uncle until she could no longer bear the silence, and then went to her own room, where she studied until it was time to go to bed. Now and then she went with the two older people to a social affair at the church, of which Henderson Woodburn was treasurer, or accompanied them to dinners at the homes of other well-to-do and respectable business men. On several occasions young men, sons of the people with whom the Woodburns dined, or students at the University, came in the evening to call. On such an occasion Clara and the young man sat in the parlor of the house and talked. After a time they grew silent and embarrassed in each other's presence. From the next room Clara could hear the rustling of the papers containing the columns of figures over which her uncle was at work. Her aunt's knitting needles clicked loudly. The young man told a tale of some football game, or if he had already gone out into the world, talked of his experiences as a traveler selling the wares manufactured or merchandized by his father. Such visits all began at the same hour, eight o'clock, and the young man left the house promptly at ten. Clara grew to feel that she was being merchandized and that they had come to look at the goods. One evening one of the men, a fellow with laughing blue eyes and kinky yellow hair, unconsciously disturbed her profoundly. All the evening he talked just as the others had talked and got out of his chair to go away at the prescribed hour. Clara walked with him to the door. She put out her hand, which he shook cordially. Then he looked at her and his eyes twinkled. "I've had a good time," he said. Clara had a sudden and almost overpowering desire to embrace him. She wanted to disturb his assurance, to startle him by kissing him on the lips or holding him tightly in her arms. Shutting the door quickly, she stood with her hand on the door-knob, her whole body trembling. The trivial by-products of her age's industrial madness went on in the next room. The sheets of paper rustled and the knitting needles clicked. Clara thought she would like to call the young man back into the house, lead him to the room where the meaningless industry went endlessly on and there do something that would shock them and him as they had never been shocked before. She ran quickly upstairs. "What is getting to be the matter with me?" she asked herself anxiously.

One evening in the month of May, during her third year at the University, Clara sat on the bank of a tiny stream by a grove of trees, far out on the edge of a suburban village north of Columbus. Beside her sat a young man named Frank Metcalf whom she had known for a year and who had once been a student in the same classes with herself. He was the son of the president of the plow manufacturing company of which her uncle was treasurer. As they sat together by the stream the afternoon light began to fade and darkness came on. Before them across an open field stood a factory, and Clara remembered that the whistle had long since blown and the men from the factory had gone home. She grew restless and sprang to her feet. Young Metcalf who had been talking very earnestly arose and stood beside her. "I can't marry for two years, but we can be engaged and that will be all the same thing as far as the right and wrong of what I want and need is concerned. It isn't my fault I can't ask you to marry me now," he declared. "In two years now, I'll inherit eleven thousand dollars. My aunt left it to me and the old fool went and fixed it so I don't get it if I marry before I'm twenty-four. I want that money. I've got to have it, but I got to have you too."

Clara looked away into the evening darkness and waited for him to finish his speech. All afternoon he had been making practically the same speech, over and over. "Well, I can't help it, I'm a man," he said doggedly. "I can't help it, I want you. I can't help it, my aunt was an old fool." He began to explain the necessity of remaining unmarried in order that he could receive the eleven thousand dollars. "If I don't get that money I'll be just the same as I am now," he declared. "I won't be any good." He grew angry and, thrusting his hands into his pockets, stared also across the field into the darkness. "Nothing keeps me satisfied," he said. "I hate being in my father's business and I hate going to school. In only two years I'll get the money. Father can't keep it from me. I'll take it and light out. I don't know just what I'll do. I'm going maybe to Europe, that's what I'm going to do. Father wants me to stay here and work in his office. To hell with that. I want to travel. I'll be a soldier or something. Anyway I'll get out of here and go somewhere and do something exciting, something alive. You can go with me. We'll cut out together. Haven't you got the nerve? Why don't you be my woman?"

Young Metcalf took hold of Clara's shoulder and tried to take her into his arms. For a moment they struggled and then, in disgust, he stepped away from her and again began to scold.

Clara walked away across two or three vacant lots and got into a street of workingmen's houses, the man following at her heels. Night had come and the people in the street facing the factory had already disposed of the evening meal. Children and dogs played in the road and a strong smell of food hung in the air. To the west across the fields, a passenger train ran past going toward the city. Its light made wavering yellow patches against the bluish black sky. Clara wondered why she had come to the out-of-the-way place with Frank Metcalf. She did not like him, but there was a restlessness in him that was like the restless thing in herself. He did not want stupidly to accept life, and that fact made him brother to herself. Although he was but twenty-two years old, he had already achieved an evil reputation. A servant in his father's house had given birth to a child by him, and it had cost a good deal of money to get her to take the child and go away without making an open scandal. During the year before he had been expelled from the University for throwing another young man down a flight of stairs, and it was whispered about among the girl students that he often got violently drunk. For a year he had been trying to ingratiate himself with Clara, had written her letters, sent flowers to her house, and when he met her on the street had stopped to urge that she accept his friendship. On the day in May she had met him on the street and he had begged that she give him one chance to talk things out with her. They had met at a street crossing where cars went past into the suburban villages that lay about the city. "Come on," he had urged, "let's take a streetcar ride, let's get out of the crowds, I want to talk to you." He had taken hold of her arm and fairly dragged her to a car. "Come and hear what I have to say," he had urged, "then if you don't want to have anything to do with me, all right. You can say so and I'll let you alone."

After she had accompanied him to the suburb of workingmen's houses, in the vicinity of which they had spent the afternoon in the fields, Clara had found he had nothing to urge upon her except the needs of his body. Still she felt there was something he wanted to say that had not been said. He was restless and dissatisfied with his life, and at bottom she felt that way about her own life. During the last three years she had often wondered why she had come to the school and what she was to gain by learning things out of books. The days and months went past and she knew certain rather uninteresting facts she had not known before. How the facts were to help her to live, she couldn't make out. They had nothing to do with such problems as her attitude toward men like John May the farm hand, the school teacher who had taught her something by holding her in his arms and kissing her, and the dark sullen young man who now walked beside her and talked of the needs of his body. It seemed to Clara that every additional year spent at the University but served to emphasize its inadequacy. It was so also with the books she read and the thoughts and actions of the older people about her. Her aunt and uncle did not talk much, but seemed to take it for granted she wanted to live such another life as they were living. She thought with horror of the probability of marrying a maker of plows or of some other dull necessity of life and then spending her days in the making of stockings for babies that did not come, or in some other equally futile manifestation of her dissatisfaction. She realized with a shudder that men like her uncle, who spent their lives in adding up rows of figures or doing over and over some tremendously trivial thing, had no conception of any outlook for their women beyond living in a house, serving them physically, wearing perhaps good enough clothes to help them make a show of prosperity and success, and drifting finally into a stupid acceptance of dullness—an acceptance that both she and the passionate, twisted man beside her were fighting against.

In a class in the University Clara had met, during that her third year there, a woman named Kate Chanceller, who had come to Columbus with her brother from a town in Missouri, and it was this woman who had given her thoughts form, who had indeed started her thinking of the inadequacy of her life. The brother, a studious, quiet man, worked as a chemist in a manufacturing plant somewhere at the edge of town. He was a musician and wanted to become a composer. One evening during the winter his sister Kate had brought Clara to the apartment where the two lived, and the three had become friends. Clara had learned something there that she did not yet understand and never did get clearly into her consciousness. The truth was that the brother was like a woman and Kate Chanceller, who wore skirts and had the body of a woman, was in her nature a man. Kate and Clara spent many evenings together later and talked of many things not usually touched on by girl students. Kate was a bold, vigorous thinker and was striving to grope her way through her own problem in life and many times, as they walked along the street or sat together in the evening, she forgot her companion and talked of herself and the difficulties of her position in life. "It's absurd the way things are arranged," she said. "Because my body is made in a certain way I'm supposed to accept certain rules for living. The rules were not made for me. Men manufactured them as they manufacture can-openers, on the wholesale plan." She looked at Clara and laughed. "Try to imagine me in a little lace cap, such as your aunt wears about the house, and spending my days knitting baby stockings," she said.

The two women had spent hours talking of their lives and in speculating on the differences in their natures. The experience had been tremendously educational for Clara. As Kate was a socialist and Columbus was rapidly becoming an industrial city, she talked of the meaning of capital and labor and the effect of changing conditions on the lives of men and women. To Kate, Clara could talk as to a man, but the antagonism that so often exists between men and women did not come into and spoil their companionship. In the evening when Clara went to Kate's house her aunt sent a carriage to bring her home at nine. Kate rode home with her. They got to the Woodburn house and went in. Kate was bold and free with the Woodburns, as with her brother and Clara. "Come," she said laughing, "put away your figures and your knitting. Let's talk." She sat in a large chair with her legs crossed and talked with Henderson Woodburn of the affairs of the plow company. The two got into a discussion of the relative merits of the free trade and protection ideas. Then the two older people went to bed and Kate talked to Clara. "Your uncle is an old duffer," she said. "He knows nothing about the meaning of what he's doing in life." When she started home afoot across the city, Clara was alarmed for her safety. "You must get a cab or let me wake up uncle's man; something may happen," she said. Kate laughed and went off, striding along the street like a man. Sometimes she thrust her hands into her skirt pockets, that were like the trouser pockets of a man, and it was difficult for Clara to remember that she was a woman. In Kate's presence she became bolder than she had ever been with anyone. One evening she told the story of the thing that had happened to her that afternoon long before on the farm, the afternoon when, her mind having been inflamed by the words of Jim Priest regarding the sap that goes up the tree and by the warm sensuous beauty of the day, she had wanted so keenly to draw close to someone. She explained to Kate how she had been so brutally jarred out of the feeling in herself that she felt was at bottom all right. "It was like a blow in the face at the hand of God," she said.

Kate Chanceller was excited as Clara told the tale and listened with a fiery light burning in her eyes. Something in her manner encouraged Clara to tell also of her experiments with the school teacher and for the first time she got a sense of justice toward men by talking to the woman who was half a man. "I know that wasn't square," she said. "I know now, when I talk to you, but I didn't know then. With the school teacher I was as unfair as John May and my father were with me. Why do men and women have to fight each other? Why does the battle between them have to go on?"

Kate walked up and down before Clara and swore like a man. "Oh, hell," she exclaimed, "men are such fools and I suppose women are as bad. They are both too much one thing. I fall in between. I've got my problem too, but I'm not going to talk about it. I know what I'm going to do. I'm going to find some kind of work and do it." She began to talk of the stupidity of men in their approach to women. "Men hate such women as myself," she said. "They can't use us, they think. What fools!

They should watch and study us. Many of us spend our lives loving other women, but we have skill. Being part women, we know how to approach women. We are not blundering and crude. Men want a certain thing from you. It is delicate and easy to kill. Love is the most sensitive thing in the world. It's like an orchid. Men try to pluck orchids with ice tongs, the fools."

Walking to where Clara stood by a table, and taking her by the shoulder, the excited woman stood for a long time looking at her. Then she picked up her hat, put it on her head, and with a flourish of her hand started for the door. "You can depend on my friendship," she said. "I'll do nothing to confuse you. You'll be in luck if you can get that kind of love or friendship from a man."

Clara kept thinking of the words of Kate Chanceller on the evening when she walked through the streets of the suburban village with Frank Metcalf, and later as the two sat on the car that took them back to the city. With the exception of another student named Phillip Grimes, who had come to see her a dozen times during her second year in the University, young Metcalf was the only one of perhaps a dozen men she had met since leaving the farm who had been attracted to her. Phillip Grimes was a slender young fellow with blue eyes, yellow hair and a not very vigorous mustache. He was from a small town in the northern end of the State, where his father published a weekly newspaper. When he came to see Clara he sat on the edge of his chair and talked rapidly. Some person he had seen in the street had interested him. "I saw an old woman on the car," he began. "She had a basket on her arm. It was filled with groceries. She sat beside me and talked aloud to herself." Clara's visitor repeated the words of the old woman on the car. He speculated about her, wondered what her life was like. When he had talked of the old woman for ten or fifteen minutes, he dropped the subject and began telling of another experience, this time with a man who sold fruit at a street crossing. It was impossible to be personal with Phillip Grimes. Nothing but his eyes were personal. Sometimes he looked at Clara in a way that made her feel that her clothes were being stripped from her body, and that she was being made to stand naked in the room before her visitor. The experience, when it came, was not entirely a physical one. It was only in part that. When the thing happened Clara saw her whole life being stripped bare. "Don't look at me like that," she once said somewhat sharply, when his eyes had made her so uncomfortable she could no longer remain silent. Her remark had frightened Phillip Grimes away. He got up at once, blushed, stammered something about having another engagement, and hurried away.

In the streetcar, homeward bound beside Frank Metcalf, Clara thought of Phillip Grimes and wondered whether or not he would have stood the test of Kate Chanceller's speech regarding love and friendship. He had confused her, but that was perhaps her own fault. He had not insisted on himself at all. Frank Metcalf had done nothing else. "One should be able," she thought, "to find somewhere a man who respects himself and his own desires but can understand also the desires and fears of a woman." The streetcar went bouncing along over railroad crossings and along residence streets. Clara looked at her companion, who stared straight ahead, and then turned to look out of the car window. The window was open and she could see the interiors of the laborers' houses along the streets. In the evening with the lamps lighted they seemed cosy and comfortable. Her mind ran back to the life in her father's house and its loneliness. For two summers she had escaped going home. At the end of her first year in school she had made an illness of her uncle's an excuse for spending the summer in Columbus, and at the end of the second year she had found another excuse for not going. This year she felt she would have to go home. She would have to sit day after day at the farm table with the farm hands. Nothing would happen. Her father would remain silent in her presence. She would become bored and weary of the endless small talk of the town girls. If one of the town boys began to pay her special attention, her father would become suspicious and that would lead to resentment in herself. She would do something she did not want to do. In the houses along the streets through which the car passed, she saw women moving about. Babies cried and men came out of the doors and stood talking to one another on the sidewalks. She decided suddenly that she was taking the problem of her own life too seriously. "The thing to do is to get married and then work things out afterward," she told herself. She made up her mind that the puzzling, insistent antagonism that existed between men and women was altogether due to the fact that they were not married and had not the married people's way of solving such problems as Frank Metcalf had been talking about all afternoon. She wished she were with Kate Chanceller so that she could discuss with her this new viewpoint. When she and Frank Metcalf got off the car she was no longer in a hurry to go home to her uncle's house. Knowing she did not want to marry him, she thought that in her turn she would talk, that she would try to make him see her point of view as all the afternoon he had been trying to make her see his.

For an hour the two people walked about and Clara talked. She forgot about the passage of time and the fact that she had not dined. Not wishing to talk of marriage, she talked instead of the possibility of friendship between men and women. As she talked her own mind seemed to her to have become clearer. "It's all foolishness your going on as you have," she declared. "I know how dissatisfied and unhappy you sometimes are. I often feel that way myself. Sometimes I think it's marriage I want. I really think I want to draw close to someone. I believe everyone is hungry for that experience. We all want something we are not willing to pay for. We want to steal it or have it given us. That's what's the matter with me, and that's what's the matter with you."

They came to the Woodburn hourse, and turning in stood on a porch in the darkness by the front door. At the back of the house Clara could see a light burning. Her aunt and uncle were at the eternal figuring and knitting. They were finding a substitute for living. It was the thing Frank Metcalf was protesting against and was the real reason for her own constant secret protest. She took hold of the lapel of his coat, intending to make a plea, to urge upon him the idea of a friendship that would mean something to them both. In the darkness she could not see his rather heavy, sullen face. The maternal instinct became strong in her and she thought of him as a wayward, dissatisfied boy, wanting love and understanding as she had wanted to be loved and understood by her father when life in the moment of the awakening of her womanhood seemed ugly and brutal. With her free hand she stroked the sleeve of his coat. Her gesture was misunderstood by the man who was not thinking of her words but of her body and of his hunger to possess it. He took her into his arms and held her tightly against his breast. She tried to struggle, to tear herself away but, although she was strong and muscular, she found herself unable to move. As he held her her uncle, who had heard the two people come up the steps to the door, threw it open. Both he and his wife had on several occasions warned Clara to have nothing to do with young Metcalf. One day when he had sent flowers to the house, her aunt had urged her to refuse to receive them. "He's a bad, dissipated, wicked man," she had said. "Have nothing to do with him." When he saw his niece in the arms of the man who had been the subject of so much discussion in his own house and in every respectable house in Columbus, Henderson Woodburn was furious. He forgot the fact that young Metcalf was the son of the president of the company of which he was treasurer. It seemed to him that some sort of personal insult had been thrown at him by a common ruffian. "Get out of here," he screamed. "What do you mean, you nasty villain? Get out of here."

Frank Metcalf went off along the street laughing defiantly, and Clara went into the house. The sliding doors that led into the living room had been thrown open and the light from a hanging lamp streamed in upon her. Her hair was disheveled and her hat twisted to one side. The man and woman stared at her. The knitting needles and a sheet of paper held in their hands suggested what they had been doing while Clara was getting another lesson from life. Her aunt's hands trembled and the knitting needles clicked together. Nothing was said and the confused and angry girl ran up a stairway to her own room. She locked herself in and knelt on the floor by the bed. She did not pray. Her association with Kate Chanceller had given her another outlet for her feelings. Pounding with her fists on the bed coverings, she swore. "Fools, damned fools, the world is filled with nothing but a lot of damned fools."

## CHAPTER X

Clara Butterworth left Bidwell, Ohio, in September of the year in which Steve Hunter's plant-setting machine company went into the hands of a receiver, and in January of the next year that enterprising young man, together with Tom Butterworth, bought the plant. In March a new company was organized and at once began making Hugh's corn-cutting machine, a success from the beginning. The failure of the first company and the sale of the plant had created a furor in the town. Both Steve and Tom Butterworth could, however, point to the fact that they had held on to their stock and lost their money in common with everyone else. Tom had indeed sold his stock because he needed ready money, as he explained, but had shown his good faith by buying again just before the failure. "Do you suppose I would have done that had I known what was up?" he asked the men assembled in the stores. "Go look at the books of the company. Let's have an investigation here. You will find that Steve and I stuck to the rest of the stockholders. We lost our money with the rest. If anyone was crooked and when they saw a failure coming went and got out from under at the expense of someone else, it wasn't Steve and me. The books of the company will show we were game. It wasn't our fault the plant-setting machine wouldn't work."

In the back room of the bank, John Clark and young Gordon Hart cursed Steve and Tom, who, they declared, had sold them out. They had lost no money by the failure, but on the other hand they had gained nothing. The four men had sent in a bid for the plant when it was put up for sale, but as they expected no competition, they had not bid very much. It had gone to a firm of Cleveland lawyers who bid a little more, and later had been resold at private sale to Steve and Tom. An investigation was started and it was found that Steve and Tom held large blocks of stock in the defunct company, while the bankers held practically none. Steve openly said that he had known of the possibility of failure for some time and had warned the larger stockholders and asked them not to sell their stock. "While I was working my head off trying to save the company, what were they up to?" he asked sharply, and his question was repeated in the stores and in the homes of the people.

The truth of the matter, and the thing the town never found out, was that from the beginning Steve had intended to get the plant for himself, but at the last had decided it would be better to take someone in with him. He was afraid of John Clark. For two or three days he thought about the matter and decided that the banker was not to be trusted. "He's too good a friend to Tom Butterworth," he told himself. "If I tell him my scheme, he'll tell Tom. I'll go to Tom myself. He's a money maker and a man who knows the difference between a bicycle and a wheelbarrow when you put one of them into bed with him."

Steve drove out to Tom's house late one evening in September. He hated to go but was convinced it would be better to do so. "I don't want to burn all my bridges behind me," he told himself. "I've got to have at least one friend among the solid men here in town. I've got to do business with these rubes, maybe all my life. I can't shut myself off too much, at least not yet a while."

When Steve got to the farm he asked Tom to get into his buggy, and the two men went for a long drive. The horse, a gray gelding with one blind eye hired for the occasion from liveryman Neighbors, went slowly along through the hill country south of Bidwell. He had hauled hundreds of young men with their sweethearts. Ambling slowly along, thinking perhaps of his own youth and of the tyranny of man that had made him a gelding, he knew that as long as the moon shone and the intense voiceless quiet continued to reign over the two people in the buggy, the whip would not come out of its socket and he would not be expected to hurry.

On the September evening, however, the gray gelding had behind him such a load as he had never carried before. The two people in the buggy on that evening were not foolish, meandering sweethearts, thinking only of love, and allowing themselves to be influenced in their mood by the beauty of the night, the softness of the black shadows in the road, and the gentle night winds that crept down over the crests of hills. They were solid business men, mentors of the new age, the kind of men who, in the future of America and perhaps of the whole world, were to be the makers of governments, the molders of public opinion, the owners of the press, the publishers of books, buyers of pictures, and in the goodness of their hearts, the feeders of an occasional starving and improvident poet, lost on other roads. In any event the two men sat in the buggy and the gray gelding meandered along through the hills. Great splashes of moonlight lay in the road. By chance it was on the same evening that Clara Butterworth left home to become a student in the State University. Remembering the kindness and tenderness of the rough old farm hand, Jim Priest, who had brought her to the station, she lay in her berth in the sleeping car and looked out at the roads, washed with moonlight, that slid away into the distance like ghosts. She thought of her father on that night and of the misunderstanding that had grown up between them. For the moment she was tender with regrets. "After all, Jim Priest and my father must be a good deal alike," she thought. "They have lived on the same farm, eaten the same food; they both love horses. There can't be any great difference between them." All night she thought of the matter. An obsession, that the whole world was aboard the moving train and that, as it ran swiftly along, it was carrying the people of the world into some strange maze of misunderstanding, took possession of her. So strong was it that it affected her deeply buried unconscious self and made her terribly afraid. It seemed to her that the walls of the sleeping-car berth were like the walls of a prison that had shut her away from the beauty of life. The walls seemed to close in upon her. The walls, like life itself, were shutting in upon her youth and her youthful desire to reach a hand out of the beauty in herself to the buried beauty in others. She sat up in the berth and forced down a desire in herself to break the car window and leap out of the swiftly moving train into the quiet night bathed with moonlight. With girlish generosity she took upon her own shoulders the responsibility for the misunderstanding that had grown up between herself and her father. Later she lost the impulse that led her to come to that decision, but during that night it persisted. It was, in spite of the terror caused by the hallucination regarding the moving walls of the berth that seemed about to crush her and that came back time after time, the most beautiful night she had ever lived through, and it remained in her memory throughout her life. She in fact came to think later of that night as the time when, most of all, it would have been beautiful and right for her to have been able to give herself to a lover. Although she did not know it, the kiss on the cheek from the be-whiskered lips of Jim Priest had no doubt something to do with that thought when it came.

And while the girl fought her battle with the strange-ness of life and tried to break through the imaginary walls that shut her off from the opportunity to live, her father also rode through the night. With a shrewd eye he watched the face of Steve Hunter. It had already begun to get a little fat, but Tom realized suddenly that it was the face of a man of ability. There was something about the jowls that made Tom, who had dealt much in livestock, think of the face of a pig. "The man goes after what he wants. He's greedy," the farmer thought. "Now he's up to something. To get what he wants he'll give me a chance to get something I want. He's going to make some kind of proposal to me in connection with the factory. He's hatched up a scheme to shut Gordon Hart and John Clark out because he doesn't want too many partners. All right, I'll go in with him. Either one of them would have done the same thing had they had the chance."

Steve smoked a black cigar and talked. As he grew more sure of himself and the affairs that absorbed him, he also became more smooth and persuasive in the matter of words. He talked for a time of the necessity of certain men's surviving and growing constantly stronger and stronger in the industrial world. "It's necessary for the good of the community," he said. "A few fairly strong men are a good thing for a town, but if they are fewer and relatively stronger it's better." He turned to look sharply at his companion. "Well," he exclaimed, "we talked there in the bank of what we would do when things went to pieces down at the factory, but there were too many men in the scheme. I didn't realize it at the time, but I do now." He knocked the ashes off his cigar and laughed. "You know what they did, don't you?" he asked. "I asked you all not to sell any of your stock. I didn't want to get the whole town bitter. They wouldn't have lost anything. I promised to see them through, to get the plant for them at a low price, to put them in the way to make some real money. They played the game in a small-town way. Some men can think of thousands of dollars, others have to think of hundreds. It's all their minds are big enough to comprehend. They snatch at a little measly advantage and miss the big one. That's what these men have done."

For a long time the two rode in silence. Tom, who had also sold his stock, wondered if Steve knew. He decided he did. "However, he's decided to deal with me. He needs someone and has chosen me," he thought. He made up his mind to be bold. After all, Steve was young. Only a year or two before he was nothing but a young upstart and the very boys in the street laughed at him. Tom grew a little indignant, but was careful to take thought before he spoke. "Perhaps, although he's young and don't look like much, he's a faster and shrewder thinker than any of us," he told himself.

"You do talk like a fellow who has something up his sleeve," he said laughing. "If you want to know, I sold my stock the same as the others. I wasn't going to take a chance of being a loser if I could help it. It may be the small-town way, but you know things maybe I don't know. You can't blame me for living up to my lights. I always did believe in the survival of the fittest and I got a daughter to support and put through college. I want to make a lady of her. You ain't got any kids yet and you're younger. Maybe you want to take chances I don't want to take. How do I know what you're up to?"

Again the two rode in silence. Steve had prepared himself for the talk. He knew there was a chance that, in its turn, the corn-cutting machine Hugh had invented might not prove practical and that in the end he might be left with a factory on his hands and with nothing to manufacture in it. He did not, however, hesitate. Again, as on the day in the bank when he was confronted by the two older men, he made a bluff. "Well, you can come in or stay out, just as you wish," he said a little sharply. "I'm going to get hold of that factory, if I can, and I'm going to manufacture corn-cutting machines. Already I have promises of orders enough to keep running for a year. I can't take you in with me and have it said around town you were one of the fellows who sold out the small investors. I've got a hundred thousand dollars of stock in the company. You can have half of it. I'll take your note for the fifty thousand. You won't ever have to pay it. The earnings of the new factory will clean you up. You got to come clean, though. Of course you can go get John Clark and come out and make an open fight to get the factory yourselves, if you want to. I own the rights to the corn-cutting machine and will take it somewhere else and manufacture it. I don't mind telling you that, if we split up, I will pretty well advertise what you three fellows did to the small investors after I asked you not to do it. You can all stay here and own your empty factory and get what satisfaction you can out of the love and respect you'll get from the people. You can do what you please. I don't care. My hands are clean. I ain't done anything I'm ashamed of, and if you want to come in with me, you and I together will pull off something in this town we don't neither one of us have to be ashamed of."

The two men drove back to the Butterworth farmhouse and Tom got out of the buggy. He intended to tell Steve to go to the devil, but as they drove along the road, he changed his mind. The young school teacher from Bidwell, who had come on several occasions to call on his daughter Clara, was on that night abroad with another young woman. He sat in a buggy with his arm around her waist and drove slowly through the hill country. Tom and Steve drove past them and the farmer, seeing in the moonlight the woman in the arms of the man, imagined his daughter in her place. The thought made him furious. "I'm losing the chance to be a big man in the town here in order to play safe and be sure of money to leave to Clara, and all she cares about is to galavant around with some young squirt," he thought bitterly. He began to see himself as a wronged and unappreciated father. When he got out of the buggy, he stood for a moment by the wheel and looked hard at Steve. "I'm as good a sport as you are," he said finally. "Bring around your stock and I'll give you the note. That's all it will be, you understand: just my note. I don't promise to back it up with any collateral and I don't expect you to offer it for sale." Steve leaned out of the buggy and took him by the hand. "I won't sell your note, Tom," he said. "I'll put it away. I want a partner to help me. You and I are going to do things together."

The young promoter drove off along the road, and Tom went into the house and to bed. Like his daughter he did not sleep. For a time he thought of her and in imagination saw her again in the buggy with the school teacher who had her in his arms. The thought made him stir restlessly about beneath the sheets. "Damn women anyway," he muttered. To relieve his mind he thought of other things. "I'll make out a deed and turn three of my farms over to Clara," he decided shrewdly. "If things go wrong we won't be entirely broke. I know

Charlie Jacobs in the courthouse over at the county seat. I ought to be able to get a deed recorded without anyone knowing it if I oil Charlie's hand a little."

Clara's last two weeks in the Woodburn household were spent in the midst of a struggle, no less intense because no words were said. Both Henderson Woodburn and his wife felt that Clara owed them an explanation of the scene at the front door with Frank Metcalf. When she did offer it they were offended. When he threw open the door and confronted the two people, the plow manufacturer had got an impression that Clara was trying to escape Frank Metcalf's embraces. He told his wife that he did not think she was to blame for the scene on the front porch. Not being the girl's father he could look at the matter coldly. "She's a good girl," he declared. "That beast of a Frank Metcalf is all to blame. I daresay he followed her home. She's upset now, but in the morning she'll tell us the story of what happened."

The days went past and Clara said nothing. During her last week in the house she and the two older people scarcely spoke. The young woman was in an odd way relieved. Every evening she went to dine with Kate Chanceller who, when she heard the story of the afternoon in the suburb and the incident on the porch, went off without Clara's knowing of it and had a talk with Henderson Woodburn in his office. After the talk the manufacturer was puzzled and just a little afraid of both Clara and her friend. He tried to tell his wife about it, but was not very clear. "I can't make it out," he said. "She is the kind of woman I can't understand, that Kate. She says Clara wasn't to blame for what happened between her and Frank Metcalf, but don't want to tell us the story, because she thinks young

Metcalf wasn't to blame either." Although he had been respectful and courteous as he listened to Kate's talk, he grew angry when he tried to tell his wife what she had said. "I'm afraid it was just a lot of mixed up nonsense," he declared. "It makes me glad we haven't a daughter. If neither of them were to blame what were they up to? What's getting the matter with the women of the new generation? When you come down to it what's the matter with Kate Chanceller?"

The plow manufacturer advised his wife to say nothing to Clara. "Let's wash our hands of it," he suggested. "She'll go home in a few days now and we will say nothing about her coming back next year. Let's be polite, but act as though she didn't exist."

Clara accepted the new attitude of her uncle and aunt without comment. In the afternoon she did not come home from the University but went to Kate's apartment. The brother came home and after dinner played on the piano. At ten o'clock Clara started home afoot and Kate accompanied her. The two women went out of their way to sit on a bench in a park. They talked of a thousand hidden phases of life Clara had hardly dared think of before. During all the rest of her life she thought of those last weeks in Columbus as the most deeply satisfactory time she ever lived through. In the Woodburn house she was uncomfortable because of the silence and the hurt, offended look on her aunt's face, but she did not spend much time there. In the morning Henderson Woodburn ate his breakfast alone at seven, and clutching his ever present portfolio of papers, was driven off to the plow factory. Clara and her aunt had a silent breakfast at eight, and then Clara also hurried away. "I'll be out for lunch and will go to Kate's for dinner," she said as she went out of her aunt's presence, and she said it, not with the air of one asking permission as had been her custom before the Frank Metcalf incident, but as one having the right to dispose of her own time. Only once did her aunt break the frigid air of offended dignity she had assumed. One morning she followed Clara to the front door, and as she watched her go down the steps from the front porch to the walk that led to the street, called to her. Some faint recollection of a time of revolt in her own youth perhaps came to her. Tears came into her eyes. To her the world was a place of terror, where wolflike men prowled about seeking women to devour, and she was afraid something dreadful would happen to her niece. "If you don't want to tell me anything, it's all right," she said bravely, "but I wish you felt you could." When Clara turned to look at her, she hastened to explain. "Mr. Woodburn said I wasn't to bother you about it and I won't," she added quickly. Nervously folding and unfolding her arms, she turned to stare up the street with the air of a frightened child that looks into a den of beasts. "O Clara, be a good girl," she said. "I know you're grown up now, but, O Clara, do be careful! Don't get into trouble."

The Woodburn house in Columbus, like the Butterworth house in the country south of Bidwell, sat on a hill. The street fell away rather sharply as one went toward the business portion of the city and the streetcar line, and on the morning when her aunt spoke to her and tried with her feeble hands to tear some stones out of the wall that was being built between them, Clara hurried along the street under the trees, feeling as though she would like also to weep. She saw no possibility of explaining to her aunt the new thoughts she was beginning to have about life and did not want to hurt her by trying. "How can I explain my thoughts when they're not clear in my own mind, when I am myself just groping blindly about?" she asked herself. "She wants me to be good," she thought. "What would she think if I told her that I had come to the conclusion that, judging by her standards, I have been altogether too good? What's the use trying to talk to her when I would only hurt her and make things harder than ever?" She got to a street crossing and looked back. Her aunt was still standing at the door of her house and looking at her. There was something soft, small, round, insistent, both terribly weak and terribly strong about the completely feminine thing she had made of herself or that life had made of her. Clara shuddered. She did not make a symbol of the figure of her aunt and her mind did not form a connection between her aunt's life and what she had become, as Kate Chanceller's mind would have done. She saw the little, round, weeping woman as a boy, walking in the tree-lined streets of a town, sees suddenly the pale face and staring eyes of a prisoner that looks out at him through the iron bars of a town jail. Clara was startled as the boy would be startled and, like the boy, she wanted to run quickly away. "I must think of something else and of other kinds of women or I'll get things terribly distorted," she told herself. "If I think of her and women like her I'll grow afraid of marriage, and I want to be married as soon as I can find the right man. It's the only thing I can do. What else is there a woman can do?"

As Clara and Kate walked about in the evening, they talked continually of the new position Kate believed women were on the point of achieving in the world. The woman who was so essentially a man wanted to talk of marriage and to condemn it, but continually fought the impulse in herself. She knew that were she to let herself go she would say many things that, while they might be true enough as regards herself, would not necessarily be true of Clara. "Because I do not want to live with a man or be his wife is not very good proof that the institution is wrong. It may be that I want to keep Clara for myself. I think more of her than of anyone else I've ever met. How can I think straight about her marrying some man and becoming dulled to the things that mean most to me?" she asked herself. One evening, when the women were walking from Kate's apartment to the Woodburn house, they were accosted by two men who wanted to walk with them. There was a small park nearby and Kate led the men to it. "Come," she said, "we won't walk with you, but you may sit with us here on a bench." The men sat down beside them and the older one, a man with a small black mustache, made some remark about the fineness of the night. The younger man who sat beside Clara looked at her and laughed. Kate at once got down to business.

"Well, you wanted to walk with us: what for?" she asked sharply. She explained what they had been doing. "We were walking and talking of women and what they were to do with their lives," she explained. "We were expressing opinions, you see. I don't say either of us had said anything that was very wise, but we were having a good time and trying to learn something from each other. Now what have you to say to us? You interrupted our talk and wanted to walk with us: what for? You wanted to be in our company: now tell us what you've got to contribute. You can't just come and walk with us like dumb things. What have you got to offer that you think will make it worth while for us to break up our conversation with each other and spend the time talking with you?"

The older man, he of the mustache, turned to look at Kate, then got up from the bench. He walked a little away and then turned and made a sign with his hand to his companion. "Come on," he said, "let's get out of here. We're wasting our time. It's a cold trail. They're a couple of highbrows. Come on, let's be on our way."

The two women again walked along the street. Kate could not help feeling somewhat proud of the way in which she had disposed of the men. She talked of it until they got to the door of the Woodburn house, and, as she went away along the street Clara thought she swaggered a little. She stood by the door and watched her friend until she had disappeared around a corner. A flash of doubt of the infallibility of Kate's method with men crossed her mind. She remembered suddenly the soft brown eyes of the younger of the two men in the park and wondered what was back of the eyes. Perhaps after all, had she been alone with him, the man might have had something to say quite as much to the point as the things she and Kate had been saying to each other. "Kate made the men look like fools, but after all she wasn't very fair," she thought as she went into the house.

Clara was in Bidwell for a month before she realized what a change had taken place in the life of her home town. On the farm things went on very much as always, except that her father was very seldom there. He had gone deeply into the project of manufacturing and selling corn-cutting machines with Steve Hunter, and attended to much of the selling of the output of the factory. Almost every month he went on trips to cities of the West. Even when he was in Bidwell, he had got into the habit of staying at the town hotel for the night. "It's too much trouble to be always running back and forth," he explained to Jim Priest, whom he had put in charge of the farm work. He swaggered before the old man who for so many years had been almost like a partner in his smaller activities. "Well, I wouldn't like to have anything said, but I think it just as well to have an eye on what's going on," he declared. "Steve's all right, but business is business. We're dealing in big affairs, he and I. I don't say he would try to get the best of me; I'm just telling you that in the future I'll have to be in town most of the time and can't think of things out here. You look out for the farm. Don't bother me with details. You just tell me about it when there is any buying or selling to do."

Clara arrived in Bidwell in the early afternoon of a warm day in June. The hill country through which her train came into town was in the full flush of its summer beauty. In the little patches of level land between the hills grain was ripening in the fields. Along the streets of the tiny towns and on dusty country roads farmers in overalls stood up in their wagons and scolded at the horses, rearing and prancing in half-pretended fright of the passing train. In the forests on the hillsides the open places among the trees looked cool and enticing. Clara put her cheek against the car window and imagined herself wandering in cool forests with a lover. She forgot the words of Kate Chanceller in regard to the independent future of women. It was, she thought vaguely, a thing to be thought about only after some more immediate problem was solved. Just what the problem was she didn't definitely know, but she did know that it concerned some close warm contact with life that she had as yet been unable to make. When she closed her eyes, strong warm hands seemed to come out of nothingness and touch her flushed cheeks. The fingers of the hands were strong like the branches of trees. They touched with the firmness and gentleness of the branches of trees nodding in a summer breeze.

Clara sat up stiffly in her seat and when the train stopped at Bidwell got off and went to her waiting father with a firm, business-like air. Coming out of the land of dreams, she took on something of the determined air of Kate Chanceller. She stared at her father and an onlooker might have thought them two strangers, meeting for the purpose of discussing some business arrangement. A flavor of something like suspicion hung over them. They got into Tom's buggy, and as Main Street was torn up for the purpose of laying a brick pavement and digging a new sewer, they drove by a roundabout way through residence streets until they got into Medina Road. Clara looked at her father and felt suddenly very alert and on her guard. It seemed to her that she was far removed from the green, unsophisticated girl who had so often walked in Bidwell's streets; that her mind and spirit had expanded tremendously in the three years she had been away; and she wondered if her father would realize the change in her. Either one of two reactions on his part might, she felt, make her happy. The man might turn suddenly and taking her hand receive her into fellowship, or he might receive her as a woman and his daughter by kissing her.

He did neither. They drove in silence through the town and passed over a small bridge and into the road that led to the farm. Tom was curious about his daughter and a little uncomfortable. Ever since the evening on the porch of the farmhouse, when he had accused her of some unnamed relationship with John May, he had felt guilty in her presence but had succeeded in transferring the notion of guilt to her. While she was away at school he had been comfortable. Sometimes he did not think of her for a month at a time. Now she had written that she did not intend to go back. She had not asked his advice, but had said positively that she was coming home to stay. He wondered what was up. Had she got into another affair with a man? He wanted to ask, had intended to ask, but in her presence found that the words he had intended to say would not come to his lips. After a long silence Clara began to ask questions about the farm, the men who worked there, her aunt's health, the usual homecoming questions. Her father answered with generalities. "They're all right," he said, "everyone and everything's all right."

The road began to lift out of the valley in which the town lay, and Tom stopped the horse and pointing with the whip talked of the town. He was relieved to have the silence broken, and decided not to say anything about the letter announcing the end of her school life. "You see there," he said, pointing to where the wall of a new brick factory arose above the trees that grew beside the river. "That's a new factory we're building. We're going to make corn-cutting machines there. The old factory's already too small. We've sold it to a new company that's going to manufacture bicycles. Steve Hunter and I sold it. We got twice what we paid for it. When the bicycle factory's started, he and I'll own the control in that too. I tell you the town's on the boom."

Tom boasted of his new position in the town and Clara turned and looked sharply at him and then looked quickly away. He was annoyed by the action and a flush of anger came to his cheeks. A side of his character his daughter had never seen before came to the surface. When he was a simple farmer he had been too shrewd to attempt to play the aristocrat with his farm hands, but often, as he went about the barns and as he drove along country roads and saw men at work in his fields, he had felt like a prince in the presence of his vassals. Now he talked like a prince. It was that that had startled Clara. There was about him an indefinable air of princely prosperity. When she turned to look at him she noticed for the first time how much his person had also changed. Like Steve Hunter he was beginning to grow fat. The lean hardness of his cheeks had gone, his jaws seemed heavier, even his hands had changed their color. He wore a diamond ring on the left hand and it glistened in the sunlight. "Things have changed," he declared, still pointing at the town. "Do you want to know who changed it? Well, I had more to do with it than anyone else. Steve thinks he did it all, but he didn't. I'm the man who has done the most. He put through the plant-setting machine company, but that was a failure. When you come right down to it, things would have gone to pieces again if I hadn't gone to John Clark and talked and bluffed him into giving us money when we wanted it. I had most to do with finding the big market for our corn-cutters, too. Steve lied to me and said he had 'em all sold for a year. He didn't have any sold at all."

Tom struck the horse with the whip and drove rapidly along the road. Even when the climb became difficult he would not let the horse walk, but kept cracking the whip over his back. "I'm a different man than I was when you went away," he declared. "You might as well know it, I'm the big man in this town. It comes pretty near being my town when you come right down to it. I'm going to take care of everyone in

Bidwell and give everyone a chance to make money, but it's my town now pretty near and you might as well know it."

Embarrassed by his own words, Tom talked to cover his embarrassment. Something he wanted very much to say got itself said. "I'm glad you went to school and fitted yourself to be a lady," he began. "I want you should marry pretty soon now. I don't know whether you met anyone at school there or not. If you did and he's all right, it's all right with me. I don't want you should marry an ordinary man, but a smart one, an educated man, a gentleman. We Butterworths are going to be bigger and bigger people here. If you get married to a good man, a smart one, I'll build a house for you; not just a little house but a big place, the biggest place Bidwell ever seen."

They came to the farm and Tom stopped the buggy in the road. He shouted to a man in the barnyard who came running for her bags. When she had got out of the buggy he immediately turned the horse about and drove rapidly away. Her aunt, a large, moist woman, met her on the steps leading to the front door, and embraced her warmly. The words her father had just spoken ran a riotous course through Clara's brain. She realized that for a year she had been thinking of marriage, had been wanting some man to approach and talk of marriage, but she had not thought of the matter in the way her father had put it. The man had spoken of her as though she were a possession of his that must be disposed of. He had a personal interest in her marriage. It was in some way not a private matter, but a family affair. It was her father's idea, she gathered, that she was to go into marriage to strengthen what he called his position in the community, to help him be some vague thing he called a big man. She wondered if he had someone in mind and could not avoid being a little curious as to who it could be. It had never occurred to her that her marriage could mean anything to her father beyond the natural desire of the parent that his child make a happy marriage. She began to grow angry at the thought of the way in which her father had approached the subject, but was still curious to know whether he had gone so far as to have someone in mind for the rôle of husband, and thought she would try to find out from her aunt. The strange farm hand came into the house with her bags and she followed him upstairs to what had always been her own room. Her aunt came puffing at her heels. The farm hand went away and she began to unpack, while the older woman, her face very red, sat on the edge of the bed. "You ain't been getting engaged to a man down there where you been to school, have you, Clara?" she asked.

Clara looked at her aunt and blushed; then became suddenly and furiously angry. Dropping the bag she had opened to the floor, she ran out of the room. At the door she stopped and turned on the surprised and startled woman. "No, I haven't," she declared furiously. "It's nobody's business whether I have or not. I went to school for an education. I didn't go to get me a man. If that's what you sent me for, why didn't you say so?"

Clara hurried out of the house and into the barnyard. She went into all of the barns, but there were no men about. Even the strange farm hand who had carried her bags into the house had disappeared, and the stalls in the horse and cattle barns were empty. Then she went into the orchard and climbing a fence went through a meadow and into the wood to which she had always fled, when as a girl on the farm she was troubled or angry. For a long time she sat on a log beneath a tree and tried to think her way through the new idea of marriage she had got from her father's words. She was still angry and told herself that she would leave home, would go to some city and get work. She thought of Kate Chanceller who intended to be a doctor, and tried to picture herself attempting something of the kind. It would take money for study. She tried to imagine herself talking to her father about the matter and the thought made her smile. Again she wondered if he had any definite person in mind as her husband, and who it could be. She tried to check off her father's acquaintances among the young men of Bidwell. "It must be some new man who has come here, someone having something to do with one of the factories," she thought.

After sitting on the log for a long time, Clara got up and walked under the trees. The imaginary man, suggested to her mind by her father's words, became every moment more and more a reality. Before her eyes danced the laughing eyes of the young man who for a moment had lingered beside her while Kate Chanceller talked to his companion that evening when they had been challenged on the streets of Columbus. She remembered the young school teacher, who had held her in his arms through a long Sunday afternoon, and the day when, as an awakening maiden, she had heard Jim Priest talking to the laborers in the barn about the sap that ran up the tree. The afternoon slipped away and the shadows of the trees lengthened. On such a day and alone there in the quiet wood, it was impossible for her to remain in the angry mood in which she had left the house. Over her father's farm brooded the passionate fulfillment of summer. Before her, seen through the trees, lay yellow wheat fields, ripe for the cutting; insects sang and danced in the air about her head; a soft wind blew and made a gentle singing noise in the tops of the trees; at her back among the trees a squirrel chattered; and two calves came along a woodland path and stood for a long time staring at her with their large gentle eyes. She arose and went out of the wood, crossed a falling meadow and came to a rail fence surrounding a corn field. Jim Priest was cultivating corn and when he saw her left his horses and came to her. He took both her hands in his and pumped her arms up and down. "Well, Lord A'mighty, I'm glad to see you," he said heartily. "Lord A'mighty, I'm glad to see you." The old farm hand pulled a long blade of grass out of the ground beneath the fence and leaning against the top rail began to chew it. He asked Clara the same question her aunt had asked, but his asking did not annoy her. She laughed and shook her head. "No, Jim," she said, "I seem to have made a failure of going away to school. I didn't get me a man. No one asked me, you see."

Both the woman and the old man became silent. Over the tops of the young corn they could see down the hillside into the distant town. Clara wondered if the man she was to marry was there. The idea of a marriage with her had perhaps been suggested to his mind also. Her father, she decided, was capable of that. He was evidently ready to go to any length to see her safely married. She wondered why. When Jim Priest began to talk, striving to explain his question, his words fitted oddly into the thoughts she was having in regard to herself. "Now about marriage," he began, "you see now, I never done it. I didn't get married at all. I don't know why. I wanted to and I didn't. I was afraid to ask, maybe. I guess if you do it you're sorry you did and if you don't you're sorry you didn't."

Jim went back to his team, and Clara stood by the fence and watched him go down the long field and turn to come back along another of the paths between the corn rows. When the horses came to where she stood, he stopped again and looked at her. "I guess you'll get married pretty soon now," he said. The horses started on again and he held the cultivating machine with one hand and looked back over his shoulder at her. "You're one of the marrying kind," he called. "You ain't like me. You don't just think about things. You do 'em. You'll be getting yourself married before very long. You are one of the kind that does."

## CHAPTER XI

If many things had happened to Clara Butterworth in the three years since that day when John Mav so rudely tripped her first hesitating girlish attempt to run out to life, things had also happened to the people she had left behind in Bidwell. In so short a space of time her father, his business associate Steve Hunter, Ben Peeler the town carpenter, Joe Wainsworth the harness maker, almost every man and woman in town had become something different in his nature from the man or woman bearing the same name she had known in her girlhood.

Ben Peeler was forty years old when Clara went to Columbus to school. He was a tall, slender, stoop-shouldered man who worked hard and was much respected by his fellow townsmen. Almost any afternoon he might have been seen going through Main Street, wearing his carpenter's apron and with a carpenter's pencil stuck under his cap and balanced on his ear. He went into Oliver Hall's hardware store and came out with a large package of nails under his arm. A farmer who was thinking of building a new barn stopped him in front of the post-office and for a half-hour the two men talked of the project. Ben put on his glasses, took the pencil out of his cap and made some notation on the back of the package of nails. "I'll do a little figuring; then I'll talk things over with you," he said. During the spring, summer and fall Ben had always employed another carpenter and an apprentice, but when Clara came back to town he was employing four gangs of six men each and had two foremen to watch the work and keep it moving, while his son, who in other times would also have been a carpenter, had become a salesman, wore fancy vests and lived in Chicago. Ben was making money and for two years had not driven a nail or held a saw in his hand. He had an office in a frame building beside the New York Central tracks, south of Main Street, and employed a bookkeeper and a stenographer. In addition to carpentry he had embarked in another business. Backed by Gordon Hart, he had become a lumber dealer and bought and sold lumber under the firm name of Peeler and Hart. Almost every day cars of lumber were unloaded and stacked under sheds in the yard back of his office. He was no longer satisfied with his income as a workman but, under the influence of Gordon Hart, demanded also a swinging profit on the building materials. Ben now drove about town in a vehicle called a buckboard and spent the entire day hurrying from job to job. He had no time now to stop for a half-hour's gossip with a prospective builder of a barn, and did not come to loaf in Birdie Spinks' drugstore at the end of the day. In the evening he went to the lumber office and Gordon Hart came over from the bank. The two men figured on jobs to be built, rows of workingmen's houses, sheds alongside one of the new factories, large frame houses for the superintendents and other substantial men of the town's new enterprises. In the old days Ben had been glad to go occasionally into the country on a barn-building job. He had liked the country food, the gossip with the farmer and his men at the noon hour and the drive back and forth to town, mornings and evenings. While he was in the country he managed to make a deal for his winter potatoes, hay for his horse, and perhaps a barrel of cider to drink on winter evenings. Now he had no time to think of such things. When a farmer came to see him he shook his head. "Get someone else to figure on your job," he advised. "You'll save money by getting a barn-building carpenter. I can't bother. I have too many houses to build." Ben and Gordon sometimes worked in the lumber office until midnight. On warm still nights the sweet smell of new-cut boards filled the air of the yard and crept in through the open windows, but the two men, intent on their figures, did not notice. In the early evening one or two teams came back to the yard to finish hauling lumber to a job where the men were to work on the next day. The voices of the men, talking and singing as they loaded their wagons, broke the silence. Later the wagons loaded high with boards went creaking away. When the two men grew tired and sleepy, they locked the office and walked through the yard to the driveway that led to a residence street. Ben was nervous and irritable. One evening they found three men, sleeping on a pile of boards in the yard, and drove them out. It gave both men something to think about. Gordon Hart went home and before he slept made up his mind that he would not let another day go by without getting the lumber in the yard more heavily insured. Ben had not handled affairs long enough to come quickly to so sensible a decision. All night he rolled and tumbled about in his bed. "Some tramp with his pipe will set the place afire," he thought. "I'll lose all the money I've made." For a long time he did not think of the simple expedient of hiring a watchman to drive sleepy and penniless wanderers away, and charging enough more for his lumber to cover the additional expense. He got out of bed and dressed, thinking he would get his shotgun out of the barn and go back to the yard and spend the night. Then he undressed and got into bed again. "I can't work all day and spend my nights down there," he thought resentfully. When at last he slept, he dreamed of sitting in the lumber yard in the darkness with the gun in his hand. A man came toward him and he discharged the gun and killed the man. With the inconsistency common to the physical aspect of dreams, the darkness passed away and it was daylight. The man he had thought dead was not quite dead. Although the whole side of his head was torn away, he still breathed. His mouth opened and closed convulsively. A dreadful illness took possession of the carpenter. He had an elder brother who had died when he was a boy, but the face of the man on the ground was the face of his brother. Ben sat up in bed and shouted. "Help, for God's sake, help! It's my own brother. Don't you see, it is Harry Peeler?" he cried. His wife awoke and shook him. "What's the matter, Ben," she asked anxiously. "What's the matter?" "It was a dream," he said, and let his head drop wearily on the pillow. His wife went to sleep again, but he stayed awake the rest of the night. When on the next morning Gordon Hart suggested the insurance idea, he was delighted. "That settles it of course," he said to himself. "It's simple enough, you see. That settles everything."

In his shop on Main Street Joe Wainsworth had plenty to do after the boom came to Bidwell. Many teams were employed in the hauling of building materials; loads of paving brick were being carted from cars to where they were to be laid on Main Street; and teams hauled earth from where the new Main Street sewer was being dug and from the freshly dug cellars of houses. Never had there been so many teams employed and so much repairing of harness to do. Joe's apprentice had left him, had been carried off by the rush of young men to the places where the boom had arrived earlier. For a year Joe had worked alone and had then employed a journeyman harness maker who had drifted into town drunk and who got drunk every Saturday evening. The new man was an odd character. He had a faculty for making money, but seemed to care little about making it for himself. Within a week after he came to town he knew everyone in Bidwell. His name was Jim Gibson and he had no sooner come to work for Joe than a contest arose between them. The contest concerned the question of who was to run the shop. For a time Joe asserted himself. He growled at the men who brought harness in to be repaired, and refused to make promises as to when the work would be done. Several jobs were taken away and sent to nearby towns. Then Jim Gibson asserted himself. When one of the teamsters who had come to town with the boom came with a heavy work harness on his shoulder, he went to meet him. The harness was thrown with a rattling crash on the floor and Jim examined it. "Oh, the devil, that's an easy job," he declared. "We'll fix that up in a jiffy. You can have it tomorrow afternoon if you want it."

For a time Jim made it a practice to come to where Joe stood at work at his bench and consult with him regarding prices to be charged for work. Then he returned to the customer and charged more than Joe had suggested. After a few weeks he stopped consulting Joe at all. "You're no good," he exclaimed, laughing. "What you're doing in business I don't know." The old harness maker stared at him for a minute and then went to his bench and to work. "Business," he muttered, "what do I know about business? I'm a harness maker, I am."

After Jim came to work for him, Joe made in one year almost twice the amount he had lost in the failure of the plant-setting machine factory. The money was not invested in stock of any factory but lay in the bank. Still he was not happy. All day Jim Gibson, whom Joe had never dared tell the tales of his triumph as a workman and to whom he did not brag as he had formerly done to his apprentices, talked of his ability to get the best of customers. He had, he declared, managed, in the last place he had worked before he came to Bidwell, to sell a good many sets of harness as handmade that were in reality made in a factory. "It isn't like the old times," he said, "things are changing. We used to sell harness only to farmers or to teamsters right in our towns who owned their own horses. We always knew the men we did business with and always would know them. Now it's different. The men now, you see, who are here in this town to work—well, next month or next year they'll be somewhere else. All they care about you and me is how much work they can get for a dollar. Of course they talk big about honesty and all that stuff, but that's only their guff. They think maybe we'll fall for it and they'll get more for the money they pay out. That's what they're up to."

Jim tried hard to make his version of how the shop should be run clear to his employer. Every day he talked for hours regarding the matter. He tried to get Joe to put in a stock of factory-made harness and when he was unsuccessful was angry. "O the devil," he cried. "Can't you understand what you're up against? The factories are bound to win. For why? Look here, there can't anyone but some old mossback who has worked around horses all his life tell the difference between hand- and machine-sewed harness. The machine-made can be sold cheaper. It looks all right and the factories are able to put on a lot of do-dads. That catches the young fellows. It's good business. Quick sales and profits, that's the story." Jim laughed and then said something that made the shivers run up and down Joe's back. "If I had the money and was steady I'd start a shop in this town and show you up," he said. "I'd pretty near run you out. The trouble with me is I wouldn't stick to business if I had the money. I tried it once and made money; then when I got a little ahead I shut up the shop and went on a big drunk. I was no good for a month. When I work for someone else I'm all right. I get drunk on Saturdays and that satisfies me. I like to work and scheme for money, but it ain't any good to me when I get it and never will be. What I want you to do here is to shut your eyes and give me a chance. That's all I ask. Just shut your eyes and give me a chance."

All day Joe sat astride his harness maker's horse, and when he was not at work, stared out through a dirty window into an alleyway and tried to understand Jim's idea of what a harness maker's attitude should be toward his customers, now that new times had come. He felt very old. Although Jim was as old in years lived as himself, he seemed very young. He began to be a little afraid of the man. He could not understand why the money, nearly twenty-five hundred dollars he had put in the bank during the two years Jim had been with him, seemed so unimportant and the twelve hundred dollars he had earned slowly after twenty years of work seemed so important. As there was much repair work always waiting to be done in the shop, he did not go home to lunch, but every day carried a few sandwiches to the shop in his pocket. At the noon hour, when Jim had gone to his boarding-house, he was alone, and if no one came in, he was happy. It seemed to him the best time of the day. Every few minutes he went to the front door to look out. The quiet Main Street, on which his shop had faced since he was a young man just come home from his trade adventures, and which had always been such a sleepy place at the noon hour in the summer, was now like a battlefield from which an army had retreated. A great gash had been cut in the street where the new sewer was to be laid. Swarms of workingmen, most of them strangers, had come into Main Street from the factories by the railroad tracks. They stood in groups in lower Main Street by Wymer's tobacco store. Some of them had gone into Ben Head's saloon for a glass of beer and came out wiping their mustaches. The men who were digging the sewer, foreign men, Italians he had heard, sat on the banks of dry earth in the middle of the street. Their dinner pails were held between their legs and as they ate they talked in a strange language. He remembered the day he had come to Bidwell with his bride, the girl he had met on his trade journey and who had waited for him until he had mastered his trade and had a shop of his own. He had gone to New York State to get her and had arrived back in Bidwell at noon on just such another summer day. There had not been many people about, but everyone had known him. On that day everyone had been his friend. Birdie Spinks rushed out of his drugstore and had insisted that he and his bride go home to dinner with him. Everyone had wanted them to come to his house for dinner. It had been a happy, joyous time.

The harness maker had always been sorry his wife had borne him no children. He had said nothing and had always pretended he did not want them and now, at last, he was glad they had not come. He went back to his bench and to work, hoping Jim would be late in getting back from lunch. The shop was very quiet after the activity of the street that had so bewildered him. It was, he thought, like a retreat, almost like a church when you went to the door and looked in on a week day. He had done that once and had liked the empty silent church better than he did a church with a preacher and a lot of people in it. He had told his wife about the matter. "It was like the shop in the evening when I've got a job of work done and the boy has gone home," he had said.

The harness maker looked out through the open door of his shop and saw Tom Butterworth and Steve Hunter going along Main Street, engaged in earnest conversation. Steve had a cigar stuck in the corner of his mouth and Tom had on a fancy vest. He thought again of the money he had lost in the plant-setting machine venture and was furious. The noon hour was spoiled and he was almost glad when Jim came back from his midday meal.

The position in which he found himself in the shop amused Jim Gibson. He chuckled to himself as he waited on the customers who came in, and as he worked at the bench. One day when he came back along Main Street from the noon meal, he decided to try an experiment. "If I lose my job what difference does it make?" he asked himself. He stopped at a saloon and had a drink of whisky. When he got to the shop he began to scold his employer, to threaten him as though he were his apprentice. Swaggering suddenly in, he walked to where Joe was at work and slapped him roughly on the back. "Come, cheer up, old daddy," he said. "Get the gloom out of you. I'm tired of your muttering and growling at things."

The employee stepped back and watched his employer. Had Joe ordered him out of the shop he would not have been surprised, and as he said later when he told Ben Head's bartender of the incident, would not have cared very much. The fact that he did not care, no doubt saved him. Joe was frightened. For just a moment he was so angry he could not speak, and then he remembered that if Jim left him he would have to wait on trade and would have to dicker with the strange teamsters regarding the repairing of the work harness. Bending over the bench he worked for an hour in silence. Then, instead of demanding an explanation of the rude familiarity with which Jim had treated him, he began to explain. "Now look here, Jim," he pleaded, "don't you pay any attention to me. You do as you please here. Don't you pay any attention to me."

Jim said nothing, but a smile of triumph lit up his face. Late in the afternoon he left the shop. "If anyone comes in, tell them to wait. I won't be gone very long," he said insolently. Jim went into Ben Head's saloon and told the bartender how his experiment had come out. The story was later told from store to store up and down the Main Street of Bidwell. "He was like a boy who has been caught with his hand in the jam pot," Jim explained. "I can't think what's the matter with him. Had I been in his shoes I would have kicked Jim Gibson out of the shop. He told me not to pay any attention to him and to run the shop as I pleased. Now what do you think of that? Now what do you think of that for a man who owns his own shop and has money in the bank? I tell you, I don't know how it is, but I don't work for Joe any more. He works for me. Some day you come in the shop casual-like and I'll boss him around for you. I'm telling you I don't know how it is that it come about, but I'm the boss of the shop as sure as the devil."

All of Bidwell was looking at itself and asking itself questions. Ed Hall, who had been a carpenter's apprentice earning but a few dollars a week with his master, Ben Peeler, was now foreman in the corn-cutter factory and received a salary of twenty-five dollars every Saturday night. It was more money than he had ever dreamed of earning in a week. On pay nights he dressed himself in his Sunday clothes and had himself shaved at Joe Trotter's barber shop. Then he went along Main Street, fingering the money in his pocket and half-fearing he would suddenly awaken and find it all a dream. He went into Wymer's tobacco store to get a cigar, and old Claude Wymer came to wait on him. On the second Saturday evening after he got his new position, the tobacconist, a rather obsequious man, called him Mr. Hall. It was the first time such a thing had happened and it upset him a little. He laughed and made a joke of it. "Don't get high and mighty," he said, and turned to wink at the men loafing in the shop. Later he thought about the matter and was sorry he had not accepted the new title without protest. "Well, I'm foreman, and a lot of the young fellows I've always known and fooled around with will be working under me," he told himself. "I can't be getting thick with them."

Ed walked along the street feeling very keenly the importance of his new place in the community. Other young fellows in the factory were getting a dollar and a half a day. At the end of the week he got twenty-five dollars, almost three times as much. The money was an indication of superiority. There could be no doubt about that. Ever since he had been a boy he had heard older men speak respectfully of men who possessed money. "Get on in the world," they said to young men, when they talked seriously. Among themselves they did not pretend that they did not want money. "It's money makes the mare go," they said.

Down Main Street to the New York Central tracks Ed went, and then turned out of the street and disappeared into the station. The evening train had passed and the place was deserted. He went into the dimly lighted waiting-room. An oil lamp, turned low, and fastened by a bracket to the wall made a little circle of light in a corner. The room was like a church in the early morning of a wintry day, cold and still. He went hurriedly to the light, and taking the roll of money from his pocket, counted it. Then he went out of the room and along the station platform almost to Main Street, but was not satisfied. On an impulse he returned to the waiting room again and, late in the evening on his way home, he stopped there for a final counting of the money before he went to bed.

Peter Fry was a blacksmith and had a son who was clerk in the Bidwell Hotel. He was a tall young fellow with curly yellow hair and watery blue eyes and smoked cigarettes, a habit that was an offense to the nostrils of the men of his times. His name was Jacob, but he was called in derision Fizzy Fry. The young man's mother was dead and he got his meals at the hotel and at night slept on a cot in the hotel office. He had a passion for gayly colored neckties and waistcoats and was forever trying unsuccessfully to attract the attention of the town girls. When he and his father met on the street, they did not speak to each other. Sometimes the father stopped and stared at his son. "How did I happen to be the father of a thing like that?" he muttered aloud.

The blacksmith was a square-shouldered, heavily built man with a bushy black beard and a tremendous voice. When he was a young man he sang in the Methodist choir, but after his wife died he stopped going to church and began putting his voice to other uses. He smoked a short clay pipe that had become black with age and that at night could not be seen against his black curly beard. Smoke rolled out of his mouth in clouds and appeared to come up out of his belly. He was like a volcanic mountain and was called, by the men who loafed in Birdie Spinks' drugstore, Smoky Pete.

Smoky Pete was in more ways than one like a mountain given to eruptions. He did not get drunk, but after his wife died he got into the habit of having two or three drinks of whisky every evening. The whisky inflamed his mind and he strode up and down Main Street, ready to quarrel with anyone his eye lighted upon. He got into the habit of roaring at his fellow citizens and making ribald jokes at their expense. Everyone was a little afraid of him and he became in an odd way the guardian of the town morals. Sandy Ferris, a house painter, became a drunkard and did not support his family. Smoky Pete abused him in the public streets and in the sight of all men. "You cheap thing, warming your belly with whisky while your children freeze, why don't you try being a man?" he shouted at the house painter, who staggered into a side street and went to sleep off his intoxication in a stall in Clyde Neighbors' livery barn. The blacksmith kept at the painter until the whole town took up his cry and the saloons became ashamed to accept his custom. He was forced to reform.

The blacksmith did not, however, discriminate in the choice of victims. His was not the spirit of the reformer. A merchant of Bidwell, who had always been highly respected and who was an elder in his church, went one evening to the county seat and there got into the company of a notorious woman known throughout the county as Nell Hunter. The two went into a little room at the back of a saloon and were seen by two Bidwell young men who had gone to the county seat for an evening of adventure. When the merchant, named Pen Beck, realized he had been seen, he was afraid the tale of his indiscretion would be carried to his home town, and left the woman to join the young men. He was not a drinking man, but began at once to buy drinks for his companions. The three got very drunk and drove home together late at night in a rig the young men had hired for the occasion from Clyde Neighbors. On the way the merchant kept trying to explain his presence in the company of the woman. "Don't say anything about it," he urged. "It would be misunderstood. I have a friend whose son has been taken in by the woman. I was trying to get her to let him alone."

The two young men were delighted that they had caught the merchant off his guard. "It's all right," they assured him. "Be a good fellow and we won't tell your wife or the minister of your church." When they had all the drinks they could carry, they got the merchant into the buggy and began to whip the horse. They had driven halfway to Bidwell and all of them had fallen into a drunken sleep, when the horse became frightened at something in the road and ran away. The buggy was overturned and they were all thrown into the road. One of the young men had an arm broken and Pen Beck's coat was almost torn in two. He paid the young man's doctor's bill and settled with Clyde Neighbors for the damage to the buggy.

For a long time the story of the merchant's adventure did not leak out, and when it did, but a few intimate friends of the young men knew it. Then it reached the ears of Smoky Pete. On the day he heard it he could hardly bear to wait until evening came. He hurried to Ben Head's saloon, had two drinks of whisky and then went to stand with the loafers before Birdie Spinks' drugstore. At half past seven Pen Beck turned into Main Street from Cherry Street, where he lived. When he was more than three blocks away from the crowd of men before the drugstore, Smoky Pete's roaring voice began to question him. "Well, Penny, my lad, so you went for a night among the ladies?" he shouted. "You've been fooling around with my girl, Nell Hunter, over at the county seat. I'd like to know what you mean. You'll have to make an explanation to me."

The merchant stopped and stood on the sidewalk, unable to decide whether to face his tormentor or flee. It was just at the quiet time of the evening when the housewives of the town had finished their evening's work and stood resting by the kitchen doors. It seemed to Pen Beck that Smoky Pete's voice could be heard for a mile. He decided to face it out and if necessary to fight the blacksmith. As he came hurriedly toward the group before the drugstore, Smoky Pete's voice took up the story of the merchant's wild night. He stepped out from the men in front of the store and seemed to be addressing himself to the whole street. Clerks, merchants, and customers rushed out of the stores. "Well," he cried, "so you made a night of it with my girl Nell Hunter. When you sat with her in the back room of the saloon you didn't know I was there. I was hidden under a table. If you'd done anything more than bite her on the neck I'd have come out and called you to time."

Smoky Pete broke into a roaring laugh and waved his arms to the people gathered in the street and wondering what it was all about. It was for him one of the really delicious spots of his life. He tried to explain to the people what he was talking about. "He was with Nell Hunter in the back room of a saloon over at the county seat," he shouted. "Edgar Duncan and Dave Oldham saw him there. He came home with them and the horse ran away. He didn't commit adultery. I don't want you to think that happened. All that happened was he bit my best girl, Nell Hunter, on the neck. That's what makes me so mad. I don't like to have her bitten by him. She is my girl and belongs to me."

The blacksmith, forerunner of the modern city newspaper reporter in his love of taking the center of the stage in order to drag into public sight the misfortunes of his fellows, did not finish his tirade. The merchant, white with anger, rushed up and struck him a blow on the chest with his small and rather fat fist. The blacksmith knocked him into the gutter and later, when he was arrested, went proudly off to the office of the town mayor and paid his fine.

It was said by the enemies of Smoky Pete that he had not taken a bath for years. He lived alone in a small frame house at the edge of town. Behind his house was a large field. The house itself was unspeakably dirty. When the factories came to town, Tom Butterworth and Steve Hunter bought the field intending to cut it into building lots. They wanted to buy the blacksmith's house and finally did secure it by paying a high price. He agreed to move out within a year but after the money was paid repented and wished he had not sold. A rumor began to run about town connecting the name of Tom Butterworth with that of Fanny Twist, the town milliner. It was said the rich farmer had been seen coming out of her shop late at night. The blacksmith also heard another story whispered in the streets. Louise Trucker, the farmer's daughter who had at one time been seen creeping through a side street in the company of young Steve Hunter, had gone to Cleveland and it was said she had become the proprietor of a prosperous house of ill fame. Steve's money, it was declared, had been used to set her up in business. The two stories offered unlimited opportunity for expansion in the blacksmith's mind, but while he was preparing himself to do what he called bringing the two men down in the sight and hearing of the whole town, a thing happened that upset his plans. His son Fizzy Fry left his place as clerk in the hotel and went to work in the corn-cutting machine factory. One day his father saw him coming from the factory at noon with a dozen other workmen. The young man had on overalls and smoked a pipe. When he saw his father he stopped, and when the other men had gone on, explained his sudden transformation. "I'm in the shop now, but I won't be there long," he said proudly. "You know Tom Butterworth stays at the hotel? Well, he's given me a chance. I got to stay in the shop for a while to learn about things. After that I'm to have a chance as shipping clerk. Then I'll be a traveler on the road." He looked at his father and his voice broke. "You haven't thought very much of me, but I'm not so bad," he said. "I don't want to be a sissy, but I'm not very strong. I worked at the hotel because there wasn't anything else I thought I could do."

Peter Fry went home to his house but could not eat the food he had cooked for himself on the tiny stove in the kitchen. He went outdoors and stood for a long time, looking out across the cow-pasture Tom Butterworth and Steve Hunter had bought and that they proposed should become a part of the rapidly growing city.

He had himself taken no part in the new impulses that had come upon the town, except that he had taken advantage of the failure of the town's first industrial effort to roar insults at those of his townsmen who had lost their money. One evening he and Ed Hall had got into a fight about the matter on Main Street, and the blacksmith had been compelled to pay another fine. Now he wondered what was the matter with him. He had evidently made a mistake about his son. Had he made a mistake about Tom Butterworth and Steve Hunter?

The perplexed man went back to his shop and all the afternoon worked in silence. His heart had been set on the creation of a dramatic scene on Main Street, when he openly attacked the two most prominent men of the town, and he even pictured himself as likely to be put in the town jail where he would have an opportunity to roar things through the iron bars at the citizens gathered in the street. In anticipation of such an event, he had prepared himself to attack the reputation of other people. He had never attacked women but, if he were locked up, he intended to do so. John May had once told him that Tom Butterworth's daughter, who had been away to college for a year, had been sent away because she was in the family way. John May had claimed he was responsible for her condition. Several of Tom's farm hands he said had been on intimate terms with the girl. The blacksmith had told himself that if he got into trouble for publicly attacking the father he would be justified in telling what he knew about the daughter.

The blacksmith did not come into Main Street that evening. As he went home from work he saw Tom Butterworth standing with Steve Hunter before the post-office. For several weeks Tom had been spending most of his time away from town, had only appeared in town for a few hours at a time, and had not been seen on the streets in the evening. The blacksmith had been waiting to catch both men on the street at one time. Now that this opportunity had come, he began to be afraid he would not dare take it. "What right have I to spoil my boy's chances?" he asked himself, as he went rather heavily along the street toward his own house.

It rained on that evening and for the first time in years Smoky Pete did not go into Main Street. He told himself that the rain kept him at home, but the thought did not satisfy him. All evening he moved restlessly about the house and at half past eight went to bed. He did not, however, sleep, but lay with his trousers on and with his pipe in his mouth, trying to think. Every few minutes he took the pipe from his mouth, blew out a cloud of smoke and swore viciously. At ten o'clock the farmer, who had owned the cow-pasture back of his house and who still kept his cows there, saw his neighbor tramping about in the rain in the field and saying things he had planned to say on Main Street in the hearing of the entire town.

The farmer also had gone to bed early, but at ten o'clock he decided that, as the rain continued to fall and as it was growing somewhat cold, he had better get up and let his cows into the barn. He did not dress, but threw a blanket about his shoulders and went out without a light. He let down the bars separating the field from the barnyard and then saw and heard Smoky Pete in the field. The blacksmith walked back and forth in the darkness, and as the farmer stood by the fence, began to talk in a loud voice. "Well, Tom Butterworth, you're fooling around with Fanny Twist," he cried into the silence and emptiness of the night. "You're sneaking into her shop late at night, eh? Steve Hunter has set Louise Trucker up in business in a house in Cleveland. Are you and Fanny Twist going to open a house here? Is that the next industrial enterprise we're to have here in this town?"

The amazed farmer stood in the rain in the darkness, listening to the words of his neighbor. The cows came through the gate and went into the barn. His bare legs were cold and he drew them alternately up under the blanket. For ten minutes Peter Fry tramped up and down in the field. Once he came quite near the farmer, who drew himself down beside the fence and listened, filled with amazement and fright. He could dimly see the tall, old man striding along and waving his arms about. When he had said many bitter, hateful things regarding the two most prominent men of Bidwell, he began to abuse Tom Butterworth's daughter, calling her a bitch and the daughter of a dog. The farmer waited until Smoky Pete had gone back to his house and, when he saw a light in the kitchen, and fancied he could also see his neighbor cooking food at a stove, he went again into his own house. He had himself never quarreled with Smoky Pete and was glad. He was glad also that the field at the back of his house had been sold. He intended to sell the rest of his farm and move west to Illinois. "The man's crazy," he told himself. "Who but a crazy man would talk that way in the darkness? I suppose I ought to report him and get him locked up, but I guess I'll forget what I heard. A man who would talk like that about nice respectable people would do anything. He might set fire to my house some night or something like that. I guess I'll just forget what I heard."

# Book Four

## CHAPTER XII

After the success of his corn-cutting machine and the apparatus for unloading coal cars that brought him a hundred thousand dollars in cash, Hugh could not remain the isolated figure he had been all through the first several years of his life in the Ohio community. From all sides men reached out their hands to him and more than one woman thought she would like to be his wife. All men lead their lives behind a wall of misunderstanding they themselves have built, and most men die in silence and unnoticed behind the walls. Now and then a man, cut off from his fellows by the peculiarities of his nature, becomes absorbed in doing something that is impersonal, useful, and beautiful. Word of his activities is carried over the walls. His name is shouted and is carried by the wind into the tiny inclosure in which other men live and in which they are for the most part absorbed in doing some petty task for the furtherance of their own comfort. Men and women stop their complaining about the unfairness and inequality of life and wonder about the man whose name they have heard.

From Bidwell, Ohio, to farms all over the Middle West, Hugh McVey's name had been carried. His machine for cutting corn was called the McVey Corn-Cutter. The name was printed in white letters against a background of red on the side of the machine. Farmer boys in the States of Indiana, Illinois, Iowa, Kansas,

Nebraska, and all the great corn-growing states saw it and in idle moments wondered what kind of man had invented the machine they operated. A Cleveland newspaper man came to Bidwell and went to Pickleville to see Hugh. He wrote a story telling of Hugh's early poverty and his efforts to become an inventor. When the reporter talked to Hugh he found the inventor so embarrassed and uncommunicative that he gave up trying to get a story. Then he went to Steve Hunter who talked to him for an hour. The story made Hugh a strikingly romantic figure. His people, the story said, came out of the mountains of Tennessee, but they were not poor whites. It was suggested that they were of the best English stock. There was a tale of Hugh's having in his boyhood contrived some kind of an engine that carried water from a valley to a mountain community; another of his having seen a clock in a store in a Missouri town and of his having later made a clock of wood for his parents; and a tale of his having gone into the forest with his father's gun, shot a wild hog and carried it down the mountainside on his shoulder in order to get money to buy school books. After the tale was printed the advertising manager of the corn-cutter factory got Hugh to go with him one day to Tom Butterworth's farm. Many bushels of corn were brought out of the corn cribs and a great mountain of corn was built on the ground at the edge of a field. Back of the mountain of corn was a corn field just coming into tassel. Hugh was told to climb up on the mountain and sit there. Then his picture was taken. It was sent to newspapers all over the West with copies of the biography cut from the Cleveland paper. Later both the picture and the biography were used in the catalogue that described the McVey Corn-Cutter.

The cutting of corn and putting it in shocks against

the time of the husking is heavy work. In recent times it has come about that much of the corn grown on mid-American prairie lands is not cut. The corn is left standing in the fields, and men go through it in the late fall to pick the yellow ears. The workers throw the corn over their shoulders into a wagon driven by a boy, who follows them in their slow progress, and it is then hauled away to the cribs. When a field has been picked, the cattle are turned in and all winter they nibble at the dry corn blades and tramp the stalks into the ground. All day long on the wide western prairies when the gray fall days have come, you may see the men and the horses working their way slowly through the fields. Like tiny insects they crawl across the immense landscapes. After them in the late fall and in the winter when the prairies are covered with snow, come the cattle. They are brought from the far West in cattle cars and after they have nibbled the corn blades all day, are taken to barns and stuffed to bursting with corn. When they are fat they are sent to the great killing-pens in Chicago, the giant city of the prairies. In the still fall nights, as you stand on prairie roads or in the barnyard back of one of the farmhouses, you may hear the rustling of the dry corn blades and then the crash of the heavy bodies of the beasts going forward as they nibble and trample the corn.

In earlier days the method of corn harvesting was different. There was poetry in the operation then as there is now, but it was set to another rhythm. When the corn was ripe men went into the fields with heavy corn knives and cut the stalks of corn close to the ground. The stalks were cut with the right hand swinging the corn knife and carried on the left arm. All day a man carried a heavy load of the stalks from which yellow ears hung down. When the load became unbearably heavy it was carried to the shock, and when all the corn was cut in a certain area, the shock was made secure by binding it with tarred rope or with a tough stalk twisted to take the place of the rope. When the cutting was done the long rows of stalks stood up in the fields like sentinels, and the men crawled off to the farmhouses and to bed, utterly weary.

Hugh's machine took all of the heavier part of the work away. It cut the corn near the ground and bound it into bundles that fell upon a platform. Two men followed the machine, one to drive the horses and the other to place the bundles of stalks against the shocks and to bind the completed shocks. The men went along smoking their pipes and talking. The horses stopped and the driver stared out over the prairies. His arms did not ache with weariness and he had time to think. The wonder and mystery of the wide open places got a little into his blood. At night when the work was done and the cattle fed and made comfortable in the barns, he did not go at once to bed but sometimes went out of his house and stood for a moment under the stars.

This thing the brain of the son of a mountain man, the poor white of the river town, had done for the people of the plains. The dreams he had tried so hard to put away from him and that the New England woman Sarah Shepard had told him would lead to his destruction had come to something. The car-dumping apparatus, that had sold for two hundred thousand dollars, had given Steve Hunter money to buy the plant-setting machine factory, and with Tom Butterworth to start manufacturing the corn-cutters, had affected the lives of fewer people, but it had carried the Missourian's name into other places and had also made a new kind of poetry in railroad yards and along rivers at the back of cities where ships are loaded. On city nights as you lie in your houses you may hear suddenly a long reverberating roar. It is a giant that has cleared his throat of a carload of coal. Hugh McVey helped to free the giant. He is still doing it. In Bidwell, Ohio, he is still at it, making new inventions, cutting the bands that have bound the giant. He is one man who had not been swept aside from his purpose by the complexity of life.

That, however, came near happening. After the coming of his success, a thousand little voices began calling to him. The soft hands of women reached out of the masses of people about him, out of the old dwellers and new dwellers in the city that was growing up about the factories where his machines were being made in ever increasing numbers. New houses were constantly being built along Turner's Pike that led down to his workshop at Pickleville. Beside Allie Mulberry a dozen mechanics were now employed in his experimental shop. They helped Hugh with a new invention, a hay-loading apparatus on which he was at work, and also made special tools for use in the corn-cutter factory and the new bicycle factory. A dozen new houses had been built in Pickleville itself. The wives of the mechanics lived in the houses and occasionally one of them came to see her husband at Hugh's shop. He found it less and less difficult to talk to people. The workmen, themselves not given to the use of many words, did not think his habitual silence peculiar. They were more skilled than Hugh in the use of tools and thought it rather an accident that he had done what they had not done. As he had grown rich by that road they also tried their hand at inventions. One of them made a patent door hinge that Steve sold for ten thousand dollars, keeping half the money for his services, as he nad done in the case of Hugh's car-dumping apparatus. At the noon hour the men hurried to their houses to eat and then came back to loaf before the factory and smoke their noonday pipes. They talked of money-making, of the price of food stuffs, of the advisability of a man's buying a house on the partial payment plan. Sometimes they talked of women and of their adventures with women. Hugh sat by himself inside the door of the shop and listened. At night after he had gone to bed he thought of what they had said. He lived in a house belonging to a Mrs. McCoy, the widow of a railroad section hand killed in a railroad accident, who had a daughter. The daughter, Rose McCoy, taught a country school and most of the year was away from home from Monday morning until late on Friday afternoon. Hugh lay in bed thinking of what his workmen had said of women and heard the old housekeeper moving about downstairs. Sometimes he got out of bed to sit by an open window. Because she was the woman whose life touched his most closely, he thought often of the school teacher. The McCoy house, a small frame affair with a picket fence separating it from Turner's Pike, stood with its back door facing the Wheeling Railroad. The section hands on the railroad remembered their former fellow workman, Mike McCoy, and wanted to be good to his widow. They sometimes dumped half decayed railroad ties over the fence into a potato patch back of the house. At night, when heavily loaded coal trains rumbled past, the brakemen heaved large chunks of coal over the fence. The widow awoke whenever a train passed. When one of the brakemen threw a chunk of coal he shouted and his voice could be heard above the rumble of the coal cars. "That's for Mike," he cried. Sometimes one of the chunks knocked a picket out of the fence and the next day Hugh put it back again. When the train had passed the widow got out of bed and brought the coal into the house. "I don't want to give the boys away by leaving it lying around in the daylight," she explained to Hugh. On Sunday mornings Hugh took a crosscut saw and cut the railroad ties into lengths that would go into the kitchen stove. Slowly his place in the McCoy household had become fixed, and when he received the hundred thousand dollars and everybody, even the mother and daughter, expected him to move, he did not do so. He tried unsuccessfully to get the widow to take more money for his board and when that effort failed, life in the McCoy household went as it had when he was a telegraph operator receiving forty dollars a month.

In the spring or fall, as he sat by his window at night, and when the moon came up and the dust in Turner's Pike was silvery white, Hugh thought of Rose McCoy, sleeping in some farmer's house. It did not occur to him that she might also be awake and thinking. He imagined her lying very still in bed. The section hand's daughter was a slender woman of thirty with tired blue eyes and red hair. Her skin had been heavily freckled in her youth and her nose was still freckled. Although Hugh did not know it, she had once been in love with George Pike, the Wheeling station agent, and a day had been set for the marriage. Then a difficulty arose in regard to religious beliefs and George Pike married another woman. It was then she became a school teacher. She was a woman of few words and she and Hugh had never been alone together, but as Hugh sat by the window on fall evenings, she lay awake in a room in the farmer's house, where she was boarding during the school season, and thought of him. She thought that had Hugh remained a telegraph operator at forty dollars a month something might have happened between them. Then she had other thoughts, or rather, sensations that had little to do with thoughts. The room in which she lay was very still and a streak of moonlight came in through the window. In the barn back of the farmhouse she could hear the cattle stirring about. A pig grunted and in the stillness that followed she could hear the farmer, who lay in the next room with his wife, snoring gently. Rose was not very stong and the physical did not rule in her nature, but she was very lonely and thought that, like the farmer's wife, she would like to have a man to lie with her. Warmth crept over her body and her lips became dry so that she moistened them with her tongue. Had you been able to creep unobserved into the room, you might have thought her much like a kitten lying by a stove. She closed her eyes and gave herself over to dreams. In her conscious mind she dreamed of being the wife of the bachelor Hugh McVey, but deep within her there was another dream, a dream having its basis in the memory of her one physical contact with a man. When they were engaged to be married George had often kissed her. On one evening in the spring they had gone to sit together on the grassy bank beside the creek in the shadow of the pickle factory, then deserted and silent, and had come near to going beyond kissing. Why nothing else had happened Rose did not exactly know. She had protested, but her protest had been feeble and had not expressed what she felt. George Pike had desisted in his effort to press love upon her because they were to be married, and he did not think it right to do what he thought of as taking advantage of a girl.

At any rate he did desist and long afterward, as she lay in the farmhouse consciously thinking of her mother's bachelor boarder, her thoughts became less and less distinct and when she had slipped off into sleep, George Pike came back to her. She stirred uneasily in bed and muttered words. Rough but gentle hands touched her cheeks and played in her hair. As the night wore on and the position of the moon shifted, the streak of moonlight lighted her face. One of her hands reached up and seemed to be caressing the moonbeams. The weariness had all gone out of her face. "Yes, George, I love you, I belong to you," she whispered.

Had Hugh been able to creep like the moonbeam into the presence of the sleeping school teacher, he must inevitably have loved her. Also he would perhaps have understood that it is best to approach human beings directly and boldly as he had approached the mechanical problems by which his days were filled. Instead he sat by his window in the presence of the moonlit night and thought of women as being utterly unlike himself. Words dropped by Sarah Shepard to the awakening boy came creeping back to his mind. He thought women were for other men but not for him, and told himself he did not want a woman.

And then in Turner's Pike something happened. A farmer boy, who had been to town and who had the daughter of a neighbor in his buggy, stopped in front of the house. A long freight train, grinding its way slowly past the station, barred the passage along the road. He held the reins in one hand and put the other about the waist of his companion. The two heads sought each other and lips met. They clung to each other. The same moon that shed its light on Rose McCoy in the distant farmhouse lighted the open place where the lovers sat in the buggy in the road. Hugh had to close his eyes and fight to put down an almost overpowering physical hunger in himself. His mind still protested that women were not for him. When his fancy made for him a picture of the school teacher Rose McCoy sleeping in a bed, he saw her only as a chaste white thing to be worshiped from afar and not to be approached, at least not by himself. Again he opened his eyes and looked at the lovers whose lips still clung together. His long slouching body stiffened and he sat up very straight in his chair. Then he closed his eyes again. A gruff voice broke the silence. "That's for Mike," it shouted and a great chunk of coal thrown from the train bounded across the potato patch and struck against the back of the house. Downstairs he could hear old Mrs. McCoy getting out of bed to secure the prize. The train passed and the lovers in the buggy sank away from each other. In the silent night Hugh could hear the regular beat of the hoofs of the farmer boy's horse as it carried him and his woman away into the darkness.

The two people, living in the house with the old woman who had almost finished her life, and themselves trying feebly to reach out to life, never got to anything very definite in relation to each other. One Saturday evening in the late fall the Governor of the state came to Bidwell. There was a parade to be followed by a political meeting and the Governor, who was a candidate for re-election, was to address the people from the steps of the town hall. Prominent citizens were to stand on the steps beside the Governor. Steve and Tom were to be there, and they had asked Hugh to come, but he had refused. He asked Rose McCoy to go to the meeting with him, and they set out from the house at eight o'clock and walked to town. Then they stood at the edge of the crowd in the shadow of a store building and listened to the speech. To Hugh's amazement his name was mentioned. The Governor spoke of the prosperity of the town, indirectly hinting that it was due to the political sagacity of the party of which he was a representative, and then mentioned several individuals also partly responsible. "The whole country is sweeping forward to new triumphs under our banner," he declared, "but not every community is so fortunate as I find you here. Labor is employed at good wages. Life here is fruitful and happy. You are fortunate here in having among you such business men as Steven Hunter and Thomas Butterworth; and in the inventor Hugh McVey you have one of the greatest intellects and the most useful men that ever lived to help lift the burden off the shoulder of labor. What his brain is doing for labor, our party is doing in another way. The protective tariff is really the father of modern prosperity."

The speaker paused and a cheer arose from the crowd. Hugh took hold of the school teacher's arm and drew her away down a side street. They walked home in silence, but when they got to the house and were about to go in, the school teacher hesitated. She wanted to ask Hugh to walk about in the darkness with her but did not have the courage of her desires. As they stood at the gate and as the tall man with the long serious face looked down at her, she remembered the speaker's words. "How could he care for me? How could a man like him care anything for a homely little school teacher like me?" she asked herself. Aloud she said something quite different. As they had come along Turner's Pike she had made up her mind she would boldly suggest a walk under the trees along Turner's Pike beyond the bridge, and had told herself that she would later lead him to the place beside the stream and in the shadow of the old pickle factory where she and George Pike had come so near being lovers. Instead she hesitated for a moment by the gate and then laughed awkwardly and passed in. "You should be proud. I would be proud if I could be spoken of like that. I don't see why you keep living here in a cheap little house like ours," she said.

On a warm spring Sunday night during the year in which Clara Butterworth came back to Bidwell to live, Hugh made what was for him an almost desperate effort to approach the school teacher. It had been a rainy afternoon and Hugh had spent a part of it in the house. He came over from his shop at noon and went to his room. When she was at home the school teacher occupied a room next his own. The mother who seldom left the house had on that day gone to the country to visit a brother. The daughter got dinner for herself and Hugh and he tried to help her wash the dishes. A plate fell out of his hands and its breaking seemed to break the silent, embarrassed mood that had possession of them. For a few minutes they were children and acted like children. Hugh picked up another plate and the school teacher told him to put it down. He refused. "You're as awkward as a puppy. How you ever manage to do anything over at that shop of yours is more than I know."

Hugh tried to keep hold of the plate which the school teacher tried to snatch away and for a few minutes they struggled laughing. Her cheeks were flushed and Hugh thought she looked bewitching. An impulse he had never had before came to him. He wanted to shout at the top of his lungs, throw the plate at the ceiling, sweep all of the dishes off the table and hear them crash on the floor, play like some huge animal loose in a tiny world. He looked at Rose and his hands trembled from the strength of the strange impulse. As he stood staring she took the plate out of his hand and went into the kitchen. Not knowing what else to do he put on his hat and went for a walk. Later he went to the shop and tried to work, but his hand trembled when he tried to hold a tool and the hay-loading apparatus on which he was at work seemed suddenly a very trivial and unimportant thing.

At four o'clock Hugh got back to the house and found it apparently empty, although the door leading to Turner's Pike was open. The rain had stopped falling and the sun struggled to work its way through the clouds. He went upstairs to his own room and sat on the edge of his bed. The conviction that the daughter of the house was in her room next door came to him, and although the thought violated all the beliefs he had ever held regarding women in relation to himself, he decided that she had gone to her room to be near him when he came in. For some reason he knew that if he went to her door and knocked she would not be surprised and would not refuse him admission. He took off his shoes and set them gently on the floor. Then he went on tiptoes out into the little hallway. The ceiling was so low that he had to stoop to avoid knocking his head against it. He raised his hand intending to knock on the door, and then lost courage. Several times he went into the hallway with the same intent, and each time returned noiselessly to his own room. He sat in the chair by the window and waited. An hour passed. He heard a noise that indicated that the school teacher had been lying on her bed. Then he heard footsteps on the stairs, and presently saw her go out of the house and go along Turner's Pike. She did not go toward town but over the bridge past his shop and into the country. Hugh drew himself back out of sight. He wondered where she could be going. "The roads are muddy. Why does she go out? Is she afraid of me?" he asked himself. When he saw her turn at the bridge and look back toward the house, his hands trembled again. "She wants me to follow. She wants me to go with her," he thought.

Hugh did presently go out of the house and along the road but did not meet the school teacher. She had in fact crossed the bridge and had gone along the bank of the creek on the farther side. Then she crossed over again on a fallen log and went to stand by the wall of the pickle factory. A lilac bush grew beside the wall and she stood out of sight behind it. When she saw Hugh in the road her heart beat so heavily that she had difficulty in breathing. He went along the road and presently passed out of sight, and a great weakness took possession of her. Although the grass was wet she sat on the ground against the wall of the building and closed her eyes. Later she put her face in her hands and wept.

The perplexed inventor did not get back to his boarding-house until late that night, and when he did he was unspeakably glad that he had not knocked on the door of Rose McCoy's room. He had decided during the walk that the whole notion that she had wanted him had been born in his own brain. "She's a nice woman," he had said to himself over and over during the walk, and thought that in coming to that conclusion he had swept away all possibilities of anything else in her. He was tired when he got home and went at once to bed. The old woman came home from the country and her brother sat in his buggy and shouted to the school teacher, who came out of her room and ran down the stairs. He heard the two women carry something heavy into the house and drop it on the floor. The farmer brother had given Mrs. McCoy a bag of potatoes. Hugh thought of the mother and daughter standing together downstairs and was unspeakably glad he had not given way to his impulse toward boldness. "She would be telling her now. She is a good woman and would be telling her now," he thought.

At two o'clock that night Hugh got out of bed. In spite of the conviction that women were not for him, he had found himself unable to sleep. Something that shone in the eyes of the school teacher, when she struggled with him for the possession of the plate, kept calling to him and he got up and went to the window. The clouds had all gone out of the sky and the night was clear. At the window next his own sat Rose McCoy. She was dressed in a nightgown and was looking away along Turner's Pike to the place where George Pike the station master lived with his wife. Without giving himself time to think, Hugh knelt on the floor and with his long arm reached across the space between the two windows. His fingers had almost touched the back of the woman's head and ached to play in the mass of red hair that fell down over her shoulders, when again self-consciousness overcame him. He drew his arm quickly back and stood upright in the room. His head banged against the ceiling and he heard the window of the room next door go softly down. With a conscious effort he took himself in hand. "She's a good woman. Remember, she's a good woman," he whispered to himself, and when he got again into his bed he refused to let his mind linger on the thoughts of the school teacher, but compelled them to turn to the unsolved problems he still had to face before he could complete his hay-loading apparatus. "You tend to your business and don't be going off on that road any more," he said, as though speaking to another person. "Remember she's a good woman and you haven't the right. That's all you have to do. Remember you haven't the right," he added with a ring of command in his voice.

## CHAPTER XIII

Hugh first saw Clara Butterworth one day in July when she had been at home for a month. She came to his shop late one afternoon with her father and a man who had been employed to manage the new bicycle factory. The three got out of Tom's buggy and came into the shop to see Hugh's new invention, the hay-loading apparatus. Tom and the man named Alfred Buckley went to the rear of the shop, and Hugh was left alone with the woman. She was dressed in a light summer gown and her cheeks were flushed. Hugh stood by a bench near an open window and listened while she talked of how much the town had changed in the three years she had been away. "It is your doing, everyone says that," she declared.

Clara had been waiting for an opportunity to talk to Hugh. She began asking questions regarding his work and what was to come of it. "When everything is done by machines, what are people to do?" she asked. She seemed to take it for granted that the inventor had thought deeply on the subject of industrial development, a subject on which Kate Chanceller had often talked during a whole evening. Having heard Hugh spoken of as one who had a great brain, she wanted to see the brain at work.

Alfred Buckley came often to her father's house and wanted to marry Clara. In the evening the two men sat on the front porch of the farmhouse and talked of the town and the big things that were to be done there. They spoke of Hugh, and Buckley, an energetic, talkative fellow with a long jaw and restless gray eyes who had come from New York City, suggested schemes for using him. Clara gathered that there was a plan on foot to get control of Hugh's future inventions and thereby gain an advantage over Steve Hunter.

The whole matter puzzled Clara. Alfred Buckley had asked her to marry him and she had put the matter off. The proposal had been a formal thing, not at all what she had expected from a man she was to take as a partner for life, but Clara was at the moment very seriously determined upon marriage. The New York man was at her father's house several evenings every week. She had never walked about with him nor had they in any way come close to each other. He seemed too much occupied with work to be personal and had proposed marriage by writing her a letter. Clara got the letter from the post-office and it upset her so that she felt she could not for a time go into the presence of anyone she knew. "I am unworthy of you, but I want you to be my wife. I will work for you. I am new here and you do not know me very well. All I ask is the privilege of proving my merit. I want you to be my wife, but before I dare come and ask you to do me so great an honor I feel I must prove myself worthy," the letter said.

Clara had driven into town alone on the day when she received it and later got into her buggy and drove south past the Butterworth farm into the hills. She forgot to go home to lunch or to the evening meal. The horse jogged slowly along, protesting and trying to turn back at every crossroad, but she kept on and did not get home until midnight. When she reached the farmhouse her father was waiting. He went with her into the barnyard and helped unhitch the horse. Nothing was said, and after a moment's conversation having nothing to do with the subject that occupied both their minds, she went upstairs and tried to think the matter out. She became convinced that her father had something to do with the proposal of marriage, that he knew about it and had waited for her to come home in order to see how it had affected her.

Clara wrote a reply that was non-committal as the proposal itself. "I do not know whether I want to marry you or not. I will have to become acquainted with you. I however thank you for the offer of marriage and when you feel that the right time has come, we will talk about it," she wrote.

After the exchange of letters, Alfred Buckley came to her father's house more often than before, but he and Clara did not become better acquainted. He did not talk to her, but to her father. Although she did not know it, the rumor that she was to marry the New York man had already run about town. She did not know whether her father or Buckley had told the tale.

On the front porch of the farmhouse through the summer evenings the two men talked of the progress of the town and the part they were taking and hoped to take in its future growth. The New York man had proposed a scheme to Tom. He was to go to Hugh and propose a contract giving the two men an option on all his future inventions. As the inventions were completed they were to be financed in New York City, and the two men would give up manufacture and make money much more rapidly as promoters. They hesitated because they were afraid of Steve Hunter, and because Tom was afraid Hugh would not fall in with their plan. "It wouldn't surprise me if Steve already had such a contract with him. He's a fool if he hasn't," the older man said.

Evening after evening the two men talked and Clara sat in the deep shadows at the back of the porch and listened. The enmity that had existed between herself and her father seemed to be forgotten. The man who had asked her to marry him did not look at her, but her father did. Buckley did most of the talking and spoke of New York City business men, already famous throughout the Middle West as giants of finance, as though they were his lifelong friends. "They'll put over anything I ask them to," he declared.

Clara tried to think of Alfred Buckley as a husband. Like Hugh McVey he was tall and gaunt but unlike the inventor, whom she had seen two or three times on the street, he was not carelessly dressed. There was something sleek about him, something that suggested a well-bred dog, a hound perhaps. As he talked he leaned forward like a greyhound in pursuit of a rabbit. His hair was carefully parted and his clothes fitted him like the skin of an animal. He wore a diamond scarf pin. His long jaw, it seemed to her, was always wagging. Within a few days after the receipt of his letter she had made up her mind that she did not want him as a husband, and she was convinced he did not want her. The whole matter of marriage had, she was sure, been in some way suggested by her father. When she came to that conclusion she was both angry and in an odd way touched. She did not interpret it as fear of some sort of indiscretion on her part, but thought that her father wanted her to marry because he wanted her to be happy. As she sat in the darkness on the front porch of the farmhouse the voices of the two men became indistinct. It was as though her mind went out of her body and like a living thing journeyed over the world. Dozens of men she had seen and had casually addressed, young fellows attending school at Columbus and boys of the town with whom she had gone to parties and dances when she was a young girl, came to stand before her. She saw their figures distinctly, but remembered them at some advantageous moment of her contact with them. At Columbus there was a young man from a town in the southern end of the state, one of the sort that is always in love with a woman. During her first year in school he had noticed Clara, had been undecided as to whether he had better pay attention to her or to a little black-eyed town girl who was in their classes. Several times he walked down the college hill and along the street with Clara. The two stood at a street crossing where she was in the habit of taking a car. Several cars went by as they stood together by a bush that grew by a high stone wall. They talked of trivial matters, a comedy club that had been organized in the school, the chances of victory for the football team. The young man was one of the actors in a play to be given by the comedy club and told Clara of his experiences at rehearsals. As he talked his eyes began to shine and he seemed to be looking, not at her face or body, but at something within her. For a time, perhaps for fifteen minutes, there was a possibility that the two people would love each other. Then the young man went away and later she saw him walking under the trees on the college campus with the little black-eyed town girl.

As she sat on the porch in the darkness in the summer evenings, Clara thought of the incident and of dozens of other swift-passing contacts she had made with men. The voices of the two men talking of money-making went on and on. Whenever she came back out of her introspective world of thought, Alfred Buckley's long jaw was wagging. He was always at work, steadily, persistently urging something on her father. It was difficult for Clara to think of her father as a rabbit, but the notion that Alfred Buckley was like a hound stayed with her. "The wolf and the wolfhound," she thought absent-mindedly.

Clara was twenty-three and seemed to herself mature. She did not intend wasting any more time going to school and did not want to be a professional woman like Kate Chanceller. There was something she did want and in a way some man, she did not know what man it would be, was concerned in the matter. She was very hungry for love, but might have got that from another woman. Kate Chanceller would have loved her. She was not unconscious of the fact that their friendship had been something more than friendship. Kate loved to hold Clara's hand and wanted to kiss and caress her. The inclination had been put down by Kate herself, a struggle had gone on in her, and Clara had been dimly conscious of it and had respected Kate for making it.

Why? Clara asked herself that question a dozen times during the early weeks of that summer. Kate Chanceller had taught her to think. When they were together Kate did both the thinking and the talking, but now Clara's mind had a chance. There was something back of her desire for a man. She wanted something more than caresses. There was a creative impulse in her that could not function until she had been made love to by a man. The man she wanted was but an instrument she sought in order that she might fulfill herself. Several times during those evenings in the presence of the two men, who talked only of making money out of the products of another man's mind, she almost forced her mind out into a concrete thought concerning women, and then it became again befogged.

Clara grew tired of thinking, and listened to the talk. The name of Hugh McVey played through the persistent conversation like a refrain. It became fixed in her mind. The inventor was not married. By the social system under which she lived that and that only made him a possibility for her purposes. She began to think of the inventor, and her mind, weary of playing about her own figure, played about the figure of the tall, serious-looking man she had seen on Main Street. When Alfred Buckley had driven away to town for the night, she went upstairs to her own room but did not get into bed. Instead, she put out her light and sat by an open window that looked out upon the orchard and from which she could see a little stretch of the road that ran past the farmhouse toward town. Every evening before Alfred Buckley went away, there was a little scene on the front porch. When the visitor got up to go, her father made some excuse for going indoors or around the corner of the house into the barnyard. "I will have Jim Priest hitch up your horse," he said and hurried away. Clara was left in the company of the man who had pretended he wanted to marry her, and who, she was convinced, wanted nothing of the kind. She was not embarrassed, but could feel his embarrassment and enjoyed it. He made formal speeches. "Well, the night is fine," he said. Clara hugged the thought that he was uncomfortable. "He has taken me for a green country girl, impressed with him because he is from the city and dressed in fine clothes," she thought. Sometimes her father stayed away five or ten minutes and she did not say a word. When her father returned Alfred Buckley shook hands with him and then turned to Clara, apparently now quite at his ease. "We have bored you, I'm afraid," he said. He took her hand and leaning over, kissed the back of it ceremoniously. Her father looked away. Clara went upstairs and sat by the window. She could hear the two men continuing their talk in the road before the house. After a time the front door banged, her father came into the house and the visitor drove away. Everything became quiet and for a long time she could hear the hoofs of Alfred Buckley's horse beating a rapid tattoo on the road that led down into town.

Clara thought of Hugh McVey. Alfred Buckley had spoken of him as a backwoodsman with a streak of genius. He constantly harped on the notion that he and Tom could use the man for their own ends, and she wondered if both of the men were making as great a mistake about the inventor as they were about her. In the silent summer night, when the sound of the horse's hoofs had died away and when her father had quit stirring about the house, she heard another sound. The corn-cutting machine factory was very busy and had put on a night shift. When the night was still, or when there was a slight breeze blowing up the hill from town, there was a low rumbling sound coming from many machines working in wood and steel, followed at regular intervals by the steady breathing of a steam engine.

The woman at the window, like everyone else in her town and in all the towns of the Midwestern country, became touched with the idea of the romance of industry. The dreams of the Missouri boy that he had fought, had by the strength of his persistency twisted into new channels so that they had expressed themselves in definite things, in corn-cutting machines and in machines for unloading coal cars and for gathering hay out of a field and loading it on wagons without aid of human hands, were still dreams and capable of arousing dreams in others. They awoke dreams in the mind of the woman. The figures of other men that had been playing through her mind slipped away and but the one figure remained. Her mind made up stories concerning Hugh. She had read the absurd tale that had been printed in the Cleveland paper and her fancy took hold of it. Like every other citizen of America she believed in heroes. In books and magazines she had read of heroic men who had come up out of poverty by some strange alchemy to combine in their stout persons all of the virtues. The broad, rich land demanded gigantic figures, and the minds of men had created the figures. Lincoln, Grant, Garfield, Sherman, and a half-dozen other men were something more than human in the minds of the generation that came immediately after the days of their stirring performance. Already industry was creating a new set of semi-mythical figures. The factory at work in the nighttime in the town of Bidwell became, to the mind of the woman sitting by the window in the farmhouse, not a factory but a powerful animal, a powerful beastlike thing that Hugh had tamed and made useful to his fellows. Her mind ran forward and took the taming of the beast for granted. The hunger of her generation found a voice in her. Like everyone else she wanted heroes, and Hugh, to whom she had never talked and about whom she knew nothing, became a hero. Her father, Alfred Buckley, Steve Hunter and the rest were after all pigmies. Her father was a schemer; he had even schemed to get her married, perhaps to further his own plans. In reality his schemes were so ineffective that she did not need to be angry with him. There was but one man of them all who was not a schemer. Hugh was what she wanted to be. He was a creative force. In his hands dead inanimate things became creative forces. He was what she wanted not herself but perhaps a son, to be. The thought, at last definitely expressed, startled Clara, and she arose from the chair by the window and prepared to go to bed. Something within her body ached, but she did not allow herself to pursue further the thoughts she had been having.

On the day when she went with her father and Alfred Buckley to visit Hugh's shop, Clara knew that she wanted to marry the man she would see there. The thought was not expressed in her but slept like a seed newly planted in fertile soil. She had herself managed that she be taken to the factory and had also managed that she be left with Hugh while the two men went to look at the half-completed hay-loader at the back of the shop.

She had begun talking to Hugh while the four people stood on the little grass plot before the shop. They went inside and her father and Buckley went through a door toward the rear. She stopped by a bench and as she continued talking Hugh was compelled to stop and stand beside her. She asked questions, paid him vague compliments, and as he struggled, trying to make conversation, she studied him. To cover his confusion he half-turned away and looked out through a window into Turner's Pike. His eyes, she decided, were nice. They were somewhat small, but there was something gray and cloudy in them, and the gray cloudiness gave her confidence in the person behind the eyes. She could, she felt, trust him. There was something in his eyes that was like the things most grateful to her own nature, the sky seen across an open stretch of country or over a river that ran straight away into the distance. Hugh's hair was coarse like the mane of a horse, and his nose was like the nose of a horse. He was, she decided, very like a horse; an honest, powerful horse, a horse that was humanized by the mysterious, hungering thing that expressed itself through his eyes. "If I have to live with an animal; if, as Kate Chanceller once said, we women have to decide what other animal we are to live with before we can begin being humans, I would rather live with a strong, kindly horse than a wolf or a wolfhound," she found herself thinking.

## CHAPTER XIV

Hugh had no suspicion that Clara had him under consideration as a possible husband. He knew nothing about her, but after she went away he began to think. She was a woman and good to look upon and at once took Rose McCoy's place in his mind. All unloved men and many who are loved play in a half-subconscious way with the figures of many women as women's minds play with the figures of men, seeing them in many situations, vaguely caressing them, dreaming of closer contacts. With Hugh the impulse toward women had started late, but it was becoming every day more active. When he talked to Clara and while she stayed in his presence, he was more embarrassed than he had ever been before, because he was more conscious of her than he had ever been of any other woman. In secret he was not the modest man he thought himself. The success of his corn-cutting machine and his car-dumping apparatus and the respect, amounting almost to worship, he sometimes saw in the eyes of the people of the Ohio town had fed his vanity. It was a time when all America was obsessed with one idea, and to the people of Bidwell nothing could be more important, necessary and vital to progress than the things Hugh had done. He did not walk and talk like the other people of the town, and his body was over-large and loosely put together, but in secret he did not want to be different even in a physical way. Now and then there came an opportunity for a test of physical strength: an iron bar was to be lifted or a part of some heavy machine swung into place in the shop. In such a test he had found he could lift almost twice the load another could handle. Two men grunted and strained, trying to lift a heavy bar off the floor and put it on a bench. He came along and did the job alone and without apparent effort.

In his room at night or in the late afternoon or evening in the summer when he walked on country roads, he sometimes felt keen hunger for recognition of his merits from his fellows, and having no one to praise him, he praised himself. When the Governor of the state spoke in praise of him before a crowd and when he made Rose McCoy come away because it seemed immodest for him to stay and hear such words, he found himself unable to sleep. After tossing in his bed for two or three hours he got up and crept quietly out of the house. He was like a man who, having an unmusical voice, sings to himself in a bathroom while the water is making a loud, splashing noise. On that night Hugh wanted to be an orator. As he stumbled in the darkness along Turner's Pike he imagined himself Governor of a state addressing a multitude of people. A mile north of Pickleville a dense thicket grew beside the road, and Hugh stopped and addressed the young trees and bushes. In the darkness the mass of bushes looked not unlike a crowd standing at attention, listening. The wind blew and played in the thick, dry growth and there was a sound as of many voices whispering words of encouragement. Hugh said many foolish things. Expressions he had heard from the lips of Steve Hunter and Tom Butterworth came into his mind and were repeated by his lips. He spoke of the swift growth that had come to the town of Bidwell as though it were an unmixed blessing, the factories, the homes of happy, contented people, the coming of industrial development as something akin to a visit of the gods. Rising to the height of egotism he shouted, "I have done it. I have done it."

Hugh heard a buggy coming along the road and fled

into the thicket. A farmer, who had gone to town for the evening and who had stayed after the political meeting to talk with other farmers in Ben Head's saloon, went homeward, asleep in his buggy. His head nodded up and down, heavy with the vapors rising from many glasses of beer. Hugh came out of the thicket feeling somewhat ashamed. The next day he wrote a letter to Sarah Shepard and told her of his progress. "If you or Henry want any money, I can let you have all you want," he wrote, and did not resist the temptation to tell her something of what the Governor had said of his work and his mind. "Anyway they must think I amount to something whether I do or not," he said wistfully.

Having awakened to his own importance in the life about him, Hugh wanted direct, human appreciation. After the failure of the effort both he and Rose had made to break through the wall of embarrassment and reserve that kept them apart, he knew pretty definitely that he wanted a woman, and the idea, once fixed in his mind, grew to gigantic proportions. All women became interesting, and he looked with hungry eyes at the wives of the workmen who sometimes came to the shop door to pass a word with their husbands, at young farm girls who drove along Turner's Pike on summer afternoons, town girls who walked in the Bidwell Main Street in the evening, at fair women and dark women. As he wanted a woman more consciously and determinedly he became more afraid of individual women. His success and his association with the workmen in his shop had made him less self-conscious in the presence of men, but the women were different. In their presence he was ashamed of his secret thoughts of them.

On the day when he was left alone with Clara, Tom Butterworth and Alfred Buckley stayed at the back of the shop for nearly twenty minutes. It was a hot day and beads of sweat stood on Hugh's face. His sleeves were rolled to his elbows and his hands and hairy arms were covered with shop grime. He put up his hand to wipe the sweat from his forehead, leaving a long, black mark. Then he became aware of the fact that as she talked the woman looked at him in an absorbed, almost calculating way. It was as though he were a horse and she were a buyer examining him to be sure he was sound and of a kindly disposition. While she stood beside him her eyes were shining and her cheeks were flushed. The awakening, assertive male thing in him whispered that the flush on her cheeks and the shining eyes were indicative of something. His mind had been taught that lesson by the slight and wholly unsatisfactory experience with the school teacher at his boarding-house.

Clara drove away from the shop with her father and Alfred Buckley. Tom drove and Alfred Buckley leaned forward and talked. "You must find out whether or not Steve has an option on the new tool. It would be foolish to ask outright and give ourselves away. That inventor is stupid and vain. Those fellows always are. They appear to be quiet and shrewd, but they always let the cat out of the bag. The thing to do is to flatter him in some way. A woman could find out all he knows in ten minutes." He turned to Clara and smiled. There was something infinitely impertinent in the fixed, animal-like stare of his eyes. "We do take you into our plans, your father and me, eh?" he said. "You must be careful not to give us away when you talk to that inventor."

From his shop window Hugh stared at the backs of the heads of the three people. The top of Tom Butterworth's buggy had been let down, and when he talked Alfred Buckley leaned forward and his head disappeared. Hugh thought Clara must look like the kind of woman men meant when they spoke of a lady. The farmer's daughter had an instinct for clothes, and Hugh's mind got the idea of gentility by way of the medium of clothes. He thought the dress she had worn the most stylish thing he had ever seen. Clara's friend Kate Chanceller, while mannish in her dress, had an instinct for style and had taught Clara some valuable lessons. "Any woman can dress well if she knows how," Kate had declared. She had taught Clara how to study and emphasize by dress the good points of her body. Beside Clara, Rose McCoy looked dowdy and commonplace.

Hugh went to the rear of his shop to where there was a water-tap and washed his hands. Then he went to a bench and tried to take up the work he had been doing. Within five minutes he went to wash his hands again. He went out of the shop and stood beside the small stream that rippled along beneath willow bushes and disappeared under the bridge beneath Turner's Pike, and then went back for his coat and quit work for the day. An instinct led him to go past the creek again and he knelt on the grass at the edge and again washed his hands.

Hugh's growing vanity was fed by the thought that Clara was interested in him, but it was not yet strong enough to sustain the thought. He took a long walk, going north from the shop along Turner's Pike for two or three miles and then by a crossroad between corn and cabbage fields to where he could, by crossing a meadow, get into a wood. For an hour he sat on a log at the wood's edge and looked south. Away in the distance, over the roofs of the houses of the town, he could see a white speck against a background of green—the Butterworth farmhouse. Almost at once he decided that the thing he had seen in Clara's eyes and that was sister to something he had seen in Rose McCoy's eyes had nothing to do with him. The mantle of vanity he had been wearing dropped off and left him naked and sad. "What would she be wanting of me?" he asked himself, and got up from the log to look with critical eyes at his long, bony body. For the first time in two or three years he thought of the words so often repeated in his presence by Sarah Shepard in the first few months after he left his father's shack by the shore of the Mississippi River and came to work at the railroad station. She had called his people lazy louts and poor white trash and had railed against his inclination to dreams. By struggle and work he had conquered the dreams but could not conquer his ancestry, nor change the fact that he was at bottom poor white trash. With a shudder of disgust he saw himself again a boy in ragged clothes that smelled of fish, lying stupid and half-asleep in the grass beside the Mississippi River. He forgot the majesty of the dreams that sometimes came to him, and only remembered the swarms of flies that, attracted by the filth of their clothes, hovered over him and over the drunken father who lay sleeping beside him.

A lump arose in his throat and for a moment he was consumed with self-pity. Then he went out of the wood, crossed the field, and with his peculiar, long, shambling gait that got him over the ground with surprising rapidity, went again along the road. Had there been a stream nearby he would have been tempted to tear off his clothes and plunge in. The notion that he could ever become a man who would in any way be attractive to a woman like Clara Butterworth seemed the greatest folly in the world. "She's a lady. What would she be wanting of me? I ain't fitten for her. I ain't fitten for her," he said aloud, unconsciously falling into the dialect of his father.

Hugh walked the entire afternoon away and in the evening went back to his shop and worked until midnight. So energetically did he work that several knotty problems in the construction of the hay-loading apparatus were cleared away.

On the second evening after the encounter with Clara, Hugh went for a walk in the streets of Bidwell. He thought of the work on which he had been engaged all day and then of the woman he had made up his mind he could under no circumstances win. As darkness came on he went into the country, and at nine returned along the railroad tracks past the corn-cutter factory. The factory was working day and night, and the new plant, also beside the tracks and but a short distance away, was almost completed. Behind the new plant was a field Tom Butterworth and Steve Hunter had bought and laid out in streets of workingmen's houses. The houses were cheaply constructed and ugly, and in all directions there was a vast disorder; but Hugh did not see the disorder or the ugliness of the buildings. The sight that lay before him strengthened his waning vanity. Something of the loose shuffle went out of his stride and he threw back his shoulders. "What I have done here amounts to something. I'm all right," he thought, and had almost reached the old corn-cutter plant when several men came out of a side door and getting upon the tracks, walked before him.

In the corn-cutter plant something had happened that excited the men. Ed Hall the superintendent had played a trick on his fellow townsmen. He had put on overalls and gone to work at a bench in a long room with some fifty other men. "I'm going to show you up," he said, laughing. "You watch me. We're behind on the work and I'm going to show you up."

The pride of the workmen had been touched, and for two weeks they had worked like demons to outdo the boss. At night when the amount of work done was calculated, they laughed at Ed. Then they heard that the piece-work plan was to be installed in the factory, and were afraid they would be paid by a scale calculated on the amount of work done during the two weeks of furious effort.

The workmen who stumbled along the tracks cursed Ed Hall and the men for whom he worked. "I lost six hundred dollars in the plant-setting machine failure and this is all I get, to be played a trick on by a young suck like Ed Hall," a voice grumbled. Another voice took up the refrain. In the dim light Hugh could see the speaker, a man with a bent back, a product of the cabbage fields, who had come to town to find employment. Although he did not recognize it, he had heard the voice before. It came from a son of the cabbage farmer Ezra French and was the same voice he had once heard complaining at night as the French boys crawled across a cabbage field in the moonlight. The man now said something that startled Hugh. "Well," he declared, "it's a joke on me. I quit Dad and made him sore; now he won't take me back again. He says I'm a quitter and no good. I thought I'd come to town to a factory and find it easier here. Now I've got married and have to stick to my job no matter what they do. In the country I worked like a dog a few weeks a year, but here I'll probably have to work like that all the time. It's the way things go. I thought it was mighty funny, all this talk about the factory work being so easy. I wish the old days were back. I don't see how that inventor or his inventions ever helped us workers. Dad was right about him. He said an inventor wouldn't do nothing for workers. He said it would be better to tar and feather that telegraph operator. I guess Dad was right."

The swagger went out of Hugh's walk and he stopped to let the men pass out of sight and hearing along the track. When they had gone a little away a quarrel broke out. Each man felt the others must be in some way responsible for his betrayal in the matter of the contest with Ed Hall and accusations flew back and forth. One of the men threw a heavy stone that ran down along the tracks and jumped into a ditch filled with dry weeds. It made a heavy crashing sound. Hugh heard heavy footsteps running. He was afraid the men were going to attack him, and climbed over a fence, crossed a barnyard, and got into an empty street. As he went along trying to understand what had happened and why the men were angry, he met Clara Butterworth, standing and apparently waiting for him under a street lamp.

Hugh walked beside Clara, too perplexed to attempt to understand the new impulses crowding in upon his mind. She explained her presence in the street by saying she had been to town to mail a letter and intended walking home by a side road. "You may come with me if you're just out for a walk," she said. The two walked in silence. Hugh's mind, unaccustomed to traveling in wide circles, centered on his companion. Life seemed suddenly to be crowding him along strange roads. In two days he had felt more new emotions and had felt them more deeply than he would have thought possible to a human being. The hour through which he had just passed had been extraordinary. He had started out from his boarding-house sad and depressed. Then he had come by the factories and pride in what he thought he had accomplished swept in on him. Now it was apparent the workers in the factories were not happy, that there was something the matter. He wondered if Clara would know what was wrong and would tell him if he asked. He wanted to ask many questions. "That's what I want a woman for. I want someone close to me who understands things and will tell me about them," he thought.

Clara remained silent and Hugh decided that she, like the complaining workmen stumbling along the tracks, did not like him. The man had said he wished Hugh had never come to town. Perhaps everyone in Bidwell secretly felt that way.

Hugh was no longer proud of himself and his achievements. Perplexity had captured him. When he and Clara got out of town into a country road, he began thinking of Sarah Shepard, who had been friendly and kind to him when he was a lad, and wished she were with him, or better yet that Clara would take the attitude toward him she had taken. Had Clara taken it into her head to scold as Sarah Shepard had done he would have been relieved.

Instead Clara walked in silence, thinking of her own affairs and planning to use Hugh for her own ends. It had been a perplexing day for her. Late that afternoon there had been a scene between her and her father and she had left home and come to town because she could no longer bear being in his presence. When she had seen Hugh coming toward her she had stopped under a street lamp to wait for him. "I could set everything straight by getting him to ask me to marry him," she thought.

The new difficulty that had arisen between Clara and her father was something with which she had nothing to do. Tom, who thought himself so shrewd and crafty, had been taken in by the city man, Alfred Buckley. A federal officer had come to town during the afternoon to arrest Buckley. The man had turned out to be a notorious swindler wanted in several cities. In New York he had been one of a gang who distributed counterfeit money, and in other states he was wanted for swindling women, two of whom he married unlawfully.

The arrest had been like a shot fired at Tom by a member of his own household. He had almost come to think of Alfred Buckley as one of his family, and as he drove rapidly along the road toward home, he had been profoundly sorry for his daughter and had intended to ask her to forgive him for his part in betraying her into a false position. That he had not openly committed himself to any of Buckley's schemes, had signed no papers and written no letters that would betray the conspiracy he had entered into against Steve, filled him with joy. He had intended to be generous, and even, if necessary, confess to Clara his indiscretion in talking of a possible marriage, but when he got to the farmhouse and had taken Clara into the parlor and had closed the door, he changed his mind. He told her of Buckley's arrest, and then started tramping excitedly up and down in the room. Her coolness infuriated him. "Don't set there like a clam!" he shouted. "Don't you know what's happened? Don't you know you're disgraced, have brought disgrace on my name?"

The angry father explained that half the town knew of her engagement to marry Alfred Buckley, and when Clara declared they were not engaged and that she had never intended marrying the man, his anger did not abate. He had himself whispered the suggestion about town, had told Steve Hunter, Gordon Hart, and two or three others, that Alfred Buckley and his daughter would no doubt do what he spoke of as "hitting it off," and they had of course told their wives. The fact that he had betrayed his daughter into an ugly position gnawed at his consciousness. "I suppose the rascal told it himself," he said, in reply to her statement, and again gave way to anger. He glared at his daughter and wished she were a son so he could strike with his fists. His voice arose to a shout and could be heard in the barnyard where Jim Priest and a young farm hand were at work. They stopped work and listened. "She's been up to something. Do you suppose some man has got her in trouble?" the young farm hand asked.

In the house Tom expressed his old dissatisfaction with his daughter. "Why haven't you married and settled down like a decent woman?" he shouted. "Tell me that. Why haven't you married and settled down? Why are you always getting in trouble? Why haven't you married and settled down?"

Clara walked in the road beside Hugh and thought that all her troubles would come to an end if he would ask her to be his wife. Then she became ashamed of her thoughts. As they passed the last street lamp and prepared to set out by a roundabout way along a dark road, she turned to look at Hugh's long, serious face. The tradition that had made him appear different from other men in the eyes of the people of Bidwell began to affect her. Ever since she had come home she had been hearing people speak of him with something like awe in their voices. For her to marry the town's hero would, she knew, set her on a high place in the eyes of her people. It would be a triumph for her and would reestablish her, not only in her father's eyes but in the eyes of everyone. Everyone seemed to think she should marry; even Jim Priest had said so. He had said she was the marrying kind. Here was her chance. She wondered why she did not want to take it.

Clara had written her friend Kate Chanceller a letter in which she had declared her intention of leaving home and going to work, and had come to town afoot to mail it. On Main Street as she went through the crowds of men who had come to loaf the evening away before the stores, the force of what her father had said concerning the connection of her name with that of Buckley the swindler had struck her for the first time. The men were gathered together in groups, talking excitedly. No doubt they were discussing Buckley's arrest. Her own name was, no doubt, being bandied about. Her cheeks burned and a keen hatred of mankind had possession of her. Now her hatred of others awoke in her an almost worshipful attitude toward Hugh. By the time they had walked together for five minutes all thought of using him to her own ends had gone. "He's not like Father or Henderson Woodburn or Alfred Buckley," she told herself. "He doesn't scheme and twist things about trying to get the best of someone else. He works, and because of his efforts things are accomplished." The figure of the farm hand Jim Priest working in a field of corn came to her mind. "The farm hand works," she thought, "and the corn grows. This man sticks to his task in his shop and makes a town grow."

In her father's presence during the afternoon Clara had remained calm and apparently indifferent to his tirade. In town in the presence of the men she was sure were attacking her character, she had been angry, ready to fight. Now she wanted to put her head on Hugh's shoulder and cry.

They came to the bridge near where the road turned and led to her father's house. It was the same bridge to which she had come with the school teacher and to which John May had followed, looking for a fight. Clara stopped. She did not want anyone at the house to know that Hugh had walked home with her. "Father is so set on my getting married, he would go to see him tomorrow," she thought. She put her arms upon the rail of the bridge and bending over buried her face between them. Hugh stood behind her, turning his head from side to side and rubbing his hands on his trouser legs, beside himself with embarrassment. There was a flat, swampy field beside the road and not far from the bridge, and after a moment of silence the voices of a multitude of frogs broke the stillness. Hugh became overwhelmingly sad. The notion that he was a big man and deserved to have a woman to live with and understand him went entirely away. For the moment he wanted to be a boy and put his head on the shoulder of the woman. He did not look at Clara but at himself. In the dim light his hands, nervously fumbling about, his long, loosely-put-together body, everything connected with his person, seemed ugly and altogether unattractive. He could see the woman's small firm hands that lay on the railing of the bridge. They were, he thought, like everything connected with her person, shapely and beautiful, just as everything connected with his own person was unshapely and ugly.

Clara aroused herself from the meditative mood that had taken possession of her, and after shaking Hugh's hand and explaining that she did not want him to go further went away. When he thought she had quite gone she came back. "You'll hear I was engaged to that Alfred Buckley who has got into trouble and has been arrested," she said. Hugh did not reply and her voice became sharp and a little challenging. "You'll hear we were going to be married. I don't know what you'll hear. It's a lie," she said and turning, hurried away.

## CHAPTER XV

Hugh and Clara were married in less than a week after their first walk together. A chain of circumstances touching their two lives hurled them into marriage, and the opportunity for the intimacy with a woman for which Hugh so longed came to him with a swiftness that made him fairly dizzy.

It was a Wednesday evening and cloudy. After dining in silence with his landlady, Hugh started along Turner's Pike toward Bidwell, but when he had got almost into town, turned back. He had left the house intending to go through town to the Medina Road and to the woman who now occupied so large a place in his thoughts, but hadn't the courage. Every evening for almost a week he had taken the walk, and every evening and at almost the same spot he turned back. He was disgusted and angry with himself and went to his shop, walking in the middle of the road and kicking up clouds of dust. People passed along the path under the trees at the side of the road and turned to stare at him. A workingman with a fat wife, who puffed as she walked at his side, turned to look and then began to scold. "I tell you what, old woman, I shouldn't have married and had kids," he grumbled. "Look at me, then look at that fellow. He goes along there thinking big thoughts that will make him richer and richer. I have to work for two dollars a day, and pretty soon I'll be old and thrown on the scrap-heap. I might have been a rich inventor like him had I given myself a chance."

The workman went on his way, grumbling at his wife who paid no attention to his words. Her breath was needed for the labor of walking, and as for the matter of marriage, that had been attended to. She saw no reason for wasting words over the matter. Hugh went to the shop and stood leaning against the door frame. Two or three workmen were busy near the back door and had lighted gas lamps that hung over the work benches. They did not see Hugh, and their voices ran through the empty building. One of them, an old man with a bald head, entertained his fellows by giving an imitation of Steve Hunter. He lighted a cigar and putting on his hat tipped it a little to one side. Puffing out his chest he marched up and down talking of money. "Here's a ten-dollar cigar," he said, handing a long stogie to one of the other workmen. "I buy them by the thousands to give away. I'm interested in uplifting the lives of workmen in my home town. That's what takes all my attention."

The other workmen laughed and the little man continued to prance up and down and talk, but Hugh did not hear him. He stared moodily at the people going along the road toward town. Darkness was coming but he could still see dim figures striding along. Over at the foundry back of the corn-cutting machine plant the night shift was pouring off, and a sudden glare of light played across the heavy smoke cloud that lay over the town. The bells of the churches began to call people to the Wednesday evening prayer-meetings. Some enterprising citizen had begun to build workmen's houses in a field beyond Hugh's shop and these were occupied by Italian laborers. A crowd of them came past. What would someday be a tenement district was growing in a field beside a cabbage patch belonging to Ezra French who had said God would not permit men to change the field of their labors.

An Italian passed under a lamp near the Wheeling Station. He wore a bright red handkerchief about his neck and was clad in a brightly colored shirt. Like the other people of Bidwell, Hugh did not like to see foreigners about. He did not understand them and when he saw them going about the streets in groups, was a little afraid. It was a man's duty, he thought, to look as much as possible like all his fellow men, to lose himself in the crowds, and these fellows did not look like other men. They loved color, and as they talked they made rapid gestures with their hands. The Italian in the road was with a woman of his own race, and in the growing darkness put his arm about her shoulder. Hugh's heart began to beat rapidly and he forgot his American prejudices. He wished he were a workman and that Clara were a workman's daughter. Then, he thought, he might find courage to go to her. His imagination, quickened by the flame of desire and running in new channels, made it possible for him, at the moment to see himself in the young Italian's place, walking in the road with Clara. She was clad in a calico dress and her soft brown eyes looked at him full of love and understanding.

The three workingmen had completed the job for which they had come back to work after the evening meal, and now turned out the lights and came toward the front of the shop. Hugh drew back from the door and concealed himself by standing in the heavy shadows by the wall. So realistic were his thoughts of Clara that he did not want them intruded upon.

The workmen went out of the shop door and stood talking. The bald-headed man was telling a tale to which the others listened eagerly. "It's all over town," he said. "From what I hear everyone say it isn't the first time she's been in such a mess. Old Tom Butterworth claimed he sent her away to school three years ago, but now they say that isn't the truth. What they say is that she was in the family way to one of her father's farm hands and had to get out of town." The man laughed. "Lord, if Clara Butterworth was my daughter she'd be in a nice fix, wouldn't she, eh?" he said, laughing. "As it is, she's all right. She's gone now and got herself mixed up with this swindler Buckley, but her father's money will make it all right. If she's going to have a kid, no one'll know. Maybe she's already had the kid. They say she's a regular one for the men."

As the man talked Hugh came to the door and stood in the darkness listening. For a time the words would not penetrate his consciousness, and then he remembered what Clara had said. She had said something about Alfred Buckley and that there would be a story connecting her name with his. She had been hot and angry and had declared the story a lie. Hugh did not know what the story was about, but it was evident there was a story abroad, a scandalous story concerning her and Alfred Buckley. A hot, impersonal anger took possession of him. "She's in trouble—here's my chance," he thought. His tall figure straightened and as he stepped through the shop door his head struck sharply against the door frame, but he did not feel the blow that at another time might have knocked him down. During his whole life he had never struck anyone with his fists, and had never felt a desire to do so, but now hunger to strike and even to kill took complete possession of him. With a cry of rage his fist shot out and the old man who had done the talking was knocked senseless into a clump of weeds that grew near the door. Hugh whirled and struck a second man who fell through the open doorway into the shop. The third man ran away into the darkness along Turner's Pike.

Hugh walked rapidly to town and through Main Street. He saw Tom Butterworth walking in the street with Steve Hunter, but turned a corner to avoid a meeting. "My chance has come," he kept saying to himself as he hurried along Medina Road. "Clara's in some kind of trouble. My chance has come."

By the time he got to the door of the Butterworth house, Hugh's new-found courage had almost left him, but before it had quite gone he raised his hand and knocked on the door. By good fortune Clara came to open it. Hugh took off his hat and turned it awkwardly in his hands. "I came out here to ask you to marry me," he said. "I want you to be my wife. Will you do it?"

Clara stepped out of the house and closed the door. A whirl of thoughts ran through her brain. For a moment she felt like laughing, and then what there was in her of her father's shrewdness came to her rescue. "Why shouldn't I do it?" she thought. "Here's my chance. This man is excited and upset now, but he is a man I can respect. It's the best marriage I'll ever have a chance to make. I do not love him, but perhaps that will come. This may be the way marriages are made."

Clara put out her hand and laid it on Hugh's arm. "Well," she said, hesitatingly, "you wait here a moment."

She went into the house and left Hugh standing in the darkness. He was terribly afraid. It seemed to him that every secret desire of his life had got itself suddenly and bluntly expressed. He felt naked and ashamed. "If she comes out and says she'll marry me, what will I do? What'll I do then?" he asked himself.

When she did come out Clara wore her hat and a long coat. "Come," she said, and led him around the house and through the barnyard to one of the barns. She went into a dark stall and led forth a horse and with Hugh's help pulled a buggy out of a shed into the barnyard. "If we're going to do it there's no use putting it off," she said with a trembling voice. "We might as well go to the county seat and do it at once."

The horse was hitched and Clara got into the buggy. Hugh climbed in and sat beside her. She had started to drive out of the barnyard when Jim Priest stepped suddenly out of the darkness and took hold of the horse's head. Clara held the buggy whip in her hand and raised it to hit the horse. A desperate determination that nothing should interfere with her marriage with Hugh had taken possession of her. "If necessary I'll ride the man down," she thought. Jim came to stand beside the buggy. He looked past Clara at Hugh. "I thought maybe it was that Buckley," he said. He put a hand on the buggy dash and laid the other on Clara's arm. "You're a woman now, Clara, and I guess you know what you're doing. I guess you know I'm your friend," he said slowly. "You been in trouble, I know. I couldn't help hearing what your father said to you about Buckley, he talked so loud. Clara, I don't want to see you get into trouble."

The farm hand stepped away from the buggy and then came back and again put his hand on Clara's arm. The silence that lay over the barnyard lasted until the woman felt she could speak without a break in her voice.

"I'm not going very far, Jim," she said, laughing nervously. "This is Mr. Hugh McVey and we're going over to the county seat to get married. We'll be back home before midnight. You put a candle in the window for us."

Hitting the horse a sharp blow, Clara drove quickly past the house and into the road. She turned south into the hill country through which lay the road to the county seat. As the horse trotted quickly along, the voice of Jim Priest called to her out of the darkness of the barnyard, but she did not stop. The afternoon and evening had been cloudy and the night was dark. She was glad of that. As the horse went swiftly along she turned to look at Hugh who sat up very stiffly on the buggy seat and stared straight ahead. The long horse-like face of the Missourian with its huge nose and deeply furrowed cheeks was ennobled by the soft darkness, and a tender feeling crept over her. When he had asked her to become his wife, Clara had pounced like a wild animal abroad seeking prey and the thing in her that was like her father, hard, shrewd and quick-witted, had led her to decide to see the thing through at once. Now she became ashamed, and her tender mood took the hardness and shrewdness away. "This man and I have a thousand things we should say to each other before we rush into marriage," she thought, and was half inclined to turn the horse and drive back. She wondered if Hugh had also heard the stories connecting her name with that of Buckley, the stories she was sure were now running from lip to lip through the streets of Bidwell, and what version of the tale had been carried to him. "Perhaps he came to propose marriage in order to protect me," she thought, and decided that if he had come for that reason she was taking an unfair advantage. "It is what Kate Chanceller would call 'doing the man a dirty, low-down trick,'" she told herself; but even as the thought came she leaned forward and touching the horse with the whip urged him even more swiftly along the road.

A mile south of the Butterworth farmhouse the road to the county seat crossed the crest of a hill, the highest point in the county, and from the road there was a magnificent view of the country lying to the south. The sky had begun to clear, and as they reached the point known as Lookout Hill, the moon broke through a tangle of clouds. Clara stopped the horse and turned to look down the hillside. Below lay the lights of her father's farmhouse—where he had come as a young man and to which long ago he had brought his bride. Far below the farmhouse a clustered mass of lights outlined the swiftly growing town. The determination that had carried Clara thus far wavered again and a lump came into her throat.

Hugh also turned to look but did not see the dark beauty of the country wearing its night jewels of lights. The woman he wanted so passionately and of whom he was so afraid had her face turned from him, and he dared to look at her. He saw the sharp curve of her breasts and in the dim light her cheeks seemed to glow with beauty. An odd notion came to him. In the uncertain light her face seemed to move independent of her body. It drew near him and then drew away. Once he thought the dimly seen white cheek would touch his own. He waited breathless. A flame of desire ran through his body.

Hugh's mind flew back through the years to his boyhood and young manhood. In the river town where he was a boy the raftsmen and hangers-on of the town's saloons, who had sometimes come to spend an afternoon on the river banks with his father John McVey, often spoke of women and marriage. As they lay on the burned grass in the warm sunlight they talked and the boy who lay half-asleep nearby listened. The voices came to him as though out of the clouds or up out of the lazy waters of the great river and the talk of women awoke his boyhood lusts. One of the men, a tall young fellow with a mustache and with dark rings under his eyes, told in a lazy, drawling voice the tale of an adventure had with a woman one night when a raft on which he was employed had tied up near the city of St. Louis, and Hugh listened enviously. As he told the tale the young man a little awoke from his stupor, and when he laughed the other men lying about laughed with him. "I got the best of her after all," he boasted. "After it was all over we went into a little room at the back of a saloon. I watched my chance and when she went to sleep sitting in a chair I took eight dollars out of her stocking."

That night in the buggy beside Clara, Hugh thought of himself lying by the river bank on the summer days. Dreams had come to him there, sometimes gigantic dreams; but there had also come ugly thoughts and desires. By his father's shack there was always the sharp rancid smell of decaying fish and swarms of flies filled the air. Out in the clean Ohio country, in the hills south of Bidwell, it seemed to him that the smell of decaying fish came back, that it was in his clothes, that it had in some way worked its way into his nature. He put up his hand and swept it across his face, an unconscious return of the perpetual movement of brushing flies away from his face as he lay half-asleep by the river.

Little lustful thoughts kept coming to Hugh and made him ashamed. He moved restlessly in the buggy seat and a lump came into his throat. Again he looked at Clara. "I'm a poor white," he thought. "It isn't fitten I should marry this woman."

From the high spot in the road Clara looked down at her father's house and below at the lights of the town, that had already spread so far over the countryside, and up through the hills toward the farm where she had spent her girlhood and where, as Jim Priest had said, "the sap had begun to run up the tree." She began to love the man who was to be her husband, but like the dreamers of the town, saw him as something a little inhuman, as a man almost gigantic in his bigness. Many things Kate Chanceller had said as the two developing women walked and talked in the streets of Columbus came back to her mind. When they had started again along the road she continually worried the horse by tapping him with the whip. Like Kate, Clara wanted to be fair and square. "A woman should be fair and square, even with a man," Kate had said. "The man I'm going to have as a husband is simple and honest," she thought. "If there are things down there in town that are not square and fair, he had nothing to do with them." Realizing a little Hugh's difficulty in expressing what he must feel, she wanted to help him, but when she turned and saw how he did not look at her but continually stared into the darkness, pride kept her silent. "I'll have to wait until he's ready. Already I've taken things too much into my own hands. I'll put through this marriage, but when it comes to anything else he'll have to begin," she told herself, and a lump came into her throat and tears to her eyes.

## CHAPTER XVI

As he stood alone in the barnyard, excited at the thought of the adventure on which Clara and Hugh had set out, Jim Priest remembered Tom Butterworth. For more than thirty years Jim had worked for Tom and they had one strong impulse that bound them together —their common love of fine horses. More than once the two men had spent an afternoon together in the grandstand at the fall trotting meeting at Cleveland. In the late morning of such a day Tom found Jim wandering from stall to stall, looking at the horses being rubbed down and prepared for the afternoon's races. In a generous mood he bought his employee's lunch and took him to a seat in the grandstand. All afternoon the two men watched the races, smoked and quarreled. Tom contended that Bud Doble, the debonair, the dramatic, the handsome, was the greatest of all race-horse drivers, and Jim Priest held Bud Doble in contempt. For him there was but one man of all the drivers he wholeheartedly admired, Pop Geers, the shrewd and silent. "That Geers of yours doesn't drive at all. He just sits up there like a stick," Tom grumbled. "If a horse can win all right, he'll ride behind him all right. What I like to see is a driver. Now you look at that Doble. You watch him bring a horse through the stretch."

Jim looked at his employer with something like pity in his eyes. "Huh," he exclaimed. "If you haven't got eyes you can't see."

The farm hand had two strong loves in his life, his employer's daughter and the race-horse driver, Geers. "Geers," he declared, "was a man born old and wise." Often he had seen Geers at the tracks on a morning before some important race. The driver sat on an upturned box in the sun before one of the horse stalls. All about him there was the bantering talk of horsemen and grooms. Bets were made and challenges given. On the tracks nearby horses, not entered in the races for that day, were being exercised. Their hoofbeats made a kind of music that made Jim's blood tingle. Negroes laughed and horses put their heads out at stall doors. The stallions neighed loudly and the heels of some impatient steed rattled against the sides of a stall.

Everyone about the stalls talked of the events of the afternoon and Jim leaned against the front of one of the stalls and listened, filled with happiness. He wished the fates had made him a racing man. Then he looked at Pop Geers, the silent one, who sat for hours dumb and uncommunicative on a feed box, tapping lightly on the ground with his racing whip and chewing straw. Jim's imagination was aroused. He had once seen that other silent American, General Grant, and had been filled with admiration for him.

That was on a great day in Jim's life, the day on which he had seen Grant going to receive Lee's surrender at Appomattox. There had been a battle with the Union men pursuing the fleeing Rebs out of Richmond, and Jim, having secured a bottle of whisky, and having a chronic dislike of battles, had managed to creep away into a wood. In the distance he heard shouts and presently saw several men riding furiously down a road. It was Grant with his aides going to the place where Lee waited. They rode to the place near where Jim sat with his back against a tree and the bottle between his legs; then stopped. Then Grant decided not to take part in the ceremony. His clothes were covered with mud and his beard was ragged. He knew Lee and knew he would be dressed for the occasion. He was that kind of a man; he was one fitted for historic pictures and occasions. Grant wasn't. He told his aides to go on to the spot where Lee waited, told them what arrangements were to be made, then jumped his horse over a ditch and rode along a path under the trees toward the spot where Jim lay.

That was an event Jim never forgot. He was fascinated at the thought of what the day meant to Grant and by his apparent indifference. He sat silently by the tree and when Grant got off his horse and came near, walking now in the path where the sunlight sifted down through the trees, he closed his eyes. Grant came to where he sat and stopped, apparently thinking him dead. His hand reached down and took the bottle of whisky. For a moment they had something between them, Grant and Jim. They both understood that bottle of whisky. Jim thought Grant was about to drink, and opened his eyes a little. Then he closed them. The cork was out of the bottle and Grant clutched it in his hand tightly. From the distance there came a vast shout that was picked up and carried by voices far away. The wood seemed to rock with it. "It's done. The war's over," Jim thought. Then Grant reached over and smashed the bottle against the trunk of the tree above Jim's head. A piece of the flying glass cut his cheek and blood came. He opened his eyes and looked directly into Grant's eyes. For a moment the two men stared at each other and the great shout again rolled over the country. Grant went hurriedly along the path to where he had left his horse, and mounting, rode away.

Standing in the race track looking at Geers, Jim thought of Grant. Then his mind came back to this other hero. "What a man!" he thought. "Here he goes from town to town and from race track to race track all through the spring, summer and fall, and he never loses his head, never gets excited. To win horse races is the same as winning battles. When I'm at home plowing corn on summer afternoons, this Geers is away somewhere at some track with all the people gathered about and waiting. To me it would be like being drunk all the time, but you see he isn't drunk. Whisky could make him stupid. It couldn't make him drunk. There he sits hunched up like a sleeping dog. He looks as though he cared about nothing on earth, and he'll sit like that through three-quarters of the hardest race, waiting, taking advantage of every little stretch of firm hard ground on the track, saving his horse, watching, watching his horse too, waiting. What a man! He works the horse into fourth place, into third, into second. The crowd in the grandstand, such fellows as Tom Butterworth, have not seen what he's doing. He sits still. By God, what a man! He waits. He looks half-asleep. If he doesn't have to do it, he makes no effort. If the horse has it in him to win without help he sits still. The people are shouting and jumping up out of their seats in the grandstand, and if that Bud Doble has a horse in the race he's leaning forward in the sulky, shouting at his horse and making a holy show of himself.

"Ha, that Geers! He waits. He doesn't think of the people but of the horse he's driving. When the time comes, just the right time, that Geers, he lets the horse know. They are one at that moment, like Grant and I were over that bottle of whisky. Something happens between them. Something inside the man says, 'now,' and the message runs along the reins to the horse's brain. It flies down into his legs. There is a rush. The head of the horse has just worked its way out in front by inches—not too soon, nothing wasted. Ha, that Geers! Bud Doble, huh!"

On the night of Clara's marriage after she and Hugh had disappeared down the county seat road, Jim hurried into the barn and, bringing out a horse, sprang on his back. He was sixty-three but could mount a horse like a young man. As he rode furiously toward Bidwell he thought, not of Clara and her adventure, but of her father. To both men the right kind of marriage meant success in life for a woman. Nothing else really mattered much if that were accomplished. He thought of Tom Butterworth, who, he told himself, had fussed with Clara just as Bud Doble often fussed with a horse in a race. He had himself been like Pop Geers. All along he had known and understood the mare colt, Clara. Now she had come through; she had won the race of life.

"Ha, that old fool!" Jim whispered to himself as he rode swiftly down the dark road. When the horse ran clattering over a small wooden bridge and came to the first of the houses of the town, he felt like one coming to announce a victory, and half expected a vast shout to come out of the darkness, as it had come in the moment of Grant's victory over Lee.

Jim could not find his employer at the hotel or in Main Street, but remembered a tale he had heard whispered. Fanny Twist the milliner lived in a little frame house in Garfield Street, far out at the eastern edge of town, and he went there. He banged boldly on the door and the woman appeared. "I've got to see Tom Butterworth," he said. "It's important. It's about his daughter. Something has happened to her."

The door closed and presently Tom came around the corner of the house. He was furious. Jim's horse stood in the road, and he went straight to him and took hold of the bit. "What do you mean by coming here?" he asked sharply. "Who told you I was here? What business you got coming here and making a show of yourself? What's the matter of you? Are you drunk or out of your head?"

Jim got off the horse and told Tom the news. For a moment the two stood looking at each other. "Hugh McVey—Hugh McVey, by crackies, are you right, Jim?" Tom exclaimed. "No missfire, eh? She's really gone and done it? Hugh McVey, eh? By crackies!"

"They're on the way to the county seat now," Jim said softly. "Missfire! Not on your life." His voice lost the cool, quiet tone he had so often dreamed of maintaining in great emergencies. "I figure they'll be back by twelve or one," he said eagerly. "We got to blow 'em out, Tom. We got to give that girl and her husband the biggest blowout ever seen in this county, and we got just about three hours to get ready for it."

"Get off that horse and give me a boost," Tom commanded. With a grunt of satisfaction he sprang to the horse's back. The belated impulse to philander that an hour before sent him creeping through back streets and alleyways to the door of Fanny Twist's house was all gone, and in its place had come the spirit of the man of affairs, the man who, as he himself often boasted, made things move and kept them on the move. "Now look here, Jim," he said sharply, "there are three livery stables in this town. You engage every horse they've got for the night. Have the horses hitched to any kind of rigs you can find, buggies, surreys, spring wagons, anything. Have them get drivers off the streets, anywhere. Then have them all brought around in front of the Bidwell House and held for me. When you've done that, you go to Henry Heller's house. I guess you can find it. You found this house where I was fast enough. He lives on Campus Street just beyond the new Baptist Church. If he's gone to bed you get him up. Tell him to get his orchestra together and have him bring all the lively music he's got. Tell him to bring his men to the Bidwell House as fast as he can get them there."

Tom rode off along the street followed by Jim Priest, running at the horse's heels. When he had gone a little way he stopped. "Don't let anyone fuss with you about prices tonight, Jim," he called. "Tell everyone it's for me. Tell 'em Tom Butterworth'll pay what they ask. The sky's the limit tonight, Jim. That's the word, the sky's the limit."

To the older citizens of Bidwell, those who lived there when every citizen's affairs were the affair of the town, that evening will be long remembered. The new men, the Italians, Greeks, Poles, Rumanians, and many other strange-talking, dark-skinned men who had come with the coming of the factories, went on with their lives on that evening as on all others. They worked in the night shift at the Corn-Cutting Machine Plant, at the foundry, the bicycle factory or at the big new Tool Machine Factory that had just moved to Bidwell from Cleveland. Those who were not at work lounged in the streets or wandered aimlessly in and out of saloons. Their wives and children were housed in the hundreds of new frame houses in the streets that now crept out in all directions. In those days in Bidwell new houses seemed to spring out of the ground like mushrooms. In the morning there was a field or an orchard on Turner Pike or on any one of a dozen roads leading out of town. On the trees in the orchard green apples hung down waiting, ready to ripen. Grasshoppers sang in the long grass beneath the trees.

Then appeared Ben Peeler with a swarm of men. The trees were cut and the song of the grasshopper choked beneath piles of boards. There was a great shouting and rattling of hammers. A whole street of houses, all alike, universally ugly, had been added to the vast number of new houses already built by that energetic carpenter and his partner Gordon Hart.

To the people who lived in these houses, the excitement of Tom Butterworth and Jim Priest meant nothing. Half-sullenly they worked, striving to make money enough to take them back to their native lands. In the new place they had not, as they had hoped, been received as brothers. A marriage or a death there meant nothing to them.

To the old townsmen however, those who remembered Tom when he was a simple farmer and when Steve Hunter was looked upon with contempt as a boasting young squirt, the night rocked with excitement. Men ran through the streets. Drivers lashed their horses along roads. Tom was everywhere. He was like a general in charge of the defenses of a besieged town. The cooks at all three of the town's hotels were sent back into their kitchens, waiters were found and hurried out to the Butterworth house, and Henry Heller's orchestra was instructed to get out there at once and to start playing the liveliest possible music.

Tom asked every man and woman he saw to the wedding party. The hotel keeper was invited with his wife and daughter and two or three keepers of stores who came to the hotel to bring supplies were asked, commanded to come. Then there were the men of the factories, the office men and superintendents, new men who had never seen Clara. They also, with the town bankers and other solid fellows with money in the banks, who were investors in Tom's enterprises, were invited. "Put on the best clothes you've got in the world and have your women folks do the same," he said laughing. "Then you get out to my house as soon as you can. If you haven't any way to get there, come to the Bidwell House. I'll get you out."

Tom did not forget that in order to have his wedding party go as he wished, he would need to serve drinks. Jim Priest went from bar to bar. "What wine you got —good wine? How much you got?" he asked at each place. Steve Hunter had in the cellar of his house six cases of champagne kept there against a time when some important guest, the Governor of the state or a congressman, might come to town. He felt that on such occasions it was up to him to see that the town, as he said, "did itself proud." When he heard what was going on he hurried to the Bidwell House and offered to send his entire stock of wine out to Tom's house, and his offer was accepted.

Jim Priest had an idea. When the guests were all assembled and when the farm kitchen was filled with cooks and waiters who stumbled over each other, he took his idea to Tom. There was, he explained, a short-cut through fields and along lanes to a point on the county seat road, three miles from the house. "I'll go there and hide myself," he said. "When they come along, suspecting nothing, I'll cut out on horseback and get here a half hour before them. You make everyone in the house hide and keep still when they drive into the yard. We'll put out all the lights. We'll give that pair the surprise of their lives."

Jim had concealed a quart bottle of wine in his pocket and, as he rode away on his mission, stopped from time to time to take a hearty drink. As his horse trotted along lanes and through fields, the horse that was bringing Clara and Hugh home from their adventure cocked his ears and remembered the comfortable stall filled with hay in the Butterworth barn. The horse trotted swiftly along and Hugh in the buggy beside Clara was lost in the same dense silence that all the evening had lain over him like a cloak. In a dim way he was resentful and felt that time was running too fast. The hours and the passing events were like the waters of a river in flood time, and he was like a man in a boat without oars, being carried helplessly forward. Occasionally he thought courage had come to him and he half-turned toward Clara and opened his mouth, hoping words would come to his lips, but the silence that had taken hold of him was like a disease whose grip on its victim could not be broken. He closed his mouth and wet his lips with his tongue. Clara saw him do the thing several times. He began to seem animal-like and ugly to her. "It's not true that I thought of her and asked her to be my wife only because I wanted a woman," Hugh reassured himself. "I've been lonely, all my life I've been lonely. I want to find my way into someone's heart, and she is the one."

Clara also remained silent. She was angry. "If he didn't want to marry me, why did he ask me? Why did he come?" she asked herself. "Well, I'm married. I've done the thing we women are always thinking about," she told herself, her mind taking another turn. The thought frightened her and a shiver of dread ran over her body. Then her mind went to the defense of Hugh. "It isn't his fault. I shouldn't have rushed things as I have. Perhaps I'm not meant for marriage at all," she thought.

The ride homeward dragged on indefinitely. The clouds were blown out of the sky, the moon came out and the stars looked down on the two perplexed people. To relieve the feeling of tenseness that had taken hold of her Clara's mind resorted to a trick. Her eyes sought out a tree or the lights of a farmhouse far ahead and she tried to count the hoofbeats of the horse until they had come to it. She wanted to hurry homeward and at the same time looked forward with dread to the night alone in the dark farmhouse with Hugh. Not once during the homeward drive did she take the whip out of its socket or speak to the horse.

When at last the horse trotted eagerly across the crest of the hill, from which there was such a magnificent view of the country below, neither Clara nor Hugh turned to look. With bowed heads they rode, each trying to find courage to face the possibilities of the night.

In the farmhouse Tom and his guests waited in wine-lit suspense, and at last Jim Priest rode shouting out of a lane to the door. "They're coming—they're coming," he shouted, and ten minutes later and after Tom had twice lost his temper and cursed the girl waitresses from the town hotels who were inclined to giggle, all was silent and dark about the house and the barnyard. When all was quiet Jim Priest crept into the kitchen, and stumbling over the legs of the guests, made his way to a front window where he placed a lighted candle. Then he went out of the house to lie on his back beneath a bush in the yard. In the house he had secured for himself a second bottle of wine, and as Clara with her husband turned in at the gate and drove into the barnyard, the only sound that broke the intense silence came from the soft gurgle of the wine finding its way down his throat.

## CHAPTER XVII

As in most older American homes, the kitchen at the rear of the Butterworth farmhouse was large and comfortable. Much of the life of the house had been led there. Clara sat in a deep window that looked out across a little gully where in the spring a small stream ran down along the edge of the barnyard. She was then a quiet child and loved to sit for hours unobserved and undisturbed. At her back was the kitchen with the warm, rich smells and the soft, quick, persistent footsteps of her mother. Her eyes closed and she slept. Then she awoke. Before her lay a world into which her fancy could creep out. Across the stream before her eyes went a small, wooden bridge and over this in the spring horses went away to the fields or to sheds where they were hitched to milk or ice wagons. The sound of the hoofs of the horses pounding on the bridge was like thunder, harnesses rattled, voices shouted. Beyond the bridge was a path leading off to the left and along the path were three small houses where hams were smoked. Men came from the wagon sheds bearing the meat on their shoulders and went into the little houses. Fires were lighted and smoke crawled lazily up through the roofs. In a field that lay beyond the smoke houses a man came to plow. The child, curled into a little, warm ball in the window seat, was happy. When she closed her eyes fancies came like flocks of white sheep running out of a green wood. Although she was later to become a tomboy and run wild over the farm and through the barns, and although all her life she loved the soil and the sense of things growing and of food for hungry mouths being prepared, there was in her, even as a child, a hunger for the life of the spirit. In her dreams women, beautifully gowned and with rings on their hands, came to brush the wet, matted hair back from her forehead. Across the little wooden bridge before her eyes came wonderful men, women, and children. The children ran forward. They cried out to her. She thought of them as brothers and sisters who were to come to live in the farmhouse and who were to make the old house ring with laughter. The children ran toward her with outstretched hands, but never arrived at the house. The bridge extended itself. It stretched out under their feet so that they ran forward forever on the bridge.

And behind the children came men and women, sometimes together, sometimes walking alone. They did not seem like the children to belong to her. Like the women who came to touch her hot forehead, they were beautifully gowned and walked with stately dignity.

The child climbed out of the window and stood on the kitchen floor. Her mother hurried about. She was feverishly active and often did not hear when the child spoke. "I want to know about my brothers and sisters: where are they, why don't they come here?" she asked, but the mother did not hear, and if she did, had nothing to say. Sometimes she stopped to kiss the child and tears came to her eyes. Then something cooking on the kitchen stove demanded attention. "You run outside," she said hurriedly, and turned again to her work.

From the chair where Clara sat at the wedding feast provided by the energy of her father and the enthusiasm of Jim Priest, she could see over her father's shoulder into the farmhouse kitchen. As when she was a child, she closed her eyes and dreamed of another kind of feast. With a growing sense of bitterness she realized that all her life, all through her girlhood and young womanhood, she had been waiting for this, her wedding night, and that now, having come, the occasion for which she had waited so long and concerning which she had dreamed so many dreams, had aborted into an occasion for the display of ugliness and vulgarity. Her father, the only other person in the room in any way related to her, sat at the other end of the long table. Her aunt had gone away on a visit, and in the crowded, noisy room there was no woman to whom she could turn for understanding. She looked past her father's shoulder and directly into the wide window seat where she had spent so many hours of her childhood. Again she wanted brothers and sisters. "The beautiful men and women of the dreams were meant to come at this time, that's what the dreams were about; but, like the unborn children that ran with outstretched hands, they cannot get over the bridge and into the house," she thought vaguely. "I wish Mother had lived, or that Kate Chanceller were here," she whispered to herself as, raising her eyes, she looked at her father.

Clara felt like an animal driven into a corner and surrounded by foes. Her father sat at the feast between two women, Mrs. Steve Hunter who was inclined to corpulency, and a thin woman named Bowles, the wife of an undertaker of Bidwell. They continually whispered, smiled, and nodded their heads. Hugh sat on the opposite side of the same table, and when he raised his eyes from the plate of food before him, could see past the head of a large, masculine-looking woman into the farmhouse parlor where there was another table, also filled with guests. Clara turned from looking at her father to look at her husband. He was merely a tall man with a long face, who could not raise his eyes. His long neck stuck itself out of a stiff white collar. To Clara he was, at the moment, a being without personality, one that the crowd at the table had swallowed up as it so busily swallowed food and wine. When she looked at him he seemed to be drinking a good deal. His glass was always being filled and emptied. At the suggestion of the woman who sat beside him, he performed the task of emptying it, without raising his eyes, and Steve Hunter, who sat on the other side of the table, leaned over and filled it again. Steve like her father whispered and winked. "On the night of my wedding I was piped, you bet, as piped as a hatter. It's a good thing. It gives a man nerve," he explained to the masculine-looking woman to whom he was telling, with a good deal of attention to details, the tale of his own marriage night.

Clara did not look at Hugh again. What he did seemed no concern of hers. Bowles the Bidwell undertaker had surrendered to the influence of the wine that had been flowing freely since the guests arrived and now got to his feet and began to talk. His wife tugged at his coat and tried to force him back into his seat, but Tom Butterworth jerked her arm away. "Ah, let him alone. He's got a story to tell," he said to the woman, who blushed and put her handkerchief over her face. "Well, it's a fact, that's how it happened," the undertaker declared in a loud voice. "You see the sleeves of her nightgown were tied in hard knots by her rascally brothers. When I tried to unfasten them with my teeth I bit big holes in the sleeves."

Clara gripped the arm of her chair. "If I can let the night pass without showing these people how much I hate them I'll do well enough," she thought grimly. She looked at the dishes laden with food and wished she could break them one by one over the heads of her father's guests. As a relief to her mind, she again looked past her father's head and through a doorway into the kitchen.

In the big room three or four cooks were busily engaged in the preparation of food, and waitresses continually brought steaming dishes and put them on the tables. She thought of her mother's life, the life led in that room, married to the man who was her own father and who no doubt, but for the fact that circumstances had made him a man of wealth, would have been satisfied to see his daughter led into just such another life.

"Kate was right about men. They want something from women, but what do they care what kind of lives we lead after they get what they want?" she thought grimly.

The more to separate herself from the feasting, laughing crowd, Clara tried to think out the details of her mother's life. "It was the life of a beast," she thought. Like herself, her mother had come to the house with her husband on the night of her marriage. There was just such another feast. The country was new then and the people for the most part desperately poor. Still there was drinking. She had heard her father and Jim Priest speak of the drinking bouts of their youth. The men came as they had come now, and with them came women, women who had been coarsened by the life they led. Pigs were killed and game brought from the forests. The men drank, shouted, fought, and played practical jokes. Clara wondered if any of the men and women in the room would dare go upstairs into her sleeping room and tie knots in her night clothes. They had done that when her mother came to the house as a bride. Then they had all gone away and her father had taken his bride upstairs. He was drunk, and her own husband Hugh was now getting drunk. Her mother had submitted. Her life had been a story of submission. Kate Chanceller had said it was so married women lived, and her mother's life had proven the truth of the statement. In the farmhouse kitchen, where now three or four cooks worked so busily, she had worked her life out alone. From the kitchen she had gone directly upstairs and to bed with her husband. Once a week on Saturady afternoons she went into town and stayed long enough to buy supplies for another week of cooking. "She must have been kept going until she dropped down dead," Clara thought, and her mind taking another turn, added, "and many others, both men and women, must have been forced by circumstances to serve my father in the same blind way. It was all done in order that prosperity and money with which to do vulgar things might be his."

Clara's mother had brought but one child into the world. She wondered why. Then she wondered if she would become the mother of a child. Her hands no longer gripped the arms of her chair, but lay on the table before her. She looked at them and they were strong. She was herself a strong woman. After the feast was over and the guests had gone away, Hugh, given courage by the drinks he continued to consume, would come upstairs to her. Some twist of her mind made her forget her husband, and in fancy she felt herself about to be attacked by a strange man on a dark road at the edge of a forest. The man had tried to take her into his arms and kiss her and she had managed to get her hands on his throat. Her hands lying on the table twitched convulsively.

In the big farmhouse dining room and in the parlor where the second table of guests sat, the wedding feast went on. Afterward when she thought of it, Clara always remembered her wedding feast as a horsey affair. Something in the natures of Tom Butterworth and Jim Priest, she thought, expressed itself that night. The jokes that went up and down the table were horsey, and Clara thought the women who sat at the tables heavy and marelike.

Jim did not come to the table to sit with the others, was in fact not invited, but all evening he kept appearing and reappearing and had the air of a master of ceremonies. Coming into the dining room he stood by the door, scratching his head. Then he went out. It was as though he had said to himself, "Well, it's all right, everything is going all right, everything is lively, you see." All his life Jim had been a drinker of whisky and knew his limitations. His system as a drinking man had always been quite simple. On Saturday afternoons, when the work about the barns was done for the day and the other employees had gone away, he went to sit on the steps of a corncrib with the bottle in his hand. In the winter he went to sit by the kitchen fire in a little house below the apple orchard where he and the other employees slept. He took a long drink from the bottle and then holding it in his hand sat for a time thinking of the events of his life. Whisky made him somewhat sentimental. After one long drink he thought of his youth in a town in Pennsylvania. He had been one of six children, all boys, and at an early age his mother had died. Jim thought of her and then of his father.

When he had himself come west into Ohio, and later when he was a soldier in the Civil War, he despised his father and reverenced the memory of his mother. In the war he had found himself physically unable to stand up before the enemy during a battle. When the report of guns was heard and the other men of his company got grimly into line and went forward, something happened to his legs and he wanted to run away. So great was the desire in him that craftiness grew in his brain. Watching his chance, he pretended to have been shot and fell to the ground, and when the others had gone on crept away and hid himself. He found it was not impossible to disappear altogether and reappear in another place. The draft went into effect and many men not liking the notion of war were willing to pay large sums to the men who would go in their places. Jim went into the business of enlisting and deserting. All about him were men talking of the necessity of saving the country, and for four years he thought only of saving his own hide. Then suddenly the war was over and he became a farm hand. As he worked all week in the fields, and in the evening sometimes, as he lay in his bed and the moon came up, he thought of his mother and of the nobility and sacrifice of her life. He wished to be such another. After having two or three drinks out of the bottle, he admired his father, who in the Pennsylvania town had borne the reputation of being a liar and a rascal. After his mother's death his father had managed to marry a widow who owned a farm. "The old man was a slick one," he said aloud, tipping up the bottle and taking another long drink. "If I had stayed at home until I got more understanding, the old man and I together might have done something." He finished the bottle and went away to sleep on the hay, or if it were winter, threw himself into one of the bunks in the bunkhouse. He dreamed of becoming one who went through life beating people out of money, living by his wits, getting the best of everyone.

Until the night of Clara's wedding Jim had never tasted wine, and as it did not bring on a desire for sleep, he thought himself unaffected. "It's like sweetened water," he said, going into the darkness of the barnyard and emptying another half bottle down his throat. "The stuff has no kick. Drinking it is like drinking sweet cider."

Jim got into a frolicsome mood and went through the crowded kitchen and into the dining room where the guests were assembled. At the moment the rather riotous laughter and storytelling had ceased and everything was quiet. He was worried. "Things aren't going well. Clara's party is becoming a frost," he thought resentfully. He began to dance a heavy-footed jig on a little open place by the kitchen door and the guests stopped talking to watch. They shouted and clapped their hands. A thunder of applause arose. The guests who were seated in the parlor and who could not see the performance got up and crowded into the doorway that connected the two rooms. Jim became extraordinarily bold, and as one of the young women Tom had hired as waitresses at that moment went past bearing a large dish of food, he swung himself quickly about and took her into his arms. The dish flew across the floor and broke against a table leg and the young woman screamed. A farm dog that had found its way into the kitchen rushed into the room and barked loudly. Henry Heller's orchestra, concealed under a stairway that led to the upper part of the house, began to play furiously. A strange animal fervor swept over Jim. His legs flew rapidly about and his heavy feet made a great clatter on the floor. The young woman in his arms screamed and laughed. Jim closed his eyes and shouted. He felt that the wedding party had until that moment been a failure and that he was transforming it into a success. Rising to their feet the men shouted, clapped their hands and beat with their fists on the table. When the orchestra came to the end of the dance, Jim stood flushed and triumphant before the guests, holding the woman in his arms. In spite of her struggles he held her tightly against his breast and kissed her eyes, cheeks, and mouth. Then releasing her he winked and made a gesture for silence. "On a wedding night someone's got to have the nerve to do a little love-making," he said, looking pointedly toward the place where Hugh sat with head bent and with his eyes staring at a glass of wine that sat at his elbow.

It was past two o'clock when the feast came to an end. When the guests began to depart, Clara stood for a moment alone and tried to get herself in hand. Something inside her felt cold and old. If she had often thought she wanted a man, and that life as a married woman would put an end to her problems, she did not think so at that moment. "What I want above everything else is a woman," she thought. All the evening her mind had been trying to clutch and hold the almost forgotten figure of her mother, but it was too vague and shadowy. With her mother she had never walked and talked late at night through streets of towns when the world was asleep and when thoughts were born in herself. "After all," she thought, "Mother may also have belonged to all this." She looked at the people preparing to depart. Several men had gathered in a group by the door. One of them told a story at which the others laughed loudly. The women standing about had flushed and, Clara thought, coarse faces. "They have gone into marriage like cattle," she told herself. Her mind, running out of the room, began to caress the memory of her one woman friend, Kate Chanceller. Often on late spring afternoons as she and Kate had walked together something very like love-making had happened between them. They went along quietly and evening came on. Suddenly they stopped in the street and Kate had put her arms about Clara's shoulders. For a moment they stood thus close together and a strange gentle and yet hungry look came into Kate's eyes. It only lasted a moment and when it happened both women were somewhat embarrassed. Kate laughed and taking hold of Clara's arm pulled her along the sidewalk. "Let's walk like the devil," she said, "come on, let's get up some speed."

Clara put her hands to her eyes as though to shut out the scene in the room. "If I could have been with Kate this evening I could have come to a man believing in the possible sweetness of marriage," she thought.

## CHAPTER XVIII

Jim Priest was very drunk, but insisted on hitching a team to the Butterworth carriage and driving it loaded with guests to town. Everyone laughed at him, but he drove up to the farmhouse door and in a loud voice declared he knew what he was doing. Three men got into the carriage and beating the horses furiously Jim sent them galloping away.

When an opportunity offered, Clara went silently out of the hot dining room and through a door to a porch at the back of the house. The kitchen door was open and the waitresses and cooks from town were preparing to depart. One of the young women came out into the darkness accompanied by a man, evidently one of the guests. They had both been drinking and stood for a moment in the darkness with their bodies pressed together. "I wish it were our wedding night," the man's voice whispered, and the woman laughed. After a long kiss they went back into the kitchen.

A farm dog appeared and going up to Clara licked her hand. She went around the house and stood back of a bush in the darkness near where the carriages were being loaded. Her father with Steve Hunter and his wife came and got into a carriage. Tom was in an expansive, generous mood. "You know, Steve, I told you and several others my Clara was engaged to Alfred Buckley," he said. "Well, I was mistaken. The whole thing was a lie. The truth is I shot off my mouth without talking to Clara. I had seen them together and now and then Buckley used to come out here to the house in the evening, although he never came except when I was here. He told me Clara had promised to marry him, and like a fool I took his word. I never even asked. That's the kind of a fool I was and I was a bigger fool to go telling the story. All the time Clara and Hugh were engaged and I never suspected. They told me about it tonight."

Clara stood by the bush until she thought the last of the guests had gone. The lie her father had told seemed only a part of the evening's vulgarity. Near the kitchen door the waitresses, cooks and musicians were being loaded into the bus that had been driven out from the Bidwell House. She went into the dining room. Sadness had taken the place of the anger in her, but when she saw Hugh the anger came back. Piles of dishes filled with food lay all about the room and the air was heavy with the smell of food. Hugh stood by a window looking out into the dark farmyard. He held his hat in his hand. "You might put your hat away," she said sharply. "Have you forgotten you're married to me and that you now live here in this house?" She laughed nervously and walked to the kitchen door.

Her mind still clung to the past and to the days when she was a child and had spent so many hours in the big, silent kitchen. Something was about to happen that would take her past away—destroy it, and the thought frightened her. "I have not been very happy in this house but there have been certain moments, certain feelings I've had," she thought. Stepping through the doorway she stood for a moment in the kitchen with her back to the wall and with her eyes closed. Through her mind went a troop of figures, the stout determined figure of Kate Chanceller who had known how to love in silence; the wavering, hurrying figure of her mother; her father as a young man coming in after a long drive to warm his hands by the kitchen fire; a strong, hard-faced woman from town who had once worked for Tom as cook and who was reported to have been the mother of two illegitimate children; and the figures of her childhood fancy walking over the bridge toward her, clad in beautiful raiment.

Back of these figures were other figures, long forgotten but now sharply remembered—farm girls who had come to work by the day; tramps who had been fed at the kitchen door; young farm hands who suddenly disappeared from the routine of the farm's life and were never seen again, a young man with a red bandana handkerchief about his neck who had thrown her a kiss as she stood with her face pressed against a window.

Once a high school girl from town had come to spend

the night with Clara. After the evening meal the two girls walked into the kitchen and stood by a window, looking out. Something had happened within them. Moved by a common impulse they went outside and walked for a long way under the stars along the silent country roads. They came to a field where men were burning brush. Where there had been a forest there was now only a stump field and the figures of the men carrying armloads of the dry branches of trees and throwing them on the fire. The fire made a great splash of color in the gathering darkness and for some obscure reason both girls were deeply moved by the sight, sound, and perfume of the night. The figures of the men seemed to dance back and forth in the light. Instinctively Clara turned her face upward and looked at the stars. She was conscious of them and of their beauty and the wide sweeping beauty of night as she had never been before. A wind began to sing in the trees of a distant forest, dimly seen far away across fields. The sound was soft and insistent and crept into her soul. In the grass at her feet insects sang an accompaniment to the soft, distant music.

How vividly Clara now remembered that night! It came sharply back as she stood with closed eyes in the farm kitchen and waited for the consummation of the adventure on which she had set out. With it came other memories. "How many fleeting dreams and half visions of beauty I have had!" she thought.

Everything in life that she had thought might in some way lead toward beauty now seemed to Clara to lead to ugliness. "What a lot I've missed," she muttered, and opening her eyes went back into the dining room and spoke to Hugh, still standing and staring out into the darkness.

"Come," she said sharply, and led the way up a stairway. The two went silently up the stairs, leaving the lights burning brightly in the rooms below. They came to a door leading to a bedroom, and Clara opened it. "It's time for a man and his wife to go to bed," she said in a low, husky voice. Hugh followed her into the room. He walked to a chair by a window and sitting down, took off his shoes and sat holding them in his hand. He did not look at Clara but into the darkness outside the window. Clara let down her hair and began to unfasten her dress. She took off an outer dress and threw it over a chair. Then she went to a drawer and pulling it out looked for a night dress. She became angry and threw several garments on the floor. "Damn!" she said explosively, and went out of the room.

Hugh sprang to his feet. The wine he had drunk had not taken effect and Steve Hunter had been forced to go home disappointed. All the evening something stronger than wine had been gripping him. Now he knew what it was. All through the evening thoughts and desires had whirled through his brain. Now they were all gone. "I won't let her do it," he muttered, and running quickly to the door closed it softly. With the shoes still held in his hand he crawled through a window. He had expected to leap into the darkness, but by chance his stocking feet alighted on the roof of the farm kitchen that extended out from the rear of the house. He ran quickly down the roof and jumped, alighting in a clump of bushes that tore long scratches on his cheeks.

For five minutes Hugh ran toward the town of Bidwell, then turned, and climbing a fence, walked across a field. The shoes were still gripped tightly in his hand and the field was stony, but he did not notice and was unconscious of pain from his bruised feet or from the torn places on his cheeks. Standing in the field he heard Jim Priest drive homeward along the road.

"My bonny lies over the ocean,
My bonny lies over the sea,
My bonny lies over the ocean,
O, bring back my bonny to me."

sang the farm hand.

Hugh walked across several fields, and when he came to a small stream, sat down on the bank and put on his shoes. "I've had my chance and missed it," he thought bitterly. Several times he repeated the words. "I've had my chance and I've missed," he said again as he stopped by a fence that separated the fields in which he had been walking. At the words he stopped and put his hand to his throat. A half-stifled sob broke from him. "I've had my chance and missed," he said again.

## CHAPTER XIX

On the day after the feast managed by Tom and Jim, it was Tom who brought Hugh back to live with his wife. The older man had come to the farmhouse on the next morning bringing three women from town who were, as he explained to Clara, to clear away the mess left by the guests. The daughter had been deeply touched by what Hugh had done, and at the moment loved him deeply, but did not choose to let her father know how she felt. "I suppose you got him drunk, you and your friends," she said. "At any rate, he's not here."

Tom said nothing, but when Clara had told the story of Hugh's disappearance, drove quickly away. "He'll come to the shop," he thought and went there, leaving his horse tied to a post in front. At two o'clock his son-in-law came slowly over the Turner's Pike bridge and approached the shop. He was hatless and his clothes and hair were covered with dust, while in his eyes was the look of a hunted animal. Tom met him with a smile and asked no questions. "Come," he said, and taking Hugh by the arm led him to the buggy. As he untied the horse he stopped to light a cigar. "I'm going down to one of my lower farms. Clara thought you would like to go with me," he said blandly.

Tom drove to the McCoy house and stopped. "You'd better clean up a little," he said without looking at Hugh. "You go in and shave and change your clothes. I'm going uptown. I got to go to a store."

Driving a short distance along the road, Tom stopped and shouted. "You might pack your grip and bring it along," he called. "You'll be needing your things. We won't be back here today."

The two men stayed together all that day, and in the evening Tom took Hugh to the farmhouse and stayed for the evening meal. "He was a little drunk," he explained to Clara. "Don't be hard on him. He was a little drunk."

For both Clara and Hugh that evening was the hardest of their lives. After the servants had gone, Clara sat under a lamp in the dining room and pretended to read a book and in desperation Hugh also tried to read.

Again the time came to go upstairs to the bedroom, and again Clara led the way. She went to the door of the room from which Hugh had fled and opening it stepped aside. Then she put out her hand. "Good-night," she said, and going down a hallway went into another room and closed the door.

Hugh's experience with the school teacher was repeated on that second night in the farmhouse. He took off his shoes and prepared for bed. Then he crept out into the hallway and went softly to the door of Clara's room. Several times he made the journey along the carpeted hallway, and once his hand was on the knob of the door, but each time he lost heart and returned to his own room. Although he did not know it Clara, like Rose McCoy on that other occasion, expected him to come to her, and knelt on the floor just inside the door, waiting, hoping for, and fearing the coming of the man.

Unlike the school teacher, Clara wanted to help Hugh. Marriage had perhaps given her that impulse, but she did not follow it, and when at last Hugh, shaken and ashamed, gave up the struggle with himself, she arose and went to her bed where she threw herself down and wept, as Hugh had wept standing in the darkness of the fields on the night before.

## CHAPTER XX

It was a hot, dusty day, a week after Hugh's marriage to Clara, and Hugh was at work in his shop at Bidwell. How many days, weeks, and months he had already worked there, thinking in iron—twisted, turned, tortured to follow the twistings and turnings of his mind—standing all day by a bench beside other workmen—before him always the little piles of wheels, strips of unworked iron and steel, blocks of wood, the paraphernalia of the inventor's trade. Beside him, now that money had come to him, more and more workmen, men who had invented nothing, who were without distinction in the life of the community, who had married no rich man's daughter.

In the morning the other workmen, skillful fellows, who knew, as Hugh had never known, the science of their iron craft, came straggling through the shop door into his presence. They were a little embarrassed before him. The greatness of his name rang in their minds.

Many of the workmen were husbands, fathers of families. In the morning they left their houses gladly but nevertheless came somewhat reluctantly to the shop. As they came along the street, past other houses, they smoked a morning pipe. Groups were formed. Many legs straggled along the street. At the door of the shop each man stopped. There was a sharp tapping sound. Pipe bowls were knocked out against the door sill. Before he came into the shop, each man looked out across the open country that stretched away to the north.

For a week Hugh had been married to a woman who had not yet become his wife. She belonged, still belonged, to a world he had thought of as outside the possibilities of his life. Was she not young, strong, straight of body? Did she not array herself in what seemed unbelievably beautiful clothes? The clothes she wore were a symbol of herself. For him she was unattainable.

And yet she had consented to become his wife, had stood with him before a man who had said words about honor and obedience.

Then there had come the two terrible evenings—when he had gone back to the farmhouse with her to find the wedding feast set in their honor, and that other evening when old Tom had brought him to the farmhouse a defeated, frightened man who hoped the woman would put out her hand, would reassure him.

Hugh was sure he had missed the great opportunity of his life. He had married, but his marriage was not a marriage. He had got himself into a position from which there was no possibility of escaping. "I'm a coward," he thought, looking at the other workmen in the shop. They, like himself, were married men and lived in a house with a woman. At night they went boldly into the presence of the woman. He had not done that when the opportunity offered, and Clara could not come to him. He could understand that. His hands had builded a wall and the passing days were huge stones put on top of the wall. What he had not done became every day a more and more impossible thing to do.

Tom, having taken Hugh back to Clara, was still concerned over the outcome of their adventure. Every day he came to the shop and in the evening came to see them at the farmhouse. He hovered about, was like a mother bird whose offspring had been prematurely pushed out of the nest. Every morning he came into the shop to talk with Hugh. He made jokes about married life. Winking at a man standing nearby he put his hand familiarly on Hugh's shoulder. "Well, how does married life go? It seems to me you're a little pale," he said laughing.

In the evening he came to the farmhouse and sat talking of his affairs, of the progress and growth of the town and his part in it. Without hearing his words both Clara and Hugh sat in silence, pretending to listen, glad of his presence.

Hugh came to the shop at eight. On other mornings, all through that long week of waiting, Clara had driven him to his work, the two riding in silence down Medina Road and through the crowded streets of the town; but on that morning he had walked.

On Medina Road, near the bridge where he had once stood with Clara and where he had seen her hot with anger, something had happened, a trivial thing. A male bird pursued a female among the bushes beside the road. The two feathered, living creatures, vividly colored, alive with life, pitched and swooped through the air. They were like moving balls of light going in and out of the dark green of foliage. There was in them a madness, a riot of life.

Hugh had been tricked into stopping by the roadside. A tangle of things that had filled his mind, the wheels, cogs, levers, all the intricate parts of the hay-loading machine, the things that lived in his mind until his hand had made them into facts, were blown away like dust. For a moment he watched the living riotous things and then, as though jerking himself back into a path from which his feet had wandered, hurried onward to the shop, looking as he went not into the branches of trees, but downward at the dust of the road.

In the shop Hugh tried all morning to refurnish the warehouse of his mind, to put back into it the things blown so recklessly away. At ten Tom came in, talked for a moment and then flitted away. "You are still there. My daughter still has you. You have not run away again," he seemed to be saying to himself.

The day grew warm and the sky, seen through the shop window by the bench where Hugh tried to work, was overcast with clouds.

At noon the workmen went away, but Clara, who on other days had come to drive Hugh to the farmhouse for lunch, did not appear. When all was silent in the shop he stopped work, washed his hands and put on his coat.

He went to the shop door and then came back to the bench. Before him lay an iron wheel on which he had been at work. It was intended to drive some intricate part of the hay-loading machine. Hugh took it in his hand and carried it to the back of the shop where there was an anvil. Without consciousness and scarcely realizing what he did he laid it on the anvil and taking a great sledge in his hand swung it over his head.

The blow struck was terrific. Into it Hugh put all of his protest against the grotesque position into which he had been thrown by his marriage to Clara.

The blow accomplished nothing. The sledge descended and the comparatively delicate metal wheel was twisted, knocked out of shape. It spurted from under the head of the sledge and shot past Hugh's head and out through a window, breaking a pane of glass. Fragments of the broken glass fell with a sharp little tinkling sound upon a heap of twisted pieces of iron and steel lying beside the anvil. . . .

Hugh did not each lunch that day nor did he go to the farmhouse or return to work at the shop. He walked, but this time did not walk in country roads where male and female birds dart in and out of bushes. An intense desire to know something intimate and personal concerning men and women and the lives they led in their houses had taken possession of him. He walked in the daylight up and down in the streets of Bidwell.

To the right, over the bridge leading out of Turner's Road, the main street of Bidwell ran along a river bank. In that direction the hills out of the country to the south came down to the river's edge and there was a high bluff. On the bluff and back of it on a sloping hillside many of the more pretentious new houses of the prosperous Bidwell citizens had been built. Facing the river were the largest houses, with grounds in which trees and shrubs had been planted and in the streets along the hill, less and less pretentious as they receded from the river, were other houses built and being built, long rows of houses, long streets of houses, houses in brick, stone, and wood.

Hugh went from the river front back into this maze of streets and houses. Some instinct led him there. It was where the men and women of Bidwell who had prospered and had married went to live, to make themselves houses. His father-in-law had offered to buy him a river front place and already that meant much in Bidwell.

He wanted to see women who, like Clara, had got

themselves husbands, what they were like. "I've seen enough of men," he thought half resentfully as he went along.

All afternoon he walked in streets, going up and down before houses in which women lived with their men. A detached mood had possession of him. For an hour he stood under a tree idly watching workmen engaged in building another house. When one of the workmen spoke to him he walked away and went into a street where men were laying a cement pavement before a completed house.

In a furtive way he kept looking about for women, hungering to see their faces. "What are they up to? I'd like to find out," his mind seemed to be saying.

The women came out of the doors of the houses and passed him as he went slowly along. Other women in carriages drove in the streets. They were well-dressed women and seemed sure of themselves. "Things are all right with me. For me things are settled and arranged," they seemed to say. All the streets in which he walked seemed to be telling the story of things settled and arranged. The houses spoke of the same things. "I am a house. I am not built until things are settled and arranged. I mean that," they said.

Hugh grew very tired. In the later afternoon a small bright-eyed woman—no doubt she had been one of the guests at his wedding feast—stopped him. "Are you planning to buy or build up our way, Mr. McVey?" she asked. He shook his head. "I'm looking around," he said and hurried away.

Anger took the place of perplexity in him. The women he saw in the streets and in the doors of the houses were such women as his own woman Clara. They had married men—"no better than myself," he told himself, growing bold.

They had married men and something had happened to them. Something was settled. They could live in streets and in houses. Their marriages had been real marriages and he had a right to a real marriage. It was not too much to expect out of life.

"Clara has a right to that also," he thought and his mind began to idealize the marriages of men and women. "On every hand here I see them, the neat, well-dressed, handsome women like Clara. How happy they are!

"Their feathers have been ruffled though," he thought angrily. "It was with them as with that bird I saw being pursued through the trees. There has been pursuit and a pretense of trying to escape. There has been an effort made that was not an effort, but feathers have been ruffled here."

When his thoughts had driven him into a half-desperate mood Hugh went out of the streets of bright, ugly, freshly built, freshly painted and furnished houses, and down into the town. Several men homeward bound at the end of their day of work called to him. "I hope you are thinking of buying or building up our way," they said heartily.

It began to rain and darkness came, but Hugh did not go home to Clara. It did not seem to him that he could spend another night in the house with her, lying awake, hearing the little noises of the night, waiting—for courage. He could not sit under the lamp through another evening pretending to read. He could not go with Clara up the stairs only to leave her with a cold "good-night" at the top of the stairs.

Hugh went up the Medina Road almost to the house and then retraced his steps and got into a field. There was a low swampy place in which the water came up over his shoetops, and after he had crossed that there was a field overgrown with a tangle of vines. The night became so dark that he could see nothing and darkness reigned over his spirit. For hours he walked blindly, but it did not occur to him that as he waited, hating the waiting, Clara also waited; that for her also it was a time of trial and uncertainty. To him it seemed her course was simple and easy. She was a white pure thing —waiting—for what? for courage to come in to him in order that an assault be made upon her whiteness and purity.

That was the only answer to the question Hugh could find within himself. The destruction of what was white and pure was a necessary thing in life. It was a thing men must do in order that life go on. As for women, they must be white and pure—and wait.

Filled with inward resentment Hugh at last did go to the farmhouse. Wet and with dragging, heavy feet he turned out of the Medina Road to find the house dark and apparently deserted.

Then a new and puzzling situation arose. When he stepped over the threshold and into the house he knew Clara was there.

On that day she had not driven him to work in the morning or gone for him at noon hour because she did not want to look at him in the light of day, did not want again to see the puzzled, frightened look in his eyes. She had wanted him in the darkness alone, had waited for darkness. Now it was dark in the house and she waited for him.

How simple it was! Hugh came into the living room, stumbled forward into the darkness, and found the hat-rack against the wall near the stairway leading to the bedrooms above. Again he had surrendered what he would no doubt have called the manhood in himself, and hoped only to be able to escape the presence he felt in the room, to creep off upstairs to his bed, to lie awake listening to noises, waiting miserably for another day to come. But when he had put his dripping hat on one of the pegs of the rack and had found the lower step with his foot thrust into darkness, a voice called to him.

"Come here, Hugh," Clara said softly and firmly, and like a boy caught doing a forbidden act he went toward her. "We have been very silly, Hugh," he heard her voice saying softly.

Hugh went to where Clara sat in a chair by a window. From him there was no protest and no attempt to escape the love-making that followed. For a moment he stood in silence and could see her white figure below him in the chair. It was like something still far away, but coming swiftly as a bird flies to him—upward to him. Her hand crept up and lay in his hand. It seemed unbelievably large. It was not soft, but hard and firm. When her hand had rested in his for a moment she arose and stood beside him. Then the hand went out of his and touched, caressed his wet coat, his wet hair, his cheeks. "My flesh must be white and cold," he thought, and then he did not think any more.

Gladness took hold of him, a gladness that came up out of the inner parts of himself as she had come up to him out of the chair. For days, weeks, he had been thinking of his problem as a man's problem, his defeat had been a man's defeat.

Now there was no defeat, no problem, no victory. In himself he did not exist. Within himself something new had been born or another something that had always lived with him had stirred to life. It was not awkward.

It was not afraid. It was a thing as swift and sure as the flight of the male bird through the branches of trees and it was in pursuit of something light and swift in her, something that would fly through light and darkness but fly not too swiftly, something of which he need not be afraid, something that without the need of understanding he could understand as one understands the need of breath in a close place.

With a laugh as soft and sure as her own Hugh took Clara into his arms. A few minutes later they went upstairs and twice Hugh stumbled on the stairway. It did not matter. His long awkward body was a thing outside himself. It might stumble and fall many times but the new thing he had found, the thing inside himself that responded to the thing inside the shell that was Clara and his wife, did not stumble. It flew like a bird out of darkness into the light. At the moment he thought the sweeping flight of life thus begun would run on forever.

# Book Six

## CHAPTER XXI

It was a summer night in Ohio and the wheat in the long, flat fields that stretched away to the north from the town of Bidwell was ripe for the cutting. Between the wheat fields lay corn and cabbage fields. In the corn fields the green stalks stood up like young trees. Facing the fields lay the white roads, once the silent roads, hushed and empty through the nights and often during many hours of the day, the night silence broken only at long intervals by the clattering hoofs of homeward-bound horses and the silence of days by creaking wagons. Along the roads on a summer evening went the young farm hand in his buggy for which he had spent a summer's wage, a long summer of sweaty toil in hot fields. The hoofs of his horse beat a soft tattoo on the roads. His sweetheart sat beside him and he was in no hurry. All day he had been at work in the harvest and on the morrow he would work again. It did not matter. For him the night would last until the cocks in isolated farmyards began to hail the dawn. He forgot the horse and did not care what turning he took. All roads led to happiness for him.

Beside the long roads was an endless procession of fields broken now and then by a strip of woodland, where the shadows of trees fell upon the roads and made pools of an inky blackness. In the long, dry grass in fence corners insects sang; in the young cabbage fields rabbits ran, flitting away like shadows in the moonlight. The cabbage fields were beautiful too.

Who has written or sung of the beauties of corn fields in Illinois, Indiana, Iowa, or of the vast Ohio cabbage fields? In the cabbage fields the broad outer leaves fall down to make a background for the shifting, delicate colors of soils. The leaves are themselves riotous with color. As the season advances they change from light to dark greens, a thousand shades of purples, blues and reds appear and disappear.

In silence the cabbage fields slept beside the roads in Ohio. Not yet had the motor cars come to tear along the roads, their flashing lights—beautiful too, when seen by one afoot on the roads on a summer night—had not yet made the roads an extension of the cities. Akron, the terrible town, had not yet begun to roll forth its countless millions of rubber hoops, filled each with its portion of God's air compressed and in prison at last like the farm hands who have gone to the cities. Detroit and Toledo had not begun to send forth their hundreds of thousands of motor cars to shriek and scream the nights away on country roads. Willys was still a mechanic in an Indiana town, and Ford still worked in a bicycle repair shop in Detroit.

It was a summer night in the Ohio country and the moon shone. A country doctor's horse went at a humdrum pace along the roads. Softly and at long intervals men afoot stumbled along. A farm hand whose horse was lame walked toward town. An umbrella mender, benighted on the roads, hurried toward the lights of the distant town. In Bidwell, the place that had been on other summer nights a sleepy town filled with gossiping berry pickers, things were astir.

Change, and the thing men call growth, was in the air. Perhaps in its own way revolution was in the air, the silent, the real revolution that grew with the growth of the towns. In the stirring, bustling town of Bidwell that quiet summer night something happened that startled men. Something happened, and then in a few minutes it happened again. Heads wagged, special editions of daily newspapers were printed, the great hive of men was disturbed, under the invisible roof of the town that had so suddenly become a city, the seeds of self-consciousness were planted in new soil, in American soil.

Before all this began, however, something else happened. The first motor car ran through the streets of Bidwell and out upon the moonlit roads. The motor car was driven by Tom Butterworth and in it sat his daughter Clara with her husband Hugh McVey. During the week before, Tom had brought the car from Cleveland, and the mechanic who rode with him had taught him the art of driving. Now he drove alone and boldly. Early in the evening he had run out to the farmhouse to take his daughter and son-in-law for their first ride. Hugh sat in the seat beside him and after they had started and were clear of the town, Tom turned to him. "Now watch me step on her tail," he said proudly, using for the first time the motor slang he had picked up from the Cleveland mechanic.

As Tom sent the car hurling over the roads, Clara sat alone in the back seat unimpressed by her father's new acquisition. For three years she had been married and she felt that she did not yet know the man she had married. Always the story had been the same, moments of light and then darkness again. A new machine that went along roads at a startlingly increased rate of speed might change the whole face of the world, as her father declared it would, but it did not change certain facts of her life. "Am I a failure as a wife, or is Hugh impossible as a husband?" she asked herself for perhaps the thousandth time as the car, having got into a long stretch of clear, straight road, seemed to leap and sail through the air like a bird. "At any rate I have married me a husband and yet I have no husband, I have been in a man's arms but I have no lover, I have taken hold of life, but life has slipped through my fingers."

Like her father, Hugh seemed to Clara absorbed in only the things outside himself, the outer crust of life. He was like and yet unlike her father. She was baffled by him. There was something in the man she wanted and could not find. "The fault must be in me," she told herself. "He's all right, but what's the matter with me?"

After that night when he ran away from her bridal bed, Clara had more than once thought the miracle had happened. It did sometimes. On that night when he came to her out of the rain it had happened. There was a wall a blow could shatter, and she raised her hand to strike the blow. The wall was shattered and then builded itself again. Even as she lay at night in her husband's arms the wall reared itself up in the darkness of the sleeping room.

Over the farmhouse on such nights dense silence brooded and she and Hugh, as had become their habit together, were silent. In the darkness she put up her hand to touch her husband's face and hair. He lay still and she had the impression of some great force holding him back, holding her back. A sharp sense of struggle filled the room. The air was heavy with it.

When words came they did not break the silence. The wall remained.

The words that came were empty, meaningless words. Hugh suddenly broke forth into speech. He spoke of his work at the shop and of his progress toward the solution of some difficult, mechanical problem. If it were evening when the thing happened the two people got out of the lighted house where they had been sitting together, each feeling darkness would help the effort they were both making to tear away the wall. They walked along a lane, past the barns and over the little wooden bridge across the stream that ran down through the barnyard. Hugh did not want to talk of the work at the shop, but could find words for no other talk. They came to a fence where the lane turned and from where they could look down the hillside and into the town. He did not look at Clara but stared down the hillside and the words, in regard to the mechanical difficulties that had occupied his mind all day, ran on and on. When later they went back to the house he felt a little relieved. "I've said words. There is something achieved," he thought.

And now after the three years as a married woman Clara sat in the motor with her father and husband and with them was sent whirling swiftly through the summer night. The car ran down the hill road from the Butterworth farm, through a dozen residence streets in town and then out upon the long, straight roads in the rich, flat country to the north. It had skirted the town as a hungry wolf might have encircled silently and swiftly the fire-lit camp of a hunter. To Clara the machine seemed like a wolf, bold and cunning and yet afraid. Its great nose pushed through the troubled air of the quiet roads, frightening horses, breaking the silence with its persistent purring, drowning the song of insects. The headlights also disturbed the slumbers of the night. They flashed into barnyards where fowls slept on the lower branches of trees, played on the sides of barns sent the cattle in fields galloping away into darkness, and frightened horribly the wild things, the red squirrels and chipmunks that live in wayside fences in the Ohio country. Clara hated the machine and began to hate all machines. Thinking of machinery and the making of machines had, she decided, been at the bottom of her husband's inability to talk with her. Revolt against the whole mechanical impulse of her generation began to take possession of her.

And as she rode another and more terrible kind of revolt against the machine began in the town of Bidwell. It began in fact before Tom with his new motor left the Butterworth farm, it began before the summer moon came up, before the gray mantle of night had been laid over the shoulders of the hills south of the farmhouse.

Jim Gibson, the journeyman harness maker who worked in Joe Wainsworth's shop, was beside himself on that night. He had just won a great victory over his employer and felt like celebrating. For several days he had been telling the story of his anticipated victory in the saloons and store, and now it had happened. After dining at his boarding-house he went to a saloon and had a drink. Then he went to other saloons and had other drinks, after which he swaggered through the streets to the door of the shop. Although he was in his nature a spiritual bully, Jim did not lack energy, and his employer's shop was filled with work demanding attention. For a week both he and Joe had been returning to their work benches every evening. Jim wanted to come because some driving influence within made him love the thought of keeping the work always on the move, and Joe because Jim made him come.

Many things were on the move in the striving, hustling town on that evening. The system of checking on piece work, introduced by the superintendent Ed Hall in the corn-cutting machine plant, had brought on Bidwell's first industrial strike. The discontented workmen were not organized, and the strike was foredoomed to failure, but it had stirred the town deeply. One day, a week before, quite suddenly some fifty or sixty men had decided to quit. "We won't work for a fellow like Ed Hall," they declared. "He sets a scale of prices and then, when we have driven ourselves to the limit to make a decent day's pay, he cuts the scale." Leaving the shop the men went in a body to Main Street and two or three of them, developing unexpected eloquence, began delivering speeches on street corners. On the next day the strike spread and for several days the shop had been closed. Then a labor organizer came from Cleveland and on the day of his arrival the story ran through the street that strikebreakers were to be brought in.

And on that evening of many adventures another element was introduced into the already disturbed life of the community. At the corner of Main and McKinley Streets and just beyond the place where three old buildings were being torn down to make room for the building of a new hotel, appeared a man who climbed upon a box and attacked, not the piece work prices at the corn-cutting machine plant, but the whole system that built and maintained factories where the wage scale of the workmen could be fixed by the whim or necessity of one man or a group of men. As the man on the box talked, the workmen in the crowd who were of American birth began to shake their heads. They went to one side and gathering in groups discussed the stranger's words. "I tell you what," said a little old workman, pulling nervously at his graying mustache, "I'm on strike and I'm for sticking out until Steve Hunter and Tom Butterworth fire Ed Hall, but I don't like this kind of talk. I'll tell you what that man's doing. He's attacking our Government, that's what he's doing." The workmen went off to their homes grumbling. The Government was to them a sacred thing, and they did not fancy having their demands for a better wage scale confused by the talk of anarchists and socialists. Many of the laborers of Bidwell were sons and grandsons of pioneers who had opened up the country where the great sprawling towns were now growing into cities. They or their fathers had fought in the great Civil War. During boyhood they had breathed a reverence for government out of the very air of the towns. The great men of whom the schoolbooks talked had all been connected with the Government. In Ohio there had been Garfield, Sherman, McPherson the fighter and others. From Illinois had come Lincoln and Grant. For a time the very ground of the mid-American country had seemed to spurt forth great men as now it was spurting forth gas and oil. Government had justified itself in the men it had produced.

And now there had come among them men who had

no reverence for government. What a speaker for the first time dared say openly on the streets of Bidwell, had already been talked in the shops. The new men, the foreigners coming from many lands, had brought with them strange doctrines. They began to make acquaintances among the American workmen. "Well," they said, "you've had great men here; no doubt you have; but you're getting a new kind of great men now. These new men are not born out of people. They're being born out of capital. What is a great man? He's one who has the power. Isn't that a fact? Well, you fellows here have got to find out that nowadays power comes with the possession of money. Who are the big men of this town? —not some lawyer or politician who can make a good speech, but the men who own the factories where you have to work. Your Steve Hunter and Tom Butterworth are the great men of this town."

The socialist, who had come to speak on the streets of Bidwell, was a Swede, and his wife had come with him. As he talked his wife made figures on a blackboard. The old story of the trick by which the citizens of the town had lost their money in the plant-setting machine company was revived and told over and over. The Swede, a big man with heavy fists, spoke of the prominent citizens of the town as thieves who by a trick had robbed their fellows. As he stood on the box beside his wife, and raising his fists shouted crude sentences condemning the capitalist class, men who had gone away angry came back to listen. The speaker declared himself a workman like themselves and, unlike the religious salvationists who occasionally spoke on the streets, did not beg for money. "I'm a workman like yourselves," he shouted. "Both my wife and myself work until we've saved a little money. Then we come out to some town like this and fight capital until we're busted. We've been fighting for years now and we'll keep on fighting as long as we live."

As the orator shouted out his sentences he raised his fist as though to strike, and looked not unlike one of his ancestors, the Norsemen, who in old times had sailed far and wide over unknown seas in search of the fighting they loved. The men of Bidwell began to respect him. "After all, what he says sounds like mighty good sense," they declared, shaking their heads. "Maybe Ed Hall isn't any worse than anyone else. We got to break up the system. That's a fact. Some of these days we got to break up the system."

Jim Gibson got to the door of Joe's shop at half past seven o'clock. Several men stood on the sidewalk and he stopped and stood before them, intending to tell again the story of his triumph over his employer. Inside the shop Joe was already at his bench and at work. The men, two of them strikers from the corn-cutting machine plant, complained bitterly of the difficulty of supporting their families, and a third man, a fellow with a big black mustache who smoked a pipe, began to repeat some of the axioms in regard to industrialism and the class war he had picked up from the socialist orator. Jim listened for a moment and then, turning, put his thumb on his buttocks and wriggled his fingers. "Oh, hell," he sneered, "what are you fools talking about? You're going to get up a union or get into the socialist party. What're you talking about? A union or a party can't help a man who can't look out for himself."

The blustering and half-intoxicated harness maker stood in the open shop door and told again and in detail the story of his triumph over his employer. Then another thought came and he spoke of the twelve hundred dollars Joe had lost in the stock of the plant-setting machine company. "He lost his money and you fellows are going to get licked in this fight," he declared. "You're all wrong, you fellows, when you talk about unions or joining the socialist party. What counts is what a man can do for himself. Character counts. Yes, sir, character makes a man what he is."

Jim pounded on his chest and glared about him. "Look at me," he said. "I was a drunkard and down and out when I came to this town; a drunkard, that's what I was and that's what I am. I came here to this shop to work, and now, if you want to know, ask anyone in town who runs this place. The socialist says money is power. Well, there's a man inside here who has the money, but you bet I've got the power."

Slapping his knees with his hands Jim laughed heartily. A week before, a traveling man had come to the shop to sell machine-made harness. Joe had ordered the man out and Jim had called him back. He had placed an order for eighteen sets of the harness and had made Joe sign the order. The harness had arrived that afternoon and was now hung in the shop. "It's hanging in the shop now," Jim cried. "Go see for yourself."

Triumphantly Jim walked up and down before the men on the sidewalk, and his voice rang through the shop where Joe sat on his harness-maker's horse under a swinging lamp hard at work. "I tell you, character's the thing that counts," the roaring voice cried. "You see I'm a workingman like you fellows, but I don't join a union or a socialist party. I get my way. My boss Joe in there's a sentimental old fool, that's what he is. All his life he's made harnesses by hand and he thinks that's the only way. He claims he has pride in his work, that's what he claims."

Jim laughed again. "Do you know what he did the

other day when that traveler had gone out of the shop and after I had made him sign that order?" he asked. "Cried, that's what he did. By God, he did—sat there and cried."

Again Jim laughed, but the workmen on the sidewalk did not join in his merriment. Going to one of them, the one who had declared his intention of joining the union, Jim began to berate him. "You think you can lick Ed Hall with Steve Hunter and Tom Butterworth back of him, eh?" he asked sharply. "Well, I'll tell you what—you can't. All the unions in the world won't help you. You'll get licked—for why?

"For why? Because Ed Hall is like me, that's for why. He's got character, that's what he's got."

Growing weary of his boasting and the silence of his audience, Jim started to walk in at the door, but when one of the workmen, a pale man of fifty with a graying mustache, spoke, he turned to listen. "You're a suck, a suck and a lickspittle, that's what you are," said the pale man, his voice trembling with passion.

Jim ran through the crowd of men and knocked the speaker to the sidewalk with a blow of his fist. Two of the other workmen seemed about to take up the cause of their fallen brother, but when in spite of their threats Jim stood his ground, they hesitated. They went to help the pale workman to his feet, and Jim went into the shop and closed the door. Climbing onto his horse he went to work, and the men went off along the sidewalk, still threatening to do what they had not done when the opportunity offered.

Joe worked in silence beside his employee and night began to settle down over the disturbed town. Above the clatter of many voices in the street outside could be heard the loud voice of the socialist orator who had taken up his stand for the evening at a nearby corner. When it had become quite dark outside, the old harness maker climbed down from his horse and going to the front door opened it softly and looked up and down the street. Then he closed it again and walked toward the rear of the shop. In his hand he held his harness-maker's knife, shaped like a half moon and with an extraordinarily sharp circular edge. The harness maker's wife had died during the year before and since that time he had not slept well at night. Often for a week at a time he did not sleep at all, but lay all night with wide-open eyes, thinking strange, new thoughts. In the daytime and when Jim was not about, he sometimes spent hours sharpening the moon-shaped knife on a piece of leather; and on the day after the incident of the placing of the order for the factory-made harness he had gone into a hardware store and bought a cheap revolver. He had been sharpening the knife as Jim talked to the workmen outside. When Jim began to tell the story of his humiliation he had stopped sewing at the broken harness in his vise and, getting up, had taken the knife from its hiding-place under a pile of leather on a bench to give its edge a few last caressing strokes.

Holding the knife in his hand Joe went with shambling steps toward the place where Jim sat absorbed in his work. A brooding silence seemed to lie over the shop and even outside in the street all noises suddenly ceased. Old Joe's gait changed. As he passed behind the horse on which Jim sat, life came into his figure and he walked with a soft, catlike tread. Joy shone in his eyes. As though warned of something impending, Jim turned and opened his mouth to growl at his employer, but his words never found their way to his lips. The old man made a peculiar half step, half leap past the horse, and the knife whipped through the air. At one stroke he had succeeded in practically severing Jim Gibson's head from his body.

There was no sound in the shop. Joe threw the knife into a corner and ran quickly past the horse where the body of Jim Gibson sat upright. Then the body fell to the floor with a thump and there was the sharp rattle of heels on the board floor. The old man locked the front door and listened impatiently. When all was again quiet he went to search for the knife he had thrown away, but could not find it. Taking Jim's knife from a bench under the hanging lamp, he stepped over the body and climbed upon his horse to turn out the lights.

For an hour Joe stayed in the shop with the dead man. The eighteen sets of harness shipped from a Cleveland factory had been received that morning, and Jim had insisted they be unpacked and hung on hooks along the shop walls. He had bullied Joe into helping hang the harnesses, and now Joe took them down alone. One by one they were laid on the floor and with Jim's knife the old man cut each strap into little pieces that made a pile of litter on the floor reaching to his waist. When that was done he went again to the rear of the shop, again stepping almost carelessly over the dead man, and took the revolver out of the pocket of an overcoat that hung by the door.

Joe went out of the shop by the back door, and having locked it carefully, crept through an alleyway and into the lighted street where people walked up and down. The next place to his own was a barber shop, and as he hurried along the sidewalk, two young men came out and called to him. "Hey," they called, "do you believe in factory-made harness now-days, Joe Wainsworth? Hey, what do you say? Do you sell factory-made harness?"

Joe did not answer, but stepping off the sidewalk, walked in the road. A group of Italian laborers passed, talking rapidly and making gestures with their hands. As he went more deeply into the heart of the growing city, past the socialist orator and a labor organizer who was addressing a crowd of men on another corner, his step became catlike as it had been in the moment before the knife flashed at the throat of Jim Gibson. The crowds of people frightened him. He imagined himself set upon by a crowd and hanged to a lamppost. The voice of the labor orator arose above the murmur of voices in the street. "We've got to take power into our hands. We've got to carry on our own battle for power," the voice declared.

The harness maker turned a corner into a quiet street, his hand caressing affectionately the revolver in the side pocket of his coat. He intended to kill himself, but had not wanted to die in the same room with Jim Gibson. In his own way he had always been a very sensitive man and his only fear was that rough hands fall upon him before he had completed the evening's work. He was quite sure that had his wife been alive she would have understood what had happened. She had always understood everything he did or said. He remembered his courtship. His wife had been a country girl and on Sundays, after their marriage, they had gone together to spend the day in the wood. After Joe had brought his wife to Bidwell they continued the practice. One of his customers, a well-to-do farmer, lived five miles north of town, and on his farm there was a grove of beech trees. Almost every Sunday for several years he got a horse from the livery stable and took his wife there. After dinner at the farmhouse, he and the farmer gossiped for an hour, while the women washed the dishes, and then he took his wife and went into the beech forest. No underbrush grew under the spreading branches of the trees, and when the two people had remained silent for a time, hundreds of squirrels and chipmunks came to chatter and play about them. Joe had brought nuts in his pocket and threw them about. The quivering little animals drew near and then with a flip of their tails scampered away. One day a boy from a neighboring farm came to the wood and shot one of the squirrels. It happened just as Joe and his wife came from the farmhouse and he saw the wounded squirrel hang from the branch of a tree, and then fall. It lay at his feet and his wife grew ill and leaned against him for support. He said nothing, but stared at the quivering thing on the ground. When it lay still the boy came and picked it up. Still Joe said nothing. Taking his wife's arm he walked to where they were in the habit of sitting, and reached in his pocket for the nuts to scatter on the ground. The farm boy, who had felt the reproach in the eyes of the man and woman, had gone out of the wood. Suddenly Joe began to cry. He was ashamed and did not want his wife to see, and she pretended she had not seen.

On the night when he had killed Jim, Joe decided he would walk to the farm and the beech forest and there kill himself. He hurried past a long row of dark stores and warehouses in the newly built section of town and came to a residence street. He saw a man coming toward him and stepped into the stairway of a store building. The man stopped under a street lamp to light a cigar, and the harness maker recognized him. It was Steve Hunter, who had induced him to invest the twelve hundred dollars in the stock of the plant-setting machine company, the man who had brought the new times to Bidwell, the man who was at the bottom of all such innovations as machine-made harnesses. Joe had killed his employee, Jim Gibson, in cold anger, but now a new kind of anger took possession of him. Something danced before his eyes and his hands trembled so that he was afraid the gun he had taken out of his pocket would fall to the sidewalk. It wavered as he raised it and fired, but chance came to his assistance. Steve Hunter pitched forward to the sidewalk.

Without stopping to pick up the revolver that had fallen out of his hand, Joe now ran up a stairway and got into a dark, empty hall. He felt his way along a wall and came presently to another stairway, leading down. It brought him into an alleyway, and going along this he came out near the bridge that led over the river and into what in the old days had been Turner's Pike, the road out which he had driven with his wife to the farm and the beech forest.

But one thing now puzzled Joe Wainsworth. He had lost his revolver and did not know how he was to manage his own death. "I must do it some way," he thought, when at last, after nearly three hours steady plodding and hiding in fields to avoid the teams going along the road he got to the beech forest. He went to sit under a tree near the place where he had so often sat through quiet Sunday afternoons with his wife beside him. "I'll rest a little and then I'll think how I can do it," he thought wearily, holding his head in his hands. "I mustn't go to sleep. If they find me they'll hurt me. They'll hurt me before I have a chance to kill myself. They'll hurt me before I have a chance to kill myself," he repeated, over and over, holding his head in his hands and rocking gently back and forth.

## CHAPTER XXII

The car driven by Tom Butterworth stopped at a town, and Tom got out to fill his pockets with cigars and incidentally to enjoy the wonder and admiration of the citizens. He was in an exalted mood and words flowed from him. As the motor under its hood purred, so the brain under the graying old head purred and threw forth words. He talked to the idlers before the drugstores in the towns and, when the car started again and they were out in the open country, his voice, pitched in a high key to make itself heard above the purring engine, became shrill. Having struck the shrill tone of the new age the voice went on and on.

But the voice and the swift-moving car did not stir Clara. She tried not to hear the voice, and fixing her eyes on the soft landscape flowing past under the moon, tried to think of other times and places. She thought of nights when she had walked with Kate Chanceller through the streets of Columbus, and of the silent ride she had taken with Hugh that night they were married. Her mind went back into her childhood and she remembered the long days she had spent riding with her father in this same valley, going from farm to farm to haggle and dicker for the purchase of calves and pigs. Her father had not talked then but sometimes, when they had driven far and were homeward bound in the failing light of evening, words did come to him. She remembered one evening in the summer after her mother died and when her father often took her with him on his drives. They had stopped for the evening meal at the house of a farmer and when they got on the road again, the moon came out. Something present in the spirit of the night stirred Tom, and he spoke of his life as a boy in the new country and of his fathers and brothers. "We worked hard, Clara," he said. "The whole country was new and every acre we planted had to be cleared." The mind of the prosperous farmer fell into a reminiscent mood and he spoke of little things concerning his life as a boy and young man; the days of cutting wood alone in the silent, white forest when winter came and it was time for getting out firewood and logs for new farm buildings, the log rollings to which neighboring farmers came, when great piles of logs were made and set afire that space might be cleared for planting. In the winter the boy went to school in the village of Bidwell and as he was even then an energetic, pushing youth, already intent on getting on in the world, he set traps in the forest and on the banks of streams and walked the trap line on his way to and from school. In the spring he sent his pelts to the growing town of Cleveland where they were sold. He spoke of the money he got and of how he had finally saved enough to buy a horse of his own.

Tom had talked of many other things on that night, of the spelling-downs at the schoolhouse in town, of huskings and dances held in the barns and of the evening when he went skating on the river and first met his wife. "We took to each other at once," he said softly. "There was a fire built on the bank of the river and after I had skated with her we went and sat down to warm ourselves.

"We wanted to get married to each other right away," he told Clara. "I walked home with her after we got tired of skating, and after that I thought of nothing but how to get my own farm and have a home of my own."

As the daughter sat in the motor listening to the shrill voice of the father, who now talked only of the making of machines and money, that other man talking softly in the moonlight as the horse jogged slowly along the dark road seemed very far away. All such men seemed very far away. "Everything worth while is very far away," she thought bitterly. "The machines men are so intent on making have carried them very far from the old sweet things."

The motor flew along the roads and Tom thought of his old longing to own and drive fast racing horses. "I used to be half crazy to own fast horses," he shouted to his son-in-law. "I didn't do it, because owning fast horses meant a waste of money, but it was in my mind all the time. I wanted to go fast: faster than anyone else." In a kind of ecstasy he gave the motor more gas and shot the speed up to fifty miles an hour. The hot, summer air, fanned into a violent wind, whistled past his head. "Where would the damned race horses be now," he called, "where would your Maud S. or your J.I.C. be, trying to catch up with me in this car?"

Yellow wheat fields and fields of young corn, tall now and in the light breeze that was blowing whispering in the moonlight, flashed past, looking like squares on a checker board made for the amusement of the child of some giant. The car ran through miles of the low farming country, through the main streets of towns, where the people ran out of the stores to stand on the sidewalks and look at the new wonder, through sleeping bits of woodlands—remnants of the great forests in which Tom had worked as a boy—and across wooden bridges over small streams, beside which grew tangled masses of elderberries, now yellow and fragrant with blossoms.

At eleven o'clock having already achieved some ninety miles Tom turned the car back. Running more sedately he again talked of the mechanical triumphs of the age in which he had lived. "I've brought you whizzing along, you and Clara," he said proudly. "I tell you what, Hugh, Steve Hunter and I have brought you along fast in more ways than one. You've got to give Steve credit for seeing something in you, and you've got to give me credit for putting my money back of your brains. I don't want to take no credit from Steve. There's credit enough for all. All I got to say for myself is that

I saw the hole in the doughnut. Yes, sir, I wasn't so blind. I saw the hole in the doughnut."

Tom stopped to light a cigar and then drove on again. "I'll tell you what, Hugh," he said, "I wouldn't say so to anyone not of my family, but the truth is, I'm the man that's been putting over the big things there in Bidwell. The town is going to be a city now and a mighty big city. Towns in this state like Columbus, Toledo and Dayton, had better look out for themselves. I'm the man has always kept Steve Hunter steady and going straight ahead down the track, as this car goes with my hand at the steering wheel.

"You don't know anything about it, and I don't want you should talk, but there are new things coming to Bidwell," he added. "When I was in Chicago last month I met a man who has been making rubber buggy and bicycle tires. I'm going in with him and we're going to start a plant for making automobile tires right in Bidwell. The tire business is bound to be one of the greatest on earth and they ain't no reason why Bidwell shouldn't be the biggest tire center ever known in the world." Although the car now ran quietly, Tom's voice again became shrill. "There'll be hundreds of thousands of cars like this tearing over every road in America," he declared. "Yes, sir, they will; and if I calculate right Bidwell'll be the great tire town of the world."

For a long time Tom drove in silence, and when he again began to talk it was a new mood. He told a tale of life in Bidwell that stirred both Hugh and Clara deeply. He was angry and had Clara not been in the car would have become violently profane.

"I'd like to hang the men who are making trouble in the shops in town," he broke forth. "You know who I mean, I mean the labor men who are trying to make trouble for Steve Hunter and me. There's a socialist talking every night on the street over there. I'll tell you, Hugh, the laws of this country are wrong." For ten minutes he talked of the labor difficulties in the shops.

"They better look out," he declared, and was so angry that his voice rose to something like a suppressed scream. "We're inventing new machines pretty fast now-days," he cried. "Pretty soon we'll do all the work by machines. Then what'll we do? We'll kick all the workers out and let 'em strike till they're sick, that's what we'll do. They can talk their fool socialism all they want, but we'll show 'em, the fools."

His angry mood passed, and as the car turned into the last fifteen-mile stretch of road that led to Bidwell, he told the tale that so deeply stirred his passengers. Chuckling softly he told of the struggle of the Bidwell harness maker, Joe Wainsworth, to prevent the sale of machine-made harness in the community, and of his experience with his employee, Jim Gibson. Tom had heard the tale in the bar-room of the Bidwell House and it had made a profound impression on his mind. "I'll tell you what," he declared, "I'm going to get in touch with Jim Gibson. That's the kind of man to handle workers. I only heard about him tonight, but I'm going to see him tomorrow."

Leaning back in his seat Tom laughed heartily as he told of the traveling man who had visited Joe Wainsworth's shop and the placing of the order for the factory-made harness. In some intangible way he felt that when Jim Gibson laid the order for the harness on the bench in the shop and by the force of his personality compelled Joe Wainsworth to sign, he justified all such men as himself. In imagination he lived in that moment with Jim, and like Jim the incident aroused his inclination to boast. "Why, a lot of cheap laboring skates can't down such men as myself any more than Joe Wainsworth could down that Jim Gibson," he declared. "They ain't got the character, you see, that's what's the matter, they ain't got the character." Tom touched some mechanism connected with the engine of the car and it shot suddenly forward. "Suppose one of them labor leaders were standing in the road there," he cried. Instinctively Hugh leaned forward and peered into the darkness through which the lights of the car cut like a great scythe, and on the back seat Clara half rose to her feet. Tom shouted with delight and as the car plunged along the road his voice rose in triumph. "The damn fools!" he cried. "They think they can stop the machines. Let 'em try. They want to go on in their old hand-made way. Let 'em look out. Let 'em look out for such men as Jim Gibson and me."

Down a slight incline in the road shot the car and swept around a wide curve, and then the jumping, dancing light, running far ahead, revealed a sight that made Tom thrust out his foot and jam on the brakes.

In the road and in the very center of the circle of light, as though performing a scene on the stage, three men were struggling. As the car came to a stop, so sudden that it pitched both Clara and Hugh out of their seats, the struggle came to an end. One of the struggling figures, a small man without coat or hat, had jerked himself away from the others and started to run toward the fence at the side of the road and separating it from a grove of trees. A large, broad-shouldered man sprang forward and catching the tail of the fleeing man's coat pulled him back into the circle of light. His fist shot out and caught the small man directly on the mouth. He fell like a dead thing, face downward in the dust of the road.

Tom ran the car slowly forward and its headlight continued to play over the three figures. From a little pocket at the side of his driver's seat he took a revolver. He ran the car quickly to a position near the group in the road and stopped.

"What's up?" he asked sharply.

Ed Hall the factory superintendent, the man who had struck the blow that had felled the little man, stepped forward and explained the tragic happenings of the evening in town. The factory superintendent had remembered that as a boy he had once worked for a few weeks on the farm of which the wood beside the road was a part, and that on Sunday afternoons the harness maker had come to the farm with his wife and the two people had gone to walk in the very place where he had just been found. "I had a hunch he would be out here," he boasted. "I figured it out. Crowds started out of town in all directions, but I cut out alone. Then I happened to see this fellow and just for company I brought him along." He put up his hand and, looking at Tom, tapped his forehead. "Cracked," he declared, "he always was. A fellow I knew saw him once in that woods," he said pointing. "Somebody had shot a squirrel and he took on about it as though he had lost a child. I said then he was crazy, and he has sure proved I was right."

At a word from her father Clara went to sit on the front seat on Hugh's knees. Her body trembled and she was cold with fear. As her father had told the story of Jim Gibson's triumph over Joe Wainsworth she had wanted passionately to kill that blustering fellow. Now the thing was done. In her mind the harness maker had come to stand for all the men and women in the world who were in secret revolt against the absorption of the age in machines and the products of machines. He had stood as a protesting figure against what her father had become and what she thought her husband had become. She had wanted Jim Gibson killed and it had been done. As a child she had gone often to Wainsworth's shop with her father or some farm hand, and she now remembered sharply the peace and quiet of the place. At the thought of the same place, now become the scene of a desperate killing, her body shook so that she clutched at Hugh's arms, striving to steady herself.

Ed Hall took the senseless figure of the old man in the road into his arms and half threw it into the back seat of the car. To Clara it was as though his rough, misunderstanding hands were on her own body. The car started swiftly along the road and Ed told again the story of the night's happenings. "I tell you, Mr. Hunter is in mighty bad shape, he may die," he said. Clara turned to look at her husband and thought him totally unaffected by what had happened. His face was quiet like her father's face. The factory superintendent's voice went on explaining his part in the adventures of the evening. Ignoring the pale workman who sat lost in the shadows in a corner of the rear seat, he spoke as though he had undertaken and accomplished the capture of the murderer single-handed. As he afterwards explained to his wife, Ed felt he had been a fool not to come alone. "I knew I could handle him all right," he explained. "I wasn't afraid, but I had figured it all out he was crazy. That made me feel shaky. When they were getting up a crowd to go out on the hunt, I says to myself, I'll go alone. I says to myself, I'll bet he's gone out to that woods on the Riggly farm where he and his wife used to go on Sundays. I started and then I saw this other man standing on a corner and I made him come with me. He didn't want to come and I wish I'd gone alone. I could have handled him and I'd got all the credit."

In the car Ed told the story of the night in the streets of Bidwell. Someone had seen Steve Hunter shot down in the street and had declared the harness maker had done it and had then run away. A crowd had gone to the harness shop and had found the body of Jim Gibson. On the floor of the shop were the factory-made harnesses cut into bits. "He must have been in there and at work for an hour or two, stayed right in there with the man he had killed. It's the craziest thing any man ever done."

The harness maker, lying on the floor of the car where Ed had thrown him, stirred and sat up. Clara turned to look at him and shivered. His shirt was torn so that the thin, old neck and shoulders could be plainly seen in the uncertain light, and his face was covered with blood that had dried and was now black with dust. Ed Hall went on with the tale of his triumph. "I found him where I said to myself I would. Yes, sir, I found him where I said to myself I would."

The car came to the first of the houses of the town, long rows of cheaply built frame houses standing in what had once been Ezra French's cabbage patch, where Hugh had crawled on the ground in the moonlight, working out the mechanical problems that confronted him in the building of his plant-setting machine. Suddenly the distraught and frightened man crouched on the floor of the car, raised himself on his hands and lurched forward, trying to spring over the side. Ed Hall caught him by the arm and jerked him back. He drew back his arm to strike again but Clara's voice, cold and intense with passion, stopped him. "If you touch him, I'll kill you," she said. "No matter what he does, don't you dare strike him again."

Tom drove the car slowly through the streets of Bidwell to the door of a police station. Word of the return of the murderer had run ahead, and a crowd had gathered. Although it was past two o'clock the lights still burned in stores and saloons, and crowds stood at every corner. With the aid of a policeman, Ed Hall, with one eye fixed cautiously on the front seat where Clara sat, started to lead Joe Wainsworth away. "Come on now, we won't hurt you," he said reassuringly, and had got his man free of the car when he broke away. Springing back into the rear seat the crazed man turned to look at the crowd. A sob broke from his lips. For a moment he stood trembling with fright, and then turning, he for the first time saw Hugh, the man in whose footsteps he had once crept in the darkness in Turner's Pike, the man who had invented the machine by which the earnings of a lifetime had been swept away. "It wasn't me. You did it. You killed Jim Gibson," he screamed, and springing forward sank his fingers and teeth into Hugh's neck.

## CHAPTER XXIII

One day in the month of October, four years after the time of his first motor ride with Clara and Tom, Hugh went on a business trip to the city of Pittsburgh. He left Bidwell in the morning and got to the steel city at noon. At three o'clock his business was finished and he was ready to return.

Although he had not yet realized it, Hugh's career as a successful inventor had received a sharp check. The trick of driving directly at the point, of becoming utterly absorbed in the thing before him, had been lost. He went to Pittsburgh to see about the casting of new parts for the hay-loading machine, but what he did in Pittsburgh was of no importance to the men who would manufacture and sell that worthy, labor-saving tool.

Although he did not know it, a young man from Cleveland, in the employ of Tom and Steve, had already done what Hugh was striving half-heartedly to do. The machine had been finished and ready to market in October three years before, and after repeated tests a lawyer had made formal application for patent. Then it was discovered that an Iowa man had already made application for and been granted a patent on a similar apparatus.

When Tom came to the shop and told him what had happened Hugh had been ready to drop the whole matter, but that was not Tom's notion. "The devil!" he said. "Do you think we're going to waste all this money and labor?"

Drawings of the Iowa man's machine were secured, and Tom set Hugh at the task of doing what he called "getting round" the other fellow's patents. "Do the best you can and we'll go ahead," he said. "You see we've got the money and that means power. Make what changes you can and then we'll go on with our manufacturing plans. We'll whipsaw this other fellow through the courts. We'll fight him till he's sick of fight and then we'll buy him out cheap. I've had the fellow looked up and he hasn't any money and is a boozer besides. You go ahead. We'll get that fellow all right."

Hugh had tried valiantly to go along the road marked out for him by his father-in-law and had put aside other plans to rebuild the machine he had thought of as completed and out of the way. He made new parts, changed other parts, studied the drawings of the Iowa man's machine, did what he could to accomplish his task.

Nothing happened. A conscientious determination not to infringe on the work of the Iowa man stood in his way.

Then something did happen. At night as he sat alone in his shop after a long study of the drawings of the other man's machine, he put them aside and sat staring into the darkness beyond the circle of light cast by his lamp. He forgot the machine and thought of the unknown inventor, the man far away over forests, lakes and rivers, who for months had worked on the same problem that had occupied his mind. Tom had said the man had no money and was a boozer. He could be defeated, bought cheap. He was himself at work on the instrument of the man's defeat.

Hugh left his shop and went for a walk, and the problem connected with the twisting of the iron and steel parts of the hay-loading apparatus into new forms was again left unsolved. The Iowa man had become a distinct, almost understandable personality to Hugh. Tom had said he drank, got drunk. His own father had been a drunkard. Once a man, the very man who had been the instrument of his own coming to Bidwell, had taken it for granted he was a drunkard. He wondered if some twist of life might not have made him one.

Thinking of the Iowa man, Hugh began to think of other men. He thought of his father and of himself. When he was striving to come out of the filth, the flies, the poverty, the fishy smells, the shadowy dreams of his life by the river, his father had often tried to draw him back into that life. In imagination he saw before him the dissolute man who had bred him. On afternoons of summer days in the river town, when Henry Shepard was not about, his father sometimes came to the station where he was employed. He had begun to earn a little money and his father wanted it to buy drinks. Why?

There was a problem for Hugh's mind, a problem

that could not be solved in wood and steel. He walked and thought about it when he should have been making new parts for the hay-loading apparatus. He had lived but little in the life of the imagination, had been afraid to live that life, had been warned and re-warned against living it. The shadowy figure of the unknown inventor in the State of Iowa, who had been brother to himself, who had worked on the same problems and had come to the same conclusions, slipped away, followed by the almost equally shadowy figure of his father. Hugh tried to think of himself and his own life.

For a time that seemed a simple and easy way out of the new and intricate task he had set for his mind. His own life was a matter of history. He knew about himself. Having walked far out of town, he turned and went back toward his shop. His way led through the new city that had grown up since his coming to Bidwell. Turner's Pike that had been a country road along which on summer evenings lovers strolled to the Wheeling Station and Pickleville was now a street. All that section of the new city was given over to workers' homes and here and there a store had been built. The Widow McCoy's place was gone and in its place was a warehouse, black and silent under the night sky. How grim the street in the late night! The berry pickers who once went along the road at evening were now gone forever. Like Ezra French's sons they had perhaps become factory hands. Apple and cherry trees once grew along the road. They had dropped their blossoms on the heads of strolling lovers. They also were gone. Hugh had once crept along the road at the heels of Ed Hall, who walked with his arm about a girl's waist. He had heard Ed complaining of his lot in life and crying out for new times. It was Ed Hall who had introduced the piece-work plan in the factories of Bidwell and brought about the strike, during which three men had been killed and ill-feeling engendered in hundreds of silent workers. That strike had been won by Tom and Steve and they had since that time been victorious in a larger and more serious strike. Ed Hall was now at the head of a new factory being built along the Wheeling tracks. He was growing fat and was prosperous.

When Hugh got to his shop he lighted his lamp and again got out the drawings he had come from home to study. They lay unnoticed on the desk. He looked at his watch. It was two o'clock. "Clara may be awake. I must go home," he thought vaguely. He now owned his own motor car and it stood in the road before the shop. Getting in he drove away into the darkness over the bridge, out of Turner's Pike and along a street lined with factories and railroad sidings. Some of the factories were working and were ablaze with lights. Through lighted windows he could see men stationed along benches and bending over huge, iron machines. He had come from home that evening to study the work of an unknown man from the faraway State of Iowa, to try to circumvent that man. Then he had gone to walk and to think of himself and his own life. "The evening has been wasted. I have done nothing," he thought gloomily as his car climbed up a long street lined with the homes of the wealthier citizens of his town and turned into the short stretch of Medina Road still left between the town and the Butterworth farmhouse.

On the day when he went to Pittsburgh, Hugh got to the station where he was to take the homeward train at three, and the train did not leave until four. He went into a big waiting-room and sat on a bench in a corner. After a time he arose and going to a stand bought a newspaper, but did not read it. It lay unopened on the bench beside him. The station was filled with men, women, and children who moved restlessly about. A train came in and a swarm of people departed, were carried into faraway parts of the country, while new people came into the station from a nearby street. He looked at those who were going out into the train shed. "It may be that some of them are going to that town in Iowa where that fellow lives," he thought. It was odd how thoughts of the unknown Iowa man clung to him.

One day, during the same summer and but a few months earlier, Hugh had gone to the town of Sandusky, Ohio, on the same mission that had brought him to Pittsburgh. How many parts for the hay-loading machine had been cast and later thrown away! They did the work, but he decided each time that he had infringed on the other man's machine. When that happened he did not consult Tom. Something within him warned him against doing that. He destroyed the part. "It wasn't what I wanted," he told Tom who had grown discouraged with his son-in-law but did not openly voice his dissatisfaction. "Oh, well, he's lost his pep, marriage has taken the life out of him. We'll have to get someone else on the job," he said to Steve, who had entirely recovered from the wound received at the hands of Joe Wainsworth.

On that day when he went to Sandusky, Hugh had several hours to wait for his homebound train and went to walk by the shores of a bay. Some brightly colored stones attracted his attention and he picked several of them up and put them in his pockets. In the station at Pittsburgh he took them out and held them in his hand. A light came in at a window, a long, slanting light that played over the stones. His roving, disturbed mind was caught and held. He rolled the stones back and forth. The colors blended and then separated again. When he raised his eyes, a woman and a child on a nearby bench, also attracted by the flashing bit of color held like a flame in his hand, were looking at him intently.

He was confused and walked out of the station into the street. "What a silly fellow I have become, playing with colored stones like a child," he thought, but at the same time put the stones carefully into his pockets.

Ever since that night when he had been attacked in the motor, the sense of some indefinable, inner struggle had been going on in Hugh, as it went on that day in the station at Pittsburgh and on the night in the shop, when he found himself unable to fix his attention on the prints of the Iowa man's machine. Unconsciously and quite without intent he had come into a new level of thought and action. He had been an unconscious worker, a doer and was now becoming something else. The time of the comparatively simple struggle with definite things, with iron and steel, had passed. He fought to accept himself, to understand himself, to relate himself with the life about him. The poor white, son of the defeated dreamer by the river, who had forced himself in advance of his fellows along the road of mechanical development, was still in advance of his fellows of the growing Ohio towns. The struggle he was making was the struggle his fellows of another generation would one and all have to make.

Hugh got into his homebound train at four o'clock and went into the smoking car. The somewhat distorted and twisted fragment of thoughts that had all day been playing through his mind stayed with him. "What difference does it make if the new parts I have ordered for the machine have to be thrown away?" he thought. "If I never complete the machine, it's all right. The one the Iowa man had made does the work."

For a long time he struggled with that thought. Tom, Steve, all the Bidwell men with whom he had been associated, had a philosophy into which the thought did not fit. "When you put your hand to the plow do not turn back," they said. Their language was full of such sayings. To attempt to do a thing and fail was the great crime, the sin against the Holy Ghost. There was unconscious defiance of a whole civilization in Hugh's attitude toward the completion of the parts that would help Tom and his business associates "get around" the Iowa man's patent.

The train from Pittsburgh went through northern Ohio to a junction where Hugh would get another train for Bidwell. Great booming towns, Youngstown, Akron, Canton, Massilon—manufacturing towns all—lay along the way. In the smoker Hugh sat, again playing with the colored stones held in his hand. There was relief for his mind in the stones. The light continually played about them, and their color shifted and changed. One could look at the stones and get relief from thoughts. Raising his eyes he looked out of the car window. The train was passing through Youngstown. His eyes looked along grimy streets of workers' houses clustered closely about huge mills. The same light that had played over the stones in his hand began to play over his mind, and for a moment he became not an inventor but a poet. The revolution within had really begun. A new declaration of independence wrote itself within him. "The gods have thrown the towns like stones over the flat country, but the stones have no color. They do not burn and change in the light," he thought.

Two men who sat in a seat in the westward-bound

train began to talk, and Hugh listened. One of them had a son in college. "I want him to be a mechanical engineer," he said. "If he doesn't do that I'll get him started in business. It's a mechanical age and a business age. I want to see him succeed. I want him to keep in the spirit of the times."

Hugh's train was due in Bidwell at ten, but did not arrive until half after eleven. He walked from the station through the town toward the Butterworth farm.

At the end of their first year of marriage a daughter had been born to Clara, and some time before his trip to Pittsburgh she had told him she was again pregnant. "She may be sitting up. I must get home," he thought, but when he got to the bridge near the farmhouse, the bridge on which he had stood beside Clara that first time they were together, he got out of the road and went to sit on a fallen log at the edge of a grove of trees.

"How quiet and peaceful the night!" he thought and leaning forward held his long, troubled face in his hands. He wondered why peace and quiet would not come to him, why life would not let him alone. "After all, I've lived a simple life and have done good work," he thought. "Some of the things they've said about me are true enough. I've invented machines that save useless labor, I've lightened men's labor."

Hugh tried to cling to that thought, but it would not stay in his mind. All the thoughts that gave his mind peace and quiet flew away like birds seen on a distant horizon at evening. It had been so ever since that night when he was suddenly and unexpectedly attacked by the crazed harness maker in the motor. Before that his mind had often been unsettled, but he knew what he wanted. He wanted men and women and close association with men and women. Often his problem was yet more simple. He wanted a woman, one who would love him and lie close to him at night. He wanted the respect of his fellows in the town where he had come to live his life. He wanted to succeed at the particular task to which he had set his hand.

The attack made upon him by the insane harness maker had at first seemed to settle all his problems. At the moment when the frightened and desperate man sank his teeth and fingers into Hugh's neck, something had happened to Clara. It was Clara who, with a strength and quickness quite amazing, had torn the insane man away. All through that evening she had been hating her husband and father, and then suddenly she loved Hugh. The seeds of a child were already alive in her, and when the body of her man was furiously attacked, he became also her child. Swiftly, like the passing of a shadow over the surface of a river on a windy day, the change in her attitude toward her husband took place. All that evening she had been hating the new age she had thought so perfectly personified in the two men, who talked of the making of machines while the beauty of the night was whirled away into the darkness with the cloud of dust thrown into the air by the flying motor. She had been hating Hugh and sympathizing with the dead past he and other men like him were destroying, the past that was represented by the figure of the old harness maker who wanted to do his work by hand in the old way, by the man who had aroused the scorn and derision of her father.

And then the past rose up to strike. It struck with claws and teeth, and the claws and teeth sank into Hugh's flesh, into the flesh of the man whose seed was already alive within her.

At that moment the woman who had been a thinker stopped thinking. Within her arose the mother, fierce, indomitable, strong with the strength of the roots of a tree. To her then and forever after Hugh was no hero, remaking the world, but a perplexed boy hurt by life. He never again escaped out of boyhood in her consciousness of him. With the strength of a tigress she tore the crazed harness maker away from Hugh, and with something of the surface brutality of another Ed Hall, threw him to the floor of the car. When Ed and the policeman, assisted by several bystanders, came running forward, she waited almost indifferently while they forced the screaming and kicking man through the crowd and in at the door of the police station.

For Clara the thing for which she had hungered had, she thought, happened. In quick, sharp tones she ordered her father to drive the car to a doctor's house and later stood by while the torn and lacerated flesh of Hugh's cheek and neck was bandaged. The thing for which Joe Wainsworth stood and that she had thought was so precious to herself no longer existed in her consciousness, and if later she was for some weeks nervous and half ill, it was not because of any thought given to the fate of the old harness maker.

The sudden attack out of the town's past had brought Hugh to Clara, had made him a living if not quite satisfying companion to her, but it had brought something quite different to Hugh. The bite of the man's teeth and the torn places on his cheeks left by the tense fingers had mended, leaving but a slight scar; but a virus had got into his veins. The disease of thinking had upset the harness maker's mind and the germ of that disease had got into Hugh's blood. It had worked up into his eyes and ears. Words men dropped thoughtlessly and that in the past had been blown past his ears, as chaff is blown from wheat in the harvest, now stayed to echo and re-echo in his mind. In the past he had seen towns and factories grow and had accepted without question men's word that growth was invariably good. Now his eyes looked at the towns, at Bidwell, Akron, Youngstown, and all the great, new towns scattered up and down Midwestern America as on the train and in the station at Pittsburgh he had looked at the colored stones held in his hand. He looked at the towns and wanted light and color to play over them as they played over the stones, and when that did not happen, his mind, filled with strange new hungers engendered by the disease of thinking, made up words over which lights played. "The gods have scattered towns over the flat lands," his mind had said, as he sat in the smoking car of the train, and the phrase came back to him later, as he sat in the darkness on the log with his head held in his hands. It was a good phrase and lights could play over it as they played over the colored stones, but it would in no way answer the problem of how to "get around" the Iowa man's patent on the hay-loading device.

Hugh did not get to the Butterworth farmhouse until two o'clock in the morning, but when he got there his wife was awake and waiting for him. She heard his heavy, dragging footsteps in the road as he turned in at the farm gate, and getting quickly out of bed, threw a cloak over her shoulders and came out to the porch facing the barns. A late moon had come up and the barnyard was washed with moonlight. From the barns came the low, sweet sound of contented animals nibbling at the hay in the mangers before them, from a row of sheds back of one of the barns came the soft bleating of sheep and in a faraway field a calf bellowed loudly and was answered by its mother.

When Hugh stepped into the moonlight around the corner of the house, Clara ran down the steps to meet him, and taking his arm, led him past the barns and over the bridge where as a child she had seen the figures of her fancy advancing towards her. Sensing his troubled state her mother spirit was aroused. He was unfilled by the life he led. She understood that. It was so with her. By a lane they went to a fence where nothing but open fields lay between the farm and the town far below. Although she sensed his troubled state, Clara was not thinking of Hugh's trip to Pittsburgh nor of the problems connected with the completion of the hay-loading machine. It may be that like her father she had dismissed from her mind all thoughts of him as one who would continue to help solve the mechanical problems of his age. Thoughts of his continued success had never meant much to her, but during the evening something had happened to Clara and she wanted to tell him about it, to take him into the joy of it. Their first child had been a girl and she was sure the next would be a man child. "I felt him tonight," she said, when they had got to the place by the fence and saw below the lights of the town. "I felt him tonight," she said again, "and oh, he was strong! He kicked like anything. I am sure this time it's a boy."

For perhaps ten minutes Clara and Hugh stood by the fence. The disease of thinking that was making Hugh useless for the work of his age had swept away many old things within him and he was not self-conscious in the presence of his woman. When she told him of the struggle of the man of another generation, striving to be born he put his arm about her and held her close against his long body. For a time they stood in silence, and then started to return to the house and sleep. As they went past the barns and the bunkhouse where several men now slept they heard, as though coming out of the past, the loud snoring of the rapidly aging farm hand, Jim Priest, and then above that sound and above the sound of the animals stirring in the barns arose another sound, a sound shrill and intense, greetings perhaps to an unborn Hugh McVey. For some reason, perhaps to announce a shift in crews, the factories of Bidwell that were engaged in night work set up a great whistling and screaming. The sound ran up the hillside and rang in the ears of Hugh as, with his arm about Clara's shoulders, he went up the steps and in at the farmhouse door.

# SELECTED STORIES

# The Contract

EDITOR'S NOTE

"The Contract," an early story which appeared first in 1921, has been selected to counterbalance "The Man Who Became a Woman." The pastoral quality of the final love scene in it, and the scene witnessed at a distance by two boys, are among the best examples of Anderson's descriptive powers. Here, as in "A Meeting South," the action of the story is not spectacular; there is little outward show of emotion, yet the feeling of being betrayed and of being trapped by love is clearly conveyed by the speeches of the man and woman. The same feeling (which in Anderson's writings is a theme) enters his novels *Many Marriages* (1923) and *Beyond Desire* (1932). The story plays on the theme with greater poignancy than the longer pieces, and one is not likely to forget the sensations of a man who "felt like a beast who in playing about at night in a forest has suddenly put his foot in a trap."

ONE evening he kissed her, and she got abruptly up from the bench in the garden back of her father's house and went to stand by a tree. How soft and still and lovely the night seemed to him! He felt absurdly set up, a little, perhaps, he thought, smiling indulgently at himself, as a warrior might feel after securing a position of advantage for a coming great battle. For the moment he had forgotten her and continued to sit alone on the bench smiling at himself. Had the stillness of the garden been broken by the blast of a trumpet and himself proclaimed some kind of a conquering male hero, he would not have been too surprised. The notion of being a conqueror clung to him, and although he laughed at himself, he went on playing with the idea. There was Napoleon following his star of destiny and Alexander sighing for more worlds to conquer! Had he not suddenly kissed her without asking permission? Had he not stormed the fortress? It was the way things were done among the bolder males. He laughed softly.

In a way she had been expecting the kiss, although she had been telling herself she did not want it. Still she was prepared for it as he was not. It was the third time they had been together.

For her the first time she had seen him had been the most stirring of all. He had come into town unheralded and then word had gone around that he was a figure of consequence in the intellectual world. He was invited to speak before an organization called the Thursday Club and she went with her father, the editor of the town's one newspaper.

His figure had swept like a flame across the field of her fancy that first evening. In what a daring way he had talked! His subject was the effect of Christianity on civilization and he spoke of Jesus, the man of Nazareth, in a way that disturbed and irritated the Thursday Club. With what fire and eloquence he talked. There was the sacred young man, a carpenter in an obscure village. He had thought his own thoughts, ignored the teachings of older men. When he was not at work at his trade, he went alone to talk in the hills. His own intense nature and the long hours and days of silent contemplation of life had made him a profound mystic. Had anyone thought, had anyone dared think, of the man Jesus as just an ordinary human being who had, in the face of the commonplace standards of life, had the courage to use his life as an adventurous experiment for the benefit of society!

The speaker before the Thursday Club, organized by her father and several other men for the purpose of studying literature, had quite startled his audience. After the meeting several of the members protested, saying the club had been organized for another purpose and that it was too bad to start a religious discussion.

They had, she felt, missed the whole point of his talk. It was not a religious discussion. As she sat beside her father and looked about at the other club members and their wives and at the few unmarried men scattered among them, a great gladness that such a man had come to live in her town swept over her. As he continued talking of the man of Galilee and how he walked up and down through many towns in a faraway country casting out devils by the power of his bold and lovely presence, she was so overcome with emotion that tears came to her eyes. The speaker was himself a man of thirty, and Jesus, the Christ of whom he talked so eloquently, had been a man of thirty when he set out on his mission to civilization. After the meeting and as the speaker walked home with herself and her father, she remained silent while the two men talked. Even then he was a little too conscious of her. She had wanted to worship from afar. She had wanted to repeat aloud the words of the officers of the Pharisees, sent to seize Jesus in the temple, the men who had returned from their mission empty-handed. "Never man spake like this man," they had said, filled with wonder.

As the three people walked under the trees, he continued to speak on the subject that had been the foundation of his talk before the club. "They evidently misunderstood," he said, laughing. "I did not intend my talk to be concerned with religion. I was thinking only of the barbaric background of the life of Jesus Christ and its dramatic possibilities. You understand what I mean, the soft smiling land of Galilee, the lake with the white cities on the shore, ruled over by the cruel Herod Antipas, the fishermen leaving their nets to follow the man who taught the strange new doctrine of peace, forgiveness and love. And then the strange crowds in the streets of the towns and in the city of Jerusalem, the paralytic at Bethesda, the pool by the Sheep-gate, the prostitute who wiped his feet with her hair as he sat at the feast, the scene in the garden on the night before the crucifixion, the crucifixion itself—why should all this not be taken as profound and beautiful literature? That is how, I am sure, it has had its greatest effect upon mankind."

As he had talked to her father during the walk homeward on that first evening, the speaker had occasionally turned to her and once he had made a feeble apology for the seriousness of the talk. "Does all this bore you?" he asked, and a chill ran over her body. She made a gesture with her hand and looked away, and as soon as they had arrived at her father's house, she excused herself and went upstairs.

The two men continued talking for a long time and she undressed and lay in bed with her door open so she could hear the voices. What an evening that had been for her! Her father, usually a rather prosaic man, was excited and talked well, and she thought the newcomer the most wonderful being that had ever come into her consciousness. His strong boyish voice ran up the stairs and through the halls of the house and she sat up in bed and listened, her whole being strangely alive. The voice had carried her out of herself and into the land of

Galilee he had described so vividly, and she stood in a vast crowd of people listening to another stranger of thirty who had suddenly come out of another place and was talking. A phrase remembered from her Bible-reading ran through her mind and she repeated it aloud. She became, not herself, but a strange woman in a strange land. "Blessed be the womb that bare Thee and the breasts that Thou hast sucked," she imagined herself shouting, quite carried away.

She saw him for the second time two weeks after that first meeting, and it was strange and also sad to think that during that second meeting he came off his pedestal with a thump.

He wrote her a note and asked her to go with him to a concert and she was stirred at the thought of sitting close beside him all evening and hearing music. Before the evening came, she went about her father's house, attending to the household affairs, with her mind floating away out of her body into a land of spiritual adventure. When her father spoke to her at the table, she was confused and her cheeks grew red. "What's the matter with you?" he asked, laughing. "You've begun acting like a schoolgirl. What's happened to you?"

After all, she was not very young and the new man was not the first who had been attracted to her. Already two men of the town had asked her to marry them—but she had never before got into such a strange exalted state. "Between him and myself it will be different. We will go along a new road into a strange beautiful place," she whispered to herself. She had no plan. It was enough, she thought, that the new man had come to town, that she could occasionally sit in silence beside him, that she could hear his voice, that she could come into the presence of his mind at work making beautiful images.

"It is quite true. There is a religion of the beautiful," she thought. Her mother, who had died when she was fifteen, had been a devout church member, and as a young girl she had also given herself, for a time, to religious enthusiasm. Later she had given up churchgoing and had thought of herself as an intellectual woman.

Now she laughed at herself. "I am a child beside him," she thought, remembering how glowingly he had talked before the Thursday Club. Contentment settled down upon her. "In every life there should be a deeply spiritual love," she told herself. "I am like that woman in the Bible who on a scorching day came down alone, out of a village, to the well in the dusty plain and found lying there on a stone bench the sacred man, he who knew the true way of life."

At the concert he did several things to disturb her. In the first place he was not at all absorbed or carried away by the music and all evening he kept looking at her with hungry eyes. As they walked homeward he did not talk, giving himself with abandon to ideas, but was silent and self-conscious.

And then he kissed her and her exalted mood went quickly away and something shrewd and determined took entire possession of her.

It was ten o'clock when they got to the house and her father was at the newspaper office. The moon shone and they went into the garden and sat together on a bench. After he had kissed her, she went to stand by the tree because it was necessary for her to make a new adjustment. She had been allowing herself to be a child and her child's hands had been building a temple. Now all the bricks and stone of the temple had fallen down and there was a great dust and racket.

To relieve the tenseness of the situation she led him

out of the garden into the street. After all, she had not finished with him. There was something she wanted. They walked down a silent street under trees and a group of young men went past them singing some foolish love-song.

Presently they came to the end of the street and into a field, and it was then she understood the depth of his stupidity. Some elders grew in a little gully beside the field and he wanted her to go in among them. When she drew back, a little startled, he was angry. "The kiss you let me take back there was a lie, then?" he asked sharply. "It didn't mean anything? You are like all the other women who give kisses having no meaning?"

It was during the third time they were together that everything between them was settled. A war had broken out between the forces sleeping in each of them, but after that third meeting peace came. One Saturday afternoon they went together to spend a day in the country. She wore a heavy sweater and stout boots and on his shoulder he carried a small bag filled with the luncheon she had prepared. She was in a smiling, confident mood and he was disturbed and unhappy. When he looked at her he felt like one condemned to beat with bare hands against a cold stone wall. The wall was as hard as adamant, but was surfaced with some warm soft growth.

For a time after they set out, things went well and then the final struggle between them began. Several times during the afternoon, as they walked in a little strip of woodland among dry leaves and under the fragrant trees just in the fullness of the new spring life, she seemed about to yield to the hunger gnawing at him, but, as evening came on and when they had eaten the luncheon and sat on the grassy bank of a small stream, she became very business-like and determined. "We must get back toward town before darkness comes," she said, leading the way across a field and into a dusty road.

The battle came to a crisis quickly. When they had got almost to town, her energetic mood left her and they got out of the road and into an orchard. He built a little fire of twigs beside a rail fence and they leaned against the fence and watched it burn in silence. The thin column of smoke went up through the branches of the trees. "It's like incense," she said, creeping close to him. Their bodies pressed against each other. As the moon was full, darkness did not come and the day passed imperceptibly into night.

Two boys from a nearby farmhouse, who had been driving cows homeward along a lane, saw them standing thus, their arms about each other. They crawled over a fence and crept along in the shadows to wait and watch.

Overcome by a sudden fear she pushed herself out of his arms and moved slowly away along the fence. He followed, pressing her close. A wavering uncertainty had taken possession of her and the battle seemed lost. She wanted to escape and at the same time did not want to escape. She was tired.

With an effort she turned and walked in a very determined way across the orchard and he stood by the fence and let her go. One of the farm boys called to the other. "Nothing's going to happen. She's going away," he called. The boys climbed a fence and ran off along a lane toward a distant barn and again silence settled over the orchard. She returned to him, her eyes shining and her hands trembling.

"You see what you have brought me to, what has happened?" she asked sharply. For a moment she felt mean, beaten, and then quickly she became quite sure of herself. The whole fact of organized life stood back of her trembling figure.

He did not understand. "There will be a scandal," she said. "I don't blame you. I blame myself. Why did I let myself make a show of myself with you?"

She tried to explain. "Of course those boys know me," she said, turning her face away. "They have seen us, in this place, holding each other in that way and kissing. It's light enough to see everything. It's horrible. You are a man, but I'm a woman. There'll be a scandal and my name will be dragged in the mud."

He watched her, perplexed and puzzled. The fact that they had been seen at the love-making had rather amused him and he had been on the point of breaking into laughter. Now he felt ashamed and penitent.

She went and put her face down on the top rail of the fence and her body shook with sobs. He stood awkwardly watching.

A thought came to him. "Well," he said hesitatingly, "we could marry, we could get married."

He looked away over her head and out into an open country washed with moonlight. A wind came up and clouds raced across the sky making fugitive shadows that played madly over the face of the fields. Some shadowy, lovely thing seemed fleeing out of him and out of her. He felt like a beast who in playing about at night in a forest has suddenly put his foot into a trap. A madness to run away from her, to flit half-crazily away over the fields like one of the cloud shadows and then to disappear forever into an unknown, mysterious distance, had possession of him, but his feet had become heavy. He was held fast, bound down to the earth, not by desire now, but by a strange hesitating sympathy with the thing that bound her to earth.

When she looked up, he took her into his arms and held her tightly while he continued looking over her head and into the distance. Her body that had been quivering with excitement became quiet. "We had better be married at once," he said. "There are things I have never understood before. Let's go back to town and be married at once, tonight. That will solve all our difficulties, you see."

# The Egg

### EDITOR'S NOTE

*The Triumph of the Egg* (1921), from which "The Egg" is taken, is a book which represents Anderson's writings in their widest range of experimentation, in transit from the pages of *The Little Review* to the more formal atmosphere of *The Dial,* which in 1920 had been "revived" for the third time since its founding in 1840 by Margaret Fuller (with the advice and friendship of Emerson) and was being published as a non-political monthly of "arts and letters" in New York. As Anderson's memoirs and autobiographies reveal, he shared the enthusiasms and fortunes of those who edited and wrote for "little magazines." His advice as well as his writings was welcomed and sought for; although he had "found himself," he enjoyed the freedom of doing short pieces in a variety of forms: further verses in the manner of his *Mid-American Chants,* descriptive pieces, and brief critical essays. In *The Little Review* he shared the company of the early Ben Hecht, W. B. Yeats, James Joyce, Ezra Pound, and H. D., and in *The Dial* the company of Vachel Lindsay, George Moore, Thomas Mann, and T. S. Eliot. He shared the fortunes of "advance-guard" writers outside as well as within Chicago—and he entered the 1920's as one who held affinities with the international reaches of the "little magazines" as well as a regional kinship with Dreiser, Sinclair Lewis, Edgar Lee Masters, Sandburg, and Ernest Hemingway. In this broad milieu "The Egg" established Anderson's individuality, his gift of humor, or what his critics called his understanding of a "tragi-comic" situation. This story, not unlike the stories which follow it in *Horses and Men,* is told with a wandering, reminiscent air. He offers his readers the luxury of relaxing with him, and throughout "The Egg" he makes it seem as though the "real plot" of the story is being withheld.

How far *The Triumph of the Egg* had taken Anderson into an "international" company of artists and writers is shown in Virginia Woolf's essay on American fiction (1925): "In *The Triumph of the Egg* there is some rearrangement of the old elements of art which makes us rub our eyes. The feeling recalls that with which we read Chekhov for the first time. . . . Mr. Anderson has bored into that deeper and warmer layer of human nature which it would be frivolous to ticket new or old, American or European."

MY FATHER was, I am sure, intended by nature to be a cheerful, kindly man. Until he was thirty-four years old he worked as a farm hand for a man named Thomas Butterworth whose place lay near the town of Bidwell, Ohio. He had then a horse of his own and on Saturday evenings drove into town to spend a few hours in social intercourse with other farm hands. In town he drank several glasses of beer and stood about in Ben Head's saloon—crowded on Saturday evenings with visiting farm hands. Songs were sung and glasses thumped on the bar. At ten o'clock father drove home along a lonely country road, made his horse comfortable for the night and himself went to bed, quite happy in his position in life. He had at that time no notion of trying to rise in the world.

It was in the spring of his thirty-fifth year that father married my mother, then a country school teacher, and in the following spring I came wriggling and crying into the world. Something happened to the two people. They became ambitious. The American passion for getting up in the world took possession of them.

It may have been that mother was responsible. Being a school teacher she had no doubt read books and magazines. She had, I presume, read of how Garfield, Lincoln, and other Americans rose from poverty to fame and greatness and as I lay beside her—in the days of her lying-in—she may have dreamed that I would some day rule men and cities. At any rate she induced father to give up his place as a farm hand, sell his horse and embark on an independent enterprise of his own. She was a tall silent woman with a long nose and troubled gray eyes. For herself she wanted nothing. For father and myself she was incurably ambitious.

The first venture into which the two people went turned out badly. They rented ten acres of poor stony land on Griggs's Road, eight miles from Bidwell, and launched into chicken raising. I grew into boyhood on the place and got my first impressions of life there. From the beginning they were impressions of disaster and if, in my turn, I am a gloomy man inclined to see the darker side of life, I attribute it to the fact that what should have been for me the happy joyous days of childhood were spent on a chicken farm.

One unversed in such matters can have no notion of the many and tragic things that can happen to a chicken. It is born out of an egg, lives for a few weeks as a tiny fluffy thing such as you will see pictured on Easter cards, then becomes hideously naked, eats quantities of corn and meal bought by the sweat of your father's brow, gets diseases called pip, cholera, and other names, stands looking with stupid eyes at the sun, becomes sick and dies. A few hens and now and then a rooster, intended to serve God's mysterious ends, struggle through to maturity. The hens lay eggs out of which come other chickens and the dreadful cycle is thus made complete. It is all unbelievably complex. Most philosophers must have been raised on chicken farms. One hopes for so much from a chicken and is so dreadfully disillusioned. Small chickens, just setting out on the journey of life, look so bright and alert and they are in fact so dreadfully stupid. They are so much like people they mix one up in one's judgments of life. If disease does not kill them they wait until your expectations are thoroughly aroused and then walk under the wheels of a wagon—to go squashed and dead back to their maker. Vermin infest their youth, and fortunes must be spent for curative powders. In later life I have seen how a literature has been built up on the subject of fortunes to be made out of the raising of chickens. It is intended to be read by the gods who have just eaten of the tree of the knowledge of good and evil. It is a hopeful literature and declares that much may be done by simple ambitious people who own a few hens. Do not be led astray by it. It was not written for you. Go hunt for gold on the frozen hills of Alaska, put your faith in the honesty of a politician, believe if you will that the world is daily growing better and that good will triumph over evil, but do not read and believe the literature that is written concerning the hen. It was not written for you.

I, however, digress. My tale does not primarily concern itself with the hen. If correctly told it will center on the egg. For ten years my father and mother struggled to make our chicken farm pay and then they gave up that struggle and began another. They moved into the town of Bidwell, Ohio, and embarked in the restaurant business. After ten years of worry with incubators that did not hatch, and with tiny—and in their own way lovely—balls of fluff that passed on into semi-naked pullethood and from that into dead henhood, we threw all aside and packing our belongings on a wagon drove down Griggs's Road toward Bidwell, a tiny caravan of hope looking for a new place from which to start on our upward journey through life.

We must have been a sad looking lot, not, I fancy, unlike refugees fleeing from a battlefield. Mother and I walked in the road. The wagon that contained our goods had been borrowed for the day from Mr. Albert Griggs, a neighbor. Out of its sides stuck the legs of cheap chairs and at the back of the pile of beds, tables, and boxes filled with kitchen utensils was a crate of live chickens, and on top of that the baby carriage in which I had been wheeled about in my infancy. Why we stuck to the baby carriage I don't know. It was unlikely other children would be born and the wheels were broken. People who have few possessions cling tightly to those they have. That is one of the facts that make life so discouraging.

Father rode on top of the wagon. He was then a bald-headed man of forty-five, a little fat and from long association with mother and the chickens he had become habitually silent and discouraged. All during our ten years on the chicken farm he had worked as a laborer on neighboring farms and most of the money he had earned had been spent for remedies to cure chicken diseases, on Wilmer's White Wonder Cholera Cure or Professor Bidlow's Egg Producer or some other preparations that mother found advertised in the poultry papers. There were two little patches of hair on father's head just above his ears. I remember that as a child I used to sit looking at him when he had gone to sleep in a chair before the stove on Sunday afternoons in the winter. I had at that time already begun to read books and have notions of my own and the bald path that led over the top of his head was, I fancied, something like a broad road, such a road as Caesar might have made on which to lead his legions out of Rome and into the wonders of an unknown world. The tufts of hair that grew above father's ears were, I thought, like forests. I fell into a half-sleeping, half-waking state and dreamed I was a tiny thing going along the road into a far beautiful place where there were no chicken farms and where life was a happy eggless affair.

One might write a book concerning our flight from the chicken farm into town. Mother and I walked the entire eight miles—she to be sure that nothing fell from the wagon and I to see the wonders of the world. On the seat of the wagon beside father was his greatest treasure. I will tell you of that.

On a chicken farm where hundreds and even thousands of chickens come out of eggs surprising things sometimes happen. Grotesques are born out of eggs as out of people. The accident does not often occur—perhaps once in a thousand births. A chicken is, you see, born that has four legs, two pairs of wings, two heads or what not. The things do not live. They go quickly back to the hand of their maker that has for a moment trembled. The fact that the poor little things could not live was one of the tragedies of life to father. He had some sort of notion that if he could but bring into henhood or roosterhood a five-legged hen or a two-headed rooster his fortune would be made. He dreamed of taking the wonder about to county fairs and of growing rich by exhibiting it to other farm hands.

At any rate he saved all the little monstrous things that had been born on our chicken farm. They were preserved in alcohol and put each in its own glass bottle. These he had carefully put into a box and on our journey into town it was carried on the wagon seat beside him. He drove the horses with one hand and with the other clung to the box. When we got to our destination the box was taken down at once and the bottles removed. All during our days as keepers of a restaurant in the town of Bidwell, Ohio, the grotesques in their little glass bottles sat on a shelf back of the counter. Mother sometimes protested but father was a rock on the subject of his treasure. The grotesques were, he declared, valuable. People, he said, liked to look at strange and wonderful things.

Did I say that we embarked in the restaurant business in the town of Bidwell, Ohio? I exaggerated a little. The town itself lay at the foot of a low hill and on the shore of a small river. The railroad did not run through the town and the station was a mile away to the north at a place called Pickleville. There had been a cider mill and pickle factory at the station, but before the time of our coming they had both gone out of business. In the morning and in the evening busses came down to the station along a road called Turner's Pike from the hotel on the main street of Bidwell. Our going to the out-of-the-way place to embark in the restaurant business was mother's idea. She talked of it for a year and then one day went off and rented an empty store building opposite the railroad station. It was her idea that the restaurant would be profitable. Traveling men, she said, would be always waiting around to take trains out of town and town people would come to the station to await incoming trains. They would come to the restaurant to buy pieces of pie and drink coffee. Now that I am older I know that she had another motive in going. She was ambitious for me. She wanted me to rise in the world, to get into a town school and become a man of the towns.

At Pickleville father and mother worked hard as they always had done. At first there was the necessity of putting our place into shape to be a restaurant. That took a month. Father built a shelf on which he put tins of vegetables. He painted a sign on which he put his name in large red letters. Below his name was the sharp command—"EAT HERE"—that was so seldom obeyed. A showcase was bought and filled with cigars and tobacco. Mother scrubbed the floor and the walls of the room. I went to school in the town and was glad to be away from the farm and from the presence of the discouraged, sad-looking chickens. Still I was not very joyous. In the evening I walked home from school along Turner's Pike and remembered the children I had seen playing in the town school yard. A troop of little girls had gone hopping about and singing. I tried that. Down along the frozen road I went hopping solemnly on one leg. "Hippity Hop To The Barber Shop," I sang shrilly. Then I stopped and looked doubtfully about. I was afraid of being seen in my gay mood. It must have seemed to me that I was doing a thing that should not be done by one who, like myself, had been raised on a chicken farm where death was a daily visitor.

Mother decided that our restaurant should remain open at night. At ten in the evening a passenger train went north past our door followed by a local freight. The freight crew had switching to do in Pickleville and when the work was done they came to our restaurant for hot coffee and food. Sometimes one of them ordered a fried egg. In the morning at four they returned northbound and again visited us. A little trade began to grow up. Mother slept at night and during the day tended the restaurant and fed our boarders while father slept. He slept in the same bed mother had occupied during the night and I went off to the town of Bidwell and to school. During the long nights, while mother and I slept, father cooked meats that were to go into sandwiches for the lunch baskets of our boarders. Then an idea in regard to getting up in the world came into his head. The American spirit took hold of him. He also became ambitious.

In the long nights when there was little to do father had time to think. That was his undoing. He decided that he had in the past been an unsuccessful man because he had not been cheerful enough and that in the future he would adopt a cheerful outlook on life. In the early morning he came upstairs and got into bed with mother. She woke and the two talked. From my bed in the corner I listened.

It was father's idea that both he and mother should try to entertain the people who came to eat at our restaurant. I cannot now remember his words, but he gave the impression of one about to become in some obscure way a kind of public entertainer. When people, particularly young people from the town of Bidwell, came into our place, as on very rare occasions they did, bright entertaining conversation was to be made. From father's words I gathered that something of the jolly innkeeper effect was to be sought. Mother must have been doubtful from the first, but she said nothing discouraging. It was father's notion that a passion for the company of himself and mother would spring up in the breasts of the younger people of the town of Bidwell. In the evening bright happy groups would come singing down Turner's Pike. They would troop shouting with joy and laughter into our place. There would be song and festivity. I do not mean to give the impression that father spoke so elaborately of the matter. He was as I have said an uncommunicative man. "They want some place to go. I tell you they want some place to go," he said over and over. That was as far as he got. My own imagination has filled in the blanks.

For two or three weeks this notion of father's invaded our house. We did not talk much, but in our daily lives tried earnestly to make smiles take the place of glum looks. Mother smiled at the boarders and I, catching the infection, smiled at our cat. Father became a little feverish in his anxiety to please. There was no doubt, lurking somewhere in him, a touch of the spirit of the showman. He did not waste much of his ammunition on the railroad men he served at night but seemed to be waiting for a young man or woman from Bidwell to come in to show what he could do. On the counter in the restaurant there was a wire basket kept always filled with eggs, and it must have been before his eyes when the idea of being entertaining was born in his brain. There was something pre-natal about the way eggs kept themselves connected with the development of his idea. At any rate an egg ruined his new impulse in life. Late one night I was awakened by a roar of anger coming from father's throat. Both mother and I sat upright in our beds. With trembling hands she lighted a lamp that stood on a table by her head. Downstairs the front door of our restaurant went shut with a bang and in a few minutes father tramped up the stairs. He held an egg in his hand and his hand trembled as though he were having a chill. There was a half-insane light in his eyes. As he stood glaring at us I was sure he intended throwing the egg at either mother or me. Then he laid it gently on the table beside the lamp and dropped on his knees beside mother's bed. He began to cry like a boy and I, carried away by his grief, cried with him. The two of us filled the little upstairs room with our wailing voices. It is ridiculous, but of the picture we made I can remember only the fact that mother's hand continually stroked the bald path that ran across the top of his head. I have forgotten what mother said to him and how she induced him to tell her of what had happened downstairs. His explanation also has gone out of my mind. I remember only my own grief and fright and the shiny path over father's head glowing in the lamp light as he knelt by the bed.

As to what happened downstairs. For some unexplainable reason I know the story as well as though I had been a witness to my father's discomfiture. One in time gets to know many unexplainable things. On that evening young Joe Kane, son of a merchant of Bidwell, came to Pickleville to meet his father, who was expected on the ten o'clock evening train from the South. The train was three hours late and Joe came into our place to loaf about and to wait for its arrival. The local freight train came in and the freight crew were fed. Joe was left alone in the restaurant with father.

From the moment he came into our place the Bidwell young man must have been puzzled by my father's actions. It was his notion that father was angry at him for hanging around. He noticed that the restaurant keeper was apparently disturbed by his presence and he thought of going out. However, it began to rain and he did not fancy the long walk to town and back. He bought a five-cent cigar and ordered a cup of coffee. He had a newspaper in his pocket and took it out and began to read. "I'm waiting for the evening train. It's late," he said apologetically.

For a long time father, whom Joe Kane had never seen before, remained silently gazing at his visitor. He was no doubt suffering from an attack of stage fright. As so often happens in life he had thought so much and so often of the situation that now confronted him that he was somewhat nervous in its presence.

For one thing, he did not know what to do with his hands. He thrust one of them nervously over the counter and shook hands with Joe Kane. "How-de-do," he said. Joe Kane put his newspaper down and stared at him. Father's eye lighted on the basket of eggs that sat on the counter and he began to talk. "Well," he began hesitatingly, "well, you have heard of Christopher Columbus, eh?" He seemed to be angry. "That Christopher Columbus was a cheat," he declared emphatically. "He talked of making an egg stand on its end. He talked, he did, and then he went and broke the end of the egg."

My father seemed to his visitor to be beside himself at the duplicity of Christopher Columbus. He muttered and swore. He declared it was wrong to teach children that Christopher Columbus was a great man when, after all, he cheated at the critical moment. He had declared he would make an egg stand on end and then when his bluff had been called he had done a trick. Still grumbling at Columbus, father took an egg from the basket on the counter and began to walk up and down. He rolled the egg between the palms of his hands. He smiled genially. He began to mumble words regarding the effect to be produced on an egg by the electricity that comes out of the human body. He declared that without breaking its shell and by virtue of rolling it back and forth in his hands he could stand the egg on its end. He explained that the warmth of his hands and the gentle rolling movement he gave the egg created a new center of gravity, and Joe Kane was mildly interested. "I have handled thousands of eggs," father said. "No one knows more about eggs than I do."

He stood the egg on the counter and it fell on its side. He tried the trick again and again, each time rolling the egg between the palms of his hands and saying the words regarding the wonders of electricity and the laws of gravity. When after a half hour's effort he did succeed in making the egg stand for a moment he looked up to find that his visitor was no longer watching. By the time he had succeeded in calling Joe Kane's attention to the success of his effort the egg had again rolled over and lay on its side.

Afire with the showman's passion and at the same time a good deal disconcerted by the failure of his first effort, father now took the bottles containing the poultry monstrosities down from their place on the shelf and began to show them to his visitor. "How would you like to have seven legs and two heads like this fellow?" he asked, exhibiting the most remarkable of his treasures. A cheerful smile played over his face. He reached over the counter and tried to slap Joe Kane on the shoulder as he had seen men do in Ben Head's saloon when he was a young farm hand and drove to town on Saturday evenings. His visitor was made a little ill by the sight of the body of the terribly deformed bird floating in the alcohol in the bottle and got up to go. Coming from behind the counter father took hold of the young man's arm and led him back to his seat. He grew a little angry and for a moment had to turn his face away and force himself to smile. Then he put the bottles back on the shelf. In an outburst of generosity he fairly compelled Joe Kane to have a fresh cup of coffee and another cigar at his expense. Then he took a pan and filling it with vinegar, taken from a jug that sat beneath the counter, he declared himself about to do a new trick. "I will heat this egg in this pan of vinegar," he said. "Then I will put it through the neck of a bottle without breaking the shell. When the egg is inside the bottle it will resume its normal shape and the shell will become hard again. Then I will give the bottle with the egg in it to you. You can take it about with you wherever you go. People will want to know how you got the egg in the bottle. Don't tell them. Keep them guessing. That is the way to have fun with this trick."

Father grinned and winked at his visitor. Joe Kane decided that the man who confronted him was mildly insane but harmless. He drank the cup of coffee that had been given him and began to read his paper again. When the egg had been heated in vinegar father carried it on a spoon to the counter and going into a back room got an empty bottle. He was angry because his visitor did not watch him as he began to do his trick, but nevertheless went cheerfully to work. For a long time he struggled, trying to get the egg to go through the neck of the bottle. He put the pan of vinegar back on the stove, intending to reheat the egg, then picked it up and burned his fingers. After a second bath in the hot vinegar the shell of the egg had been softened a little but not enough for his purpose. He worked and worked and a spirit of desperate determination took possession of him. When he thought that at last the trick was about to be consummated the delayed train came in at the station and Joe Kane started to go nonchalantly out at the door. Father made a last desperate effort to conquer the egg and make it do the thing that would establish his reputation as one who knew how to entertain guests who came into his restaurant. He worried the egg. He attempted to be somewhat rough with it. He swore and the sweat stood out on his forehead. The egg broke under his hand. When the contents spurted over his clothes, Joe Kane, who had stopped at the door, turned and laughed.

A roar of anger rose from my father's throat. He danced and shouted a string of inarticulate words. Grabbing another egg from the basket on the counter, he threw it, just missing the head of the young man as he dodged through the door and escaped.

Father came upstairs to mother and me with an egg in his hand. I do not know what he intended to do. I imagine he had some idea of destroying it, of destroying all eggs, and that he intended to let mother and me see him begin. When, however, he got into the presence of mother something happened to him. He laid the egg gently on the table and dropped on his knees by the bed as I have already explained. He later decided to close the restaurant for the night and to come upstairs and get into bed. When he did so he blew out the light and after much muttered conversation both he and mother went to sleep. I suppose I went to sleep also, but my sleep was troubled. I awoke at dawn and for a long time looked at the egg that lay on the table. I wondered why eggs had to be and why from the egg came the hen who again laid the egg. The question got into my blood. It has stayed there, I imagine, because I am the son of my father. At any rate, the problem remains unsolved in my mind. And that, I conclude, is but another evidence of the complete and final triumph of the egg—at least as far as my family is concerned.

# I'm a Fool

## EDITOR'S NOTE

"I'm a Fool" and "The Man Who Became a Woman" (p. 478) are reprinted from *Horses and Men* (1923). Scenes from the race track provide the general setting for the book, and the title of one of its stories, "An Ohio Pagan," became a phrase, a name for Anderson himself; as in *The Triumph of the Egg* Anderson's "tragi-comic" spirit prevails throughout the volume. The stories "I'm a Fool" and "The Man Who Became a Woman" are told in a reminiscent, yet high-spirited fashion—their seriousness is more than half concealed. "I'm a Fool" is one of Anderson's masterpieces in the art of making a dramatic monologue turn into a story; it is the best of his very short short stories. Even its touches of rural slang have an air of permanence because they display the character of the boy who tells the story, his eagerness to be glib, quick-witted, up-to-date, and to hide his innocence behind a guise of being tough and worldly.

Of Anderson's world of the race track, Virginia Woolf has written: "It is a world in which the senses flourish; it is dominated by instincts rather than by ideas; race-horses make the hearts of little boys beat high; corn-fields flow around the cheap towns like golden seas, illimitable and profound. . . . Anderson will leave what he has found exposed, defenseless, naked to scorn and laughter."

In describing the reminiscent air with which Anderson tells the story of "The Man Who Became a Woman" Mrs. Woolf also spoke of the "shell-less" quality of his stories, as though they were "wrapped about in a soft caressing envelope, which always seems a little bit too loose to fit the shape." It is the "shell-less" quality that makes the bar-room scene in this story so effective, the scene in which the boy looks in the mirror across the bar and fears that his own face has become that of a woman; it is here that the boy has found himself "exposed, defenseless, naked to scorn and laughter."

IT WAS a hard jolt for me, one of the most bitterest I ever had to face. And it all came about through my own foolishness, too. Even yet sometimes, when I think of it, I want to cry or swear or kick myself. Perhaps, even now, after all this time, there will be a kind of satisfaction in making myself look cheap by telling of it.

It began at three o'clock one October afternoon as I sat in the grandstand at the fall trotting and pacing meet at Sandusky, Ohio.

To tell the truth, I felt a little foolish that I should be sitting in the grandstand at all. During the summer before I had left my home town with Harry Whitehead and, with a nigger named Burt, had taken a job as swipe with one of the two horses Harry was campaigning through the fall race meets that year. Mother cried and my sister Mildred, who wanted to get a job as a school teacher in our town that fall, stormed and scolded about the house all during the week before I left. They both thought it something disgraceful that one of our family should take a place as a swipe with race horses. I've an idea Mildred thought my taking the place would stand in the way of her getting the job she'd been working so long for.

But after all I had to work, and there was no other work to be got. A big lumbering fellow of nineteen couldn't just hang around the house and I had got too big to mow people's lawns and sell newspapers. Little chaps who could get next to people's sympathies by their sizes were always getting jobs away from me. There was one fellow who kept saying to everyone who wanted a lawn mowed or a cistern cleaned, that he was saving money to work his way through college, and I used to lay awake nights thinking up ways to injure him without being found out. I kept thinking of wagons running over him and bricks falling on his head as he walked along the street. But never mind him.

I got the place with Harry and I liked Burt fine. We got along splendid together. He was a big nigger with a lazy sprawling body and soft, kind eyes, and when it came to a fight he could hit like Jack Johnson. He had Bucephalus, a big black pacing stallion that could do 2.09 or 2.10, if he had to, and I had a little gelding named Doctor Fritz that never lost a race all fall when Harry wanted him to win.

We set out from home late in July in a box car with the two horses and after that, until late November, we kept moving along to the race meets and the fairs. It was a peachy time for me, I'll say that. Sometimes now I think that boys who are raised regular in houses, and never have a fine nigger like Burt for best friend, and go to high schools and college, and never steal anything, or get drunk a little, or learn to swear from fellows who know how, or come walking up in front of a grandstand in their shirt sleeves and with dirty horsey pants on when the races are going on and the grandstand is full of people all dressed up—What's the use of talking about it? Such fellows don't know nothing at all. They've never had no opportunity.

But I did. Burt taught me how to rub down a horse and put the bandages on after a race and steam a horse out and a lot of valuable things for any man to know. He could wrap a bandage on a horse's leg so smooth that if it had been the same color you would think it was his skin, and I guess he'd have been a big driver, too, and got to the top like Murphy and Walter Cox and the others if he hadn't been black.

Gee whizz, it was fun. You got to a county seat town, maybe say on a Saturday or Sunday, and the fair began the next Tuesday and lasted until Friday afternoon. Doctor Fritz would be, say in the 2.25 trot on Tuesday afternoon and on Thursday afternoon Bucephalus would knock 'em cold in the "free-for-all" pace. It left you a lot of time to hang around and listen to horse talk, and see Burt knock some yap cold that got too gay, and you'd find out about horses and men and pick up a lot of stuff you could use all the rest of your life, if you had some sense and salted down what you heard and felt and saw.

And then at the end of the week when the race meet was over, and Harry had run home to tend up to his livery stable business, you and Burt hitched the two horses to carts and drove slow and steady across country, to the place for the next meeting, so as to not overheat the horses, etc., etc., you know.

Gee whizz, Gosh amighty, the nice hickorynut and beechnut and oaks and other kinds of trees along the roads, all brown and red, and the good smells, and Burt singing a song that was called Deep River, and the country girls at the windows of houses and everything. You can stick your colleges up your nose for all me. I guess I know where I got my education.

Why, one of those little burgs of towns you come to

on the way, say now on a Saturday afternoon, and Burt says, "let's lay up here." And you did.

And you took the horses to a livery stable and fed them, and you got your good clothes out of a box and put them on.

And the town was full of farmers gaping, because they could see you were race-horse people, and the kids maybe never see a nigger before and was afraid and run away when the two of us walked down their main street.

And that was before prohibition and all that foolishness, and so you went into a saloon, the two of you, and all the yaps come and stood around, and there was always someone pretended he was horsey and knew things and spoke up and began asking questions, and all you did was to lie and lie all you could about what horses you had, and I said I owned them, and then some fellow said, "will you have a drink of whisky" and Burt knocked his eye out the way he could say, offhand-like, "Oh well, all right, I'm agreeable to a little nip. I'll split a quart with you." Gee whizz.

But that isn't what I want to tell my story about. We got home late in November and I promised mother I'd quit the race horses for good. There's a lot of things you've got to promise a mother because she don't know any better.

And so, there not being any work in our town any more than when I left there to go to the races, I went off to Sandusky and got a pretty good place taking care of horses for a man who owned a teaming and delivery and storage and coal and real estate business there. It was a pretty good place with good eats, and a day off each week, and sleeping on a cot in a big barn, and mostly just shoveling in hay and oats to a lot of big good-enough skates of horses, that couldn't have trotted a race with a toad. I wasn't dissatisfied and I could send money home.

And then, as I started to tell you, the fall races come to Sandusky and I got the day off and I went. I left the job at noon and had on my good clothes and my new brown derby hat, I'd just bought the Saturday before, and a stand-up collar.

First of all I went downtown and walked about with the dudes. I've always thought to myself, "put up a good front" and so I did it. I had forty dollars in my pocket and so I went into the West House, a big hotel, and walked up to the cigar stand. "Give me three twenty-five cent cigars," I said. There was a lot of horsemen and strangers and dressed-up people from other towns standing around in the lobby and in the bar, and I mingled amongst them. In the bar there was a fellow with a cane and a Windsor tie on, that it made me sick to look at him. I like a man to be a man and dress up, but not to go put on that kind of airs. So I pushed him aside, kind of rough, and had me a drink of whisky. And then he looked at me, as though he thought maybe he'd get gay, but he changed his mind and didn't say anything. And then I had another drink of whisky, just to show him something, and went out and had a hack out to the races, all to myself, and when I got there I bought myself the best seat I could get up in the grandstand, but didn't go in for any of these boxes. That's putting on too many airs.

And so there I was, sitting up in the grandstand as gay as you please and looking down on the swipes coming out with their horses, and with their dirty horsey pants on and the horse blankets swung over their shoulders, same as I had been doing all the year before. I liked one thing about the same as the other, sitting up there and feeling grand and being down there and looking up at the yaps and feeling grander and more important, too. One thing's about as good as another, if you take it just right. I've often said that.

Well, right in front of me, in the grandstand that day, there was a fellow with a couple of girls and they was about my age. The young fellow was a nice guy all right. He was the kind maybe that goes to college and then comes to be a lawyer or maybe a newspaper editor or something like that, but he wasn't stuck on himself. There are some of that kind are all right and he was one of the ones.

He had his sister with him and another girl and the sister looked around over his shoulder, accidental at first, not intending to start anything—she wasn't that kind—and her eyes and mine happened to meet.

You know how it is. Gee, she was a peach! She had on a soft dress, kind of a blue stuff and it looked carelessly made, but was well sewed and made and everything. I knew that much. I blushed when she looked right at me and so did she. She was the nicest girl I've ever seen in my life. She wasn't stuck on herself and she could talk proper grammar without being like a school teacher or something like that. What I mean is, she was O. K. I think maybe her father was well-to-do, but not rich to make her chesty because she was his daughter, as some are. Maybe he owned a drugstore or a drygoods store in their home town, or something like that. She never told me and I never asked.

My own people are all O. K. too, when you come to that. My grandfather was Welsh and over in the old country, in Wales he was— But never mind that.

The first heat of the first race come off and the young fellow setting there with the two girls left them and went down to make a bet. I knew what he was up to, but he didn't talk big and noisy and let everyone around know he was a sport, as some do. He wasn't that kind. Well, he come back and I heard him tell the two girls what horse he'd bet on, and when the heat was trotted they all half got to their feet and acted in the excited, sweaty way people do when they've got money down on a race, and the horse they bet on is up there pretty close at the end, and they think maybe he'll come on with a rush, but he never does because he hasn't got the old juice in him, come right down to it.

And then, pretty soon, the horses came out for the 2.18 pace and there was a horse in it I knew. He was a horse Bob French had in his string but Bob didn't own him. He was a horse owned by a Mr. Mathers down at Marietta, Ohio.

This Mr. Mathers had a lot of money and owned some coal mines or something, and he had a swell place out in the country, and he was stuck on race horses, but was a Presbyterian or something, and I think more than likely his wife was one, too, maybe a stiffer one than himself. So he never raced his horses hisself, and the story round the Ohio race tracks was that when one of his horses got ready to go to the races he turned him over to Bob French and pretended to his wife he was sold.

So Bob had the horses and he did pretty much as he pleased and you can't blame Bob, at least, I never did. Sometimes he was out to win and sometimes he wasn't. I never cared much about that when I was swiping a horse. What I did want to know was that my horse had the speed and could go out in front, if you wanted him to.

And, as I'm telling you, there was Bob in this race with one of Mr. Mathers' horses, was named "About

Ben Ahem" or something like that, and was fast as a streak. He was a gelding and had a mark of 2.21, but could step in .08 or .09.

Because when Burt and I were out, as I've told you, the year before, there was a nigger, Burt knew, worked for Mr. Mathers and we went out there one day when we didn't have no race on at the Marietta Fair and our boss Harry was gone home.

And so everyone was gone to the fair but just this one nigger and he took us all through Mr. Mathers' swell house and he and Burt tapped a bottle of wine Mr. Mathers had hid in his bedroom, back in a closet, without his wife knowing, and he showed us this Ahem horse. Burt was always stuck on being a driver but didn't have much chance to get to the top, being a nigger, and he and the other nigger gulped that whole bottle of wine and Burt got a little lit up.

So the nigger let Burt take this About Ben Ahem and step him a mile in a track Mr. Mathers had all to himself, right there on the farm. And Mr. Mathers had one child, a daughter, kinda sick and not very good-looking, and she came home and we had to hustle and get About Ben Ahem stuck back in the barn.

I'm only telling you to get everything straight. At Sandusky, that afternoon I was at the fair, this young fellow with the two girls was fussed, being with the girls and losing his bet. You know how a fellow is that way. One of them was his girl and the other his sister. I had figured that out.

"Gee whizz," I says to myself, "I'm going to give him the dope."

He was mighty nice when I touched him on the shoulder. He and the girls were nice to me right from the start and clear to the end. I'm not blaming them.

And so he leaned back and I give him the dope on About Ben Ahem. "Don't bet a cent on this first heat because he'll go like an oxen hitched to a plow, but when the first heat is over go right down and lay on your pile." That's what I told him.

Well, I never saw a fellow treat anyone sweller. There was a fat man sitting beside the little girl, that had looked at me twice by this time, and I at her, and both blushing, and what did he do but have the nerve to turn and ask the fat man to get up and change places with me so I could set with his crowd.

Gee whizz, craps amighty. There I was. What a chump I was to go and get gay up there in the West House bar, and just because that dude was standing there with a cane and that kind of a necktie on, to go and get all balled up and drink that whisky, just to show off.

Of course she would know, me setting right beside her and letting her smell of my breath. I could have kicked myself right down out of that grandstand and all around that race track and made a faster record than most of the skates of horses they had there that year.

Because that girl wasn't any mutt of a girl. What wouldn't I have give right then for a stick of chewing gum to chew, or a lozenger, or some liquorice, or most anything. I was glad I had those tweny-five cent cigars in my pocket and right away I give that fellow one and lit one myself. Then that fat man got up and we changed places and there I was, plunked right down beside her.

They introduced themselves and the fellow's best girl, he had with him, was named Miss Elinor Woodbury, and her father was a manufacturer of barrels from a place called Tiffin, Ohio. And the fellow himself was named Wilbur Wessen and his sister was Miss Lucy Wessen.

I suppose it was their having such swell names got me off my trolley. A fellow, just because he has been a swipe with a race horse, and works taking care of horses for a man in the teaming, delivery, and storage business, isn't any better or worse than anyone else. I've often thought that, and said it too.

But you know how a fellow is. There's something in that kind of nice clothes, and the kind of nice eyes she had, and the way she had looked at me, awhile before, over her brother's shoulder, and me looking back at her, and both of us blushing.

I couldn't show her up for a boob, could I?

I made a fool of myself, that's what I did. I said my name was Walter Mathers from Marietta, Ohio, and then I told all three of them the smashingest lie you ever heard. What I said was that my father owned the horse About Ben Ahem and that he had let him out to this Bob French for racing purposes, because our family was proud and had never gone into racing that way, in our own name, I mean. Then I had got started and they were all leaning over and listening, and Miss Lucy Wessen's eyes were shining, and I went the whole hog.

I told about our place down at Marietta, and about the big stables and the grand brick house we had on a hill, up above the Ohio River, but I knew enough not to do it in no bragging way. What I did was to start things and then let them drag the rest out of me. I acted just as reluctant to tell as I could. Our family hasn't got any barrel factory, and, since I've known us, we've always been pretty poor, but not asking anything of anyone at that, and my grandfather, over in Wales— But never mind that.

We set there talking like we had known each other for years and years, and I went and told them that my father had been expecting maybe this Bob French wasn't on the square, and had sent me up to Sandusky on the sly to find out what I could.

And I bluffed it through I had found out all about the 2.18 pace, in which About Ben Ahem was to start.

I said he would lose the first heat by pacing like a lame cow and then he would come back and skin 'em alive after that. And to back up what I said I took thirty dollars out of my pocket and handed it to Mr. Wilbur Wessen and asked him, would he mind, after the first heat, to go down and place it on About Ben Ahem for whatever odds he could get. What I said was that I didn't want Bob French to see me and none of the swipes.

Sure enough the first heat come off and About Ben Ahem went off his stride, up the back stretch, and looked like a wooden horse or a sick one, and come in to be last. Then this Wilbur Wessen went down to the betting place under the grandstand and there I was with the two girls, and when that Miss Woodbury was looking the other way once, Lucy Wessen kinda, with her shoulder you know, kinda touched me. Not just tucking down, I don't mean. You know how a woman can do. They get close, but not getting gay either. You know what they do. Gee whizz.

And then they give me a jolt. What they had done, when I didn't know, was to get together, and they had decided Wilbur Wessen would bet fifty dollars, and the two girls had gone and put in ten dollars each, of their own money, too. I was sick then, but I was sicker later.

About the gelding, About Ben Ahem, and their winning their money, I wasn't worried a lot about that. It come out O. K. Ahem stepped the next three heats like a bushel of spoiled eggs going to market before they could be found out, and Wilbur Wessen had got nine to two for the money. There was something else eating at me.

Because Wilbur come back, after he had bet the money, and after that he spent most of his time talking to that Miss Woodbury, and Lucy Wessen and I was left alone together like on a desert island. Gee, if I'd only been on the square or if there had been any way of getting myself on the square. There ain't any Walter Mathers, like I said to her and them, and there hasn't ever been one, but if there was, I bet I'd go to Marietta, Ohio, and shoot him tomorrow.

There I was, big boob that I am. Pretty soon the race was over, and Wilbur had gone down and collected our money, and we had a hack downtown, and he stood us a swell supper at the West House, and a bottle of champagne beside.

And I was with that girl and she wasn't saying much, and I wasn't saying much either. One thing I know. She wasn't stuck on me because of the lie about my father being rich and all that. There's a way you know. . . . Craps amighty. There's a kind of girl, you see just once in your life, and if you don't get busy and make hay, then you're gone for good and all, and might as well go jump off a bridge. They give you a look from inside of them somewhere, and it ain't no vamping, and what it means is—you want that girl to be your wife, and you want nice things around her like flowers and swell clothes, and you want her to have the kids you're going to have, and you want good music played and no rag-time. Gee whizz.

There's a place over near Sandusky, across a kind of bay, and it's called Cedar Point. And after we had supper we went over to it in a launch, all by ourselves. Wilbur and Miss Lucy and that Miss Woodbury had to catch a ten o'clock train back to Tiffin, Ohio, because, when you're out with girls like that you can't get careless and miss any trains and stay out all night, like you can with some kinds of Janes.

And Wilbur blowed himself to the launch and it cost him fifteen cold plunks, but I wouldn't never have knew if I hadn't listened. He wasn't no tin horn kind of a sport.

Over at the Cedar Point place, we didn't stay around where there was a gang of common kind of cattle at all.

There was big dance halls and dining places for yaps, and there was a beach you could walk along and get where it was dark, and we went there.

She didn't talk hardly at all and neither did I, and I was thinking how glad I was my mother was all right, and always made us kids learn to eat with a fork at table, and not swill soup, and not be noisy and rough like a gang you see around a race track that way.

Then Wilbur and his girl went away up the beach and Lucy and I sat down in a dark place, where there was some roots of old trees, the water had washed up, and after that the time, till we had to go back in the launch and they had to catch their trains, wasn't nothing at all. It went like winking your eye.

Here's how it was. The place we were setting in was dark, like I said, and there was the roots from that old stump sticking up like arms, and there was a watery smell, and the night was like—as if you could put your hand out and feel it—so warm and soft and dark and sweet like an orange.

I most cried and I most swore and I most jumped up and danced, I was so mad and happy and sad.

When Wilbur come back from being alone with his

girl, and she saw him coming, Lucy she says, "we got to go to the train now," and she was most crying too, but she never knew nothing I knew, and she couldn't be so all busted up. And then, before Wilbur and Miss Woodbury got up to where we was, she put her face up and kissed me quick and put her head up against me and she was all quivering and—Gee whizz.

Sometimes I hope I have cancer and die. I guess you know what I mean. We went in the launch across the bay to the train like that, and it was dark, too. She whispered and said it was like she and I could get out of the boat and walk on the water, and it sounded foolish, but I knew what she meant.

And then quick we were right at the depot, and there was a big gang of yaps, the kind that goes to the fairs, and crowded and milling around like cattle, and how could I tell her? "It won't be long because you'll write and I'll write to you." That's all she said.

I got a chance like a hay barn afire. A swell chance I got.

And maybe she would write me, down at Marietta that way, and the letter would come back, and stamped on the front of it by the U.S.A. "there ain't any such guy," or something like that, whatever they stamp on a letter that way.

And me trying to pass myself off for a bigbug and a swell—to her, as decent a little body as God ever made. Craps amighty—a swell chance I got!

And then the train come in, and she got on it, and Wilbur Wessen he come and shook hands with me, and that Miss Woodbury was nice too and bowed to me, and I at her, and the train went and I busted out and cried like a kid.

Gee, I could have run after that train and made Dan

Patch look like a freight train after a wreck but, socks amighty, what was the use? Did you ever see such a fool?

I'll bet you what—if I had an arm broke right now or a train had run over my foot—I wouldn't go to no doctor at all. I'd go set down and let her hurt and hurt—that's what I'd do.

I'll bet you what—if I hadn't a drunk that booze I'd a never been such a boob as to go tell such a lie—that couldn't never be made straight to a lady like her.

I wish I had that fellow right here that had on a Windsor tie and carried a cane. I'd smash him for fair. Gosh darn his eyes. He's a big fool—that's what he is.

And if I'm not another you just go find me one and I'll quit working and be a bum and give him my job. I don't care nothing for working, and earning money, and saving it for no such boob as myself.

# The Man Who Became a Woman[1]

MY FATHER was a retail druggist in our town, out in Nebraska, which was so much like a thousand other towns I've been in since that there's no use fooling around and taking up your time and mine trying to describe it.

Anyway I became a drug clerk and after father's death the store was sold and mother took the money and went west, to her sister in California, giving me four

[1] For Editor's Note, see p. 463.

hundred dollars with which to make my start in the world. I was only nineteen years old then.

I came to Chicago, where I worked as a drug clerk for a time, and then, as my health suddenly went back on me, perhaps because I was so sick of my lonely life in the city and of the sight and smell of the drugstore, I decided to set out on what seemed to me then the great adventure and became for a time a tramp, working now and then, when I had no money, but spending all the time I could loafing around out of doors or riding up and down the land on freight trains and trying to see the world. I even did some stealing in lonely towns at night—once a pretty good suit of clothes that someone had left hanging out on a clothesline, and once some shoes out of a box in a freight car—but I was in constant terror of being caught and put into jail so realized that success as a thief was not for me.

The most delightful experience of that period of my life was when I once worked as a groom, or swipe, with race horses and it was during that time I met a young fellow of about my own age who has since become a writer of some prominence.

The young man of whom I now speak had gone into race track work as a groom, to bring a kind of flourish, a high spot, he used to say, into his life.

He was then unmarried and had not been successful as a writer. What I mean is he was free and I guess, with him as with me, there was something he liked about the people who hang about a race track, the touts, swipes, drivers, niggers and gamblers. You know what a gaudy undependable lot they are—if you've ever been around the tracks much—about the best liars I've ever seen, and not saving money or thinking about morals, like most druggists, drygoods merchants and the others who used to be my father's friends in our Nebraska town—and not bending the knee much either, or kowtowing to people, they thought must be grander or richer or more powerful than themselves.

What I mean is, they were an independent, go-to-the-devil, come-have-a-drink-of-whisky, kind of a crew and when one of them won a bet, "knocked 'em off," we called it, his money was just dirt to him while it lasted. No king or president or soap manufacturer—gone on a trip with his family to Europe—could throw on more dog than one of them, with his big diamond rings and the diamond horseshoe stuck in his necktie and all.

I liked the whole blamed lot pretty well and he did too.

He was groom temporarily for a pacing gelding named Lumpy Joe owned by a tall black-mustached man named Alfred Kreymborg and trying the best he could to make the bluff to himself he was a real one. It happened that we were on the same circuit, doing the West Pennsylvania county fairs all that fall, and on fine evenings we spent a good deal of time walking and talking together.

Let us suppose it to be a Monday or Tuesday evening and our horses had been put away for the night. The racing didn't start until later in the week, maybe Wednesday, usually. There was always a little place called a dining-hall, run mostly by the Woman's Christian Temperance Associations of the towns, and we would go there to eat where we could get a pretty good meal for twenty-five cents. At least then we thought it pretty good.

I would manage it so that I sat beside this fellow, whose name was Tom Means and when we had got through eating we would go look at our two horses again and when we got there Lumpy Joe would be eating his hay in his box stall and Alfred Kreymborg would be standing there, pulling his mustache and looking as sad as a sick crane.

But he wasn't really sad. "You two boys want to go downtown to see the girls. I'm an old duffer and way past that myself. You go along. I'll be setting here anyway, and I'll keep an eye on both the horses for you," he would say.

So we would set off, going, not into the town to try to get in with some of the town girls, who might have taken up with us because we were strangers and race track fellows, but out into the country. Sometimes we got into a hilly country and there was a moon. The leaves were falling off the trees and lay in the road so that we kicked them up with the dust as we went along.

To tell the truth I suppose I got to love Tom Means, who was five years older than me, although I wouldn't have dared say so, then. Americans are shy and timid about saying things like that and a man here don't dare own up he loves another man, I've found out, and they are afraid to admit such feelings to themselves even. I guess they're afraid it may be taken to mean something it don't need to at all.

Anyway we walked along and some of the trees were already bare and looked like people standing solemnly beside the road and listening to what we had to say. Only I didn't say much. Tom Means did most of the talking.

Sometimes we came back to the race track and it was late and the moon had gone down and it was dark. Then we often walked round and round the track, sometimes a dozen times, before we crawled into the hay to go to bed.

Tom talked always on two subjects, writing and race horses, but mostly about race horses. The quiet sounds about the race tracks and the smells of horses, and the things that go with horses, seemed to get him all excited. "Oh, hell, Herman Dudley," he would burst out suddenly, "don't go talking to me. I know what I think. I've been around more than you have and I've seen a world of people. There isn't any man or woman, not even a fellow's own mother, as fine as a horse, that is to say a thoroughbred horse."

Sometimes he would go on like that a long time, speaking of people he had seen and their characteristics. He wanted to be a writer later and what he said was that when he came to be one he wanted to write the way a well bred horse runs or trots or paces. Whether he ever did it or not I can't say. He has written a lot, but I'm not too good a judge of such things. Anyway I don't think he has.

But when he got on the subject of horses he certainly was a darby. I would never have felt the way I finally got to feel about horses or enjoyed my stay among them half so much if it hadn't been for him. Often he would go on talking for an hour maybe, speaking of horses' bodies and of their minds and wills as though they were human beings. "Lord help us, Herman," he would say, grabbing hold of my arm, "don't it get you up in the throat? I say now, when a good one, like that Lumpy Joe I'm swiping, flattens himself at the head of the stretch and he's coming, and you know he's coming, and you know his heart's sound, and he's game, and you know he isn't going to let himself get licked—don't it get you Herman, don't it get you like the old Harry?"

That's the way he would talk, and then later, sometimes, he'd talk about writing and get himself all het up about that too. He had some notions about writing I've never got myself around to thinking much about but just the same maybe his talk, working in me, has led me to want to begin to write this story myself.

There was one experience of that time on the tracks that I am forced, by some feeling inside myself, to tell.

Well, I don't know why but I've just got to. It will be kind of like confession is, I suppose, to a good Catholic, or maybe, better yet, like cleaning up the room you live in, if you are a bachelor, like I was for so long. The room gets pretty mussy and the bed not made some days and clothes and things thrown on the closet floor and maybe under the bed. And then you clean all up and put on new sheets, and then you take off all your clothes and get down on your hands and knees, and scrub the floor so clean you could eat bread off it, and then take a walk and come home after a while and your room smells sweet and you feel sweetened-up and better inside yourself too.

What I mean is, this story has been on my chest, and I've often dreamed about the happenings in it, even after I married Jessie and was happy. Sometimes I even screamed out at night and so I said to myself, "I'll write the dang story," and here goes.

Fall had come on and in the mornings now when we crept out of our blankets, spread out on the hay in the tiny lofts above the horse stalls, and put our heads out to look around, there was a white rime of frost on the ground. When we woke the horses woke too. You know how it is at the tracks—the little barnlike stalls with the tiny lofts above are all set along in a row and there are two doors to each stall, one coming up to a horse's breast and then a top one, that is only closed at night and in bad weather.

In the mornings the upper door is swung open and

fastened back and the horses put their heads out. There is the white rime on the grass over inside the gray oval the track makes. Usually there is some outfit that has six, ten or even twelve horses, and perhaps they have a Negro cook who does his cooking at an open fire in the clear space before the row of stalls and he is at work now and the horses with their big fine eyes are looking about and whinnying, and a stallion looks out at the door of one of the stalls and sees a sweet-eyed mare looking at him and sends up his trumpet-call, and a man's voice laughs, and there are no women anywhere in sight or no sign of one anywhere, and everyone feels like laughing and usually does.

It's pretty fine but I didn't know how fine it was until I got to know Tom Means and heard him talk about it all.

At the time the thing happened of which I am trying to tell now Tom was no longer with me. A week before his owner, Alfred Kreymborg, had taken his horse Lumpy Joe over into the Ohio Fair Circuit and I saw no more of Tom at the tracks.

There was a story going about the stalls that Lumpy Joe, a big rangy brown gelding, wasn't really named Lumpy Joe at all, that he was a ringer who had made a fast record out in Iowa and up through the northwest country the year before, and that Kreymborg had picked him up and had kept him under wraps all winter and had brought him over into the Pennsylvania country under this new name and made a clean-up in the books.

I know nothing about that and never talked to Tom about it but anyway he, Lumpy Joe and Kreymborg were all gone now.

I suppose I'll always remember those days, and Tom's talk at night, and before that in the early September evenings how we sat around in front of the stalls, and Kreymborg sitting on an upturned feed box and pulling at his long black mustache and sometimes humming a little ditty one couldn't catch the words of. It was something about a deep well and a little gray squirrel crawling up the sides of it, and he never laughed or smiled much but there was something in his solemn gray eyes, not quite a twinkle, something more delicate than that.

The others talked in low tones and Tom and I sat in silence. He never did his best talking except when he and I were alone.

For his sake—if he ever sees my story—I should mention that at the only big track we ever visited, at Readville, Pennsylvania, we saw old Pop Geers, the great racing driver, himself. His horses were at a place far away across the tracks from where we were stabled. I suppose a man like him was likely to get the choice of all the good places for his horses.

We went over there one evening and stood about and there was Geers himself, sitting before one of the stalls on a box tapping the ground with a riding whip. They called him, around the tracks, "The silent man from Tennessee" and he was silent—that night anyway. All we did was to stand and look at him for maybe a half hour and then we went away and that night Tom talked better than I had ever heard him. He said that the ambition of his life was to wait until Pop Geers died and then write a book about him, and to show in the book that there was at least one American who never went nutty about getting rich or owning a big factory or being any other kind of a hell of a fellow. "He's satisfied I think to sit around like that and wait until the big moments of his life come, when he heads a fast one into the stretch and then, darn his soul, he can give all of himself to the thing right in front of him," Tom said, and then he was so worked up he began to blubber. We were walking along the fence on the inside of the tracks and it was dusk and, in some trees nearby, some birds, just sparrows maybe, were making a chirping sound, and you could hear insects singing and, where there was a little light, off to the west between some trees, motes were dancing in the air. Tom said that about Pop Geers, although I think he was thinking most about something he wanted to be himself and wasn't, and then he went and stood by the fence and sort of blubbered and I began to blubber too, although I didn't know what about.

But perhaps I did know, after all. I suppose Tom wanted to feel, when he became a writer, like he thought old Pop must feel when his horse swung around the upper turn, and there lay the stretch before him, and if he was going to get his horse home in front he had to do it right then. What Tom said was that any man had something in him that understands about a thing like that but that no woman ever did except up in her brain. He often got off things like that about women but I notice he later married one of them just the same.

But to get back to my knitting. After Tom had left, the stable I was with kept drifting along through nice little Pennsylvania county seat towns. My owner, a strange excitable kind of a man from over in Ohio, who had lost a lot of money on horses but was always thinking he would maybe get it all back in some big killing, had been playing in pretty good luck that year. The horse I had, a tough little gelding, a five-year-old, had been getting home in front pretty regular and so he took some of his winnings and bought a three-year-old black pacing stallion named "O My Man." My gelding was called "Pick-it-boy" because when he was in a race and had got into the stretch my owner always got half wild with excitement and shouted so you could hear him a mile and a half. "Go, pick it boy, pick it boy, pick it boy," he kept shouting and so when he had got hold of this good little gelding he had named him that.

The gelding was a fast one, all right. As the boys at the tracks used to say, he "picked 'em up sharp and set 'em down clean," and he was what we called a natural race horse, right up to all the speed he had, and didn't require much training. "All you got to do is to drop him down on the track and he'll go," was what my owner was always saying to other men, when he was bragging about his horse.

And so you see, after Tom left, I hadn't much to do evenings and then the new stallion, the three-year-old, came on with a Negro swipe named Burt.

I liked him fine and he liked me but not the same as Tom and me. We got to be friends all right and I suppose Burt would have done things for me, and maybe me for him, that Tom and me wouldn't have done for each other.

But with a Negro you couldn't be close friends like you can with another white man. There's some reason you can't understand but it's true. There's been too much talk about the difference between whites and blacks and you're both shy, and anyway no use trying and I suppose Burt and I both knew it and so I was pretty lonesome.

Something happened to me that happened several times, when I was a young fellow, that I have never exactly understood. Sometimes now I think it was all because I had got to be almost a man and had never been with a woman. I don't know what's the matter with me. I can't ask a woman. I've tried it a good many times in my life but every time I've tried the same thing happened.

Of course, with Jessie now, it's different, but at the time of which I'm speaking Jessie was a long ways off and a good many things were to happen to me before I got to her.

Around a race track, as you may suppose, the fellows who are swipes and drivers and strangers in the towns do not go without women. They don't have to. In any town there are always some fly girls will come around a place like that. I suppose they think they are fooling with men who lead romantic lives. Such girls will come along by the front of the stalls where the race horses are and, if you look all right to them, they will stop and make a fuss over your horse. They rub their little hands over the horse's nose and then is the time for you—if you aren't a fellow like me who can't get up the nerve—then is the time for you to smile and say, "Hello, kid," and make a date with one of them for that evening uptown after supper. I couldn't do that, although the Lord knows I tried hard enough, often enough. A girl would come along alone, and she would be a little thing and give me the eye, and I would try and try but couldn't say anything. Both Tom, and Burt afterwards, used to laugh at me about it sometimes but what I think is that, had I been able to speak up to one of them and had managed to make a date with her, nothing would have come of it. We would probably have walked around the town and got off together in the dark somewhere, where the town came to an end, and then she would have had to knock me over with a club before it got any further.

And so there I was, having got used to Tom and our talks together, and Burt of course had his own friends among the black men. I got lazy and mopey and had a hard time doing my work.

It was like this. Sometimes I would be sitting, perhaps under a tree in the late afternoon when the races were over for the day and the crowds had gone away. There were always a lot of other men and boys who hadn't any horses in the races that day and they would be standing or sitting about in front of the stalls and talking.

I would listen for a time to their talk and then their voices would seem to go far away. The things I was looking at would go far away too. Perhaps there would be a tree, not more than a hundred yards away, and it would just come out of the ground and float away like a thistle. It would get smaller and smaller, away off there in the sky, and then suddenly—bang, it would be back where it belonged, in the ground, and I would begin hearing the voices of the men talking again.

When Tom was with me that summer the nights were splendid. We usually walked about and talked until pretty late and then I crawled up into my hole and went to sleep. Always out of Tom's talk I got something that stayed in my mind, after I was off by myself, curled up in my blanket. I suppose he had a way of making pictures as he talked and the pictures stayed by me as Burt was always saying pork chops did by him. "Give me the old pork chops, they stick to the ribs," Burt was always saying and with the imagination it was always that way about Tom's talks. He started something inside you that went on and on, and your mind played with it like walking about in a strange town and seeing the sights, and you slipped off to sleep and had splendid dreams and woke up in the morning feeling fine.

And then he was gone and it wasn't that way any more and I got into the fix I have described. At night I kept seeing women's bodies and women's lips and things in my dreams, and woke up in the morning feeling like the old Harry.

Burt was pretty good to me. He always helped me cool Pick-it-boy out after a race and he did the things himself that take the most skill and quickness, like getting the bandages on a horse's leg smooth, and seeing that every strap is setting just right, and every buckle drawn up to just the right hole, before your horse goes out on the track for a heat.

Burt knew there was something wrong with me and put himself out not to let the boss know. When the boss was around he was always bragging about me. "The brightest kid I've ever worked with around the tracks," he would say and grin, and that at a time when I wasn't worth my salt.

When you go out with the horses there is one job that always takes a lot of time. In the late afternoon, after your horse has been in a race and after you have washed him and rubbed him out, he has to be walked slowly, sometimes for hours and hours, so he'll cool out slowly and won't get musclebound. I got so I did that job for both our horses and Burt did the more important things. It left him free to go talk or shoot dice with the other niggers and I didn't mind. I rather liked it and after a hard race even the stallion, O My Man, was tame enough, even when there were mares about.

You walk and walk and walk, around a little circle, and your horse's head is right by your shoulder, and all around you the life of the place you are in is going on, and in a queer way you get so you aren't really a part of it at all. Perhaps no one ever gets as I was then, except boys that aren't quite men yet and who like me have never been with girls or women—to really be with them, up to the hilt, I mean. I used to wonder if young girls got that way too before they married or did what we used to call "go on the town."

If I remember it right though, I didn't do much

thinking then. Often I would have forgotten supper if Burt hadn't shouted at me and reminded me, and sometimes he forgot and went off to town with one of the other niggers and I did forget.

There I was with the horse, going slow slow slow, around a circle that way. The people were leaving the fair grounds now, some afoot, some driving away to the farms in wagons and fords. Clouds of dust floated in the air and over to the west, where the town was, maybe the sun was going down, a red ball of fire through the dust. Only a few hours before the crowd had been all filled with excitement and everyone shouting. Let us suppose my horse had been in a race that afternoon and I had stood in front of the grandstand with my horse blanket over my shoulder, alongside of Burt perhaps, and when they came into the stretch my owner began to call, in that queer high voice of his that seemed to float over the top of all the shouting up in the grandstand. And his voice was saying over and over, "Go, pick it boy, pick it boy, pick it boy," the way he always did, and my heart was thumping so I could hardly breathe, and Burt was leaning over and snapping his fingers and muttering, "Come, little sweet. Come on home. Your Mama wants you. Come get your 'lasses and bread, little Pick-it-boy."

Well, all that was over now and the voices of the people left around were all low. And Pick-it-boy—I was leading him slowly around the little ring, to cool him out slowly, as I've said—he was different too. Maybe he had pretty nearly broken his heart trying to get down to the wire in front, or getting down there in front, and now everything inside him was quiet and tired, as it was nearly all the time those days in me, except in me tired but not quiet.

You remember I've told you we always walked in

a circle, round and round and round. I guess something inside me got to going round and round and round too. The sun did sometimes and the trees and the clouds of dust. I had to think sometimes about putting down my feet so they went down in the right place and I didn't get to staggering like a drunken man.

And a funny feeling came that it is going to be hard to describe. It had something to do with the life in the horse and in me. Sometimes, these late years, I've thought maybe Negroes would understand what I'm trying to talk about now better than any white man ever will. I mean something about men and animals, something between them, something that can perhaps only happen to a white man when he has slipped off his base a little, as I suppose I had then. I think maybe a lot of horsey people feel it sometimes though. It's something like this, maybe—do you suppose it could be that something we whites have got, and think such a lot of, and are so proud about, isn't much of any good after all?

It's something in us that wants to be big and grand and important maybe and won't let us just be, like a horse or a dog or a bird can. Let's say Pick-it-boy had won his race that day. He did that pretty often that summer. Well, he was neither proud, like I would have been in his place, or mean in one part of the inside of him either. He was just himself, doing something with a kind of simplicity. That's what Pick-it-boy was like and I got to feeling it in him as I walked with him slowly in the gathering darkness. I got inside him in some way I can't explain and he got inside me. Often we would stop walking for no cause and he would put his nose up against my face.

I wished he was a girl sometimes or that I was a girl and he was a man. It's an odd thing to say but it's a fact.

Being with him that way, so long, and in such a quiet way, cured something in me a little. Often after an evening like that I slept all right and did not have the kind of dreams I've spoken about.

But I wasn't cured for very long and couldn't get cured. My body seemed all right and just as good as ever but there wasn't no pep in me.

Then the fall got later and later and we came to the last town we were going to make before my owner laid his horses up for the winter, in his home town over across the state line in Ohio, and the track was up on a hill, or rather in a kind of high plain above the town.

It wasn't much of a place and the sheds were rather rickety and the track bad, especially at the turns. As soon as we got to the place and got stabled it began to rain and kept it up all week so the fair had to be put off.

As the purses weren't very large a lot of the owners shipped right out but our owner stayed. The fair owners guaranteed expenses, whether the races were held the next week or not.

And all week there wasn't much of anything for Burt and me to do but clean manure out of the stalls in the morning, watch for a chance when the rain let up a little to jog the horses around the track in the mud and then clean them off, blanket them and stick them back in their stalls.

It was the hardest time of all for me. Burt wasn't so bad off as there were a dozen or two blacks around and in the evening they went off to town, got liquored up a little and came home late, singing and talking, even in the cold rain.

And then one night I got mixed up in the thing I'm trying to tell you about.

It was a Saturday evening and when I look back at it now it seems to me everyone had left the tracks but just me. In the early evening swipe after swipe came over to my stall and asked me if I was going to stick around. When I said I was he would ask me to keep an eye out for him, that nothing happened to his horse. "Just take a stroll down that way now and then, eh, kid," one of them would say, "I just want to run up to town for an hour or two."

I would say "yes" to be sure, and so pretty soon it was dark as pitch up there in that little ruined fair-ground and nothing living anywhere around but the horses and me.

I stood it as long as I could, walking here and there in the mud and rain, and thinking all the time I wished I was someone else and not myself. "If I were some-one else," I thought, "I wouldn't be here but down there in town with the others." I saw myself going into sa-loons and having drinks and later going off to a house maybe and getting myself a woman.

I got to thinking so much that, as I went stumbling around up there in the darkness, it was as though what was in my mind was actually happening.

Only I wasn't with some cheap woman, such as I would have found had I had the nerve to do what I wanted but with such a woman as I thought then I should never find in this world. She was slender and like a flower and with something in her like a race horse too, something in her like Pick-it-boy in the stretch, I guess.

And I thought about her and thought about her un-til I couldn't stand thinking any more. "I'll do something anyway," I said to myself.

So, although I had told all the swipes I would stay

and watch their horses, I went out of the fair grounds and down the hill a ways. I went down until I came to a little low saloon, not in the main part of the town itself but halfway up the hillside. The saloon had once been a residence, a farmhouse perhaps, but if it was ever a farmhouse I'm sure the farmer who lived there and worked the land on that hillside hadn't made out very well. The country didn't look like a farming country, such as one sees all about the other county-seat towns we had been visiting all through the late summer and fall. Everywhere you looked there were stones sticking out of the ground and the trees mostly of the stubby, stunted kind. It looked wild and untidy and ragged, that's what I mean. On the flat plain, up above, where the fair ground was, there were a few fields and pastures, and there were some sheep raised and in the field right next to the tracks, on the furtherest side from town, on the back stretch side, there had once been a slaughterhouse, the ruins of which were still standing. It hadn't been used for quite some time but there were bones of animals lying all about in the field, and there was a smell coming out of the old building that would curl your hair.

The horses hated the place, just as we swipes did, and in the morning when we were jogging them around the track in the mud, to keep them in racing condition, Pick-it-boy and O My Man both raised old Ned every time we headed them up the back stretch and got near to where the old slaughterhouse stood. They would rear and fight at the bit, and go off their stride and run until they got clear of the rotten smells, and neither Burt nor I could make them stop it. "It's a hell of a town down there and this is a hell of a track for racing," Burt kept saying. "If they ever have their danged old fair someone's going to get spilled and maybe killed back here."

Whether they did or not I don't know as I didn't stay for the fair, for reasons I'll tell you pretty soon, but Burt was speaking sense all right. A race horse isn't like a human being. He won't stand for it to have to do his work in any rotten ugly kind of a dump the way a man will, and he won't stand for the smells a man will either.

But to get back to my story again. There I was, going down the hillside in the darkness and the cold soaking rain and breaking my word to all the others about staying up above and watching the horses. When I got to the little saloon I decided to stop and have a drink or two. I'd found out long before that about two drinks upset me so I was two-thirds piped and couldn't walk straight, but on that night I didn't care a tinker's dam.

So I went up a kind of path, out of the road, toward the front door of the saloon. It was in what must have been the parlor of the place when it was a farmhouse and there was a little front porch.

I stopped before I opened the door and looked about a little. From where I stood I could look right down into the main street of the town, like being in a big city, like New York or Chicago, and looking down out of the fifteenth floor of an office building into the street.

The hillside was mighty steep and the road up had to wind and wind or no one could ever have come up out of the town to their plagued old fair at all.

It wasn't much of a town I saw—a main street with a lot of saloons and a few stores, one or two dinky moving-picture places, a few fords, hardly any women or girls in sight and a raft of men. I tried to think of the girl I had been dreaming about, as I walked around in the mud and darkness up at the fair ground, living in the place but I couldn't make it. It was like trying to think of Pick-it-boy getting himself worked up to the state I was in then, and going into the ugly dump I was going into. It couldn't be done.

All the same I knew the town wasn't all right there in sight. There must have been a good many of the kinds of houses Pennsylvania miners live in back in the hills, or around a turn in the valley in which the main street stood.

What I suppose is that, it being Saturday night and raining, the women and kids had all stayed at home and only the men were out, intending to get themselves liquored up. I've been in some other mining towns since and if I was a miner and had to live in one of them, or in one of the houses they live in with their women and kids, I'd get out and liquor myself up too.

So there I stood looking, and as sick as a dog inside myself, and as wet and cold as a rat in a sewer pipe. I could see the mass of dark figures moving about down below, and beyond the main street there was a river that made a sound you could hear distinctly, even up where I was, and over beyond the river were some railroad tracks with switch engines going up and down. I suppose they had something to do with the mines in which the men of the town worked. Anyway, as I stood watching and listening there was, now and then, a sound like thunder rolling down the sky, and I suppose that was a lot of coal, maybe a whole carload, being let down plunk into a coal car.

And then besides there was, on the side of a hill far away, a long row of coke ovens. They had little doors, through which the light from the fire within leaked out and as they were set closely, side by side, they looked like the teeth of some big man-eating giant lying and waiting over there in the hills.

The sight of it all, even the sight of the kind of hell-holes men are satisfied to go on living in, gave me the fantods and the shivers right down in my liver, and on that night I guess I had in me a kind of contempt for all men, including myself, that I've never had so thoroughly since. Come right down to it, I suppose women aren't so much to blame as men. They aren't running the show.

Then I pushed open the door and went into the saloon. There were about a dozen men, miners I suppose, playing cards at tables in a little long dirty room, with a bar at one side of it, and with a big red-faced man with a mustache standing back of the bar.

The place smelled, as such places do where men hang around who have worked and sweated in their clothes and perhaps slept in them too, and have never had them washed but have just kept on wearing them. I guess you know what I mean if you've ever been in a city. You smell that smell in a city, in streetcars on rainy nights when a lot of factory hands get on. I got pretty used to that smell when I was a tramp and pretty sick of it too.

And so I was in the place now, with a glass of whisky in my hand, and I thought all the miners were staring at me, which they weren't at all, but I thought they were and so I felt just the same as though they had been. And then I looked up and saw my own face in the old cracked looking-glass back of the bar. If the miners had been staring, or laughing at me, I wouldn't have wondered when I saw what I looked like.

It—I mean my own face—was white and pasty-looking, and for some reason, I can't tell exactly why, it wasn't my own face at all. It's a funny business I'm trying to tell you about and I know what you may be thinking of me as well as you do, so you needn't suppose I'm innocent or ashamed. I'm only wondering. I've thought about it a lot since and I can't make it out. I know I was never that way before that night and I know I've never been that way since. Maybe it was lonesomeness, just lonesomeness, gone on in me too long. I've often wondered if women generally are lonesomer than men.

The point is that the face I saw in the looking-glass back of that bar, when I looked up from my glass of whisky that evening, wasn't my own face at all but the face of a woman. It was a girl's face, that's what I mean. That's what it was. It was a girl's face, and a lonesome and scared girl too. She was just a kid at that.

When I saw that the glass of whisky came pretty near falling out of my hand but I gulped it down, put a dollar on the bar, and called for another. "I've got to be careful here—I'm up against something new," I said to myself. "If any of these men in here get on to me there's going to be trouble." When I had got the second drink in me I called for a third and I thought, "When I get this third drink down I'll get out of here and back up the hill to the fair ground before I make a fool of myself and begin to get drunk."

And then, while I was thinking and drinking my third glass of whisky, the men in the room began to laugh and of course I thought they were laughing at me. But they weren't. No one in the place had really paid any attention to me.

What they were laughing at was a man who had just come in at the door. I'd never seen such a fellow. He was a huge big man, with red hair, that stuck straight up like bristles out of his head, and he had a red-haired kid in his arms. The kid was just like himself, big, I mean, for his age, and with the same kind of stiff red hair.

He came and set the kid up on the bar, close beside me, and called for a glass of whisky for himself and all the men in the room began to shout and laugh at him and his kid. Only they didn't shout and laugh when he was looking, so he could tell which ones did it, but did all their shouting and laughing when his head was turned the other way. They kept calling him "cracked." "The crack is getting wider in the old tin pan," someone sang and then they all laughed.

I'm puzzled you see, just how to make you feel as I felt that night. I suppose, having undertaken to write this story, that's what I'm up against, trying to do that. I'm not claiming to be able to inform you or to do you any good. I'm just trying to make you understand some things about me, as I would like to understand some things about you, or anyone, if I had the chance. Anyway the whole blamed thing, the thing that went on I mean in that little saloon on that rainy Saturday night, wasn't like anything quite real. I've already told you how I had looked into the glass back of the bar and had seen there, not my own face but the face of a scared young girl. Well, the men, the miners, sitting at the tables in the half-dark room, the red-faced bartender, the unholy looking big man who had come in and his queer-looking kid, now sitting on the bar—all of them were like characters in some play, not like real people at all.

There was myself, that wasn't myself—and I'm not any fairy. Anyone who has ever known me knows better than that.

And then there was the man who had come in. There was a feeling came out of him that wasn't like the feeling you get from a man at all. It was more like the feeling you get maybe from a horse, only his eyes weren't like a horse's eyes. Horses' eyes have a kind of calm something in them and his hadn't. If you've ever carried a lantern through a wood at night, going along a path, and then suddenly you felt something funny in the air and stopped, and there ahead of you somewhere were the eyes of some little animal, gleaming out at you from a dead wall of darkness— The eyes shine big and quiet but there is a point right in the center of each, where there is something dancing and wavering. You aren't afraid the little animal will jump at you, you are afraid the little eyes will jump at you—that's what's the matter with you.

Only of course a horse, when you go into his stall at night, or a little animal you had disturbed in a wood that way, wouldn't be talking and the big man who had come in there with his kid was talking. He kept talking all the time, saying something under his breath, as they say, and I could only understand now and then a few words. It was his talking made him kind of terrible. His eyes said one thing and his lips another. They didn't seem to get together, as though they belonged to the same person.

For one thing the man was too big. There was about him an unnatural bigness. It was in his hands, his arms, his shoulders, his body, his head, a bigness like you might see in trees and bushes in a tropical country perhaps. I've never been in a tropical country but I've seen pictures. Only his eyes were small. In his big head they looked like the eyes of a bird. And I remember that his lips were thick, like Negroes' lips.

He paid no attention to me or to the others in the room but kept on muttering to himself, or to the kid sitting on the bar—I couldn't tell to which.

First he had one drink and then, quick, another. I stood staring at him and thinking—a jumble of thoughts, I suppose.

What I must have been thinking was something like this. "Well he's one of the kind you are always seeing about towns," I thought. I meant he was one of the cracked kind. In almost any small town you go to you will find one, and sometimes two or three cracked people, walking around. They go through the street, muttering to themselves and people generally are cruel to them. Their own folks make a bluff at being kind, but they aren't really, and the others in the town, men and boys, like to tease them. They send such a fellow, the mild silly kind, on some fool errand after a round square or a dozen post-holes or tie cards on his back saying "Kick me," or something like that, and then carry on and laugh as though they had done something funny.

And so there was this cracked one in that saloon and I could see the men in there wanted to have some fun putting up some kind of horseplay on him, but they didn't quite dare. He wasn't one of the mild kind, that was a cinch. I kept looking at the man and at his kid, and then up at that strange unreal reflection of myself in the cracked looking-glass back of the bar. "Rats, rats, digging in the ground—miners are rats, little jack-rabbit," I heard him say to his solemn-faced kid. I guess, after all, maybe he wasn't so cracked.

The kid sitting on the bar kept blinking at his father, like an owl caught out in the daylight, and now the father was having another glass of whisky. He drank six glasses, one right after the other, and it was cheap ten-cent stuff. He must have had cast-iron insides all right.

Of the men in the room there were two or three (maybe they were really more scared than the others so had to put up a bluff of bravery by showing off) who kept laughing and making funny cracks about the big man and his kid and there was one fellow was the worst of the bunch. I'll never forget that fellow because of his looks and what happened to him afterwards.

He was one of the showing-off kind all right, and he was the one that had started the song about the crack getting bigger in the old tin pan. He sang it two or three times, and then he grew bolder and got up and began walking up and down the room singing it over and over. He was a showy kind of man with a fancy vest, on which there were brown tobacco spots, and he wore glasses. Every time he made some crack he thought was funny, he winked at the others as though to say, "You see me. I'm not afraid of this big fellow," and then the others laughed.

The proprietor of the place must have known what was going on, and the danger in it, because he kept leaning over the bar and saying, "Shush, now quit it," to the showy-off man, but it didn't do any good. The fellow kept prancing like a turkey-cock and he put his hat on one side of his head and stopped right back of the big man and sang that song about the crack in the old tin pan. He was one of the kind you can't shush until they get their blocks knocked off, and it didn't take him long to come to it that time anyhow.

Because the big fellow just kept on muttering to his kid and drinking his whisky, as though he hadn't heard anything, and then suddenly he turned and his big hand flashed out and he grabbed, not the fellow who had been showing off, but me. With just a sweep of his arm he brought me up against his big body. Then he shoved me over with my breast jammed against the bar and looking right into his kid's face and he said, "Now you watch him, and if you let him fall I'll kill you," in just quiet ordinary tones as though he was saying "good morning" to some neighbor.

Then the kid leaned over and threw his arms around my head, and in spite of that I did manage to screw my head around enough to see what happened.

It was a sight I'll never forget. The big fellow had whirled around, and he had the showy-off man by the shoulder now, and the fellow's face was a sight. The big man must have had some reputation as a bad man in the town, even though he was cracked for the man with the fancy vest had his mouth open now, and his hat had fallen off his head, and he was silent and scared. Once, when I was a tramp, I saw a kid killed by a train. The kid was walking on the rail and showing off before some other kids, by letting them see how close he could let an engine come to him before he got out of the way. And the engine was whistling and a woman, over on the porch of a house nearby, was jumping up and down and screaming, and the kid let the engine get nearer and nearer, wanting more and more to show off, and then he stumbled and fell. God, I'll never forget the look on his face, in just the second before he got hit and killed, and now, there in that saloon, was the same terrible look on another face.

I closed my eyes for a moment and was sick all through me and then, when I opened my eyes, the big man's fist was just coming down in the other man's face. The one blow knocked him cold and he fell down like a beast hit with an axe.

And then the most terrible thing of all happened. The big man had on heavy boots, and he raised one of them and brought it down on the other man's shoulder, as he lay white and groaning on the floor. I could hear the bones crunch and it made me so sick I could hardly stand up, but I had to stand up and hold on to that kid or I knew it would be my turn next.

Because the big fellow didn't seem excited or anything, but kept on muttering to himself as he had been doing when he was standing peacefully by the bar drinking his whisky, and now he had raised his foot again, and maybe this time he would bring it down in the other man's face and, "just eliminate his map for keeps," as sports and prize-fighters sometimes say. I trembled, like I was having a chill, but thank God at that moment the kid, who had his arms around me and one hand clinging to my nose, so that there were the marks of his fingernails on it the next morning, at that moment the kid, thank God, began to howl, and his father didn't bother any more with the man on the floor but turned around, knocked me aside, and taking the kid in his arms tramped out of that place, muttering to himself as he had been doing ever since he came in.

I went out too but I didn't prance out with any dignity, I'll tell you that. I slunk out like a thief or a coward, which perhaps I am, partly anyhow.

And so there I was, outside there in the darkness, and it was as cold and wet and black and Godforsaken a night as any man ever saw. I was so sick at the thought of human beings that night I could have vomited to think of them at all. For a while I just stumbled along in the mud of the road, going up the hill, back to the fair ground, and then, almost before I knew where I was, I found myself in the stall with Pick-it-boy.

That was one of the best and sweetest feelings I've ever had in my whole life, being in that warm stall alone with that horse that night. I had told the other swipes that I would go up and down the row of stalls now and then and have an eye on the other horses, but I had altogether forgotten my promise now. I went and stood with my back against the side of the stall, thinking how mean and low and all balled-up and twisted-up human beings can become, and how the best of them are likely to get that way any time, just because they are human beings and not simple and clear in their minds, and inside themselves, as animals are, maybe.

Perhaps you know how a person feels at such a moment. There are things you think of, odd little things you had thought you had forgotten. Once, when you were a kid, you were with your father, and he was all dressed up, as for a funeral or Fourth of July, and was walking along a street holding your hand. And you were going past a railroad station, and there was a woman standing. She was a stranger in your town and was dressed as you had never seen a woman dressed before, and never thought you would see one, looking so nice. Long afterwards you knew that was because she had lovely taste in clothes, such as so few women have really, but then you thought she must be a queen. You had read about queens in fairy stories and the thoughts of them thrilled you. What lovely eyes the strange lady had and what beautiful rings she wore on her fingers.

Then your father came out, from being in the railroad station, maybe to set his watch by the station clock, and took you by the hand and he and the woman smiled at each other, in an embarrassed kind of way, and you kept looking longingly back at her, and when you were out of her hearing you asked your father if she really were a queen. And it may be that your father was one who wasn't so very hot on democracy and a free country and talked-up bunk about a free citizenry, and he said he hoped she was a queen, and maybe, for all he knew, she was.

Or maybe, when you get jammed up as I was that night, and can't get things clear about yourself or other people and why you are alive, or for that matter why anyone you can think about is alive, you think, not of people at all but of other things you have seen and felt

—like walking along a road in the snow in the winter, perhaps out in Iowa, and hearing soft warm sounds in a barn close to the road, or of another time when you were on a hill and the sun was going down and the sky suddenly became a great soft-colored bowl, all glowing like a jewel-handled bowl, a great queen in some faraway mighty kingdom might have put on a vast table out under the tree, once a year, when she invited all her loyal and loving subjects to come and dine with her.

I can't, of course, figure out what you try to think about when you are as desolate as I was that night. Maybe you are like me and inclined to think of women, and maybe you are like a man I met once, on the road, who told me that when he was up against it he never thought of anything but grub and a big nice clean warm bed to sleep in. "I don't care about anything else and I don't ever let myself think of anything else," he said. "If I was like you and went to thinking about women sometime I'd find myself hooked up to some skirt, and she'd have the old double cross on me, and the rest of my life maybe I'd be working in some factory for her and her kids."

As I say, there I was anyway, up there alone with that horse in that warm stall in that dark lonesome fair ground and I had that feeling about being sick at the thought of human beings and what they could be like.

Well, suddenly I got again the queer feeling I'd had about him once or twice before, I mean the feeling about our understanding each other in some way I can't explain.

So having it again I went over to where he stood and began running my hands all over his body, just because I loved the feel of him and as sometimes, to tell the plain truth, I've felt about touching with my hands the body of a woman I've seen and who I thought was lovely too. I ran my hands over his head and neck and then down over his hard firm round body and then over his flanks and down his legs. His flanks quivered a little I remember and once he turned his head and stuck his cold nose down along my neck and nipped my shoulder a little, in a soft playful way. It hurt a little but I didn't care.

So then I crawled up through a hole into the loft above thinking that night was over anyway and glad of it, but it wasn't, not by a long sight.

As my clothes were all soaking wet and as we race track swipes didn't own any such things as nightgowns or pajamas I had to go to bed naked, of course.

But we had plenty of horse blankets and so I tucked myself in between a pile of them and tried not to think any more that night. The being with Pick-it-boy and having him close right under me that way made me feel a little better.

Then I was sound asleep and dreaming and—bang like being hit with a club by someone who has sneaked up behind you—I got another wallop.

What I suppose is that, being upset the way I was, I had forgotten to bolt the door to Pick-it-boy's stall down below and two Negro men had come in there, thinking they were in their own place, and had climbed up through the hole where I was. They were half lit-up but not what you might call dead drunk, and I suppose they were up against something a couple of white swipes, who had some money in their pockets, wouldn't have been up against.

What I mean is that a couple of white swipes, having liquored themselves up and being down there in the town on a bat, if they wanted a woman or a couple of women would have been able to find them. There is always a few women of that kind can be found around any town I've ever seen or heard of, and of course a bartender would have given them the tip where to go.

But a Negro, up there in that country, where there aren't any, or anyway mighty few Negro women, wouldn't know what to do when he felt that way and would be up against it.

It's so always. Burt and several other Negroes I've known pretty well have talked to me about it, lots of times. You take now a young Negro man—not a race track swipe or a tramp or any other low-down kind of a fellow—but, let us say, one who has been to college, and has behaved himself and tried to be a good man, the best he could, and be clean, as they say. He isn't any better off, is he? If he has made himself some money and wants to go sit in a swell restaurant, or go to hear some good music, or see a good play at the theater, he gets what we used to call on the tracks, "the messy end of the dung fork," doesn't he?

And even in such a lowdown place as what people call a "bad house" it's the same way. The white swipes and others can go into a place where they have Negro women fast enough, and they do it too, but you let a Negro swipe try it the other way around and see how he comes out.

You see, I can think this whole thing out fairly now, sitting here in my own house and writing, and with my wife Jessie in the kitchen making a pie or something, and I can show just how the two Negro men who came into that loft, where I was asleep, were justified in what they did, and I can preach about how the Negroes are up against it in this country, like a daisy, but I tell you what, I didn't think things out that way that night.

For, you understand, what they thought, they being half liquored-up, and when one of them had jerked the blankets off me, was that I was a woman. One of them carried a lantern but it was smoky and dirty and didn't give out much light. So they must have figured it out—my body being pretty white and slender then, like a young girl's body I suppose—that some white swipe had brought me up there. The kind of girls around a town that will come with a swipe to a race track on a rainy night aren't very fancy females but you'll find that kind in the towns all right. I've seen many a one in my day.

And so, I figure, these two big buck niggers, being piped that way, just made up their minds they would snatch me away from the white swipe who had brought me out there, and who had left me lying carelessly around.

"Jes' you lie still honey. We ain't gwine hurt you none," one of them said, with a little chuckling laugh that had something in it besides a laugh, too. It was the kind of laugh that gives you the shivers.

The devil of it was I couldn't say anything, not even a word. Why I couldn't yell out and say "What the hell," and just kid them a little and shoo them out of there I don't know, but I couldn't. I tried and tried so that my throat hurt but I didn't say a word. I just lay there staring at them.

It was a mixed-up night. I've never gone through another night like it.

Was I scared? Lord Almighty, I'll tell you what, I was scared.

Because the two black faces were leaning right over me now, and I could feel their liquored-up breaths on my cheeks, and their eyes were shining in the dim light from that smoky lantern, and right in the center of their eyes was that dancing flickering light I've told you about your seeing in the eyes of wild animals, when you were carrying a lantern through the woods at night.

It was a puzzler! All my life, you see—me never having had any sisters, and at that time never having had a sweetheart either—I had been dreaming and thinking about women, and I suppose I'd always been dreaming about a pure innocent one, for myself, made for me by God, maybe. Men are that way. No matter how big they talk about "let the women go hang," they've always got that notion tucked away inside themselves, somewhere. It's a kind of chesty man's notion, I suppose, but they've got it and the kind of up-and-coming women we have nowadays who are always saying, "I'm as good as a man and will do what the men do," are on the wrong trail if they really ever want to, what you might say "hog-tie" a fellow of their own.

So I had invented a kind of princess, with black hair and a slender willowy body to dream about. And I thought of her as being shy and afraid to ever tell anything she really felt to anyone but just me. I suppose I fancied that if I ever found such a woman in the flesh I would be the strong sure one and she the timid shrinking one.

And now I was that woman, or something like her, myself.

I gave a kind of wriggle, like a fish you have just taken off the hook. What I did next wasn't a thought-out thing. I was caught and I squirmed, that's all.

The two niggers both jumped at me but somehow—the lantern having been kicked over and having gone out the first move they made—well in some way, when they both lunged at me they missed.

As good luck would have it my feet found the hole, where you put hay down to the horse in the stall below, and through which we crawled up when it was time to go to bed in our blankets up in the hay, and down

I slid, not bothering to try to find the ladder with my feet but just letting myself go.

In less than a second I was out of doors in the dark and the rain and the two blacks were down the hole and out the door of the stall after me.

How long or how far they really followed me I suppose I'll never know. It was black dark and raining hard now and a roaring wind had begun to blow. Of course, my body being white, it must have made some kind of a faint streak in the darkness as I ran, and anyway I thought they could see me and I knew I couldn't see them and that made my terror ten times worse. Every minute I thought they would grab me.

You know how it is when a person is all upset and full of terror as I was. I suppose maybe the two niggers followed me for a while, running across the muddy race track and into the grove of trees that grew in the oval inside the track, but likely enough, after just a few minutes, they gave up the chase and went back, found their own place and went to sleep. They were liquored-up, as I've said, and maybe partly funning too.

But I didn't know that, if they were. As I ran I kept hearing sounds, sounds made by the rain coming down through the dead old leaves left on the trees and by the wind blowing, and it may be that the sound that scared me most of all was my own bare feet stepping on a dead branch and breaking it or something like that.

There was something strange and scary, a steady sound, like a heavy man running and breathing hard, right at my shoulder. It may have been my own breath, coming quick and fast. And I thought I heard that chuckling laugh I'd heard up in the loft, the laugh that sent the shivers right down through me. Of course every tree I came close to looked like a man standing there, ready to grab me, and I kept dodging and going—bang

—into other trees. My shoulders kept knocking against trees in that way and the skin was all knocked off, and every time it happened I thought a big black hand had come down and clutched at me and was tearing my flesh.

How long it went on I don't know, maybe an hour, maybe five minutes. But anyway the darkness didn't let up, and the terror didn't let up, and I couldn't, to save my life, scream or make any sound.

Just why I couldn't I don't know. Could it be because at the time I was a woman, while at the same time I wasn't a woman? It may be that I was too ashamed of having turned into a girl and being afraid of a man to make any sound. I don't know about that. It's over my head.

But anyway I couldn't make a sound. I tried and tried and my throat hurt from trying and no sound came.

And then, after a long time, or what seemed like a long time, I got out from among the trees inside the track and was on the track itself again. I thought the two black men were still after me, you understand, and I ran like a madman.

Of course, running along the track that way, it must have been up the back stretch, I came after a time to where the old slaughterhouse stood, in that field, beside the track. I knew it by its ungodly smell, scared as I was. Then, in some way, I managed to get over the high old fair ground fence and was in the field, where the slaughterhouse was.

All the time I was trying to yell or scream, or be sensible and tell those two black men that I was a man and not a woman, but I couldn't make it. And then I heard a sound like a board cracking or breaking in the fence and thought they were still after me.

So I kept on running like a crazy man, in the field, and just then I stumbled and fell over something. I've told you how the old slaughterhouse field was filled with bones, that had been lying there a long time and had all been washed white. There were heads of sheep and cows and all kinds of things.

And when I fell and pitched forward I fell right into the midst of something, still and cold and white.

It was probably the skeleton of a horse lying there. In small towns like that, they take an old worn-out horse, that has died, and haul him off to some field outside of town and skin him for the hide, that they can sell for a dollar or two. It doesn't make any difference what the horse has been, that's the way he usually ends up. Maybe even Pick-it-boy, or O My Man, or a lot of other good fast ones I've seen and known have ended that way by this time.

And so I think it was the bones of a horse lying there and he must have been lying on his back. The birds and wild animals had picked all his flesh away and the rain had washed his bones clean.

Anyway I fell and pitched forward and my side got cut pretty deep and my hands clutched at something. I had fallen right in between the ribs of the horse and they seemed to wrap themselves around me close. And my hands, clutching upwards, had got hold of the cheeks of that dead horse and the bones of his cheeks were cold as ice with the rain washing over them. White bones wrapped around me and white bones in my hands.

There was a new terror now that seemed to go down to the very bottom of me, to the bottom of the inside of me, I mean. It shook me like I have seen a rat in a barn shaken by a dog. It was a terror like a big wave that hits you when you are walking on a seashore, maybe.

You see it coming and you try to run and get away but when you start to run inshore there is a stone cliff you can't climb. So the wave comes high as a mountain, and there it is, right in front of you and nothing in all this world can stop it. And now it had knocked you down and rolled and tumbled you over and over and washed you clean, clean, but dead maybe.

And that's the way I felt—I seemed to myself dead with blind terror. It was a feeling like the finger of God running down your back and burning you clean, I mean.

It burned all that silly nonsense about being a girl right out of me.

I screamed at last and the spell that was on me was broken. I'll bet the scream I let out of me could have been heard a mile and a half.

Right away I felt better and crawled out from among the pile of bones, and then I stood on my own feet again and I wasn't a woman, or a young girl any more but a man and my own self, and as far as I know I've been that way ever since. Even the black night seemed warm and alive now, like a mother might be to a kid in the dark.

Only I couldn't go back to the race track because I was blubbering and crying and was ashamed of myself and of what a fool I had made of myself. Someone might see me and I couldn't stand that, not at that moment.

So I went across the field, walking now, not running like a crazy man, and pretty soon I came to a fence and crawled over and got into another field, in which there was a straw stack, I just happened to find in the pitch darkness.

The straw stack had been there a long time and some sheep had nibbled away at it until they had made a pretty deep hole, like a cave, in the side of it. I found the hole and crawled in and there were some sheep in there, about a dozen of them.

When I came in, creeping on my hands and knees, they didn't make much fuss, just stirred around a little and then settled down.

So I settled down amongst them too. They were warm and gentle and kind, like Pick-it-boy, and being in there with them made me feel better than I would have felt being with any human person I knew at that time.

So I settled down and slept after a while, and when I woke up it was daylight and not very cold and the rain was over. The clouds were breaking away from the sky now and maybe there would be a fair the next week but if there was I knew I wouldn't be there to see it.

Because what I expected to happen did happen. I had to go back across the fields and the fair ground to the place where my clothes were, right in the broad daylight, and me stark naked, and of course I knew someone would be up and would raise a shout, and every swipe and every driver would stick his head out and would whoop with laughter.

And there would be a thousand questions asked, and I would be too mad and too ashamed to answer, and would perhaps begin to blubber, and that would make me more ashamed than ever.

It all turned out just as I expected, except that when the noise and the shouts of laughter were going it the loudest, Burt came out of the stall where O My Man was kept, and when he saw me he didn't know what was the matter but he knew something was up that wasn't on the square and for which I wasn't to blame.

So he got so all-fired mad he couldn't speak for a

minute, and then he grabbed a pitchfork and began prancing up and down before the other stalls, giving that gang of swipes and drivers such a royal old dressing-down as you never heard. You should have heard him sling language. It was grand to hear.

And while he was doing it I sneaked up into the loft, blubbering because I was so pleased and happy to hear him swear that way, and I got my wet clothes on quick and got down, and gave Pick-it-boy a good-bye kiss on the cheek and lit out.

The last I saw of all that part of my life was Burt, still going it, and yelling out for the man who had put up a trick on me to come out and get what was coming to him. He had the pitchfork in his hand and was swinging it around, and every now and then he would make a kind of lunge at a tree or something, he was so mad through, and there was no one else in sight at all. And Burt didn't even see me cutting out along the fence through a gate and down the hill and out of the race-horse and the tramp life for the rest of my days.

# A Meeting South

## EDITOR'S NOTE

"A Meeting South" first appeared between the covers of a book among "articles written during the author's life as a story-teller" in *Sherwood Anderson's Notebook* (1926). And in 1933 it was reprinted in Anderson's last book of stories, *Death in the Woods and Other Stories.* It was written in 1924, during the period in which Anderson employed his widest variations on the short story form, and the following year it was published in *The Dial.* Was the piece an essay, a fragment of autobiography, or a story? It had the character of being all three in one—but Anderson's final decision to call the piece a story was correct. It is, properly speaking, a story about a young post-World War I southern writer and a woman, and it is one of the finest examples of Anderson's art in lightly sketching characters. The woman has been transplanted from the Middle West to New Orleans, and she shared with Anderson a spirit of agelessness and an almost maternal concern for the young half-crippled ex-aviator, who drinks heavily and has come home to die.

In "A Meeting South" Anderson re-creates the romantic atmosphere of the South and makes it seem inevitable that the lives of Aunt Sally, who once kept a disreputable "hotel," and the young writer should cross. Anderson's references to the Shelley-like spirit of the young writer bring to mind Shelley's lines on "the sensitive plant," and through this association the lyrical lightness of the story is sustained.

HE TOLD me the story of his ill-fortune—a crack-up in an airplane—with a very gentlemanly little smile on his very sensitive, rather thin, lips. Such things happened. He might well have been speaking of another. I liked his tone and I liked him.

This happened in New Orleans, where I had gone to live. When he came, my friend, Fred, for whom he was looking, had gone away, but immediately I felt a strong desire to know him better and so suggested we spend the evening together. When we went down the stairs from my apartment I noticed that he was a cripple. The slight limp, the look of pain that occasionally drifted across his face, the little laugh that was intended to be jolly, but did not quite achieve its purpose, all these things began at once to tell me the story I have now set myself to write.

"I shall take him to see Aunt Sally," I thought. One does not take every caller to Aunt Sally. However, when she is in fine feather, when she has taken a fancy to her visitor, there is no one like her. Although she has lived in New Orleans for thirty years, Aunt Sally is Middle Western, born and bred.

However I am plunging a bit too abruptly into my story.

First of all I must speak more of my guest, and for convenience's sake I shall call him David. I felt at once that he would be wanting a drink and, in New Orleans—dear city of Latins and hot nights—even in Prohibition times such things can be managed. We achieved several and my own head became somewhat shaky but I could see that what we had taken had not affected him. Evening was coming, the abrupt waning of the day and the quick smoky soft-footed coming of night, characteristic of the semitropic city, when he produced a bottle from his hip pocket. It was so large that I was amazed. How had it happened that the carrying of so large a bottle had not made him look deformed? His body was very small and delicately built. "Perhaps, like the kangaroo, his body has developed some kind of a natural pouch for taking care of supplies," I thought. Really he walked as one might fancy a kangaroo would walk when out for a quiet evening stroll. I went along thinking of Darwin and the marvels of Prohibition. "We are a wonderful people, we Americans," I thought. We were both in fine humor and had begun to like each other immensely.

He explained the bottle. The stuff, he said, was made

by a Negro man on his father's plantation somewhere over in Alabama. We sat on the steps of a vacant house deep down in the old French Quarter of New Orleans —the Vieux Carré—while he explained that his father had no intention of breaking the law—that is to say, in so far as the law remained reasonable. "Our nigger just makes whisky for us," he said. "We keep him for that purpose. He doesn't have anything else to do, just makes the family whisky, that's all. If he went selling any, we'd raise hell with him. I dare say Dad would shoot him if he caught him up to any such unlawful trick, and you bet, Jim, our nigger, I'm telling you of, knows it too.

"He's a good whisky-maker, though, don't you think?" David added. He talked of Jim in a warm friendly way. "Lord, he's been with us always, was born with us. His wife cooks for us and Jim makes our whisky. It's a race to see which is best at his job, but I think Jim will win. He's getting a little better all the time and all of our family—well, I reckon we just like and need our whisky more than we do our food."

Do you know New Orleans? Have you lived there in the summer when it is hot, in the winter when it rains, and through the glorious late fall days? Some of its own, more progressive, people scorn it now. In New Orleans there is a sense of shame because the city is not more like Chicago or Pittsburgh.

It, however, suited David and me. We walked slowly, on account of his bad leg, through many streets of the Old Town, Negro women laughing all around us in the dusk, shadows playing over old buildings, children with their shrill cries dodging in and out of old hallways. The old city was once almost altogether French, but now it is becoming more and more Italian. It however remains Latin. People live out of doors. Families were sitting down to dinner within full sight of the street—all doors and windows open. A man and his wife quarreled in Italian. In a patio back of an old building a Negress sang a French song.

We came out of the narrow little streets and had a drink in front of the dark cathedral and another in a little square in front. There is a statue of General Jackson, always taking off his hat to Northern tourists who in winter come down to see the city. At his horse's feet an inscription—"The Union must and will be preserved." We drank solemnly to that declaration and the general seemed to bow a bit lower. "He was sure a proud man," David said, as we went over toward the docks to sit in the darkness and look at the Mississippi. All good New Orleanians go to look at the Mississippi at least once a day. At night it is like creeping into a dark bedroom to look at a sleeping child—something of that sort—gives you the same warm nice feeling, I mean. David is a poet and so in the darkness by the river we spoke of Keats and Shelley, the two English poets all good Southern men love.

All of this, you are to understand, was before I took him to see Aunt Sally.

Both Aunt Sally and myself are Middle Westerners. We are but guests down here, but perhaps we both in some queer way belong to this city. Something of the sort is in the wind. I don't quite know how it has happened.

A great many Northern men and women come down our way and, when they go back North, write things about the South. The trick is to write nigger stories. The North likes them. They are so amusing. One of the best-known writers of nigger stories was down here recently and a man I know, a Southern man, went to call on him.

The writer seemed a bit nervous. "I don't know much about the South or Southerners," he said. "But you have your reputation," my friend said. "You are so widely known as a writer about the South and about Negro life." The writer had a notion he was being made sport of. "Now look here," he said, "I don't claim to be a highbrow. I'm a business man myself. At home, up North, I associate mostly with business men and when I am not at work I go out to the country club. I want you to understand I am not setting myself up as a highbrow.

"I give them what they want," he said. My friend said he appeared angry. "About what now, do you fancy?" he asked innocently.

However, I am not thinking of the Northern writer of Negro stories. I am thinking of the Southern poet, with the bottle clasped firmly in his hands, sitting in the darkness beside me on the docks facing the Mississippi.

He spoke at some length of his gift for drinking. "I didn't always have it. It is a thing built up," he said. The story of how he chanced to be a cripple came out slowly. You are to remember that my own head was a bit unsteady. In the darkness the river, very deep and very powerful off New Orleans, was creeping away to the gulf. The whole river seemed to move away from us and then to slip noiselessly into the darkness like a vast moving sidewalk.

When he had first come to me, in the late afternoon, and when we had started for our walk together I had noticed that one of his legs dragged as we went along and that he kept putting a thin hand to an equally thin cheek.

Sitting over by the river he explained, as a boy would

explain when he has stubbed his toe running down a hill.

When the World War broke out he went over to England and managed to get himself enrolled as an aviator, very much, I gathered, in the spirit in which a countryman, in a city for a night, might take in a show.

The English had been glad enough to take him on. He was one more man. They were glad enough to take anyone on just then. He was small and delicately built but after he got in he turned out to be a first-rate flyer, serving all through the War with a British flying squadron, but at the last got into a crash and fell.

Both legs were broken, one of them in three places, the scalp was badly torn and some of the bones of the face had been splintered.

They had put him into a field hospital and had patched him up. "It was my fault if the job was rather bungled," he said. "You see it was a field hospital, a hell of a place. Men were torn all to pieces, groaning and dying. Then they moved me back to a base hospital and it wasn't much better. The fellow who had the bed next to mine had shot himself in the foot to avoid going into a battle. A lot of them did that, but why they picked on their own feet that way is beyond me. It's a nasty place, full of small bones. If you're ever going to shoot yourself don't pick on a spot like that. Don't pick on your feet. I tell you it's a bad idea.

"Anyway, the man in the hospital was always making a fuss and I got sick of him and the place too. When I got better I faked, said the nerves of my leg didn't hurt. It was a lie, of course. The nerves of my leg and of my face have never quit hurting. I reckon maybe, if I had told the truth, they might have fixed me up all right."

I got it. No wonder he carried his drinks so well. When I understood, I wanted to keep on drinking with him, wanted to stay with him until he got tired of me as he had of the man who lay beside him in the base hospital over there somewhere in France.

The point was that he never slept, could not sleep, except when he was a little drunk. "I'm a nut," he said smiling.

It was after we got over to Aunt Sally's that he talked most. Aunt Sally had gone to bed when we got there, but she got up when we rang the bell and we all went to sit together in the little patio back of her house. She is a large woman with great arms and rather a paunch, and she had put on nothing but a light flowered dressing-gown over a thin, ridiculously girlish, night-gown. By this time the moon had come up and, outside, in the narrow street of the Vieux Carré, three drunken sailors from a ship in the river were sitting on a curb and singing a song,

*"I've got to get it,*
*You've got to get it,*
*We've all got to get it*
*In our own good time."*

They had rather nice boyish voices and every time they sang a verse and had done the chorus they all laughed together heartily.

In Aunt Sally's patio there are many broad-leafed banana plants and a Chinaberry tree throwing its soft purple shadows on a brick floor.

As for Aunt Sally, she is as strange to me as he was. When we came and when we were all seated at a little table in the patio, she ran into her house and presently came back with a bottle of whisky. She, it seemed, had understood him at once, had understood without unnecessary words that the little Southern man lived always in the black house of pain, that whisky was good to him, that it quieted his throbbing nerves, temporarily at least. "Everything is temporary, when you come to that," I can fancy Aunt Sally saying.

We sat for a time in silence, David having shifted his allegiance and taken two drinks out of Aunt Sally's bottle. Presently he rose and walked up and down the patio floor, crossing and recrossing the network of delicately outlined shadows on the bricks. "It's really all right, the leg," he said, "something just presses on the nerves, that's all." In me there was a self-satisfied feeling. I had done the right thing. I had brought him to Aunt Sally. "I have brought him to a mother." She has always made me feel that way since I have known her.

And now I shall have to explain her a little. It will not be so easy. That whole neighborhood in New Orleans is alive with tales concerning her.

Aunt Sally came to New Orleans in the old days, when the town was wild, in the wide-open days. What she had been before she came no one knew, but anyway she opened a place. That was very, very long ago when I was myself but a lad, up in Ohio. As I have already said Aunt Sally came from somewhere up in the Middle-Western country. In some obscure subtle way it would flatter me to think she came from my state.

The house she had opened was one of the older places in the French Quarter down here, and when she had got her hands on it, Aunt Sally had a hunch. Instead of making the place modern, cutting it up into small rooms, all that sort of thing, she left it just as it was and spent her money rebuilding falling old walls, mending winding broad old stairways, repairing dim high-ceilinged old rooms, soft-colored old marble mantels. After all, we do seem attached to sin and there are so many people busy making sin unattractive. It is good to find someone who takes the other road. It would have been so very much to Aunt Sally's advantage to have made the place modern, that is to say, in the business she was in at that time. If a few old rooms, wide old stairways, old cooking ovens built into the walls, if all these things did not facilitate the stealing in of couples on dark nights, they at least did something else. She had opened a gambling and drinking house, but one can have no doubt about the ladies stealing in. "I was on the make all right," Aunt Sally told me once.

She ran the place and took in money, and the money she spent on the place itself. A falling wall was made to stand up straight and fine again, the banana plants were made to grow in the patio, the Chinaberry tree got started and was helped through the years of adolescence. On the wall the lovely Rose of Montana bloomed madly. The fragrant Lantana grew in a dense mass at a corner of the wall.

When the Chinaberry tree, planted at the very center of the patio, began to get up into the light it filled the whole neighborhood with fragrance in the spring.

Fifteen, twenty years of that, with Mississippi River gamblers and race-horse men sitting at tables by windows in the huge rooms upstairs in the house that had once, no doubt, been the town house of some rich planter's family—in the boom days of the Forties. Women stealing in, too, in the dusk of evenings. Drinks being sold. Aunt Sally raking down the kitty from the game, raking in her share, quite ruthlessly.

At night, getting a good price too from the lovers. No questions asked, a good price for drinks. Moll Flanders might have lived with Aunt Sally. What a pair they would have made! The Chinaberry tree beginning to be lusty. The Lantana blossoming—in the fall the Rose of Montana.

Aunt Sally getting hers. Using the money to keep the old house in fine shape. Salting some away all the time.

A motherly soul, good, sensible Middle-Western woman, eh? Once a race-horse man left twenty-four thousand dollars with her and disappeared. No one knew she had it. There was a report the man was dead. He had killed a gambler in a place down by the French Market and while they were looking for him he managed to slip in to Aunt Sally's and leave his swag. Some time later a body was found floating in the river and it was identified as the horseman but in reality he had been picked up in a wire-tapping haul in New York City and did not get out of his Northern prison for six years.

When he did get out, naturally, he skipped for New Orleans. No doubt he was somewhat shaky. She had him. If he squealed there was a murder charge to be brought up and held over his head. It was night when he arrived and Aunt Sally went at once to an old brick oven built into the wall of the kitchen and took out a bag. "There it is," she said. The whole affair was part of the day's work for her in those days.

Gamblers at the tables in some of the rooms upstairs, lurking couples, from the old patio below the fragrance of growing things.

When she was fifty, Aunt Sally had got enough and had put them all out. She did not stay in the way of sin too long and she never went in too deep, like that Moll Flanders, and so she was all right and sitting pretty. "They wanted to gamble and drink and play with the ladies. The ladies liked it all right. I never saw none of them come in protesting too much. The worst was in the morning when they went away. They looked so sheepish and guilty. If they felt that way, what made them come? If I took a man, you bet I'd want him and no monkey-business or nothing doing.

"I got a little tired of all of them, that's the truth." Aunt Sally laughed. "But that wasn't until I had got what I went after. Oh, pshaw, they took up too much of my time, after I got enough to be safe."

Aunt Sally is now sixty-five. If you like her and she likes you she will let you sit with her in her patio gossiping of the old times, of the old river days. Perhaps—well, you see there is still something of the French influence at work in New Orleans, a sort of matter-of-factness about life—what I started to say is that if you know Aunt Sally and she likes you, and if, by chance, your lady likes the smell of flowers growing in a patio at night—really, I am going a bit too far. I only meant to suggest that Aunt Sally at sixty-five is not harsh. She is a motherly soul.

We sat in the garden talking, the little Southern poet, Aunt Sally and myself—or rather they talked and I listened. The Southerner's great-grandfather was English, a younger son, and he came over here to make his fortune as a planter, and did it. Once he and his sons owned several great plantations with slaves, but now his father had but a few hundred acres left, about one of the old houses—somewhere over in Alabama. The land is heavily mortgaged and most of it has not been under cultivation for years. Negro labor is growing more and more expensive and unsatisfactory since so many Negroes have run off to Chicago, and the poet's father and the one brother at home are not much good at working the land. "We aren't strong enough and we don't know how," the poet said.

The Southerner had come to New Orleans to see Fred, to talk with Fred about poetry, but Fred was out of town. I could only walk about with him, help him drink his home-made whisky. Already I had taken nearly a dozen drinks. In the morning I would have a headache.

I drew within myself, listening while David and Aunt Sally talked. The Chinaberry tree had been so and so many years growing—she spoke of it as she might have spoken of a daughter. "It had a lot of different sicknesses when it was young, but it pulled through." Someone had built a high wall on one side of her patio so that the climbing plants did not get as much sunlight as they needed. The banana plants, however, did very well and now the Chinaberry tree was big and strong enough to take care of itself. She kept giving David drinks of whisky and he talked.

He told her of the place in his leg where something, a bone perhaps, pressed on the nerve, and of the place on his left cheek. A silver plate had been set under the skin. She touched the spot with her fat old fingers. The moonlight fell softly down on the patio floor. "I can't sleep except somewhere out of doors," David said.

He explained how that, at home on his father's plantation, he had to be thinking all day whether or not he would be able to sleep at night.

"I go to bed and then I get up. There is always a bottle of whisky on the table downstairs and I take three or four drinks. Then I go out doors." Often very nice things happened.

"In the fall it's best," he said. "You see the niggers are making molasses." Every Negro cabin on the place had a little clump of ground back of it where cane grew and in the fall the Negroes were making their 'lasses. "I take the bottle in my hand and go into the fields, unseen by the niggers. Having the bottle with me, that way, I drink a good deal and then lie down on the ground. The mosquitoes bite me some, but I don't mind much. I reckon I get drunk enough not to mind. The little pain makes a kind of rhythm for the great pain—like poetry.

"In a kind of shed the niggers are making the 'lasses, that is to say, pressing the juice out of the cane and boiling it down. They keep singing as they work. In a few years now I reckon our family won't have any land. The banks could take it now if they wanted it. They don't want it. It would be too much trouble for them to manage, I reckon.

"In the fall, at night, the niggers are pressing the cane. Our niggers live pretty much on 'lasses and grits.

"They like working at night and I'm glad they do. There is an old mule going round and round in a circle and beside the press a pile of the dry cane. Niggers come, men and women, old and young. They build a fire outside the shed. The old mule goes round and round.

"The niggers sing. They laugh and shout. Sometimes the young niggers with their gals make love on the dry cane pile. I can hear it rattle.

"I have come out of the big house, me and my bottle, and I creep along, low on the ground, 'til I get up close. There I lie. I'm a little drunk. It all makes me happy. I can sleep some, on the ground like that, when the niggers are singing, when no one knows I'm there.

"I could sleep here, on these bricks here," David said, pointing to where the shadows cast by the broad leaves of the banana plants were broadest and deepest.

He got up from his chair and went limping, dragging one foot after the other, across the patio and lay down on the bricks.

For a long time Aunt Sally and I sat looking at each other, saying nothing, and presently she made a sign with her fat finger and we crept away into the house.

"I'll let you out at the front door. You let him sleep, right where he is," she said. In spite of her huge bulk and her age she walked across the patio floor as soft as a kitten. Beside her I felt awkward and uncertain. When we had got inside she whispered to me. She had some champagne left from the old days, hidden away somewhere in the old house. "I'm going to send a magnum up to his dad when he goes home," she explained.

She, it seemed, was very happy, having him there, drunk and asleep on the brick floor of the patio. "We used to have some good men come here in the old days too," she said. As we went into the house through the kitchen door I had looked back at David, asleep now in the heavy shadows at a corner of the wall. There was no doubt he also was happy, had been happy ever since I had brought him into the presence of Aunt Sally. What a small huddled figure of a man he looked, lying thus on the brick, under the night sky, in the deep shadows of the banana plants.

I went into the house and out at the front door and into a dark narrow street, thinking. Well, I was, after all, a Northern man. It was possible Aunt Sally had become completely Southern, being down here so long.

I remembered that it was the chief boast of her life that once she had shaken hands with John L. Sullivan and that she had known P. T. Barnum.

"I knew Dave Gears. You mean to tell me you don't know who Dave Gears was? Why, he was one of the biggest gamblers we ever had in this city."

As for David and his poetry—it is in the manner of Shelley. "If I could write like Shelley I would be happy. I wouldn't care what happened to me," he had said during our walk of the early part of the evening.

I went along enjoying my thoughts. The street was dark and occasionally I laughed. A notion had come to me. It kept dancing in my head and I thought it very delicious. It had something to do with aristocrats, with such people as Aunt Sally and David. "Lordy," I thought, "maybe I do understand them a little. I'm from the Middle West myself and it seems we can produce our aristocrats too." I kept thinking of Aunt Sally and of my native state, Ohio. "Lordy, I hope she comes from up there, but I don't think I had better inquire too closely into her past," I said to myself, as I went smiling away into the soft smoky night.

# Death in the Woods

### EDITOR'S NOTE

Anderson rewrote the story "Death in the Woods" several times until he was at last content with the version which gave the title to his last book of selected stories (1933). As Paul Rosenfeld observed in his introduction to *The Sherwood Anderson Reader* (1947), among Anderson's favorite books was Turgenev's *Memoirs of a Sportsman,* and he quoted Anderson's remark that Turgenev's writings were "like low fine music." It is more than likely that among other examples Anderson held in mind as he rewrote "Death in the Woods," the example of Turgenev's long short story, "A Lear of the Steppes," was not forgotten. Turgenev's "low fine music" sounds throughout it, and the view of the peasant in Turgenev's "Lear" has the same clarity that Anderson achieved in his description of the old woman who met her death in the woods. Turgenev's story was also a story-teller's story, and its overtones are not unlike those over which Anderson had masterly control. Those who read Anderson for his "universal" qualities, qualities which make him seem European as well as American have their proof of what they have discovered in "Death in the Woods."

SHE was an old woman and lived on a farm near the town in which I lived. All country and small-town people have seen such old women, but no one knows much about them. Such an old woman comes into town driving an old worn-out horse or she comes afoot carrying a basket. She may own a few hens and have eggs to sell. She brings them in a basket and takes them to a grocer. There she trades them in. She gets some salt pork and some beans. Then she gets a pound or two of sugar and some flour.

Afterwards she goes to the butcher's and asks for some dog-meat. She may spend ten or fifteen cents, but when she does she asks for something. Formerly the butchers gave liver to anyone who wanted to carry it away. In our family we were always having it. Once one of my brothers got a whole cow's liver at the slaughterhouse near the fair grounds in our town. We had it until we were sick of it. It never cost a cent. I have hated the thought of it ever since.

The old farm woman got some liver and a soup-bone. She never visited with anyone, and as soon as she got what she wanted she lit out for home. It made quite a load for such an old body. No one gave her a lift. People drive right down a road and never notice an old woman like that.

There was such an old woman who used to come into town past our house one summer and fall when I was a young boy and was sick with what was called inflammatory rheumatism. She went home later carrying a heavy pack on her back. Two or three large gaunt-looking dogs followed at her heels.

The old woman was nothing special. She was one of the nameless ones that hardly anyone knows, but she got into my thoughts. I have just suddenly now, after all these years, remembered her and what happened. It is a story. Her name was Grimes, and she lived with her husband and son in a small unpainted house on the bank of a small creek four miles from town.

The husband and son were a tough lot. Although the son was but twenty-one, he had already served a term in jail. It was whispered about that the woman's husband stole horses and ran them off to some other county. Now and then, when a horse turned up missing, the man had also disappeared. No one ever caught him. Once, when I was loafing at Tom Whitehead's livery-barn, the man came there and sat on the bench in front. Two or three other men were there, but no one spoke to him. He sat for a few minutes and then got up and went away. When he was leaving he turned around and stared at the men. There was a look of defiance in his eyes. "Well, I have tried to be friendly. You don't want to talk to me. It has been so wherever I have gone in this town. If, some day, one of your fine horses turns up missing, well, then what?" He did not say anything actually. "I'd like to bust one of you on the jaw," was about what his eyes said. I remember how the look in his eyes made me shiver.

The old man belonged to a family that had had money once. His name was Jake Grimes. It all comes back clearly now. His father, John Grimes, had owned a sawmill when the country was new, and had made money. Then he got to drinking and running after women. When he died there wasn't much left.

Jake blew in the rest. Pretty soon there wasn't any more lumber to cut and his land was nearly all gone.

He got his wife off a German farmer, for whom he went to work one June day in the wheat harvest. She was a young thing then and scared to death. You see, the farmer was up to something with the girl—she was, I think, a bound girl and his wife had her suspicions. She took it out on the girl when the man wasn't around. Then, when the wife had to go off to town for supplies, the farmer got after her. She told young Jake that nothing really ever happened, but he didn't know whether to believe it or not.

He got her pretty easy himself, the first time he was out with her. He wouldn't have married her if the German farmer hadn't tried to tell him where to get off. He got her to go riding with him in his buggy one night when he was threshing on the place, and then he came for her the next Sunday night.

She managed to get out of the house without her employer's seeing, but when she was getting into the buggy he showed up. It was almost dark, and he just popped up suddenly at the horse's head. He grabbed the horse by the bridle and Jake got out his buggy-whip.

They had it out all right! The German was a tough one. Maybe he didn't care whether his wife knew or not. Jake hit him over the face and shoulders with the buggy-whip, but the horse got to acting up and he had to get out.

Then the two men went for it. The girl didn't see it. The horse started to run away and went nearly a mile down the road before the girl got him stopped. Then she managed to tie him to a tree beside the road. (I wonder how I know all this. It must have stuck in my mind from small-town tales when I was a boy.) Jake found her there after he got through with the German. She was huddled up in the buggy seat, crying, scared to death. She told Jake a lot of stuff, how the German had tried to get her, how he chased her once into the barn, how another time, when they happened to be alone in the house together, he tore her dress open clear down the front. The German, she said, might have got her that time if he hadn't heard his old woman drive in at the gate. She had been off to town for supplies. Well, she would be putting the horse in the barn. The German managed to sneak off to the fields without his wife seeing. He told the girl he would kill her if she told. What could she do? She told a lie about ripping her dress in the barn when she was feeding the stock. I remember now that she was a bound girl and did not know where her father and mother were. Maybe she did not have any father. You know what I mean.

Such bound children were often enough cruelly treated. They were children who had no parents, slaves really. There were very few orphan homes then. They were legally bound into some home. It was a matter of pure luck how it came out.

## II

She married Jake and had a son and daughter, but the daughter died.

Then she settled down to feed stock. That was her job. At the German's place she had cooked the food for the German and his wife. The wife was a strong woman with big hips and worked most of the time in the fields with her husband. She fed them and fed the cows in the barn, fed the pigs, the horses and the chickens. Every moment of every day, as a young girl, was spent feeding something.

Then she married Jake Grimes and he had to be fed. She was a slight thing, and when she had been married for three or four years, and after the two children were born, her slender shoulders became stooped.

Jake always had a lot of big dogs around the house, that stood near the unused sawmill near the creek. He was always trading horses when he wasn't stealing something and had a lot of poor bony ones about. Also he kept three or four pigs and a cow. They were all pastured in the few acres left of the Grimes place and Jake did little enough work.

He went into debt for a threshing outfit and ran it for several years, but it did not pay. People did not trust him. They were afraid he would steal the grain at night. He had to go a long way off to get work and it cost too much to get there. In the winter he hunted and cut a little firewood, to be sold in some nearby town. When the son grew up he was just like the father. They got drunk together. If there wasn't anything to eat in the house when they came home the old man gave his old woman a cut over the head. She had a few chickens of her own and had to kill one of them in a hurry. When they were all killed she wouldn't have any eggs to sell when she went to town, and then what would she do?

She had to scheme all her life about getting things fed, getting the pigs fed so they would grow fat and could be butchered in the fall. When they were butchered her husband took most of the meat off to town and sold it. If he did not do it first the boy did. They fought sometimes and when they fought the old woman stood aside trembling.

She had got the habit of silence anyway—that was fixed. Sometimes, when she began to look old—she wasn't forty yet—and when the husband and son were both off, trading horses or drinking or hunting or stealing, she went around the house and the barnyard muttering to herself.

How was she going to get everything fed?—that was her problem. The dogs had to be fed. There wasn't enough hay in the barn for the horses and the cow. If she didn't feed the chickens how could they lay eggs? Without eggs to sell how could she get things in town, things she had to have to keep the life of the farm going? Thank heaven, she did not have to feed her husband—in a certain way. That hadn't lasted long after their marriage and after the babies came. Where he went on his long trips she did not know. Sometimes he was gone from home for weeks, and after the boy grew up they went off together.

They left everything at home for her to manage and she had no money. She knew no one. No one ever talked to her in town. When it was winter she had to gather sticks of wood for her fire, had to try to keep the stock fed with very little grain.

The stock in the barn cried to her hungrily, the dogs followed her about. In the winter the hens laid few enough eggs. They huddled in the corners of the barn and she kept watching them. If a hen lays an egg in the barn in the winter and you do not find it, it freezes and breaks.

One day in winter the old woman went off to town with a few eggs and the dogs followed her. She did not get started until nearly three o'clock and the snow was heavy. She hadn't been feeling very well for several days and so she went muttering along, scantily clad, her shoulders stooped. She had an old grain bag in which she carried her eggs, tucked away down in the bottom. There weren't many of them, but in winter the price of eggs is up. She would get a little meat in exchange for the eggs, some salt pork, a little sugar, and some coffee perhaps. It might be the butcher would give her a piece of liver.

When she had got to town and was trading in her eggs the dogs lay by the door outside. She did pretty well, got the things she needed, more than she had hoped. Then she went to the butcher and he gave her some liver and some dog-meat.

It was the first time anyone had spoken to her in a friendly way for a long time. The butcher was alone in his shop when she came in and was annoyed by the thought of such a sick-looking old woman out on such a day. It was bitter cold and the snow, that had let up during the afternoon, was falling again. The butcher said something about her husband and her son, swore at them, and the old woman stared at him, a look of mild surprise in her eyes as he talked. He said that if either the husband or the son were going to get any of the liver or the heavy bones with scraps of meat hanging to them that he had put into the grain bag, he'd see him starve first.

Starve, eh? Well, things had to be fed. Men had to be fed, and the horses that weren't any good but maybe could be traded off, and the poor thin cow that hadn't given any milk for three months.

Horses, cows, pigs, dogs, men.

III

The old woman had to get back before darkness came if she could. The dogs followed at her heels, sniffing at the heavy grain bag she had fastened on her back. When she got to the edge of town she stopped by a fence and tied the bag on her back with a piece of rope she had carried in her dress-pocket for just that purpose. That was an easier way to carry it. Her arms ached. It was hard when she had to crawl over fences and once she fell over and landed in the snow. The dogs went frisking about. She had to struggle to get to her feet again, but she made it. The point of climbing over the fences was that there was a short cut over a hill and through a woods. She might have gone around by the road, but it was a mile farther that way. She was afraid she couldn't make it. And then, besides, the stock had to be fed. There was a little hay left and a little corn. Perhaps her husband and son would bring some home when they came. They had driven off in the only buggy the Grimes family had, a rickety thing, a rickety horse hitched to the buggy, two other rickety horses led by halters. They were going to trade horses, get a little money if they could. They might come home drunk. It would be well to have something in the house when they came back.

The son had an affair on with a woman at the county seat, fifteen miles away. She was a rough enough woman, a tough one. Once, in the summer, the son had brought her to the house. Both she and the son had been drinking. Jake Grimes was away and the son and his woman ordered the old woman about like a servant. She didn't mind much; she was used to it. Whatever happened she never said anything. That was her way of getting along. She had managed that way when she was a young girl at the German's and ever since she had married Jake. That time her son brought his woman to the house they stayed all night, sleeping together just as though they were married. It hadn't shocked the old woman, not much. She had got past being shocked early in life.

With the pack on her back she went painfully along across an open field, wading in the deep snow, and got into the woods.

There was a path, but it was hard to follow. Just beyond the top of the hill, where the woods was thickest, there was a small clearing. Had someone once thought of building a house there? The clearing was as large as a building lot in town, large enough for a house and a garden. The path ran along the side of the clearing, and when she got there the old woman sat down to rest at the foot of a tree.

It was a foolish thing to do. When she got herself placed, the pack against the tree's trunk, it was nice, but what about getting up again? She worried about that for a moment and then quietly closed her eyes.

She must have slept for a time. When you are about so cold you can't get any colder. The afternoon grew a little warmer and the snow came thicker than ever. Then after a time the weather cleared. The moon even came out.

There were four Grimes dogs that had followed Mrs. Grimes into town, all tall gaunt fellows. Such men as Jake Grimes and his son always keep just such dogs. They kick and abuse them, but they stay. The Grimes dogs, in order to keep from starving, had to do a lot of foraging for themselves, and they had been at it while the old woman slept with her back to the tree at the side of the clearing. They had been chasing rabbits in the woods and in adjoining fields and in their ranging had picked up three other farm dogs.

After a time all the dogs came back to the clearing. They were excited about something. Such nights, cold and clear and with a moon, do things to dogs. It may be that some old instinct, come down from the time when they were wolves and ranged the woods in packs on winter nights, comes back into them.

The dogs in the clearing, before the old woman, had caught two or three rabbits and their immediate hunger had been satisfied. They began to play, running in circles in the clearing. Round and round they ran, each dog's nose at the tail of the next dog. In the clearing, under the snow-laden trees and under the wintry moon they made a strange picture, running thus silently, in a circle their running had beaten in the soft snow. The dogs made no sound. They ran around and around in the circle.

It may have been that the old woman saw them doing that before she died. She may have awakened once or twice and looked at the strange sight with dim old eyes.

She wouldn't be very cold now, just drowsy. Life hangs on a long time. Perhaps the old woman was out of her head. She may have dreamed of her girlhood, at the German's, and before that, when she was a child and before her mother lit out and left her.

Her dreams couldn't have been very pleasant. Not many pleasant things had happened to her. Now and then one of the Grimes dogs left the running circle and came to stand before her. The dog thrust his face close to her face. His red tongue was hanging out.

The running of the dogs may have been a kind of death ceremony. It may have been that the primitive instinct of the wolf, having been aroused in the dogs by the night and the running, made them somehow afraid.

"Now we are no longer wolves. We are dogs, the servants of men. Keep alive, man! When man dies we become wolves again."

When one of the dogs came to where the old woman sat with her back against the tree and thrust his nose close to her face he seemed satisfied and went back to run with the pack. All the Grimes dogs did it at some time during the evening, before she died. I knew all about it afterward, when I grew to be a man, because once in a woods in Illinois, on another winter night, I saw a pack of dogs act just like that. The dogs were waiting for me to die as they had waited for the old woman that night when I was a child, but when it happened to me I was a young man and had no intention whatever of dying.

The old woman died softly and quietly. When she was dead and when one of the Grimes dogs had come to her and had found her dead all the dogs stopped running.

They gathered about her.

Well, she was dead now. She had fed the Grimes dogs when she was alive, what about now?

There was the pack on her back, the grain bag containing the piece of salt pork, the liver the butcher had given her, the dog-meat, the soup bones. The butcher in town, having been suddenly overcome with a feeling of pity, had loaded her grain bag heavily. It had been a big haul for the old woman.

It was a big haul for the dogs now.

## IV

One of the Grimes dogs sprang suddenly out from among the others and began worrying the pack on the old woman's back. Had the dogs really been wolves that one would have been the leader of the pack. What he did, all the others did.

All of them sank their teeth into the grain bag the old woman had fastened with ropes to her back.

They dragged the old woman's body out into the open clearing. The worn-out dress was quickly torn from her shoulders. When she was found, a day or two later, the dress had been torn from her body clear to the hips, but the dogs had not touched her body. They had got the meat out of the grain bag, that was all. Her body was frozen stiff when it was found, and the shoulders were so narrow and the body so slight that in death it looked like the body of some charming young girl.

Such things happened in towns of the Middle West, on farms near town, when I was a boy. A hunter out after rabbits found the old woman's body and did not touch it. Something, the beaten round path in the little snow-covered clearing, the silence of the place, the place where the dogs had worried the body trying to pull the grain bag away or tear it open—something startled the man and he hurried off to town.

I was in Main Street with one of my brothers who was town newsboy and who was taking the afternoon papers to the stores. It was almost night.

The hunter came into a grocery and told his story. Then he went to a hardware shop and into a drugstore. Men began to gather on the sidewalks. Then they started out along the road to the place in the woods.

My brother should have gone on about his business of distributing papers but he didn't. Everyone was going to the woods. The undertaker went and the town marshal. Several men got on a dray and rode out to where the path left the road and went into the woods, but the horses weren't very sharply shod and slid about on the slippery roads. They made no better time than those of us who walked.

The town marshal was a large man whose leg had been injured in the Civil War. He carried a heavy cane and limped rapidly along the road. My brother and I followed at his heels, and as we went other men and boys joined the crowd.

It had grown dark by the time we got to where the old woman had left the road but the moon had come out. The marshal was thinking there might have been a murder. He kept asking the hunter questions. The hunter went along with his gun across his shoulders, a dog following at his heels. It isn't often a rabbit hunter has a chance to be so conspicuous. He was taking full advantage of it, leading the procession with the town marshal. "I didn't see any wounds. She was a beautiful young girl. Her face was buried in the snow. No, I didn't know her." As a matter of fact, the hunter had not looked closely at the body. He had been frightened. She might have been murdered and someone might spring out from behind a tree and murder him. In a woods, in the late afternoon, when the trees are all bare and there is white snow on the ground, when all is silent, something creepy steals over the mind and body. If something strange or uncanny has happened in the neighborhood all you think about is getting away from there as fast as you can.

The crowd of men and boys had got to where the old woman had crossed the field and went, following the marshal and the hunter, up the slight incline and into the woods.

My brother and I were silent. He had his bundle of papers in a bag slung across his shoulder. When he got back to town he would have to go on distributing his papers before he went home to supper. If I went along, as he had no doubt already determined I should, we would both be late. Either mother or our older sister would have to warm our supper.

Well, we would have something to tell. A boy did not get such a chance very often. It was lucky we just happened to go into the grocery when the hunter came in. The hunter was a country fellow. Neither of us had ever seen him before.

Now the crowd of men and boys had got to the clearing. Darkness comes quickly on such winter nights, but the full moon made everything clear. My brother and I stood near the tree, beneath which the old woman had died.

She did not look old, lying there in that light, frozen and still. One of the men turned her over in the snow and I saw everything. My body trembled with some strange mystical feeling and so did my brother's. It might have been the cold.

Neither of us had ever seen a woman's body before. It may have been the snow, clinging to the frozen flesh, that made it look so white and lovely, so like marble. No woman had come with the party from town; but one of the men, he was the town blacksmith, took off his overcoat and spread it over her. Then he gathered her into his arms and started off to town, all the others following silently. At that time no one knew who she was.

## V

I had seen everything, had seen the oval in the snow, like a miniature race track, where the dogs had run, had seen how the men were mystified, had seen the white bare young-looking shoulders, had heard the whispered comments of the men.

The men were simply mystified. They took the body to the undertaker's, and when the blacksmith, the hunter, the marshal and several others had got inside they closed the door. If father had been there perhaps he could have got in, but we boys couldn't.

I went with my brother to distribute the rest of his papers and when we got home it was my brother who told the story.

I kept silent and went to bed early. It may have been I was not satisfied with the way he told it.

Later, in the town, I must have heard other fragments of the old woman's story. She was recognized the next day and there was an investigation.

The husband and son were found somewhere and brought to town and there was an attempt to connect them with the woman's death, but it did not work. They had perfect enough alibis.

However, the town was against them. They had to get out. Where they went I never heard.

I remember only the picture there in the forest, the men standing about, the naked girlish-looking figure, face down in the snow, the tracks made by the running dogs and the clear cold winter sky above. White fragments of clouds were drifting across the sky. They went racing across the little open space among the trees.

The scene in the forest had become for me, without my knowing it, the foundation for the real story I am now trying to tell. The fragments, you see, had to be picked up slowly, long afterwards.

Things happened. When I was a young man I worked on the farm of a German. The hired-girl was afraid of her employer. The farmer's wife hated her.

I saw things at that place. Once later, I had a half-uncanny, mystical adventure with dogs in an Illinois forest on a clear, moonlit winter night. When I was a schoolboy, and on a summer day, I went with a boy friend out along a creek some miles from town and came to the house where the old woman had lived. No one had lived in the house since her death. The doors were broken from the hinges; the window lights were all broken. As the boy and I stood in the road outside, two dogs, just roving farm dogs no doubt, came running around the corner of the house. The dogs were tall, gaunt fellows and came down to the fence and glared through at us, standing in the road.

The whole thing, the story of the old woman's death, was to me as I grew older like music heard from far off. The notes had to be picked up slowly one at a time. Something had to be understood.

The woman who died was one destined to feed animal life. Anyway, that is all she ever did. She was feeding animal life before she was born, as a child, as a young woman working on the farm of the German, after she married, when she grew old and when she died. She fed animal life in cows, in chickens, in pigs, in horses, in dogs, in men. Her daughter had died in childhood and with her one son she had no articulate relations. On the night when she died she was hurrying homeward, bearing on her body food for animal life.

She died in the clearing in the woods and even after her death continued feeding animal life.

You see it is likely that, when my brother told the story, that night when we got home and my mother and sister sat listening, I did not think he got the point. He was too young and so was I. A thing so complete has its own beauty.

I shall not try to emphasize the point. I am only explaining why I was dissatisfied then and have been ever since. I speak of that only that you may understand why I have been impelled to try to tell the simple story over again.

# MEN AND WOMEN

## EDITOR'S NOTE

In *Horses and Men* and in *Sherwood Anderson's Notebook* there are brief lyrical portraits of writers, Dreiser, Gertrude Stein, Ring Lardner, Paul Rosenfeld, Sinclair Lewis. These portraits are, as he properly called them, "impressions"; and in his remarks on Ring Lardner what he has to say about Mark Twain very nearly overshadows the subject of the sketch. The "impressions" are his moments of glancing at his subjects, and in that glance perceiving something that he alone has the candor to express. In *Sherwood Anderson's Memoirs* there is another portrait, titled "The Death of D. H. Lawrence"—and again one receives a strange "shock of recognition." It also shows Anderson's courtesy to his fellow writers, and his chivalry—a chivalry, by the way, which he extended also to his treatment of women in his novels, stories, and autobiographies. It is almost an understatement to say that Anderson was no prude when he discussed and portrayed sexual relationships, an affinity which he held with George Moore and D. H. Lawrence, but it is equally significant that his candor never modified his chivalrous attitude in his personal relationships with men and women. It was that chivalrous quality in Anderson which Gertrude Stein in writing of him called "sweetness," a chivalry removed from all taint of hypocrisy.

# Four American Impressions:

## Gertrude Stein, Paul Rosenfeld, Ring Lardner, Sinclair Lewis[1]

ONE who thinks a great deal about people and what they are up to in the world comes inevitably in time to relate them to experiences connected with his own life. The round hard apples in this old orchard are the breasts of my beloved. The curved round hill in the distance is the body of my beloved, lying asleep. I cannot avoid practicing this trick of lifting people out of the spots on which in actual life they stand and transferring them to what seems at the moment some more fitting spot in the fanciful world.

And I get also a kind of aroma from people. They are green healthy growing things or they have begun to decay. There is something in this man, to whom I have just talked, that has sent me away from him smiling and in an odd way pleased with myself. Why has this other man, although his words were kindly and his deeds apparently good, spread a cloud over my sky?

In my own boyhood in an Ohio town I went about delivering newspapers at kitchen doors, and there were certain houses to which I went—old brick houses with immense old-fashioned kitchens—in which I loved to linger. On Saturday mornings I sometimes managed to collect a fragrant cooky at such a place but there was

[1] These sketches were written in 1919 and published in *The New Republic.*

something else that held me. Something got into my mind connected with the great light kitchens and the women working in them that came sharply back when, last year, I went to visit an American woman, Miss Gertrude Stein, in her own large room in the house at 27 rue de Fleurus in Paris. In the great kitchen of my fanciful world in which, ever since that morning, I have seen Miss Stein standing there is a most sweet and gracious aroma. Along the walls are many shining pots and pans, and there are innumerable jars of fruits, jellies and preserves. Something is going on in the great room, for Miss Stein is a worker in words with the same loving touch in her strong fingers that was characteristic of the women of the kitchens of the brick houses in the town of my boyhood. She is an American woman of the old sort, one who cares for the handmade goodies and who scorns the factory-made foods, and in her own great kitchen she is making something with her materials, something sweet to the tongue and fragrant to the nostrils.

That her materials are the words of our English speech and that we do not, most of us, know or care too much what she is up to does not greatly matter to me. The impression I wish now to give you of her is of one very intent and earnest in a matter most of us have forgotten. She is laying word against word, relating sound to sound, feeling for the taste, the smell, the rhythm of the individual word. She is attempting to do something for the writers of our English speech that may be better understood after a time, and she is not in a hurry.

And I have always that picture of the woman in the great kitchen of words, standing there by a table, clean, strong, with red cheeks and sturdy legs, always quietly and smilingly at work. If her smile has in it something of the mystery, to the male at least, of the Mona Lisa, I remember that the women in the kitchens on the wintry mornings wore often that same smile.

She is making new, strange and to my ears sweet combinations of words. As an American writer I admire her because she, in her person, represents something sweet and healthy in our American life, and because I have a kind of undying faith that what she is up to in her word kitchen in Paris is of more importance to writers of English than the work of many of our more easily understood and more widely accepted word artists.

## II

When it comes to our Mr. Ring Lardner, here is something else again. Here is another word fellow, one who cares about the words of our American speech and who is perhaps doing more than any other American to give new force to the words of our everyday life.

There is something I think I understand about Mr. Ring Lardner. The truth is that I believe there is something the matter with him and I have a fancy I know what it is. He is afraid of the highbrows. They scare him to death. I wonder why. For it is true that there is often, in a paragraph of his, more understanding of life, more human sympathy, more salty wisdom than in hundreds of pages of, say Mr. Sinclair Lewis's dreary prose—and I am sure Mr. Lewis would not hesitate to outface any highbrow in his lair.

I said that I thought I knew what was the matter with Mr. Ring Lardner. He comes from out in my country, from just such another town as the one in which I spent my own boyhood, and I remember certain shy lads of my own town who always made it a point to consort mostly with the town toughs—and for a reason. There was in them something extremely sensitive that did not want to be hurt. Even to mention the fact that there was in such a one a real love of life, a quick sharp stinging hunger for beauty, would have sent a blush of shame to his cheeks. He was intent upon covering up, concealing from everyone, at any cost, the shy hungry child he was carrying about within himself.

And I always see our Mr. Ring Lardner as such a fellow. He is covering up, sticking to the gang, keeping out of sight. And that is all right too, if in secret and in his suburban home he is really using his talent for sympathetic understanding of life, if in secret he is being another Mark Twain and working in secret on his own *Huckleberry Finn.* Mark Twain wrote and was proclaimed for writing his *Innocents Abroad, Following the Equator, Roughing It,* etc., etc., and was during his lifetime most widely recognized for such secondary work. And Mark Twain was just such another shy lad, bluffed by the highbrows—and even the glorious Mark had no more sensitive understanding of the fellow in the street, in the hooch joint, the ball-park and the city suburb than our Mr. Ring Lardner.

III

Which brings me to a man who, it seems to me, of all our American writers, is the one who is most unafraid, Mr. Paul Rosenfeld. Here is an American writer actually unashamed of being fine and sensitive in his work. To me it seems that he has really freed himself from both the high and the low brows and has made of himself a real aristocrat among writers of prose.

To be sure, to the man in the street, accustomed to the sloppiness of hurried newspaper writing, the Rosenfeld prose is sometimes difficult. His vocabulary is immense and he cares very, very much for just the shade of meaning he is striving to convey. Miss Jean Heap recently spoke of him as "our well-dressed writer of prose," and I should think Paul Rosenfeld would not too much resent the connotations of that. For, after all, Rosenfeld is our man of distinction, the American, it seems to me, who is unafraid and unashamed to live for the things of the spirit as expressed in the arts. I get him as the man walking cleanly and boldly and really accepting, daring to accept, the obligations of the civilized man. To my ears that acceptance has made his prose sound clearly and sweetly across many barren fields. To me it is often like soft bells heard ringing at evening across fields long let go to the weeds of carelessness and the general slam-it-through-ness of so much of our American writing.

## IV

Of the four American writers concerning whose handling of our speech I have had the temerity to express my own feeling there is left Mr. Sinclair Lewis.

The texture of the prose written by Mr. Lewis gives me but faint joy and I cannot escape the conviction that for some reason Lewis has himself found but little joy, either in life among us or in his own effort to channel his reactions to our life into prose. There can be no doubt that this man, with his sharp journalistic nose for news of the outer surface of our lives, has found out a lot of things about us and the way we live in our towns and cities, but I am very sure that in the life of every man woman and child in the country there are forces at work that seem to have escaped the notice of Mr. Lewis. Mr. Ring Lardner has seen them and in his writing there is sometimes real laughter, but one has the feeling that Lewis never laughs at all, that he is in an odd way too serious about something to laugh.

For after all, even in Gopher Prairie or in Indianapolis, Indiana, boys go swimming in the creeks on summer afternoons, shadows play at evening on factory walls, old men dig angleworms and go fishing together, love comes to at least a few men and women, and everything else failing, the baseball club comes from a neighboring town and Tom Robinson gets a home run. That's something. There is an outlook on life across which even the cry of a child, choked to death by its own mother, would be something. Life in our American towns and cities is barren enough and there are enough people saying that with the growth of industrialism it has become continually more and more ugly, but Mr. Paul Rosenfeld and Mr. Ring Lardner apparently do not find it altogether barren and ugly. For them and for a growing number of men and women in America there is something like a dawn that Mr. Lewis has apparently sensed but little, for there is so little sense of it in the texture of his prose. Reading Mr. Sinclair Lewis, one comes inevitably to the conclusion that here is a man writing who, wanting passionately to love the life about him, cannot bring himself to do so, and who, wanting perhaps to see beauty descend upon our lives like a rainstorm, has become blind to the minor beauties our lives hold.

And is it not just this sense of dreary spiritual death in the man's work that is making it so widely read? To one who is himself afraid to live there is, I am sure, a kind of joy in seeing other men as dead. In my own feeling for the man from whose pen has come all of this prose over which there are so few lights and shades, I have come at last to sense, most of all, the man fighting terrifically and ineffectually for a thing about which he really does care. There is a kind of fighter living inside Mr. Sinclair Lewis and there is, even in this dull, unlighted prose of his, a kind of dawn coming. In the dreary ocean of this prose, islands begin to appear. In *Babbitt* there are moments when the people of whom he writes, with such amazing attention to the outer details of lives, begin to think and feel a little, and with the coming of life into his people a kind of nervous, hurried beauty and life flits, like a lantern carried by a night watchman past the window of a factory as one stands waiting and watching in a grim street on a night of December.

# Dreiser

*Heavy, heavy, hangs over thy head,*
*Fine, or superfine?*

THEODORE DREISER is old—he is very, very old. I do not know how many years he has lived, perhaps forty, perhaps fifty, but he is very old. Something gray and bleak and hurtful, that has been in the world perhaps forever, is personified in him.

When Dreiser is gone men shall write books, many of them, and in the books they shall write there will be so many of the qualities Dreiser lacks. The new, the younger men shall have a sense of humor, and everyone knows Dreiser has no sense of humor. More than that, American prose writers shall have grace, lightness of touch, a dream of beauty breaking through the husks of life.

O, those who follow him shall have many things that Dreiser does not have. That is a part of the wonder and beauty of Theodore Dreiser, the things that others shall have, because of him.

Long ago, when he was editor of the *Delineator*, Dreiser went one day, with a woman friend, to visit an orphan asylum. The woman once told me the story of that afternoon in the big, ugly gray building, with Dreiser, looking heavy and lumpy and old, sitting on a platform, folding and refolding his pocket-handkerchief and watching the children—all in their little uniforms, trooping in.

"The tears ran down his cheeks and he shook his head," the woman said, and that is a real picture of Theodore Dreiser. He is old in spirit and he does not know what to do with life, so he tells about it as he sees it, simply and honestly. The tears run down his cheeks and he folds and refolds the pocket-handkerchief and shakes his head.

Heavy, heavy, the feet of Theodore. How easy to pick some of his books to pieces, to laugh at him for so much of his heavy prose.

The feet of Theodore are making a path, the heavy brutal feet. They are tramping through the wilderness of lies, making a path. Presently the path will be a street, with great arches overhead and delicately carved spires piercing the sky. Along the street will run children, shouting, "Look at me. See what I and my fellows of the new day have done"—forgetting the heavy feet of Dreiser.

The fellows of the ink-pots, the prose writers in America who follow Dreiser, will have much to do that he has never done. Their road is long but, because of him, those who follow will never have to face the road through the wilderness of Puritan denial, the road that Dreiser faced alone.

*Heavy, heavy, hangs over thy head,*
*Fine, or superfine?*

# REPORTAGE AND EDITORIAL

# The American County Fair

EDITOR'S NOTE

*The American County Fair* appeared in paper covers (a limited edition of pamphlets) in 1930. Of impressionistic writers in America none has greater descriptive powers than Anderson at his best, particularly when he holds before the eyes of his readers the view of a racecourse, a Midwestern pastoral, an evening in New Orleans (as in "A Meeting South"), or a county fair. The scene in its descriptive detail takes on an unmistakable life of its own; it is not a "still life," but one with air and light between objects seen and heard—and between the very phrases of Anderson's prose.

IT IS an odd time in a town. The fair ground commonly is a deserted place. It stands on a hill.

The land rolls away. Now the fair is being held. From the grandstand, where you sit to watch the races, you can see, over a high board fence, into distant hills.

The fair is held sometimes at the end of August but sometimes not until late October or early November. It makes a difference in the color of the hills.

Hills are at their best when white farmhouses cling to their sides. Nature untouched by man is too terrible. It is too difficult of approach. You become terrorized. The pioneers, who go into lands where man has not been, must be very brave or very dull. Perhaps they are only dull.

You are always wanting man in nature—woman in nature. You can get it at the fair. What a place for pictures. You will do well, at the country fairs, not to draw too close.

What a scene it is. Suppose you go up into the high grandstand. There is the bright grandstand, yellow in the afternoon light. The hills in the distance are blue.

Thousands of cars are parked in a great field at the rear of the grandstand. A cloud of dust arises. Nowadays people come to a fair from two or three counties.

The shows are here—in the open space between the field where the cars are parked and the grandstand. There is the snake tamer, the fat woman, the hoochy-coochy girls, the woman buried alive, the man with the web feet and hands, a calf with two heads. The gamblers are out in force.

They have all sorts of little wheels. They are shrewd-looking, hard-faced young men and they have their women with them. The women whirl the wheels while the men implore the men in the crowd, begging them to come up and win money. Win money indeed. These men and women are young but already they know a thousand foxy tricks to get money.

The fair is something special in the county. In spite of all the talk about improving agriculture, etc., it is a pagan outbreak.

See the women going about, the girls from the towns and from the farms. They walk boldly. Now is the time to get yourself a man. They all feel that. It shows in the way they walk. It is in their eyes. They will stay at the fair all day and far into the night. They are tireless.

The men all act a little puzzled. They wander aimlessly about.

The state agricultural department has brought fine

cattle to be shown. Some of the rich farmers have also brought fine fat cattle, huge horses, sheep and pigs.

The older men go down to the sheds to look. They stand about and talk, spitting on the ground. The young fellows do not go and the women do not go.

The older women go into the buildings and sheds where women's work is shown. An amazing number of the older women are fat. Fat bodies rubbing against each other, fat still faces.

The children are tired, become tired early in the day. They cry. The tears make little streaks in the tiny dusty faces. The mothers carry the children into the field where the cars are parked and lay them on the car seats. They sleep there. When they waken they again cry.

Now it is time for the races. A bell rings. The judges of the races are in the judges' stand that is directly in front of the grandstand. There is a race starter who has a voice like an auctioneer. He shouts through a megaphone.

It is difficult to clear the track for the races. Thousands of people have gathered there. The starter of the races, with his megaphone, shouts, the county sheriff, a large man, appears and shouts. The people move back slowly, reluctantly.

And now, here are the horses—the trotters and pacers. This is something to wait for.

The horses are moving down the tracks, swiftly and smoothly. What has man done more noble than this?

He has developed these fine beasts.

They have been taught to go at a certain gait, the trot or pace, faster, faster, faster. They are hitched to little carts, very delicately made, and the driver sits up close to the horse. The moving flanks of the horse are almost in the driver's lap.

The drivers are young and old men. Some of them, many of them in fact, are quiet respectable men at other times during the year, excepting only in the fall when the fairs are being held. Now they shout, they lean forward over their horses.

There is no money to be made racing horses at the fairs. The horses cost too much. It costs too much to train them.

Professional trainers must be employed. There is feed to be bought, harness, racing carts and other equipment. The trainer's salary must be paid and there are grooms, in our part of the country a black for each horse.

The owners are country bankers, farmers, doctors and merchants.

The horses race for a purse of say two hundred dollars. A hundred dollars is given the winner and the other hundred is distributed between the second, third, and fourth horse.

And now the doctors, bankers, merchants, prosperous farmers have become something other than doctors, bankers, merchants, farmers. They have put on little gaily colored caps and gaily colored coats. The horses are brought out hitched to their carts.

The respectable citizen, who has become a jockey, is on the track, before the grandstand walking up and down.

Now the crowd is all attention. The shows are deserted, the band stops playing.

People crowd into the grandstand, they crowd to the fences.

The jockeys have mounted the little sulkies with the delicate bicycle wheels and the horses are being warmed up.

They dash up and down. The horses also are excited and the drivers are tense.

The drivers try to appear cool. After all this is dangerous business. These horses, so highly bred, so finely trained, sometimes lose their heads.

The horses must score down past the grandstand and the judges' stand until the race starter decides it is a fair start. Each driver tries to crowd to the front, to give his horse an advantage.

If it is not a fair start a bell rings and they must try again.

In the Grand Circuit, to which the fastest of all the trotters and pacers go, where the purses are larger, nearly all driving is done by professional drivers but at these little fairs—here the owner himself has a chance.

What would Mr. Harry Sinclair give if he could himself ride one of his beautiful thoroughbreds, or Mr. Harry Payne Whitney, or Mr. Bradley?

It can't be done. The rider of the thoroughbred must weigh almost nothing. He must be a mere slip of a boy.

On the Grand Circuit where the fastest of all trotters and pacers go the amount of money involved is large. They are racing for ten thousand dollars, not for two hundred.

But these men, these country bankers, doctors, lawyers, farmers, who are horse lovers, have also invested their money. The horses here are often but a few seconds slower than those on the Grand Circuit. Some of them are sons and daughters of great sires. At the stables, over there under that hill, you will hear names of kings bandied about "He is a son of Grayson Gravy 2.01 1/2. All the sons of that fellow go fast."

There is talk too of the art of driving. There is a certain horse you must "tuck in" until you get to the head of the stretch. He is a stretch trotter. Wait. Wait. Wait. Then ask him for it.

Ask him softly or with a gentle tap of the whip. "Now, now, now."

Or he may be one who will take his punishment like a soldier. Give it to him. Lay the whip to him. Shout. "Ata boy. Ata boy." A wild cry.

You have to put your own excitement into the nerves of some of the horses, make them feel it, tell them what you want.

You want all they have got, every ounce. The horse to keep his head, not to lose the smooth rhythm of the trot or pace, not to leap into the air, to keep on trotting or pacing.

The stride to be lengthened more and more, the legs to reach, reach, reach.

All the very fast ones have that smooth long rhythmical stride. They have courage too. They know what they are doing.

It is something to be the driver of such a horse. Everything is in the driver. If he is timid or weak-hearted the horse will know it now.

The horse will lose confidence, he will never win.

Something like love between the man and the horse. You feel it when you go to the stables. Watch the way that man over there, that merchant, touches his horse. It is the touch of a lover.

Do you think he touches the goods in his store that way.

And what about his wife?

A wife is a wife but a horse is a horse.

Do you think there are many wives in America as beautiful as Mary Rose, who this afternoon, at our fair, won the 2.18 trot? Will they respond as courageously when you call on them?

Why Mary Rose will not cry, she will not sulk. She is what she is. Look at her.

This afternoon, in the 2.18 trot, after she had won two heats, in the third heat that great raw-looking gray there challenged her on the back stretch.

The gray came with a terrific burst of speed and passed Mary Rose.

She was tired, tired. Already she had gone, at top speed, to win two grueling heats.

But that man there, that not-too-slender merchant from a neighboring town, who owns her, who was risking his precious neck driving her—he called upon her.

There was something pleading in his voice.

"Mary, Mary."

He touched her with the whip too.

Did you see how her ears lay back, did you hear how the breath whistled through her nostrils? Why you could hear it clear across the tracks, in the grandstand here, in the intense silence.

All these thousands of people silent, all staring.

Mary Rose seemed to get smaller. She flattened. Her body went down closer to earth. Her stride lengthened and quickened.

She went faster than she could go. That merchant sat up there and plead with her. He was like a determined, half-angry, hopeful boy.

She never went back on him though. She raced the gray through the stretch to the wire, neck and neck, and then, forty yards from the wire, she made him cough it up.

He broke his stride. Mary Rose won of course.

Can you imagine any wife doing that?

Is the man, that merchant, in love? Of course he is. He is a lover. What else?

And so the fair again. Every year a moment like that. Something pagan, everyone feeling it.

In the evenings, now-days, traveling musical comedy companies come, "Revue" they call them. Young girls come out and dance, and show their legs.

Fat comedians get off stale Broadway jokes. The people laugh, year after year, at the same jokes.

And then the fireworks.

It is best, in the evening, to go a little away, up the track, into the darkness.

See it from there, the moving lights, the moving pictures.

In the dark stables Mary Rose is resting now. It would be interesting to go there. You will find that man, that merchant, hanging about.

He is going home, to his store in another town, on the late train.

However he has come back for a last look. He goes into Mary Rose's stall, touches her once more in the darkness. She puts her head on his shoulder.

He is going away now, back to his store, but next week, at the next town where a fair is being held, and where there is racing, next Thursday he will be back again.

He will be driving Mary Rose in another race. She will not last long, three, four, five years, but perhaps she will drop a fast colt.

There is, after all, the uncertainty of this sort of thing. You have to take chances in life.

# In Washington

EDITOR'S NOTE

In his lecture on "A Writer's Conception of Realism" Anderson spoke of "bad art—although it may possibly be very good journalism." Yet one side of Anderson's gift for writing was journalism of a kind that enabled him to own and write for two small-town papers, one Republican in politics, the other Democratic, both in Marion, Virginia, in 1925. The results of this adventure were published in *Hello Towns!* in 1929. In these writings Anderson became an elder version of his own George Willard of *Winesburg, Ohio*—it was his proof perhaps that, as Oscar Wilde once said, "life imitated art." In being owner of both papers he also showed an indifference to political names and slogans, a vehement indifference, overtones of which were heard in his lecture on Realism in 1939: "Since I have been here [he spoke at Olivet College in Michigan] I do not believe I have heard the word 'capitalist' or 'proletariat' used once. What a relief." But his books, *Perhaps Women* (1931), *No Swank* (1934), and *Puzzled America* (1935) were extended editorials on American life and culture.

As editor-reporter of his Marion, Virginia, newspapers, he visited Washington, D. C. and Mr. Herbert Hoover in 1927, and what he saw was not merely Mr. Hoover, a future President, but areas of Washington, including the Freer Gallery and Whistler's Peacock

Room. The piece is a burlesque of the usual "newspaper interview," yet it does not fail to contain its "editorial" commentary.

NEWS

IN WASHINGTON, where I have been sent to interview the Secretary of Commerce, Mr. Hoover. I do not like the job much. Why did I take it?

I am always undertaking something the Lord never intended me to do.

I have arrived in the city in the early morning and am not to see the man until late afternoon. It is bitter cold. When I saw Washington last, some fifteen or twenty years ago, it was merely a great straggling town. Now it has become a modern city.

I have been at a big hotel and have left my bag. I begin wondering what I shall do with my day.

We who live in country towns miss certain things. The radio and the phonograph can bring us music by the best orchestras—if there are any bests—we can hear speakers talk, but there are things we cannot get.

We cannot see the best players on the stage and we cannot see paintings.

I decided to go to a museum.

There are days for everything. Was this a day to see paintings? I should, no doubt, have gone to talk to some politician, but I knew no politicians as politicians. No one ever talks politics to me. I went to the new Freer Gallery.

The Freer Gallery, named for its builder, was built by a rich man of Detroit and was intended primarily to house the paintings of the American painter Whistler.

In it are housed, as well, many old and rare objects of Chinese and Japanese art.

I went to the gallery in the morning and it was quite empty but for the attendants. There was a hushed quiet over the place. The walls and the attendants seemed crying out at me "be careful, walk quietly, this is a sacred place."

Sacred, indeed. What a strange thing is the life of the artist.

Standing in the gallery and looking at these paintings, conscious all the time of the uniformed attendants watching me, afraid perhaps I might steal some of these sacred objects, an odd feeling of annoyance creeping over me.

Such a man as Whistler lives. His work is condemned or praised by the men of his own time. It has been the fate of some men, who have produced the greatest art, made the greatest discoveries in science, the greatest contributions to scholarship, to live and die unknown. They are perhaps the lucky men.

Such a man as Whistler, fighting for fame. He was always a great fighter. Once he wrote a book called *The Gentle Art of Making Enemies.* He knew how to do that all right.

Much of his energy must have been spent in fighting for fame. Well, he has won. He has fame. Fame, in the end, does not always mean worth. If you keep insisting that you are a great man after a time people will believe. It doesn't necessarily mean you are great.

James McNeill Whistler was not one of the great painters of the world. His fighting and his personality got him somewhere. A rich patron of the arts, Mr. Freer, became devoted to him. He has spent hundreds of thousands of dollars, his time, his own energy, in making Mr. Whistler's fame secure. Mr. Freer, because of his devotion to another, may possibly be a finer and a greater man than Mr. Whistler.

As for myself, I could not get over the feeling that much of Mr. Whistler's work is vastly overestimated. Many of these paintings, carefully guarded by paid attendants, housed in this great stone building, are commonplace enough.

I went out of the famous Peacock Room and into the room where the older art treasures are housed. There were the old Chinese and Japanese things.

Objects of art come out of a day when there is no such thing as publicity—paintings by reticent, devoted men. Whistler has been rather widely advertised as having brought over into his own day much of the fineness of these older painters. He has not brought over so much.

Such a short time ago, some fifty years, and Whistler's house in London was being sold over his head. Many of these paintings, so sumptuously housed now, were sold then for a few shillings. Have they increased in value so much?

The value of the older Chinese and Japanese things is fixed. Money cannot express it. There is "The Waves at Matsushinea," painted by some unknown man called "Satatsu" in the seventeenth century. In another painting the Chinese Emperor Ming Huang is with his concubine Kuei-fei in a garden. What a charming lady! It is spring. She is singing to make the flowers bloom for her emperor.

And there is another painting. The Emperor Weu, of the Chow Dynasty, is meeting the sage, Chiang Tzu-ya. The two men are meeting on an island in a winding lake. All nature seems hushed and quiet. Clouds are standing still in the sky, as though intent on the scene below. There is a sense in the painting of infinite time, space, distance.

Mr. Hoover and I did not meet on an island in a winding lake. There were no fleecy clouds floating in the sky; no sense of infinite time, space, distance.

It may be that Mr. Hoover has in him the making of an emperor, but I am no sage.

If I had been a sage I would not have been where I was.

I was in a great office building in the modern city of Washington. Before me sat a well-dressed man of perhaps fifty. Like myself, he was a bit too fat. He had leaned too long over a desk, over figures and plans, and I had leaned too long over a typewriter. Besides that Mr. Hoover had just been to a dentist.

And he did not want to be interviewed.

"Are you an interviewer?" he asked. "Yes," I said doubtfully. I had never been such a thing before. I am a writer of books, sometimes a teller of tales. I run a country weekly. Country weeklies are not newspapers. We do not interview people. I am not a politically minded man. Always I am asking myself the question, "Why does any man want to be President? Why does any man want power?"

By my philosophy power is the forerunner of corruption.

To be a bright, intelligent newspaper interviewer, I should have asked Mr. Hoover some embarrassing questions. He was a member of the cabinet of Mr. Harding, sat cheek by jowl with Mr. Fall and Mr. Daugherty. A stench arose from that sitting. What about it?

The question trembled on my lips.

Other questions crowding into my mind. "What of the League of Nations, our attitude toward the small republics of Central America?"

Better that I should not ask such questions. The man would twist me about his little finger. "It is just possible he knows something about leagues of nations and all such things, but what do you know?" I was now asking myself.

A fragment of song floated up into my mind, even then, at that unfortunate moment. The song was like the clouds floating above that island when the Emperor Weu went to meet Chiang Tzu-ya.

My freedom sleeps in a mulberry bush.
My country is in the shivering legs of a little lost dog.

"I am not going to be interviewed," Mr. Hoover said again. "I don't care," I said. As a matter of fact, I did not care two straws. I had made a futile trip to Washington. Well, it was not futile. I had seen the Emperor Ming Huang with his concubine Kuei-fei walking in a garden.

The Emperor Ming Huang had walked in his garden with Kuei-fei in another age than my own. There were no factories in that age. Men did not rush through the streets in automobiles. There were no radios, no airplanes.

Just the same men fought wars, men were cruel and greedy, as in my own age.

My mind full of things far removed from Mr. Hoover and his age, I was going out the door, having got nothing from him, having failed as a modern newspaper correspondent—a task that no such man as myself should have undertaken—when Mr. Hoover called me back.

"I will not be interviewed, but we can talk," he said. Mr. Hoover was being kind. He must have felt my incompetence. I understood what he meant. He meant only that things were to be in his own hands. We were to speak only of those things that Mr. Hoover cared to discuss.

He began to talk now, first of the Mississippi problem. It was a huge problem, he said, but it could be met. There was a way out.

There was the river cutting down through the heart of the country, twisting and winding. Had I not spent days and weeks on the great river? I told him I had. "It is uncontrollable," I said. "The Mississippi is a thing in nature. It is nature." But did not Joshua make the sun stand still? I remembered a summer when I took the Mississippi as a god, became a river worshiper.

I was in a boat fishing on the Mississippi when a flood came. I felt its power, it put the fear of God into my heart.

But Mr. Hoover had been down there and was not afraid. He spoke of spillways. There was to be a new river bed creeping down westward of the Mississippi—all through the lower country.

Then when great floods came rampaging and tearing down and Mother Mississippi was on a spree, she was to be split in two. Two Mother Mississippis, gentled now, going down to the sea. "What a man," I said to myself.

And could he also handle like that the industrial age?

There was the question. That also had become to me like a thing in nature.

I had after all got down to the heart of what I wanted to ask Mr. Hoover.

The industrial age has been sweeping forward ever since I was a boy. I have seen the river of it swell and swell. It has swept over the entire land. The industrialists may not be Ming Huangs but they are in power.

They have raised this Mr. Hoover up out of the ranks of men as perhaps the finest Republican example of manhood and ability in present-day American political and industrial life. He is, apparently, a man very sure of himself. His career has been a notable one. From a small beginning he has risen steadily in power. There has never been any check. I felt, looking at him, that he has never known failure.

It is too bad never to have known that. Never to have known miserable nights of remorse, feeling the world too big and strange and difficult for you.

Well, power also, when it is sure of itself, can gentle a man. Mr. Hoover has nice eyes, a clear, cool voice. He gave me long rows of figures showing how the industrialists have improved things for the common man. We spoke of Mr. Ford and he was high in his praise of the man. "When I go to ride in an automobile," he said, "it does not matter to me that there are a million automobiles on the road just like mine. I am going somewhere and want to get there in what comfort I can and at the lowest cost."

That, it seemed to me, summed up Mr. Hoover's philosophy of life.

When you have a man's philosophy of life, why stay about? Why bother the man?

Mr. Hoover spoke of the farmers. It is quite true that, in the distribution of the good things the industrial age has brought, the industrialists and the financiers have got rather the best of it. Labor has been able to take good care of itself, Mr. Hoover thinks. The farmer is another problem. Here is one place where the modern system has not quite worked.

It is a matter, he said, of too much waste between the farmer and the consumer. I gathered that the whole system of merchandising would have to be brought up into the new age.

"Something like the systems of chain stores," I suggested. He fended me off there. I presume any man in political life has to be cautious. The merchant class is a large class. There are votes there. My mind flopped back to my own town. Voters gathered in the evening at the back of the drug store, the hardware store, the grocery store. The small, individual merchant, who is, I gather, at the bottom of the farmer's troubles, has power, too—in his own store.

There had been something hanging in my mind for a long time. I thought I would at least take a shot at it. All of this industrialism and standardization growing up in my day. I had seen it grow and grow. A whole nation riding in the same kind of cars, smoking the same kind of cigars, wearing the same kind of clothes, thinking the same thoughts.

Individualism, among the masses of the people, gradually dying.

You get a few men, drawn up and become powerful because they control the mass needs and the mass thought. No questions asked any more. All doubting men thrown aside.

Young men, buried yet down in the mass, squirming about. They not liking too well the harness of industrialism and standardization. Men coming into power, not as Lincoln came, nor yet as Napoleon came.

At the bottom of it all, a growing number of the younger men feeling hopeless boredom.

Is the heavy boredom of a standardized civilization true for Mr. Hoover as it is sometimes true for me? I asked Mr. Hoover that question and for the first time during our talk he did not seem comfortable.

But power is power. He fended off again. After all the age and the system of the age that may destroy one man may make another. Mr. Hoover has been made by his age. Apparently, he is satisfied with it.

I got out of Mr. Hoover's presence feeling we had got nowhere. Surely it wasn't his fault. I went walking for a long time in the streets of Washington. The more I walked the more sure I was that Mr. Hoover is the ideal among Republican men to be the present-day President of the United States—if he can make them see it.

Other men feel that. I asked several men I had never seen before.

I asked a man who drove a streetcar, one who opened oysters, another who scrubbed the floor in the lobby of a hotel.

"He is the ideal man," they all said. They were afraid the politicians would not give him the chance. The reason given was that he has too much brains.

But these men's opinions have also been made by the standardized newspaper opinion of the age in which they live. Their expression of doubt was merely resentment. Mr. Hoover is the blameless man. In Mr. Hoover's head has developed the ideal brain for his time. Are the other leaders of his party afraid of him? Surely theirs are not the nameless fears of such men as myself.

It would be a little odd if, the age having produced a perfect thing, a man who does so very well and with such fine spirit just what everyone apparently believes they want done—should be thrown aside, being too perfect.

There is no doubt in my own mind. I am convinced Mr. Hoover would make the ideal Republican President.

No one will ever sing songs about Mr. Hoover after he is President—if they decide to give him the chance. There will be no paintings made of him walking at evening in a garden while a lovely lady sings to make the flowers bloom.

But it is not an age of painting, not an age of song.

And so there was I walking in the streets of Washington, having made a failure of my day. I had tried to be smart and had not been smart. I had got myself into a false position. What happens to the age in which a man lives is like the Mississippi, a thing in nature. It is no good quarreling with the age in which you live.

I had come to Washington, I think wanting to like Mr. Hoover, and had ended by admiring him. He had not warmed me. I went over past the White House and tried to think of Lincoln living there. Then I went back to the Freer Gallery for another look at Ming Huang walking in his garden and listening to the voice of Kuei-fei—but it was closed for the night.

# A SELECTION OF LETTERS

## EDITOR'S NOTE

No selection of Sherwood Anderson's writings can be called complete without a selection from his letters, and through the courtesy of Mrs. Anderson, Miss Frances Steloff of The Gotham Book Mart in New York, and Mr. James Schevill of Berkeley, California, I have been able to gather together a group of letters that have not hitherto appeared between the covers of of a book.

That air of personal candor which Anderson cultivated, and not always successfully, in many pages of his autobiographies has its best and, I believe, most enduring expression in this present selection of his letters. Here he is far less concerned with the problems of subjective and objective truths than in his other autobiographical writings, and throughout the letters one feels his strong temperamental affinity with his British contemporary, D. H. Lawrence. When Anderson wrote to Stieglitz of his own "display of unhealthy egotism" he was very close to what Lawrence felt when he spoke of "the world that is tainted with myself," and this likeness of feeling is not derived from any literary influences that Lawrence's writings may have had upon Anderson. Both Lawrence and Anderson, with totally different sources of experience, maintained a watchful distrust of merely political movements and motives; yet both frequently felt the need of writing manifestoes, Lawrence in his *Pansies*, Anderson in his letters; and both contradicted their sanctions of large ideological movements in favor of thinking for themselves. Both writers were, of course, strongly Protestant in their convictions; they were "protesters" in favor of the arts, and they belonged to that branch of Protestantism that is commonly called heretical and is self-consciously unorthodox.

To the social as well as the literary historian these letters of Anderson's reflect the thinking and emotional reflexes of the period (1925-1940) through which he moved—most clearly perhaps the letters to John Anderson, to Theodore Dreiser, to John L. Lewis, to Edmund Wilson, and to Gilbert Wilson.

These letters are arranged, as nearly as possible, in chronological order. Where Anderson dated his letters the dates are given. Most times, however, Anderson did not date his letters. When it has been possible to assign dates, these are given in parentheses.

### TO ALFRED STIEGLITZ[1]

New Orleans, La.,
July 10, 1925.

Dear Stieglitz:

I just got back from my trip on the river and found the two letters from you and one from Paul. I wish I could see and talk with you and did not have to try

[1] Alfred Stieglitz (1864-1946) was a gifted photographer, and one of the most perceptive of American pioneers in introducing modern art in painting to the American public. In New York, his gallery, "An American Place," in which the early paintings of Arthur B. Dove, John Marin, Georgia O'Keefe (Mrs. Alfred Stieglitz), and Marsden Hartley were exhibited, became the center of a group which included Van Wyck Brooks, Paul Rosenfeld, Waldo Frank, Lewis Mumford, and the Stettheimer sisters.

to say in a letter what your letter made me feel. The trip up the river was a sort of turning point. What has happened to me this year, has happened before. I turn in on myself, spend hours analyzing myself and my attitude toward life and finally get myself into a state where I am half insane. Then something happens to clarify the atmosphere. I realize anew that if I do my job the best I can at the time, it isn't up to me to decide on its ultimate merit.

The whole thing is a display of unhealthy egotism on my part, and when I come out from under it, I am always intensely relieved. In this case I have probably been able to come out from under it because of E.

Naturally I wish that your own health might go on for twenty years yet without your body giving you pain or uneasiness. There is a way in which you are so like a father to many of us, that when you are depressed, it depresses us too.

Paul's letter, however, reports you as flying around and working again. I am so glad Georgia is working. Her work last year meant so much to me.

It has been very hot here and Elizabeth and I are going away to the country somewhere. I think we can probably find a place in the mountains of Virginia or North Carolina. Will write you as soon as we have an address.

Love to all of you.

Sincerely yours,

TO JOHN ANDERSON[1]

Hamburg-Amerika Line
(1927)

My dear John,

There were so many things I wanted to say to you while I was still in Paris and that I did not get said. It was really too bad that we had to be together at a time when I was a good deal upset in regard to any of my own work. If you go on with the arts—and I suspect you will—you will know such times.

There seems to be no escape. You would think that a greater command of your metier, what is called "fame," etc., would satisfy and quiet the thing inside but it doesn't. Sometimes I suspect that only dull people ever really are satisfied with themselves.

What I really wanted to say was how much I am pleased with you. I like your attitude toward life and work. You have all of my affection.

Naturally I hope you will find for yourself an outlet in painting. It is one of the most subtile and difficult of all the arts. A lifetime will not teach you half you want to know. It would indeed be pretty fine if during this year you could get a conviction, inside, that you know what you want to do in life. Perhaps it will turn out so. I hope so.

I think, John, you are a bit inclined to take your own health, etc., too seriously. I do it myself. Try not to think about illness.

You have also perhaps some inclination to stay too much away from people. Go about a good deal. Never hesitate to use the fact you are my son if it will help

[1] Son of Sherwood Anderson; a young painter.

you to see some man in whose work you are interested. You have natural good taste—will not vulgarize opportunities. Do not hesitate to take them.

About money. I want you not merely to be careful about it, but, on the other hand, if something comes up you would like to do and that would take another $100, do not hesitate to ask for it.

The great thing I really want to say is that I am satisfied with you—and very proud to be your father.

As always,

S. A.

P.S. For three or four weeks I will be traveling and speaking almost every day. I may not write often. After I get to the farm I will. A good passage, so far. E. pretty well. However we are just out—long miles to go.

(1927)

Dear John,

I have been intending to write you for several days but have been absorbed in work. I just this morning got your note from the Seine boat. The movement of my story has stopped for a time. I will write you in the interval.

I've a notion that, in America, you will be less bothered with homosexually inclined men. However the arts have always been a refuge for such men.

They are, as I think you have guessed, the less vigorous men. There is some distinct challenge of life they do not want to meet, and can't meet.

However they can't escape sex. They seem to me to try to throw a kind of artificial glamor over it, plunge into fake mysticism, etc. Some of them have delicate minds.

On the other hand American men cannot understand love between man and man. We have all of the same types in America but—except in the big cities—they hide themselves away. All kinds of lonely queer figures here. We have them in the country as well as in the cities.

If you have, in life, such experiences as I have had, I think you will find that finding a few real companions is the most difficult thing on earth. You will have to take what you can get, here and there.

On the other hand it is a great mistake to draw away too much.

Paul Rosenfeld has been here for three weeks. He is a real man, vigorous, full of life but extremely delicate-minded. He is rather afraid of people. I've been watching him. Lord, how much he misses of association, little flashing things picked up, by not being able to meet people, quite frankly. Some men get their sensibilities hurt and hurt. They can't stand it any more. That's why I suppose real achievement in the arts calls for a reserve of physical power.

To heal hurt nerves—try again.

The brain both makes and destroys. I think you have to meet the challenge of the brain's development or sink into idiocracy. It's the challenge David Prall was talking about in his essay.

To the artist it means not to shrink from human life —no matter what its complications—a large order.

However a man doesn't make himself all at once—by a resolution.

Artists have a thing called style. It's what makes an artist distinctive. The style is himself. What is he?

He is, I dare say, what his relations with himself and others make him.

To keep my relationships—not to shrink from them and yet keep personal dignity.

Homosexuality dodges. It isn't in the main current.

Artists use the phrase—speaking of a certain man—"He is in the tradition."

The old tradition of the arts is really health. The artist man should really, I think, be the most masculine and manly of all men.

I have tried to get at that somewhat in *A Story-Teller's Story*. You'll get more out of that when you read it again.

If it's there. A man never quite knows whether or not he has got down the inner meaning he was going toward.

I think also, John, that manliness—maleness really—implies tenderness. Dreiser is perhaps the most important writer living—because, in spite of unspeakable prose crudeness, he has in him the most male tenderness.

If my own senses are as acute as I hope they are, I would not be surprised if you would find—if you live long and become an artist—you'll be an artist in spirit whether you are in fact or not—you'll find a decided drift toward a kind of decadence.

Hatred, cruelty—taking the place of tenderness and the attempt at understanding. It's easier.

A good many things may make it so. Industrialism, city life.

The growth of advertising and publicity.

Fake figures always being built up by publicity—in the arts—in government—everywhere.

Everyone really knowing.

The answer being cynicism.

That's the easy way out.

You'll come however to realize the arts are old and old and old. There is a kind of underlying brotherhood. The signs of it are pretty faint sometimes.

I suppose the only value of being in Europe—for a young American—is because you may feel old men through old work.

The true thing in some way stays.

The half men—all homos are that—at bottom avoid the whole challenge. They are likely to be clever, sensitive in certain directions.

Then they turn and muss everything up.

Such a one in life always goes to books, pictures, other men's work.

There is no relationship with life itself.

You could use the word "God" or "Nature." Sometimes I just call the central thing "it."

That thing for which all men of parts have always been willing to go any length.

To work and be modest and wait and work again.

Not too much talk in cafes, not too much association with second-rate men.

Not quitting while there is life left in the body.

I don't know what it's all about. I've not many real illusions about my own value to "the tradition." As far as I see, though, John, it's the only thing there is.

S. A.

Ripshin Farm
Grant, Virginia
(1927)

Dear John,

Something I should have said in my letter yesterday. In relation to painting.

Don't be carried off your feet by anything because it is modern—the latest thing.

Go to the Louvre often and spend a good deal of time before the Rembrandts, the Delacroixs.

Learn to draw. Try to make your hand so unconsciously adept that it will put down what you feel without your having to think of your hands.

Then you can think of the thing before you.

Draw things that have some meaning to you. An apple, what does it mean?

The object drawn doesn't matter so much. It's what you feel about it, what it means to you.

A masterpiece could be made of a dish of turnips.

Draw, draw hundreds of drawings.

Try to remain humble. Smartness kills everything.

The object of art is not to make salable pictures. It is to save yourself.

Any clearness I have in my own life is due to my feeling for words.

The fools who write articles about me think that one morning I suddenly decided to write and began to produce masterpieces.

There is no special trick about writing or painting either. I wrote constantly for fifteen years before I produced anything with any solidity to it.

For days, weeks, and months now I can't do it.

You saw me in Paris this winter. I was in a dead blank time. You have to live through such times all your life.

The thing, of course, is to make yourself alive. Most people remain all of their lives in a stupor.

The point of being an artist is that you may live.

Such things as you suggested in your letter the other day. I said "Don't do what you would be ashamed to tell me about."

I was wrong.

You can't depend on me. Don't do what you would be ashamed of before a sheet of white paper—or a canvas.

The materials have to take the place of God.

About color. Be careful. Go to nature all you can. Instead of paint shops—other men's palettes—look at the sides of buildings in every light. Learn to observe little things—a red apple lying on a grey cloth.

Trees—trees against hills—everything. I know little enough. It seems to me that if I wanted to learn about color I would try always to make a separation. There is a plowed field here before me, below it a meadow, half decayed cornstalks in the meadow making yellow lines, stumps, sometimes like looking into an ink bottle, sometimes almost blue.

The same in nature is a composition.

You look at it thinking—what made up that color. I have walked over a piece of ground, after seeing it from a distance—trying to see what made the color I saw.

Light makes so much difference.

You won't arrive. It is an endless search.

I write as though you were a man. Well, you must know my heart is set on you.

It isn't your success I want. There is a possibility of your having a decent attitude toward people and work. That alone may make a man of you.

S. A.

P.S. Tell Church that David Prall finally got the Cezanne prints.

Also tell the man at the shop where you go for the Picasso book—or if you have been there, drop him a note—the shop I mean.

(1927)

Dear John,

Your letter outlining something of your hours—perhaps sometimes days and weeks—of hopelessness about yourself falls in strangely with what I am writing about just now.

First of all I do think that this growing sensitiveness to the danger of cleverness and prettiness is a big achievement in itself.

Whatever you do in life you are going to find people all around you faking and getting away with it apparently.

If you have time some day, read again the last section of my *Story Teller's Story*—about the man who wrote football stories.

Fake men being acclaimed everywhere, fake furniture in houses, fake house building, city building.

Vast sums being acquired by men from fakiness.

That doesn't matter.

You can't fake raising corn in a field.

Life comes back to the substance in the sod.

The reason for being an artist is that it is the finest challenge there is.

It's a man's only possible approach to God.

I mean to humbleness, decency.

I suppose you can be an artist in your attitude no matter what you do. I don't know.

It depends on what you feel. I happen to have given myself the challenge of a prose writer. I am going to stick to it while I live.

And it isn't because of success or fame or anything else. I would chuck all that fast enough.

It's because that is my challenge to myself—what Mr. Prall meant in his article.

I think it would draw us a bit closer together if you really knew that I—at fifty—am much closer to your position than you know.

You have torn up some drawings. Within the last year I have torn up twenty-five starts at novels—some of them going to 20,000 words.

It's nothing.

I had faked as you had—was perhaps showing off.

Or I had listened to someone else. I hadn't found my own truth for the man I was writing about.

Something in your letter I think is wrong.

You say, "It is my world."

It isn't.

Your Uncle Earl who might have made a fine artist went wrong there. He got that idea fixed. It destroyed him.

What you felt, when you sat down to write me, a hundred, say a thousand, say ten or five, other young men might at that very moment have been feeling—in Paris.

Men and women walking along the streets. What do you know of them? Study them—don't be afraid—go, man. Make drawings of their faces.

Don't listen too much to what people say. Try to think what they are thinking and feeling.

You are made ashamed by something in yourself when you go near people. You draw away—more and more.

Your Uncle Earl did that for fifteen years. He loved me and I loved him. He hid himself from me.

It was fifteen years lost. It brought about his death. I sat beside him before he died. I know what did it.

Refusing love because you won't pay the price of misunderstanding, your own confusion.

You have got to pay it all. What you were feeling

when you wrote this letter you have got to pay over and over and over.

There's no dodging a damn thing.

In a book of mine *Many Marriages* I came somewhere near saying it.

Your life is like a filled cup you have got to carry in the midst of crowds.

I would go to school and I would try to get what they had to give. Any skill of any kind helps. I would go among people constantly and try to understand them.

Another person is as important as a tree or a mountain.

Don't dodge.

You are pretty young yet. So much to learn. For Christ's sake avoid intolerance.

For example, dear John, you write me, often constructing sentences in a slovenly way, putting in capitals at the wrong place, saying "are" when you mean "is." That's important too—something to learn.

If for nothing else—that my sense of words be not offended.

You see, John, I don't give a damn about your being just a painter. I want you to do whatever in the end gives you most happiness.

But I do want you to avoid intolerance, self-absorption—fear.

There's a hell of a lot more to say. I'll send your letter back.

While you are there anyway draw.

Draw, draw, and draw.

See if you can't begin to find a bit of light on everything out through the end of your pencil. If you can I know you won't quit.

S. A.

### TO BURTON EMMETT[1]

May 12, 1927

My Dear Burton Emmett,

It all makes me feel a little woozy. We had better talk of it some time. If you come here I could show you how I work. Much, nowadays all, of my work is done in longhand. When I actually write I get too excited for a typewriter.

I used to use it. Much of my stuff went down that way first.

The pen is more direct. I throw aside a terrific lot of stuff. Novels started that never get into the right key.

Everything is in the tone. Does it belong to me? Is it coming straight out of me?

Often things break dead off. I might go on but would have to force my stroke.

I start again.

I get ideas. An idea is not a theme.

Theme and the prose surface have to fit.

I am thinking of all this MS. that never gets anywhere.

Has that sort of stuff value?

We ought to think of real values.

I can't quite think you haven't the artist's impulse. I value you because you respond. Frankly I'm a bit afraid of the collector's impulse. I don't understand.

Let's forget the money matter, for the time anyway. Money is an odd thing. I hardly understand that either. When I have a few hundred dollars in hand I feel rich until it is spent. Then, I admit, I worry.

[1] Burton Emmett and his wife Mary were close friends of the Andersons, well known as art collectors and patrons.

What a little frightens me about the collector's impulse is that it must have in it at bottom possessiveness. I may be wrong. Some day we will talk it out.

And then the gamble. There is no proof anything of mine will have permanent value. I'm not working for that. Oblivion doesn't scare me. Often it seems the sweetest of all ideas.

I am driving at some indefinite thing—the "it." The mystic in me arises there.

Don't bother to think of it now. What I have in the way of MS. will be here.

Do try sometime this summer to drive down for a few days. We'll go into the woods, sit on a log and talk.

Sincerely,

TO FERDINAND SCHEVILL[1]

Marion, Virginia, December, 1930.

It has been an odd year. I am at any rate a good deal amused at myself. This winter I have had opportunity to make three or four thousand dollars but can't make any of it. I'm becoming a nut. When I am offered money for anything it becomes spoiled for me. It doesn't matter so much as I spend little.

I've about concluded that it is wrong for me to go on thinking of myself as an artist at all. I can't be professional, it seems. On the other hand I can't quite go to work at some commercial thing.

Perhaps it will work. I think I will try to get someone to back me in devoting myself to the country press.

[1] American historian and contemporary of Anderson.

It seems I do believe, after three years down here, that the country press offers the biggest opportunity in America for educational work in a real sense. All the big universities now have journalistic schools. Why could I not do a good thing toward directing some of the younger talent and energy away from the cities and to the little weeklies? I would like to go into propaganda work for something of this sort. The country press was once quite a powerful thing but it has gone to seed. It has got into the hands of the petty bourgeoisie. In a way I think we have proved down here that it doesn't need to be quite that. I believe that I am enough of a figure to attract attention to the idea. I might take it up as a work I could do. If I do I should get someone with money to put up a fund. It wouldn't need be so much. The money would not need to be given, just the interest, for it to keep me going at it, pay a secretary, etc. If I went into it I would write and lecture on the subject. I wouldn't mind doing that. What I hated about the other kind of lecturing I did was that it had to be devoted to the arts and indirectly to myself, a kind of exhibitionism. I have a kind of growing conviction that these little country papers, once they got into the hands of live young men and women, could do rather wonders. I believe we all believe now that there must come a kind of change in our civilization. The alert, well-educated young men, or women, with a kind of flair—and there must be many such—could get a feeling on a country paper they can never get buried on the big dailies. Twenty or thirty such people in a state, say like Illinois or Virginia, could do a lot in ten years. They could check a lot of brutality, wipe out a lot of ignorance, and the young men and women doing it might well feel they were going somewhere. At that they could make a living doing it.

I believe it wants but someone of some little prominence pushing the idea. What do you think?

TO EDMUND WILSON[1]

(Summer, 1931)

Dear Wilson,

I got a wire from Tom Tippitt at Charleston—I guess it was after you left there—wanting me to come over and address the strikers from the courthouse steps. I didn't go. I had engaged to go down South.

I might have gone just the same but was uncertain. I have a queer guilty feeling just now about taking any part in pulling people out on strike. We go and stir them up. Out they come and presently get licked. Then we go comfortably off. It seems to me that if we, of what I presume you might call the intelligentsia, are to go in at all with the workers perhaps we should be ready to go all the way. I mean that we should be willing to go live with them in their way and take it in the neck with them.

I suppose the Negroes are good communist material but they will be making a mistake, won't they, if they take the material just because it is easy.

There are no *New Republics* sold here. I have sent

[1] This letter to Edmund Wilson was written during the period (1926-1931) when Wilson, as literary editor of *The New Republic,* made that publication the most highly respected and influential critical journal in the United States; not a little of its influence was due to the essays contributed by Wilson himself, which were later collected and published in his three volumes of criticism, *Axel's Castle, The Triple Thinkers, The Wound and the Bow.*

a subscription and have asked for the number containing your article on West Virginia.

I sent for the books on Lenin, Stalin, etc. They are interesting but certainly impersonal. The books make them seem hardly human.

I have had a bad week's slump but am feeling more like writing again. It was great fun seeing you. I hope you will come this way again. Some of these days we'll do that stunt, get in the car and go off bumming together. Love to Mrs. Wilson.

As always,
Sherwood

TO ———[1]

I will not try to answer the questions in your recent letter in detail. To an observer, who stands a little aside in such a civilization as has been built up in America—a part of it and yet not wholly a part—an artist—the American culture does not seem a thing made yet. Everything here is as yet in flux, in movement.

There has been and is this tremendous energy here. It has taken and still takes the form of mechanical development of life. This has been carried to ridiculous lengths. Life has got out of gear. The production of goods has been carried to extreme lengths and every conceivable method used to foist the goods upon the people. The plan has largely succeeded. We Americans are flooded with goods, we are drowned in goods. . . . The idea seemed to be that things could go on so forever. We could make cheap cars, mechanical clothes, washing machines, iceless refrigerators, etc., for all the

[1] Addressee and date are unknown.

world while we stayed at home and rode about in somewhat better cars—something of that sort. We have clung to the idea until we have got ourselves disliked over much of the world. The truth is that we are people like all other people. Do not judge us by the rich boaster you see taking his vacation in Paris, throwing his money about there.

The thing draws to its logical end. A part of the mechanical development here has been the automatic machines. This is constantly throwing men out of work. We stand idly by, our hands useless, while the goods still pour out of the machines. There is little growth of socialistic feeling here yet. We cannot yet quite face the fact that the American scheme isn't going to work. A curious part of the situation is this—it is an undoubtable fact that a man's hands, having been separated from materials in his work, become ineffective.

Men, more than they yet realize, live through their hands. When the hands become useless something happens also to the mind. The real danger in modern automatic machinery lies in the fact that it produces impotence.

But the American people are not impotent, not yet. If we can avoid war, that so burns up young energy without results, I expect the readjustment to take place. I expect new impulses in art and literature, new political leadership, new facing of the problems that are becoming real in America as in the rest of the world. I expect America to draw nearer Europe, nearer all the rest of the world. I expect youth to be heard over here.

Sherwood Anderson

TO DOROTHY DUDLEY[1]

(Early spring, 1933)

Dear Dorothy Dudley:

I am in the mood to answer your letter at once but you will have to put up with the job of untangling my script. There are many provocative things in your letter.

In the first place don't tell me you are poor. I thought you Dudleys were well heeled. You amaze and shock me. You can't buy my book and I have no money to buy and send it. I never made any money out of writing except once. *Dark Laughter*. That I took and with it built a grand stone house in the Blue Ridge mountains of Virginia—spending it all in one grand, gorgeous building splurge and I haven't been able to afford to live there since.

I'm going to try again this summer. The place is big enough for ten or twelve people to live and I'm going to get a cook, plant a big garden and try some kind of co-operative scheme. A number of us could go there summers and live, I believe, for a few dollars a week. Better get you a blanket, sheets and cat and come there and start that book.

And as regards Sandburg, Dreiser, etc. First of all you should know what damn crazy egotists all poets seem to be and you were making Dreiser bigger and more significant than any of the rest of us—which he probably was and is—but I fancy old Carl didn't like it.

And I do think you are mistaken in thinking that

[1] A close friend of Theodore Dreiser and the author of a study of his writings, *Forgotten Frontiers*.

Dreiser has gone over to externals. I think he is like the rest of us in America now—confused and baffled. My dear woman, when you see at first hand what is going on here it's hard not to become a rampant red and cry "anything but this."

You know, my dear, it is not only the hunger and destitution—it's something gone out of America—an old faith lost and no new one got. It's youth not given a break—youth licked before it starts.

Well Dorothy Dudley—if you haven't any money go somewhere and get some and get at that book. You can't ask whether or not they want it. I think that—in the Dreiser book—you did show a detached attitude and a real ability to grasp things. And as regards this other thing, you brought it out clearly in your book—the place in which we Americans have failed most dismally—suspicion of one another—lack of any real belief in comradeship—failure to say a word to one another. My dear, it is a common experience of my own. How many times it has happened to me. I write a book—tear it out of my very guts, and there is the same old patronizing senseless patter about it in public. Often the same men who chatter in public about my "groping" "vagueness" etc etc etc will write me a private letter saying just the opposite.

As though if we dared love and help each other we had in some way sinned. Is that Puritanism, I dunno.

Anyway we have to begin and again begin and again to try to help each other, and work together, and make if we can a few little cells of good feeling and hope.

Sherwood Anderson

TO BURTON AND MARY EMMETT[1]

Chicago,
September 15, 1933

Dear Burt and Mary:

I came up here to Chicago with Eleanor who had to come to a meeting of government officials—to discuss means of enforcing the minimum wage. I tell her she ought to bring up the matter of author's wage, but she won't. We are going home tomorrow, pack up and go on to New York.

We went for an evening to the Fair and it rained but I thought it rather wonderful, and oddly cheap and gaudy too—a mixture, like everything now—some kind of old life among us gone and the new life not born.

It is marvelous to think of being in your house but I can't help wishing you were there, we dropping in on you, doing things together, talking, etc. Perhaps you don't know what it means to us but you will know when I tell you I haven't made a cent this year.

It's because everything I've done this year has been for the future—the play on which there must still be work done and then this new book.

I want to tell—in story form—half story and half reflection—the tale of what happened to a young American business man that reversed everything in him—attitude toward his fellows, toward sex, toward the arts and his adventuring in the American field of intellectuals and artists, and have got nearly 40,000 words of it done. I am calling it "I Build my House," the house being not necessarily a physical house but rather the house of a man's self—with all the good

[1] See note, p. 597.

and bad, kindness and hard selfishness that he is.

All of them requiring great frankness and work in trying to see a little clearly.

The hardest thing of all to see—a man's self.

Chicago itself is much more exciting to me than its World's Fair. What a city it is, folks—how amazing, changing, undisciplined, odd flashes of a new world, remnants of an old.

I took Eleanor with me and we went pretending we were a couple seeking rooms—I think the landlady was Suspicious. She may have thought I had made a pick-up on the street.

We went to the old rooming house and to the room where I wrote *Winesburg.*

Afterwards we wanted to go there—sleep there while we were here, but I wouldn't. Our going was such a success—old dreams coming back—faces popping up. "No," I said, "let me have it just as it is."

How I'd like to talk with you both, be with you both, here in Chicago, where you two also had a life.

Dear people, you can't imagine all it means your offering the house to us for the winter.

Love,
Sherwood

TO THEODORE DREISER[1]

Marion, Virginia
January 2, 1936

Dear Teddy:

For the last year or two I have had something in my mind that you and I should have spoken about and during the last year or two it has been sharpened in

[1] The novelist.

my mind by the suicide of fellows like Hart Crane, Vachel Lindsay, and others, to say nothing of the bitterness of a Masters. In your play, *American Tragedy,* the play ends by the pronouncement that we can forgive a murderer but that society cannot be forgiven. To tell the truth, Ted, I think it nonsense to talk this way about society. I doubt if there is any such thing. If there has been a betrayal in America I think it is our betrayal of each other.

I do not believe that we—and by the word "we" I mean artists, writers, singers, etc.—have really stood by each other. There is a curious thing in America. The land is very vast. I think for example that French society has been able to attain to a real culture because we can say that Paris is France . . . as we could say London is England.

Now we know that New York is not America, Chicago is not America, San Francisco is not America. We have a curious situation. We are too much separated. I have hinted at this matter to you before and I take it to you because you are one of the least guilty, in the way I mean, of any of us. I know of no one more willing than you to put out a hand to others, more ready to give yourself. I know of no man among us with less bitterness in his nature. One of the reasons I love you is because in your presence I never do feel this bitterness.

Now what I have been thinking is that we need here among us some kind of new building up of a relationship between man and man. I feel so strongly on this matter that I am thinking of trying to get my thoughts and those of others who also feel this thing into form. I think even of a general letter or pamphlet that I might call "American Man to American Man." I think it is our loneliness for each other that has made most of us throw too much on woman and I also think that this is so much true that we are habitually making women carry more than their load.

I do not think that it is necessarily unfair to women to say frankly that the imaginative world is naturally the male province, but look what we do. We try to compensate for our loneliness for each other by throwing ourselves into the arms of woman. I believe it is in the nature of things that this is not sound. Instead of demanding of women we should be giving. Woman really wants personal beauty, one might almost say showered down upon her, that can only come out of the imaginative life. We have all been shirking our jobs but I do not believe that our shirking is due primarily to our own weakness but to our confusion and that our confusion comes partly from the tremendous size of the country. I even think that our Civil War was brought on by the impossibility or seeming impossibility of man finding man.

I have written you something about this before but have not amplified my idea as I am trying to do in this letter. I have been trying to think my way through this problem and the thought has occurred to me that in a country like this where personal relations in any sustained way between men working in the imaginative field are almost impossible, that it would help for all of us to return to the old habit of letter writing between man and man that has at certain periods existed in the world.

For example, Ted, suppose that every morning when you go to your desk to work you would begin your day's work by writing, let's say, one letter to one other man working in the same field as you are. Suppose we did, by this effort, produce less as writers. There is probably too much being produced. I am suggesting this as the only way out I can see in the situation. It isn't that I want you to write to me. I could give you names and addresses of others who need you and whom you need. I think it possible to build up a kind of network of relationships, something closer say between writers and painters, painters and song makers, etc., etc.

I think now that we are too much confused by the political. I think this need of man for man in the imaginative world is more important. I think that if it had existed, men like Crane and Lindsay would not have committed suicide. I would like to issue a pamphlet, or a general letter, on this subject, not for publication in some magazine where the idea might be muddled by all sorts of sentimentality, but where it might reach out to all sorts of men needing what I am talking about here.

Teddy, the truth is that although I am addressing this letter to you, I am only doing it because you may possibly be the most distinguished man among us and I tell you frankly that I may use this letter as the basis of what I want to say to many others.

If I do this, I will ask you and several others to whom I may send copies of this letter to send me letters expressing their feelings in the matter to be included in the pamphlet.

I will say no more about all this today. I am writing of this on New Year's day. The project is very close to me. I think it may be to you.

Sincerely yours,
Sherwood Anderson

NOTES

I am holding the above letter. It is interesting to me that on the day after I wrote the above I had two letters, one from Edgar Lee Masters, rather blaming the East and its attitude toward the West for the very thing I have tried to express above, and one from Malcolm Cowley[1] blaming the small bickerings, jealousies and cowardice of our little literary and intellectual groups in our cities.

* * *

Jasper Deeter of Hedgerow Theatre passed through our Virginia country and spent a night at a neighboring town. We gathered in a room and talked until late. Jap laughed and said that the great crime in this country was to be serious about anything.

I do know that he is persistently, and I believe in a fine impersonal way, serious about the theatre.

He objected that such a plan would bring down upon any one of us a flood of letters.

Well we all know about such letters. They come, in ninety-five per cent of cases, from young men and women who want to push themselves forward by crawling into bed with some man, or men, who they think has, as the saying is, arrived.

It's pretty grubby, most of it.

At the same time, tremendously needed.

I think it may be possible that the above idea, if it amounts to anything, may have to be a matter for each man to handle for himself, that the best that can be done is a general recognition of the need.

* * *

This we all know. We have very little real and

[1] Former literary editor of *The New Republic*, critic, poet, and author of *Exile's Return*.

sharply sustained criticism. How many of you constantly get letters asking you to go to bat for some book. What really basic cheapness in this whole idea.

One wonders sometimes if maleness is going out of our American life. It is amusing, is it not, that our most distinguished critic is a woman — Mary Colum.[1]

* * *

Something is constantly happening here. New men of talent come along. The critics are constantly trying to use the new man of talent to kill off the old—as though the minds of the critics could not hold the thought that two talented men, in the same art, could exist within the same country.

Today, for example, Hemingway is the new man. What praise lavished on him. Look out, Hemmy, they'll be trying to kill you off tomorrow.

Or it is Bill Faulkner, or Thomas Wolfe.

* * *

This I believe to be true—that any man of talent, whose talent has come to life and form in any sound piece of work, is never dead again until he is completely and finally physically dead. We all have lapses, go off into the political, get Hollywood-caught, money hunger comes.

We lose touch, do bad, rotten work.

O. K. We live in difficult times.

Can you believe that Vachel Lindsay would have taken . . . if on that day he had got even two or three letters from some of the rest of us?

"Keep shooting, lad. Do not let them put the bee on

[1] Author of *From These Roots* and *Life and the Dream*.

you. You have done good work and will do good work again. We need you." You all know what I mean.

* * *

I am a little afraid, writing all of the above. Will my fellows be saying, "Well, well, Sherwood is down"?

No, I am not. I do not believe any man in American letters has been as well treated by his contemporaries as I have. It just happens that I know so many others who, because of some shyness, resentment over past treatment, too much crowing by the destroyers over some not quite up to snuff piece of work done, have this terrible feeling of isolation that the rest of us too often do nothing to buck.

* * *

The question in my own mind is this—is it possible to do anything about all this? Do you think—my general notion—that intellectuals, artists, etc., in this country lead peculiarly lonely lives? Would it only lead to a lot of sentimental gush to try to do anything about it?

S. A.

*Note.* How insulting women are sometimes in their day of triumph. "The way to a man's heart is through his belly." There's a sample of it for you.

### TO JOHN L. LEWIS[1]

(1936)

John L. Lewis:

I have been wondering why something is not being done to draw the American intellectuals closer to American labor. Here we have "The friends of Soviet Russia," "Friends of New Spain," etc., etc., more or less organized groups of intellectuals, and united, trying, let's say, to give people a clearer view of what is going on in other countries.

Why not an organization here, let's say "Friends of American Workers"?

To be sure there is the Authors' League, more or less a trade union, but rather too conservative even for the A. F. of L.

And then there are some smaller, probably communist controlled groups.

Writers, for example, like Sinclair Lewis, Theodore Dreiser and a whole host of other men and women are not communists, nor are they conservatives. They are probably sincere believers in democracy and if it is true that labor is now at the parting of the roads, labor more and more to be felt as a real power in national affairs, wouldn't it be a smart move for your organization to attempt an organization of writers?

Get some man who knows how to organize such a group. Get a few big names among writers to serve as a sort of advisory board. None of the real writers would probably be worth a damn at building such an organization.

[1] John L. Lewis of the United Mine Workers of America. There is some doubt that this letter was ever mailed.

The idea, however, being for some of your fellows, in the midst of the struggle, to meet occasionally with groups of writers having real power, letting them in on what you are doing, getting acquainted with them personally, etc.

The idea being a more or less loose organization of the writers in closer touch with labor, the idea itself sponsored by your group.

TO HENRY GODDARD LEACH[1]

(June 1936)

Dear Leach,

I have read with interest the discussion between Drs. Harry Laidler and Eustace Seligman. I am afraid it only adds to my confusion. The difficulty with me is that when I hear anything that seems like a defense of capitalism, I become communistic and when I hear communistic arguments, I become somewhat tender toward capitalism.

I don't believe anyone quite knows what makes wars.

I don't believe anyone can really think clearly on any subject involving whole peoples.

I do think that our present passion for getting at everything through economics is a little insane. When again, if ever, we can all begin to at least try to think small, in little circles, a family, a few acquaintances, getting at what makes wars there, not forever jumping off into these huge pronouncements . . . God help me, I'm always doing it too. . . .

[1] Editor of *The Forum* (1923-1940); Anderson's letter is obviously a reply to a series of questions sent to him by that journal of controversial opinions.

When as individuals we can learn more of the ways of peace, we will have taken a great step toward universal peace.

TO MARY BLAIR[1]

New York
Friday
(Oct. 30, 1936)

Dear Mary Blair,

I think you are entirely justified, entirely right. How it happened I don't know because I remember so vividly your work.

I think it must be just one of those things that happen to us—in American life. You are not now in the public eye. Past work, no matter how fine, is forgotten. Apparently we'll all fall into the pattern—the immediate.

I hope you can find it in your heart to forgive me. I feel very humble and ashamed.

Sherwood Anderson

TO JAMES BOYD[2]

(1937)

Dear Jim,

All sorts of things in the head, dancing about. A man becomes, outwardly, stolid, middle-aged, and remains a colt inside. I'm thinking of things I wish I had

[1] Mary Blair (1895-1947) was a highly gifted actress, whose career was associated with the Provincetown Playhouse in New York; she was also the wife of Edmund Wilson.

[2] James Boyd (1888-1944) was a historical novelist whose best-known books were *Drums* and *Marching On.*

talked over with you but, as suggested, too many ideas. Sometimes I wish I were like a Brisbane, talking, talking, all sorts of wisdom, into a graphophone.

It was rather a longer drive than I thought but we got into New Orleans at four Sunday, all hotel rooms taken, prices up, the outlook for any prolonged stay here thin. We get off tomorrow morning (Wednesday) for Corpus Christi, Texas.

Tom Wolfe had just been here, evidently being made much a hero and social lion. Wish I had seen him. I tried to call him, hearing he had holed-up at Pass Christian but he had left there, they said, for N. C. From all my friends here say, he is evidently troubled, rather distraught and upset. Aint it hell? You keep thinking of the other fellow as going on, eating, drinking, perpetually working and happy. I have been having a grand time thinking of Wolfe in that way, a kind of "roll river" man and now to find that he also gets upset, perhaps even discouraged . . . it's disillusioning. Perhaps you'd better write him. If I had found him here I'd have taken him off to Texas where, as far as I know, no one is literary.

After tonight we will have had three evenings here . . . too much drinking, talk until two or three, etc., and will be glad to consort with Kansas wheat farmers, down on the coast in their trailers. Wish you and Mrs. Boyd (am tempted to write "Kate") were along.

We had such a good and satisfying time there.

I took Paul's[1] *Rising Sun* play as well as the Virginia Woolf and will return them in one package.

My idea of the letters I wrote you and Paul and didn't send, after my first visit, was I guess a kind of confessional letter writing, as between several of us,

[1] Paul Green, playwright, author of *Johnny Johnson*.

working now, trying each in his own way to outline to the others his own difficulties, always of course in respect to work and living.

The two being so damned inseparable.

Such ideas seem so far-reaching and all right often until you try to explain definitely to another just what you mean. I presume I seek a feeling of some sort of more or less compact body of us, with some sense not only of working together to hold on to something, but also of keeping each other alive.

It may all be silly. If you do see Wolfe and if I have suggested anything at all to you by these words, talk it over with him.

You are very very fine people. It seems so foolish that I have not known you both longer. Anyway I'm grateful to you for being.

Sherwood Anderson

2700 Rincon St.
Corpus Christi, Texas
Feb. 21, 1937

Dear Jim,

I am writing you at Eleanor's hand because I just came out the hospital here after a two weeks' illness.

I was pretty sick beginning with a bad flu that upset my guts. There are too many yards of guts. It is one of God's mistakes, and every inch of mine sore as an ulcerated tooth.

I was terribly sorry to miss Wolfe as I believe so much in his basic soundness and sweetness. I think he will be more and more perhaps our great novelist. This tremendous fertility and richness of his has glorious value.

I wish we had gone to the Bahamas. Does it cost much there? I always have to think of that as I make so little money. Here we live really in a little auto camp at the water's edge having kitchen, sitting room, dining room and bedroom all miraculously crowded into one room. Can walk straight down along a little pier from the door and catch fish to eat. Eleanor does the cooking. The whole thing costing sixteen a week. (E. says this is a lie.)

Got both your Brownsville letters and the one here but, alas, your script is as hard to read as my own although yours seems somewhat more distinguished.

Glad you are reading Borrow, as I love his gusto, and don't mind his prejudice.

What I think hurt me a little about Green[1] was his bunking himself about Hollywood. After all an artist should be an artist in the sense that he accepts the artist's morality. I sometimes think it is the only true morality and that it is closely allied with what should be the morality of the craftsman or worker.

Jim, I do not believe that a man will come to save us. We must in some way save ourselves and others through brotherhood. You see, this terrible spiritual poverty comes back to men's breaking faith as it were with their own hands and bodies—as a woman may find God through her body in children so man must sometime come to realize again that he can only find God through his own body as expressed in work.

Does this seem far-fetched? It isn't. It is one thing I know with my whole soul.

And I do not feel proud that I also have never gone for something like the Hollywood thing—that is to say cheapening of my attitude toward figures in an imaginative world for money. I have never been greatly

[1] Paul Green.

tempted. No one ever offered me big money. So I cannot, too much, condemn Green, for example, for going back to that trash.

I guess you know that I say all this loving very much something fine in Green.

Oh, keep clinging to this idea of a possible group of men who might help each other in this matter. I was full of it after the first evening with you and Paul and wrote many pages that I didn't send. One grows skeptical and even afraid. It seems an impertinence to be warning others although I kept wanting to shout at Green as though following him along the street and shouting, "Don't, don't!"

It is so hard on the other hand to accept poverty. How much more work I could do if I could afford, for example, a paid secretary. One places such horrible limitations on himself by poverty, too. I keep saying to myself, for example, that I will live only for the week or month, but occasional fears come to paralyze me, the fear, for example, of old age and dependence. And it seems so simple to settle it all by going for a time to some place like Hollywood and raking in some cash. What is not realized is that the artist's obligation to people in the imaginative world is the same as a man's obligation to real people in a real world. You see the demand always made is to sell out these imaginative people. Of course all this is a deep subject, but to us at least, who are artists, the spiritual wreck we are in in some way has its basis here.

I wonder, Jim, can we help each other? Could you and I make Paul see and understand this? Is some sort of male grouping of American artists in our own age and time possible? Can we give this kind of love? It is thinking of it that continually half paralyzes me. I so much want it to begin to happen.

When will you be back in Southern Pines? I hope it may be possible for us to see each other this spring.

Give my best to Kate. It may sound impertinent calling her Kate but I think of her so. I was much charmed by a fine quality I felt in her.

I think I shall be better now and hope I shall do some work. Write me often.

Sherwood
by EA

Saturday
(1937)

Dear Jim:

It is uncertain how long we will be here. It depends largely upon Eleanor, who seems to have got herself tied up here.

How have you escaped? I seem to have become a kind of stuffed shirt for all sorts of things. People keep coming to me, wanting me to sign this or that manifesto for Cultural Freedom, for Peace and Democracy, for this and that. I do it and find myself involved.

From time to time an impulse comes to me. I would like to write the story of a man during an hour of his life, without physical action, the man sitting, or standing, or just walking about. All that he is that made him what he is. I have this temptation and at the same time realize that man is best understood by his actions.

Sometimes my feeling about inanimate objects goes, I'm afraid, to too great lengths. I remember a room in which I once lived in Chicago. Some men came to see me one evening and something vile happened. It was largely stuff going on in the men. It seemed to me to make the room vile. I had worked pretty well there but after it happened couldn't work. I got the notion they had put something into the very furniture of the room, into the walls and the wall paper. I carry it too far I think sometimes.

Your letter was something fine to me, the quality of the mind back of it so finely shown. We are working in a tough time, Jim. There are so many forces pulling away from the real point. It is good to have you thus unload your mind to me. I am grateful.

Sherwood A

TO PAUL APPEL[1]

The Miller Hotel
Brownsville, Texas
April 1, 1938

Dear Paul Appel,

Your letter of March 10, with enclosure, just caught up with me. I'd say that it is pretty hard to answer most of the questions you are putting up to yourselves. I'd say that the central difficulty, in all publishing, in all of its forms, is that there is a pretense of an interest, say in literature, or science, or in truth, while there is, at the same time, the fact that the whole set-up is a business set-up.

But how are you going to avoid this in the modern world? You have the same thing in the churches, in politics, in the colleges. It all seems to me to go with our kind of civilization. We have to thread our way through it as best we can. What we have got is an almost universal control of all of the channels of public expression by business and the central idea of business is profits.

I think that the whole set-up, from the writer's point

[1] A young novelist and short story writer.

of view, is hardest on the young, on the new writers as they come on. It is pretty hard for them to realize how hard-boiled it all is. It confuses, puzzles and defeats them.

But how are you going to change it without changing the whole civilization? That is what you are up against.

Sherwood Anderson

TO ALFRED STIEGLITZ

August Sixth
1938

Dear Stieglitz,

I have written asking for the photograph. It is a way to remind myself how rich I am. Already I have some twelve or fifteen men looking down from the wall of the room. It is just possible that the whole thing will be too much for many people. There is such a richness of life, of character.

I was shocked to hear of your illness. It doesn't seem right. Illness in you is too much like a mountain running from the moon.

But I know this—that the life in you is real life. I have made an epitaph for my own grave—"Life not Death is the Adventure."

You shall always mean sweet life to me.

As always,

TO MAXWELL PERKINS[1]

(September 20, 1938)

Dear Max,

I was terribly upset by Tom's illness and death. Such a grand young talent gone. Eleanor thought I should go down to Asheville, to his funeral, but hating funerals, I didn't. I did however send his mother a wire. It's bad business. Tom had so much of the thing needed —vitality—great and rich talent.

To tell the truth however, Max, when he separated himself from you, I was afraid for him. I had a friend once, strangely like Tom, who, after years of tearing himself to pieces, much as Tom did, ended by drinking himself insane. Naturally, Max, I never mentioned this to anyone—a curious likeness in the two men—the same violence—talent—Mississippi River kind of force —and I speak of it to you only because, in spite of everything, you remained, to the end, closer to Tom than anyone else. I was often frankly afraid Tom would drive himself into the black hole of insanity as my other friend did, but my saying this is just for you.

The loss to literature is just a bitter fact. It hurts. We don't get many in Tom's class.

As regards the book on writing . . . Max, it is true that an amazing number of the younger writers have gone out of their way to say practically that I have shown them the way. They have written to tell me so. If it would be in decent taste to use some of the things said for the book on writing to introduce it, it ought to count—whether or not it would be in good taste to

[1] Friend and editor of Thomas Wolfe.

use these expressions of esteem, in private letters, for example from such men as Tom, I a good deal doubt. It is something we could talk about anyway.

I keep going on with the other book—I have now given the title "Men and Their Women"—in the loose form I have told you about. Anyway, Max, it is the form that seems best fitted to what talent I have.

I wish we had got you down here this summer. I'll not be satisfied until you know this beautiful country. I'm sure, if you come once, you would come again.

I'll be in New York sometime in October.

As always,

TO JAMES BOYD

April 10, 1939

Dear Jim:

I just got your letter yesterday. I was mighty sorry not to see you and Katherine when I was on my way South. Southern Pines and particularly your place were so lovely that spring morning. A colored girl came to the door and I asked her for a little slip of paper. I wrote my name on the paper leaning against the nose of my car. Filled with sadness that you weren't there. I knew there were a lot of trotting horses in training over at that track where we once went together. I thought we might have a morning together over there watching them step.

In your letter I like particularly your saying that about the business of writing—that it is the highest business there is, although I wasn't so hot, Jim, on your using the word "business" to get at your meaning and between us, Jim, I don't think that talent has a great deal to do with it either.

The country and our civilization has lost its morality and what is man without morality?

You see, Jim, it is my notion that we American writers, all of us, are pretty lousy. Who among us really takes upon his shoulders the responsibility of what you speak of as the business of writing? We do make a business of it.

I guess it is pretty much my notion that man's real life is lived out there in the imaginative world and that is where we sell him out. That's what we writers haven't found out. That is what we will some day have to find out if we are really ever to take on the responsibility implied in your saying that writing is the highest business there is.

I know you agree with me, Jim. I am mighty sorry I did not see you. I haven't yet read your new book. Tell Max to send me a copy.

With my best wishes to you both,

Sherwood

TO ETTIE STETTHEIMER[1]

Marion, Virginia
August 14, 1939

Dear Ettie Stettheimer:

I am sorry I did not get in to see you before I left New York. I wasn't well, wasn't working and came home here expecting to return to New York before finally coming for the summer but simply stayed here, Mrs. Anderson coming later.

We have been having guests. There is held here annually what they call a musical festival. It is held on

[1] Author of the novel *Love-Days,* written under the pseudonym of Henrie Waste.

one of the highest mountains east of the Mississippi, a mountain only some twenty miles from here. The idea is that the mountaineers, men and women, will come trooping up into the mountain. They will burst into song. There is a kind of man or woman who goes in for heavy FOLK . . . Percy MacKaye[1] and others. They all come.

They have had a good deal of trouble. Young men from New York's eastside put on faded overalls, tie red handkerchiefs about their necks and get all the prizes. Some of these New York eastsiders are wonderful in FOLK.

A good many Folk seekers usually get washed up on our doorsteps. It is wonderful. Two or three years ago Mrs. Roosevelt was here. There must have been at least ten thousand people that year all seeking the lonely mountain singer. You should come down and see us here. Really the country is very beautiful.

I hear from Paul Rosenfeld that you have moved. Lewis Galantière[2] was here with his tall beautiful wife. Ferdinand Schevill is coming in September and perhaps if he can get away from his Virgin Islands, Robert Lovett will come.

I am writing only short stories. I have a lot I want to tell you if I can. I would like to have news of you.

Sherwood Anderson

[1] Poet and dramatist, author of *Kentucky Mountain Fantasies*, etc.
[2] Author, translator of modern French and German works.

## TO GILBERT WILSON[1]

Denver, Colorado
October 26, 1939

Dear Gilbert Wilson:

Your letter reached me only yesterday at Denver, Colorado. I have been wandering around since you left our place and mail has been following me from place to place in the meantime. Your letter puzzles me, and of course I do not know how to answer it nor can I tell you what to do. In the first place, however, let me say that the letter from Alexander seems to me very fair and sympathetic. It seems a shame to let them down, and the first thought that occurred to me when I read that you were out living with Art and going off by yourself was to wonder why instead you didn't go to Antioch and sit down before that mural and do your thinking about it rather than about yourself.

Of course I know that you are terribly puzzled and it seems to me also that all of those who accepted as a kind of mission the changing of human beings through some big national movement have been let down most terribly by recent events.

I expect this has upset you. My own theory as to the position of the working artist that I expounded to you when you were with me may be also a dodging of the issue, but at least in the absorption in other individuals you are not let down so terribly as you are in these big attempts that take in great masses of people.

I do not know whether or not, when you were at my

[1] A painter, best known for his murals.

place, you took much note of the man who runs my farm and who, with his son, was building the barn. He is a simple country man and can barely read and write, but I must say gives me more satisfaction as a companion and friend than most of the artists who come to me and who are so terribly concerned about their genius and their missions.

Frankly, I do not believe this sort of thing concerns me at all. I have no feeling of being a public figure and do not want to be one, and often I think that my own interest in the lives of people about me has at bottom more integrity than this ambitious effort to think of masses of people, where they are going and what is best for them. . . .

You have talked to me a great deal of what Art means to you. You come to me and to Dreiser. I do not think we can really help. The truth is that we are probably wanting what you say you want, but have had experience enough to know that few men get it. I really think there is some danger of surrender to self-pity and also perhaps too much clutching at others. There is too much emphasis on what you can get from others and not enough on giving. This may sound like preaching, but it is pretty sound.

The truth is, all I can see for you, if you play fair, is to return to Antioch and face your problem there.

I am sorry not to be more helpful. I do not know what else to say.

As always,
Sherwood Anderson

New York,
March 20, 1940

Dear Gilbert Wilson:[1]

The other day I received a copy of the little magazine *Unquote* containing the correspondence between you and White. It is certainly revealing.

However, I do not wonder that the man is puzzled. Who isn't nowadays? Have the Communists really hooked up with the Fascists? It makes a sick-looking picture.

Am I right in thinking that every effort we make to think our way through these big world movements is bound to come to nothing just now, so that a man must work in his own back yard, hoping that these big power-hungry ones will kill each other off and a little sanity come back into life?

Anyway you know what I mean when we talked of a man working in the small, trying to save a little of the feeling of man for man.

Sincerely,
Sherwood Anderson

TO ANITA LOOS[2]

The Royalton
December 1, 1940

Dear Anita:

. . . Eleanor and I will be here, at least by present plans, until the 15th or 20th of December. We will then,

[1] At the time of this letter, Wilson had returned to Antioch College.

[2] The author of the famous *Gentlemen Prefer Blondes*; "John" refers to her husband, John Emerson.

I presume, go home for the holidays. And I expect we will be off to South America about the middle of January. There was some talk of my going down there, with Rockefeller money, on a kind of cultural mission, to get in touch with South American writers, but now I believe I will probably be sent by one of the magazines. This kind of a trip would be much less official and would be more in my line. Eleanor will go with me if we pull it off and I think we will.

I am glad to hear that you were out for Roosevelt. I did not do much but Eleanor was hot on the job. She even made several street-corner speeches here in New York, and had some good stories to tell of her experiences.

Naturally, Anita, I am keenly interested in what you say of Hakim, the producer of *Baker's Wife.* I may have told you that when *The Baker's Wife* opened in New York two or three of the critics said something to the effect that it was the kind of movie that Sherwood Anderson could do, and when I saw it I felt a little bit that way myself. As regards the material, I think I would suggest, first of all, two stories. In *Winesburg, Ohio* there is the story called "A Man of Ideas." I am pretty sure that a figure of this story, Jo Welling, could be worked up into something both very amusing and very human. It would have to be built up, to be sure, but the story in *Winesburg* could, I am also sure, give the key to how to work it up.

And then there is the title story to the book called *The Triumph of the Egg.* With another fellow helping me I once made a little play out of this story that was produced by the old Provincetown theatre. Gene O'Neill had a two-act play, *Different,* and we filled out the evening with the *Egg.* I think the figure here of the poor little restaurant keeper trying to be a public entertainer could also be made into something rather grand if handled right.

I think these two stories are the ones I would tell Mr. Hakim to look at. *Winesburg, Ohio* is in the Modern Library and therefore could be got in any bookstore. I believe *Triumph of the Egg* is now out of print but under other cover today I am sending you one.

I just made a change of publishers, leaving Scribner's and going to Harcourt Brace. I am doing a book of memoirs, in which by the way I hope to do John justice, and Harcourt Brace were so enthusiastic about the project and made such a good offer on it that I am going over to them.

Some time ago a friend of mine here recommended to me a Hollywood agent named Ned Brown. I know very little about him but he seems to write intelligent letters and to be anxious to get to work on my material, so I may ask him to go to see Mr. Hakim, but before he does so I am going to take the liberty of asking him to first call you on the telephone as I think it would be much nicer if the first suggestions to Hakim in regard to the stories came from you.

I wish, Anita, that it were possible for you and John to take the trip to South America with us for this winter. Perhaps we can do it together next winter.

Sincerely yours,
Sherwood

P.S. Both Eleanor and myself are struggling with the Spanish language. I bought an outfit called "Linguaphone." I put the records on the phonograph so that I may hear the actual spoken language. I think the outfit would be a big help to you.